SIGNALS FROM A LAMPLESS BEACON:

BEASTS OF BURDEN

PAUL TRAYWICK

iUNIVERSE, INC.
NEW YORK   BLOOMINGTON

Signals from a Lampless Beacon:
Beasts of Burden

Copyright © 2009 Paul Traywick

iUniverse books may be ordered through booksellers or by contacting:

iUniverse
1663 Liberty Drive
Bloomington, IN 47403
www.iuniverse.com
1-800-Authors (1-800-288-4677)

ISBN: 978-1-4401-2639-0 (pbk)
ISBN: 978-1-4401-2640-6 (ebk)

Printed in the United States of America

iUniverse rev. date: 3/23/2009

"On other occasions an incident had been
repeated to him and he had explained it,
a problem had been put to him and he had
solved it. Now, for the first time in his life,
he had to pick out his own questions and
answer them himself."

Margery Allingham: *The Crime at Black Dudley*, Ch. 7

My thanks are due Professor Stephen Della Lana for translation of the brief conversation in German within Chapter III. (His German is far too good for either of the interlocutors!) PT

To Suzy

I

"He spoke thus, and when Dream heard his word, he went forth."
Iliad : 2.16 (tr. PT)

"The third man was your son."
"You could see his face?"
"Not then. But I knew him."

The World, again! Consuming itself in war again. Before, that dark word, sprung from dynastic greed and jealousy abroad, had spread from empire to kingdom and colony. Now, mankind, it seems, must be delivered from a misbegotten yeoman turned to madness, and confirmed in it by a folk driven by humiliation to equal madness.

The New World has felt already, from across both oceans, the sting of the whiphand.

Will this war be in any way a better one to fight? In any way less distressing to undertake or to endure? That is, because we are waging it against an aggressor who, in victory, would degrade all of our life? No; it is there, ineluctable; it is dusk seeping away. The workman gathers his tools, and prepares for night.

And this time around, he and Grace had a son to offer up, Robert, a Naval

Lieutenant. For a few days, he had been at home with them, at home on leave. Over multiple though minor objections, without giving any reason, he had insisted upon coming to them for these particular days. Yet once at home, he had seemed entirely himself. Until the Hammonds had asked him to dinner on the Wednesday evening.

On Thursday morning, Thomas Strikestraw had got up and was waiting for his wife to awaken. They would talk together about the things he had just been thinking through. They would speak and listen to each other, yet saying nothing. He knew she had been awake through most of the night, waiting for Robert to return. Robert had not returned. She would ask Thomas about that, but he would have no answer. Unless the answer lay in the shocked sorrow of the osprey whom he watched, wheeling and banking about her towering but plundered nest, her cloud-dark, lofty, pillaged nest.

Grace stirred. She was awake; they didn't talk to each other, after all. This day might prove the first of their childlessness. No words. On the morning of the first day, nothing was said; it was yet too soon. Grace remained in bed. Sometimes she did this, either because she was afraid to arise, or because she saw no point in it. But on this day she wanted specifically to work the sympathetic magic of the women of the Old Northwest. They had used this practice on days when their men went out to hunt the whale. She lay on her side, facing inland from the direction of the sea, compelling herself to breathe deeply, very slowly, soundlessly, and to envisage, if not calm, then at least not turmoil—the turmoil, say, of threshing tail and drowning torrent.

All her bedroom windows were open. New Brunswick at midsummer was often cooled in early morning—as it was on this first morning—by the riverwind, even though July sun would later bore its way through any defect in a canopy of shade.

Thomas had gone to sit in the library downstairs. The family had thought it pretentious to continue calling it the "drawing room," too outmoded (and, really, somehow questionable) to call it the "parlor." So bookshelves had been installed. From here, for a time, he could keep an eye on the front gates, with their forged curves and reverses, one of the treasures of the little Town.

About this time he usually had a cup of coffee in his study, which was at the back of the house, and read over the morning papers, but on this morning of the first day he suspended many of his habits, preferring to sit still, to do nothing until there came to him either some messenger or some sign that all was well.

At five minutes before eight, Rhodë (pronounced in two syllables) was exactly five minutes away from the house where Grace and Thomas were waiting—that is, about three blocks. She usually held to the side of the street upon which brick walls or white picket fences kept in the gardens lining the western side of Front Street. But she had abandoned herself to the splendor of the day and crossed to the modest esplanade on the other side. This ran along the ridge of a bluff, beside the Great River. In a few brisk strides Rhodë had then crossed back and stepped onto the brick-paved driveway that led through other gates of ironwork directly to the back of the grounds, where they parked their cars. Mr. Robert's car was not there. Rhodë thought it ought to have been; when things were not as she thought they ought to be, she fretted. When she fretted, she was very particular about keeping her own counsel, and this extended to ritual silence. In the kitchen, as she took up her duties, she was careful to let no vessels strike together; she opened the taps slowly and only far enough to let the water spill in soundless, slender streams.

In the first thin, fluid filaments Rhodë could see the Thread of Fate. By five minutes past eight it had started to come in a series of abortive spurts, then stopped. Had it merely been checked? Would it begin presently to run again? Or had it been parted? Or was it simply yet too soon to know? The house, after all, was full of vagaries of plumbing, and they were being allowed to get worse. Like the washbasin in the downstairs bathroom, where the cold water could not be controlled from the tap—only by means of the shutoff valve near the floor.

She went into the library. "Good morning, Father. Here is your second cup."

"Good morning, Rhodë. It smells wonderful!" For coffee of good quality was scarce.

"What about Miss Grace?"

"She hasn't come down, yet?"

"Not yet."

"Then I think the best thing is to leave her."

"What about Mr. Robert?"

What about Robert? What? What at all? "He didn't return home last night."

"I noticed his car wasn't out back." She waited. "I didn't think he'd be gone again so early." And again she waited. Thomas drank a little of the coffee.

"I don't mean to ask what's no business of mine."

Thomas smiled up at her and then drained his cup. "Rhodë, if anything should ever happen in this house that's not your business, then"—he searched for a sturdy enough circumstance to support so unlikely a condition—"then it will be after we're all dead and gone. But you've put your finger on the trouble: Robert didn't come home last night, and although he told us he might be later than usual, he didn't say why. He was emphatic about telling his mother not to stay awake, that he would definitely be coming home.

"Since he hasn't returned, I suppose we're all very much afraid, to tell you the truth. And Miss Grace did lie awake all night, I believe. I imagine it must be the War."

"Partly the War, Father. But Miss Grace has never slept while Mr. Robert was out, not until he'd come home."

"Did she tell you that?"

"She let me know it."

Upstairs the bedroom windows still stood open wide, but the climbing sun now posed serious challenge to the riverwind, to the atmosphere altogether, to everything that had had respite during the hours of darkness—darkness that allowed frenetic molecular collisions to lose some of their reaction and momentum.

But Grace continued to lie quite still, made herself imagine a glass-blue ocean folded just by the lightest of swells, of an almost windless calm, of a luminous mist drifting slowly onshore, temple-veil, to conceal and sanctify the self-sacrifice of the revered, even beloved Leviathan, beneficent, for the preservation of the tribal community; sacrifice—quick and merciful slaughter-stroke. She had almost succeeded in dreaming: Light craft emerging from the sheltering vapor into safety.

Rhodë sat about in the kitchen. She did not want to appear to be eavesdropping, under cover of bustling about the house with broom and duster. Under no circumstances, of course, must the vacuum cleaner be operated, for the one the Strikestraws owned generated a howl equal to the scream of Harpys. Finally she returned to the library where Thomas still sat looking out through the window.

"Father, since Miss Grace hasn't come down, will you want your lunch in your study or in the breakfast room?"

"I think I'd better have it in the dining room, actually. I suppose it doesn't seem sensible, but for a little longer I feel I ought to be able to watch the gates."

"Earlier, I first took your coffee into the study and I wondered why I didn't find you." She waited once more; Thomas could think of nothing to say. "Are we expecting anybody?"

"We may be. But I don't know whom."

"Might it be somebody who would come around to the back?"

"Possibly. I simply don't know."

Grace's doggedness fell in upon itself before Thomas's did. *Enough of this,* she said to herself, *is enough. I've lain here for hours, and still no word has come.* So taking what seemed to her a more practical approach she sat up, lifted the Prayer Book and Hymnal from her bedside table, and read over the words of the Navy Hymn. The church bells sounded the noon hour; the morning of the first day was over.

After his lunch Thomas met Rhodë in the back hallway. She took his plate from him, and he said: "I enjoyed my lunch, Rhodë."

"I'm glad you did, Father." Now they heard Grace's footfalls in the room above, followed by the sound of water running into the bath.

"I've been staring so long at those gates, I think I'm beginning to see things. Maybe I'm finally losing my mind."

"Oh, no, Father." For Thomas was but fifty-six years old.

"As the sun has been getting higher, I've noticed them—the gates, ironwork you know—reflecting little brilliances. Then little shadows, moving across those."

"But, Father, that's normal and natural, isn't it?"

"But the brightnesses and shadows have begun to overlap each other, very quickly, changing back and forth—the whole thing has seemed to be twinkling."

"You're tired, Father, and worried. That's what it is."

"But that's not even the craziest part. There were beings at the gates, like people. They weren't real people, Rhodë, you understand. Just in my imagination. And there were two sorts: One sort were Dreads, the other, Expectations."

"What were they doing?" Rhodë asked, nearly voraciously, taking Thomas a little by surprise.

"They were all elbowing each other to see who would be let in first. Anyway, I'm going into my study now. It's time I did something about all this. I'm going to let them in, one at a time—Dreads and Expectations—and look each one square in the eye. Then, if I haven't settled upon any better plan, I'm going to telephone Mr. Hammond."

"I think I heard mention that Mr. and Mrs. Hammond were planning to go into Wilmington for the day."

"It can't hurt to try. Mr. Robert was supposed to have dinner with them yesterday evening."

Then Rhodë climbed the stairs. "Can I help you with anything, Miss Grace?"

"Oh, Rhodë, please just sit on the foot of the bed and talk to me!"

"Yes, Ma'am." Grace could be heard splashing about in the bath, and then the scent of hyacinths floated out upon the caustic summer air. Rhodë said: "Father Thomas has seen a vision."

"A vision! Are you entirely sure! What makes you think so?"

"Well, Ma'am, I'm not *entirely* sure. But he told me he saw forms of people—not *real* people, of course…"

"Of course."

"…standing outside the front gates. Dreads and Expectations, he called them, and you know as well as I do what *that* means!"

"As a matter of fact, Rhodë, I'm afraid I've no idea what it means." More splashing, more hyacinths. "You must explain it to me."

Knowing Rhodë to be a devout Christian, Grace might have expected her to avoid superstition; yet, on the other hand, given the extent to which Christian doctrine is rooted in the supernatural—a thing which Grace knew to have begun to trouble her husband sorely—it was perhaps the greater wonder that Rhodë hadn't taken it all a good deal further.

"The Dreads are devils, and the Expectations are angels."

"That doesn't sound very much like my husband's way of looking at things."

"No, Ma'am, but the Almighty will sometimes poke a hole in the way you're looking at things, and then show you what you never had suspected."

"Now, he would certainly agree with that."

"And a different way has been shown Father. And he's not used to it, Miss Grace. I believe he thinks too much. Not all the time, mind, but for a lot of the time."

"That is possible. Rhodë, could you shut your eyes and help me out of this dismal warm bath?" Rhodë took up a large bath towel and, holding it before herself like a mantle, went into the bathroom. "I really don't—thank you—imagine that Father Thomas thinks he's seen devils. You see, Rhodë, he doesn't think there are any. He doesn't even think there's Satan."

"But where does he think evil comes from?"

"You're not ready for this, Rhodë. We'll talk about it when things have settled down a bit."

" 'Things,' Miss Grace, may never 'settle down'."

"I know."

Far off, a Hag leaned back in her great chair, resting upon her knee the hand in which she held the silver scissors.

In the study the only ugly thing was the telephone set; but it was a prodigy of ugliness. Thomas spun the crank-handle twice, pausing momentarily between. This process was meant to be facilitated by a small ferrule that ran free on the end of the handle. After many years it still kept a faint phenolic smell about it. Thomas took up the receiver.

Presently, a meticulously depersonalized voice came over the line: "Number, please."

"One-six-J," Thomas answered Sarah Elkin, as blandly as he could, in an effort to keep up the feeling of metropolitan anonymity which the telephone network seemed to have inspired, even in these early years. He expected to hear a series of electrical disconnections and re-connections, but instead there was an uncertain pause. Then, in her normal voice, Sarah said: "I'll be glad to ring it for you, Canon Strikestraw, but I believe they may be away for the day."

"Thank you, Sarah; it can't hurt to try." Then the expected electrical interferences did occur.

In fact, John and Helen Hammond had planned an excursion (neither of them remembered mentioning it to anybody else), but had then abandoned the plan. For they were being visited by their own misgivings. So John Hammond was there to answer the telephone when it rang. But even so, when it did, he started slightly.

"Hello?"

"John?"

"Yes?"

"This is Thomas Strikestraw."

"Hello, Tommy. How are you?"

"A little worried, actually. Did Robert keep his engagement with you last evening?"

"Of course. Otherwise we would have called you. Why?"

"He didn't come home last night. We were expecting him."

"I wonder what can have happened? Could he have driven back to Norfolk overnight?"

"He hadn't planned to; he was going to return tomorrow. Did he say anything to make you think he would?"

"No."

"Well, I'm at a complete loss. And tormented. Did anything happen, that you noticed?"

"At dinner? Several odd things happened, now you mention it—just very small things—things I wouldn't even bring up if I knew he were with you now."

"What sort of things?"

"Well, not really much of anything, as I said. First, we got to thinking that dinner with old godparents might be dull for him, so Helen invited Louisa—made an even number at table, and so on. Afterward, we both felt

Robert had been a little edgy, and of course Helen is convinced he thought we were trying to make a match. And then we really were fairly mortified—I mean, its being so soon after Anne."

"Oh, I think Helen should put that straight out of her thoughts. Louisa and Robert have known each other from childhood—they're pals."

"I didn't set much store by all that, either. There were a couple of other things I noticed but ignored…until now. Can I call you back in a few minutes?"

"Could you possibly hurry and finish it up now? Soon I'll have to deal with Grace; she's just got up."

"Of course. It's just that I have a problem of, ah, a like nature. Hold the line for a minute." Evidently Helen had come into the room. Thomas could hear muffled conversation.

He reflected for an instant upon the telephone apparatus. Leaving the magneto box out of account, it looked like an obscene, fat black flower, the mouthpiece its corolla. Idly, Thomas unscrewed this, mainly because it came away easily, and inspected and smelt it. Because of less direct exposure to air, about the threads the phenolic smell was stronger, yet cleaner. Going on with his analogy, Thomas seemed to hold in his hand a deformed pod plucked in desperate harvest from the dark and turgid stalk, which supported the whole. Then, distantly, because he had taken the receiver away in order to despise completely the way it looked, he heard John Hammond's voice calling to him. He put the instrument back against his ear.

"As I was saying, one or two other things did strike me last night as being perhaps out of the ordinary. First, when I heard Bob drive up—and he got here before Louisa—I went out to meet him. He had switched off the motor and got out of the car. And he had just finished locking the trunk. Now, of course, that's perfectly normal, isn't it?"

"No."

"I thought not."

"What else?"

"Just this: Around nine o'clock we were still at table—hadn't had dessert yet. That's a little late for us. Bob started glancing down at his watch. There's an old clock on the chimneypiece, but it has to be wound up, and nobody ever does—wind it, that is—except my sister, when she's here. She says time stands still in her absence. Says it whenever she visits. It's one of the things I detest most about her; there are plenty of others.

"At any rate, Bobby was very discreet, just looked down into his lap several times. I've noticed he wears his watch inside the wrist; I think that is a military fashion. I'm pretty sure that was what he was doing. Checking the hour. Finally Helen stood up, and Bob came around to me and asked to use the telephone. I said Of course. But the thing is just outside the dining room door, in the hallway.

"Helen always picks up more than you think she does. She said we ought to take coffee out onto the verandah, because it had got at least a little cooler. So we left Bobby with the telephone and some privacy. I was last out of the room; I heard him instructing the operator to reverse the charges, so I know it was a long distance call. But that's all I know."

"What did he do afterward?"

"He joined us outside for coffee and looked a lot more at ease. From then onward, he seemed in no hurry to leave."

"I hope he didn't wear out his welcome."

"An impossibility, so far as Helen and I are concerned. And I must tell you, Louisa wasn't *at all* impatient. She was absolutely bubbling over; Bob was a good sport about it, of course. All of that is what I think got Helen concerned about being thought a shameless matchmaker. Not that there's any other kind."

"But there will be no more...he's alone now forever, I think."

"Who knows? Anyway," John Hammond went on, "The moon was starting to drain the marsh; the land breeze brought its sweetness to us. Yes, after all, it was very pleasant."

Rainfall in the West, they say, makes the mountains weep. The leaning tree will lead a droplet down toward the living moss (upon which it falls, silent and soft as paper-ash) that grows at the base of some transpiring stone—itself living, according to the terms of its creation. Runnels form, turning into that way from this hindrance, and sheets of water slip from beneath stretches of leaf-mold, all gathering like an army katabatic, all seeking downward courses, as mass and gravity coöperate to find a plane of lower energy, to dissipate more and more the force that first lifted the water high into the atmosphere.

Creeks come into being. At first each is called just "The Creek." Then with names they are first seen on quadrangles within the Geologic Survey, later even on road maps. And at villages and crossroads, or away in the wilderness, they confound their waters, some having flowed past stately Thorbiskope, or olden Ellerslie, or half-ruined Cool Spring (with its vaulted attic, where once a dance was held; then that family began as often as possible to speak of "The Ballroom at Cool Spring"). The ghosts of dreams travel along rivers with their everflowing waters. Drift in a boat at midnight of the full moon, and you will see. Hear. And you will know.

The army of waters presses on to its port of embarkation; miles above Cape Fear it finds a gracious channel, broad but kept in by the banks, deep, passing Wilmington, Orton's Point, New Brunswick, Southport. No longer broken by Bald Head Island, it offers its flood to the Ocean, which at the dictates of the sun and of the moon accepts the tribute with more or less instant thirst.

Now that the sun had mounted up near to the zenith and shone from a particular angle upon the face of the waters flowing by New Brunswick, a network of trembling light floated upon the library ceiling inside the Strikestraw house. Thomas came into the room. He saw Grace sitting sidewise in a chair she seldom used, leafing with studied absorption through a monograph having to do with theoretical physics. Thomas selected the sofa and sat down. But he leaned forward, with his elbows on his knees, clasping his hands together. Eventually Grace, without looking up, said casually, as she believed: "You and John Hammond certainly went on for a long time."

"I know we did. I'm sorry to have left you so long. But he had some things to tell me about last night—some things about Robert."

The movement Grace made in attempting to set the pamphlet onto a tea-stand beside her began as fluid and voluntary, but fine motor adjustment was quickly lost. She struck a silver phial holding a single rose in loosening bud. Thomas thought irrelevantly as he watched it topple onto the floor and the water spill out that it was *'Désprez à fleurs jaunes.'* There was only a little water. It formed into beads, like mercury, upon the carpet, sought channels among the knotted tufts—what was left of them after a century of wear— and had just started to flow accordingly, but was suddenly soaked up and vanished, as Grace's sorrow surpassed her fear and expressed from her a cry of anguish: "What! What did he tell you? Tell me!" And her sorrow wounded her husband, for he loved her.

"Nothing so very much; nothing especially good, and nothing especially bad." He gave the clearest account he could of their conversation. As his wife listened, she was able to compose herself.

"I wonder," Grace said when he had finished, "what this thing of your seeing visions means?"

"I expect Rhodë told you about the Hopes and Fears?"

"She said 'Dreads' and 'Expectations'—as though these constituted a tenth and an eleventh Order of Angels."

"About that I can assure you I was speaking purely figuratively, or at least I thought I was. I might have foreseen that she'd take up the most sensational part."

"Rhodë is a very sensible woman." (Sensible, and cultivated. Thomas's mother was English. She thought all young women, Black or White, ought to be brought up as ladies. The idea was ahead of its time, so that Rhodë's mother had been her only adherent among the Colored Folk, and Rhodë herself her mother's only taker.)

"But a devout Christian. They're forever making up gods for themselves. And a proportion of them are, without knowing it, devil-worshippers. They make those up, too, of course."

"If you keep up that kind of talk, you will lose your job."

"What difference would it make?" Thomas had long since leaned back into the sofa. Now for a while he stared, clearly rapt. Then he turned again to Grace. "And I suppose she forgot to say anything about the front gates?"

"What might she have said about them?"

Thomas then glanced all round the room. "I told her that the gates twinkled in the sunlight—bright reflections, bars of shadow, and that these kept changing places with each other."

"I'm hardly surprised she didn't mention it! She probably thought by then that you had simply gone crazy."

"At first that's what I thought, too. But something has finally dawned on me about it. What I was seeing were dashes and dots!" Grace was not encouraged by this reply.

"Dashes and dots? Do you mean dots and dashes? The kind that make up Morse Code?"

"Yes. I know Morse Code. Did you know I did? I learned it at the beginning of the Great War. I thought it might make me useful somehow, but it didn't."

"And you haven't forgotten it?"

"No. I still practice every few days; you've seen my keys, on the shelf beside the old trigger-guards."

"I didn't know exactly what they were, but yes, I have seen them I think. They look like little nautical instruments—Those?"

"Yes. There are just a few, but mine are elegantly designed for their use and finely made. Anyway, dashes and dots always register in my mind as letters. It just happens automatically."

"And are you telling me you were receiving some message from the front gates? Or from beyond?"

"Please don't make fun of me, Grace. This is not a time for it. And you will just burst into tears."

"Truly, I don't mean to. I meant, did the letters make up any message?"

"If they did, it was enciphered."

By the time the telephone in the study had rung twice, Rhodë had answered it. Grace and Thomas heard her speak briefly, and then she came into the library. "Mr. Hammond is on the telephone and would like to speak to Canon Strikestraw." Thomas went out, and Rhodë sat down near Grace. "Everything's going to be all right, Miss Grace, so try not to feel too bad just now," and she patted Grace's knee.

"How do you *know* it's going to be all right, Rhodë?" She hoped—she knew it was a vain hope—that John Hammond might have said something to Rhodë, the merest favorable news. Rhodë looked out through the garden window and after a while she spoke:

"It just has to be, Miss Grace." And then, "It has to be."

Where am I? Am I wrecked?

Thomas sat down to the telephone mouthpiece and placed the receiver against his ear. "John?"

"Tommy, I've found Robert's car."

Not "Robert," nor yet "Robert and his car," which was probably all to the good, but "Robert's car."

"Where is it? Is it wrecked?"

"No, not wrecked." Then, "Helen didn't want me to disturb you again."

"You haven't disturbed me the first time yet. I telephoned you, remember."

"She didn't want Grace to be distressed further, or not now."

"I think she's past distressing further. She—and certainly I...anything we can know.... The car...?"

"I began to think they couldn't have simply vanished from the earth, and it wasn't up to me to start going about asking questions. So I decided to look for them."

"Them?"

"Bob and the car,"

"Ah."

"I knew they had got to the end of our lane—I had stood on the verandah to wave Goodbye. You know the road to Southport and Fort Caswell? Coming from Town? It makes a bend right at our gate, then continues directly south. Thinking back, I couldn't remember having seen Bob's headlight beams swing around back northward, as they would have if he had made the sharp left turn to go back home. So today I went the way he must have gone, at least at first, mainly just to have that stretch of road out of the way. I was looking for the car or for a place where it might have been parked out of sight. I didn't see anything; I wondered why I was continuing, to tell you the truth. There seemed no point in going into Southport. So I turned off onto the road around to Oak Island. Just after the Inland Waterway, on the right, is a clump of sand-cypresses. I turned around and went back to it. There was a dirt track. I followed it, and there was the car.

"It looked perfectly intact. It was open, and there was nothing in it."

"The glove compartment?"

"It wasn't locked; there was nothing in it out of the ordinary. Then I found the keys. They were on top of the front tire on the driver's side, up under the fender. That's where a lot of the young people seem to put them when they don't want to leave them in the ignition switch."

"Clever of you to know that."

"Anyway, that's where they were."

"Just the keys to the car?"

"No. A whole ring of different kinds of keys. You'll want to know about the trunk, of course. I opened it, but there was nothing except the spare, jack, and lug-wrench. And there was no sign of the cuttings."

"Cuttings?"

"I rooted five cuttings of *Grüss an Aachen* for you. One should thrive, I'd say. Except now we'll have to call it *regards à Aix-la-Chapelle*."

"Thank you. I wonder where they are."

"Who's to say?"

"Is the car still there where you found it?"

"No. I went back for Helen, and now I've brought it here."

"Thank you, John. Thank you very much. For what you've done, and for letting me know. I really am at a loss to make any sense of all this. And I'm ashamed to ask you another favor."

"Don't be absurd."

"Could you bring the car here? And would you mind waiting until after dark? I mean, to suppress as much speculation as we can?"

" 'Speculation' is a nice word for it. But, certainly. I'll be there around eight-thirty, if that suits."

"And then I can take you back in our car."

Thomas went again into the library. Grace was pitiful to see. Rhodë had her arms around her. She seemed able to hold her head up only in the expectation of some encouragement, no matter how tenuous, no matter how far-fetched. And of course there was none. "John has found Robert's car, but no trace of Robert himself."

Her head fell forward, as she finally and fully submitted to sorrow. Thomas took her under one arm, Rhodë, the other, in order to help her up to bed. She was deadweight. Conscious, though, her eyes open, fixed before her, frail shoulders wracked by what must have been half-born sobs.

Let her consciousness go with her strength! This thought was a prayer.

They helped her upstairs to her bedroom. All the time she tended to stare vacantly straight before her, but now and then nodded in diminished response, tried weakly to smile. They got her to the bed, and Rhodë's work was done; she left the house. Thomas sat beside Grace, and helped her to lie down. He said: "Dear Grace, our boy has either gone away or been taken away. I don't think there is anything we can do to fetch him back."

Thomas came, after dusk, into the back hallway of his house and laid his son's keys along with his own in a china pin-tray already full of other keys—odd ones—of coins, of little objects that belonged nowhere in particular. He picked up some of the loose keys by turns, holding them against the lamplight and examining their jagged and dissimilar bits. Surely they unlocked something. Surely they could tell him something. Perhaps, he guessed, against a stronger light, sometime. One of them.

Upstairs he lay down beside Grace and took her hand. It, and indeed her entire arm and whole body, seemed entirely without tone or strength.

They said nothing, did nothing to fend off darkness and silence, which crept in and wrapped themselves about them, finally displacing everything, even watching, so that then they slept.

When Rhodë returned next morning, the Friday, she found them so. Since neither had come downstairs, she had brought early tea. When she first saw them there, she watched long enough to see that each was breathing then she set the tea tray down upon the bench at the foot of the bed. She withdrew in silence, her face shining from the tears flowing over it. And when outside in the hallway she bent down to the burnished rimlatch to take care it made no noise in catching, her tears fell free and onto the floorboard, which had tasted this salt before.

At nine o'clock Thomas came downstairs clean-shaven and carefully dressed and groomed. When he met Rhodë he said: "Just when you have the time, Rhodë, would you take a light breakfast up to Miss Grace. She is better this morning—she has got up and dressed. Now she has lain down again. She told me she had 'some thinking to do.' "

"I reckon she has, the poor Thing; we've never been in a fix like this. Let me get her some breakfast."

Thomas had begun to reason a little. For him to report a missing person to the police would be idle and worse. If they knew where Robert was they would have let him know by now, *especially if they had found him injured… or anything of that kind.* And it would do no good to have news of Robert's disappearance—for that was what it must now be acknowledged to be—put about town. It would be put about, too; next, someone would convince himself that good could come of passing the news on to another.

On the other hand, if he telephoned to the Naval Base in Norfolk, then he needn't make any announcement, but merely an enquiry. Thomas looked at his desk calendar and observed that today was the tenth of July, 1942, Friday; by this hour a full complement of personnel ought to be at their places on post. He rang the number at Robert's quarters, but without expecting an answer; and he got none. Then he rang the Base and asked to speak to Lieutenant Strikestraw. He thought he noticed a brief pause or check of some kind, after which the voice at the other end of the line said: "Who shall I tell Lieutenant Strikestraw is calling?"

"His father, if you please." There came a click, then another. Thomas assumed at first that he had been disconnected. It happened so often these days. Yet he kept the receiver to his ear, and while he waited it occurred to him that someone might be listening on the line. Then he decided he was imagining things. Ultimately, another voice answered, this one more authoritative, or more military—or peremptory?

"Mr. Strikestraw?"

"Yes?"

"I'm afraid you can't speak with your son right now. If you'll give me your number, I'll ask him to telephone back." At this, instead of following his impulse, Thomas said only:

"He has the number, as it is that of his childhood home. I wonder when you are expecting him in, or whether you are. Alternatively, could you tell me where else I might try to reach him."

"Hold on a minute." An officer, perhaps, but not necessarily a gentleman. This time, though, the delay was not so long; the speaker had clearly simply clapped a hand over the mouthpiece and now was muttering to someone nearby. Then: "I'm afraid I can't tell you how to reach him, but could you give me a number anyway? It may become necessary for me to call you back myself."

The Friday was as bright and as hot as the Thursday had been, and again the window sashes in Grace's bedroom stood open wide. Grace herself, though, was determined not to spend another day paralyzed and in a void. There was little she could do, but she proposed to do that little. She had finished her breakfast and had settled herself to "do the thinking" she had mentioned to her husband. She was glad that Thomas had not asked her what she planned to think about, because by then she hadn't decided—just that it be something quite agreeable, involving scenes with pleasant associations, which she could capture in her mind's eye as they unfolded.

In January she had driven down to Southport to watch the Great River enter the sea. She would think about that. She had arrived in the afternoon. The air had been bright and clear, for the sun had had more than a month to climb out of solstitial gloom. Grace had friends in the village but had found her way down to the waterfront without crossing paths with any of them, which on this day had been her intent. She had sat down on a park bench to gaze out across the mouth of the River, the breadth of which had never failed to cause the stirring of awe within her. At high water—as now—it had resembled vast meadowland. The breeze was raking the surface as uniformly as grasses grow in a plowed but fallow field. Beneath, no skein of current could be sensed.

And now began the spectacle that Grace had come to witness, an everyday pageant produced in concert by man and nature, one that she had always permitted to astonish her—often though she had watched it—with its "surprise" ending: Shipping held the channel close to the western bank, running down past Southport and away from Oak Island. And now as she watched, a freighter was steering this way, steaming toward the open sea. Until the very last moment she appeared to hold a course that would take her right past and away from the embrace of land—Grace had even sometimes thought away from earth itself.

Now it appeared that just this very thing was going to happen, for the first time and unaccountably. Abruptly, however, the vessel came hard aport and ran some distance eastward and out to sea. Grace had watched until the ship vanished over the horizon.

Apart from land, maybe apart from earth.

If she heard it, Grace did not register a knock upon the door downstairs at the back of the hallway. The knock was in itself surprising, for people who entered the house by this way were ordinarily not expected to knock. But Rhodë came out of the kitchen and answered the door just as she would have the front. It seemed to her curious that it was young Harry Weston. She said: "Good evening, Mr. Harry"—she used this formula after three o'clock or thereabout.

"Hello, Rhodë. Is Canon Strikestraw at home, and may I see him?"

"Let me just go and find out," and she stepped across the hallway to the study door, which was closed, as it was usually not, and she rapped softly. Then she entered. "Father, Mr. Harry Weston is here to see you; may I show him in?"

"Big Harry or Little Harry? And why did he come around this way?"

"It's young Mr. Weston, Father, and he knows something about our trouble."

"How do you know?"

"Well, he *did* come around to the back. And he's acting as solemn as a judge."

"Ask him to come in."

Rhodë had not quite prepared Thomas for the pitch of the young man's agitation and distress. They shook hands. Harry's was cold, sweaty, and trembled slightly. "Hello, Harry. How are you; how are your family?"

"We're all well, thank you, Canon. But I have something I must talk to you about right away." Less than normally ceremonious, Thomas noted. The young man was clearly very uncomfortable.

"Please sit down and talk to me." But Harry did not sit down. "I've got something to show you, too." With this, he looked outside the room, then stepped quickly onto the back porch—actually a small loggia. He returned immediately with a duffle bag hefted onto his shoulder and did not set it down until he had glanced about and found a place where it could rest out of sight from the doorway.

To begin with, Harry said nothing, but walked around the room, glancing as he went, out through each of the four tall windows as he passed them. He seemed dissatisfied that all of them were open. The basement storey of the house, though, raised the room and the two men in it well above the plane of being overheard from outside the house. Thomas, taking note of this behavior, gathered that he himself might at least close the door. Then they sat down upon chairs covered in old leather worn supple, redolent of saddle soap, and Harry began to disclose his inexplicable tidings:

"I guess you know I've closed my office and enlisted. Now I'm waiting to be called up. But the waiting is getting on my nerves. I ought to be doing something. Or if I'm forced to do nothing, then at least I want it to be active nothing, not passive nothing. I've taken to patrolling, for whatever it's worth."

"To patrolling what?"

"Any coastline, the beaches, even the river bank up as far as here, and on up to Orton's Point."

"Are you doing this patrolling on your own? Have you associated yourself with the Coast Guard?"

"Not officially. Not yet. I could be called up at any time. But I know they've started sending out their own patrols. Sometimes I meet them."

"Have you seen anything?"

"That's why I've come. I have."

"What?"

"Robert.

"It's confusing. I can't understand what was happening."

Thomas was momentarily struck dumb. After a little while, during which the dreamlike state of the day before lapsed closer toward nightmare, he said: "Well, then, can you describe what *seemed* to be happening?"

"I'll try. On Wednesday night I couldn't sleep. I got up and drove down to Oak Island, thinking I might do well to scout over part of the shoreline near the old beacon range."

The priest was seized with alarm at the mention of the name of the place, for it had been upon a dirt track off the road onto Oak Island that his son's car had been found. He waited, and Harry went on: "You hear things, of course, and you see all kinds of things. Movement. Everywhere. I try not to let my imagination get away with me.

"I parked off the road and started walking. But when I got close to the old range, at first I thought—then I was sure—I saw people moving about, ahead of me. So I left the beach and went into the dunes. In a way I felt foolish. But the War is real."

"Yes, real indeed."

"I knelt down and edged toward them. Eventually, I could hear their voices. But I couldn't make out what they were saying.

"I waited for a while. When I was pretty sure they hadn't noticed me, I got nearer and climbed a high dune."

Rhodë tapped on the door then put her head inside. "Excuse me, Father, but Miss Grace has told me to go along home. So I've brought you your evening drink." There were two tumblers on the little tray she held, and a decanter. "I thought maybe Mr. Harry might like to join you." Each man drank off a glass of whiskey, before realizing he had done it. Thomas, who ordinarily had only one, immediately poured two more from the decanter, and with these they settled back. They drank slowly for a time in silence.

"Are you sure it was Robert you saw? Was he with these people?"

"I wasn't at first; later, I was. And, yes, Sir. He was with them."

The room, being at the back of the house, which was westward, had grown strangely cool and unexpectedly darker. The little arrangement of silver and crystal and amber spirit that Rhodë had left behind glinted lazily in the waning light. So did Thomas's eyes. So did Harry's. To cover panic and the knowledge of disaster.

"I looked all around. I counted six men in all. Three were in swimsuits."

"But, what time was it?" By this point, Thomas was speaking automatically, as though he were outside himself. Listening to himself. Even seeing himself, through alien eyes.

"About eleven, I think. Two of the three in swimsuits were farther off, dragging a box about four feet long into the dunes beyond me. That would be east of where I was. The box seemed to be heavy. And it wasn't the first one they'd dragged there. I could see furrows in the sand from another one—or from other ones—I wasn't close enough to tell. It was dark—darker than I recall as being usual, even down there. The other man stayed at the water's edge, with his foot on the bowline of an inflatable rubber boat, to keep it from washing away. I think they had brought the boxes in it, because that's where the furrows started."

"Brought them from where?"

"I don't know. I kept looking out to sea. It was very dark." Harry stopped, then continued, but in voice of a different register. Thomas rather wanted him to digress, to stall, to defer. And at the same time he wanted him to go straight to the point. For himself, of course, the point of the story was Robert. If only he could be sure of being ready! "Canon, have you ever been looking for something you didn't really expect to find, then thought you'd found it after all? But then not been able to believe it was what you thought it was, when you *did* find it?"

"Possibly, I think."

"Well, out at sea, not far out, dark as it was, I kept thinking I saw something glimmering."

"And you couldn't make out anything in particular about it?"

"No, Sir. I'm not even sure I saw it. It was as though it—or something— were...rolling slightly, so that as soon as I would seem to see it, the glimmering would be gone. Do you see what I mean?"

"In a general way, yes, I think so."

"Anyhow, the men who'd been dragging the box, after they'd got it over the dunes, went back down to the water and hung about with the one keeping the boat. Light surf was breaking, washing over their feet. I guess the boat was empty by then because the water took it lightly first before them, then behind again, as the surf slid back. One of the three had a flashlight. It was turned on, but he kept his hand over the glass. You could just see a red glow. And all three of them, I think, had handguns."

"Are you sure?"

"No, but almost sure—pistols, I think, not revolvers."

"Where was the one you took for Robert?" Harry glanced upward at the priest. Then down again.

"He was one of the other three. These other three men were dressed—one I had never seen before, as far as I could tell, another of them seemed to be somebody I either knew or knew about. I can't tell you what made me think I knew who he was.

"The third one was Bob."

"You could see his face?"

"Not then. But I knew him. I don't think he was as thick with the other two as they were with each other."

"But they were all talking among themselves?"

"Yes, Sir. It was mostly the others—not Bob—but every once in a while he'd put in a word."

"What were they talking about?"

"I couldn't tell. The breeze kept shifting quarters; their voices rose and fell with it. Anyway, they weren't speaking English."

"None of them?"

"If you mean Bob, Canon, yes, he was speaking the foreign language too."

Leaning forward Thomas said: "Listen to me, Harry. Nothing much less fortunate than this can have happened. It looks rather grim for Robert. Even so, you must go right away and make a full report. No one must be allowed to retrieve those boxes, assuming it's not already too late."

"I don't think it is. I stayed on until the shore was clear. And I went back to watch before daybreak. Then I sent some friends there to play Badminton yesterday morning, and some others later for a picnic. I don't think anybody will have been around there trying to retrieve boxes."

"That's a relief. And good thinking, too, but now some authority has got to be informed. Did you drive here?"

"Yes, Sir."

"Then go over to the Coast Guard station and give them full particulars."

Harry stood. Thomas stood. Neither spoke. In back of the garden crickets began to sing. Harry did not want to finish the story; Thomas did not wish to hear the rest. But Necessity had enjoined it, fatal filament running.

In a yet more hushed voice Harry said: "The one doing most of the talking said something sharp to Bob. Bob took a mailing tube or a small map case—something like that—out of the jacket he was wearing and handed it over. Then the three of them huddled together. The head man opened the cylinder and took out some papers. They were trying to unroll them and read them, I think. Unroll them against the breeze. One of the men—I couldn't tell which—took out a flashlight, a small one, and very bright, when he switched it on—that's when I saw Robert's face. I could swear an oath on it." Thomas winced, but inwardly. "The last of them—the one who seemed in a way familiar—took him by the elbow..."

"Who? Robert?"

"No. The head man. He took him away a little distance and talked quietly to him. Then the head man gave the other what I think was a sealed envelope and sent him away. He passed below me going west, heading for the road. It had got late—in all, an hour and a half must have gone by. I remember thinking after they'd all gone away: *'Maybe none of it really happened'*."

"No, Son, it really happened, I'm afraid. And Robert's car has been found."

"But *I* found it. It's one of the things I came to tell you."

"Somebody else found it first and found the keys, so he was able to move it. Now come to the end."

"That duffle has his uniform in it; there was nothing in any of the pockets. It was in the trunk."

"Harry, it's time to get on."

"The one I've been calling the 'head man' whistled—a low-pitched whistle, like wind in the telephone wires—and two of the men in swimsuits, I think they were the same two—the ones dragging the crate—came up to them, then they all went down to the water. Bob too. I think they were holding a gun on him. All five got into the boat and they pulled away. They disappeared. It was dark over the ocean. I watched, but I saw nothing more… nothing more at all."

On that night, after a little time, while broken waves slid up and back over the footprints, imprint of the bowline in the wet sand, other marks near the water, the tide ebbed, far enough eventually so that scattered pieces and heaps of rip-rap emerged—part of a groin once, or of some other work of man. But there is no bulwark against the sea.

Back and forth across the roughly dressed and now weed-covered stones, as they stood out into the air, sand-fiddlers scuttered. Softly as they went, they rattled and ticked. Their courses wrote pentagrams—no, dodecagrams. No, no figure either of geometric or of runic meaning.

So much racked by sorrow and fear, Grace had slipped into a languor, through which at intervals she had heard the two men talking in the room below. She stared stuporously out through her bedroom windows, and though now the passage of half a year had brought her to midsummer, the westering sun approximated in her memory to the angle it had held on the January afternoon in the fishing village downriver. Besides, a breeze suddenly filled the curtains like sails, filled the decks of the room in the same moment, a ship, and Grace definitely sea-borne.

She arose and packed a small suitcase then sat down and sipped at a glass of tepid tea while she waited for her husband to appear. When he came to the doorway of their bedroom, she said: "Tommy, I am going away for a while. I'm sure—if you've thought about it—that this is what you will have expected of me. I'll take Robert's car and leave you ours."

"Do you want me to come with you?"

"No. You would be miserable if you ran away. I have to run away because here I don't know where to turn. It would be toward the wrong point— I'm sure of that. There is no right; our life seems to have become horribly deformed. And all in just a moment." She took her suitcase from the luggage rack under the window. "Do you know what Rhodë said to me this evening when she left?"

"I think I could guess."

"That's right: 'I will see you in the morning, if life lasts and nothing happens.' It's what she says most afternoons. Can you imagine? *'If nothing happens'!"*

For that matter, 'If life lasts.' Thomas was thinking not of his son but of his wife. He and Grace went downstairs. He carried her suitcase. Then she drove away.

Thomas found Rhodë in the breakfast room next morning—Saturday morning—setting out bacon, eggs, toast, marmalade. "I thought, Father," she said, "that you might want to build up your strength." He sat down to it all gratefully. "And, Sir? I feel that I ought to pray for Mr. Robert in the presence of the Holy Sacrament. If that would be all right. Later on." At that time, Rhodë was the only Colored Episcopalian in New Brunswick, a direct result of old Mrs. Strikestraw's exertions. She tended to be rather High-Church.

"Of course I want you to do as you think fit, Rhodë. Go whenever you wish. The church is open. The Sacrament is there, on the side-altar as usual. But the Creator (This is how Thomas was referring to the Godhead at that period) will surely receive your prayers, no matter from where you make them, don't you think?"

"Let it be a far thing from me to tell you about matters like this. But with things as they are, I'd fall down amid a multitude and try to touch the hem of the Savior's garment if I had the chance."

"Yes, I see now how it stands. And, Rhodë …."

"Sir?"

"Did Miss Grace tell you yesterday where she would be going?"

"Yes, Sir. To Aberdeen, to stay with her sister. And, do you know, in all these years I never have heard one word about her sister in Aberdeen!" And she went off into the kitchen.

Now Grace Strikestraw had no sister at all. She was at this time a woman of fifty-three years. She had been thought remarkably pretty as a young girl; her slender form and lovely features had paled into a ghostly over-refinement. In her youth she had been slightly neurasthenic. But she had been successful in her schooling and other endeavors, and widely sought after by her peers, from whom the neurasthenia had been concealed. It was in any case never pervasive—just a small, jagged crack running across the pane through which her character had to be looked at.

For example, although brought up to exhibit a practically Oriental deference toward her elders, she had once, when her mother had suggested some minor change in her technique at the piano, slammed the cover down over the keyboard and stormed away.

Years afterward she told her husband about it. This was during her mother's funeral when, like most in that circumstance, she had been trying to remember, and to expiate, all offenses to the dead.

"What were you playing?"

"Something by Debussy, I think. Why?"

"Well, because there—little as I know about it—I believe technique and interpretation are more important."

"More than what?"

"Than in Bach."

"What do you mean by that?"

"Oh, I don't know. It's probably idle to discuss it."

"Well, I don't see what you mean; probably I don't want to. I'm just so terribly sorry to have wounded her."

"I expect you wounded her less gravely than you think."

"Why?"

"She was your mother; mothers usually love their children without qualification—fathers, too, though less regularly."

"Do you think unqualified love is good…or right?"

"I think that love, if genuine, will be unqualified."

Later still, when this same subject had again arisen, Thomas told Grace that if she had been playing Bach the question would probably never have come up.

"Why not?"

"Because Bach's music always tells it own tale."

"Bach's music doesn't tell 'tales.' "

"Yes it does, and they can't be so readily distorted by technique or interpretation. Their existences are very close to their essences."

"Where did you get that?"

"Not from a musicologist."

Since Thomas was widely considered to be a good shepherd and to know his sheep, Grace was generally felt to be the power behind the crook. That is how it was in those days in the South.

Yet now she fled from an affliction that she thought she might not be able to withstand. She journeyed again to the fishing village, not in rêverie this time, but indeed, and put up for the night on Friday in a small motor hotel just at the waterfront. More for camouflage than for disguise, she had packed the kind of clothes she never wore: Trousers, overshirts with embroidery and long tails, straw sunhat, smoked glasses—wear more probable in Rockport than in Southport. Besides, anyone looking for her would be looking either in New Brunswick or in Aberdeen!

In the morning, she went out and found a place upon the same park bench. The village was now sheathed in green; heat and shadow everywhere. But the great expanse of water that was the River surging into the ocean looked much the same as before. Leaning sunlight flecked the surface, which was riffled only by a midsummer breeze. Grace waited for a ship to come steaming, to turn at the last moment, to run a space, to turn again, to cross the bar. And for the River, grown so great after its passage through confining banks and forest gloom, overhung by bowing trees, hobbled by rocks and shallows in the uplands and, nearer the coast choked by fallen trestles and towers and drowned pilings—unremembered and uncharted—to spill free into the ocean, clear of land, and be always in the sun.

No ship came, however. None came, and suddenly as she watched—No, not suddenly; so overwhelming a thing could not have appeared suddenly, not if one had been watching—a shattering rainstorm broke. It had been heralded. The light from the sky had been not so much clouded-over as cancelled away by a low and heavy, lurid stratum of mist, and anything at all obscure to begin with—the inside of a boathouse seen through open doors, the shade beneath a grove, the space between two houses standing close together—had now been seized by lampless dark.

Then silence had settled over everything. It was as though one had gone abruptly deaf, had expected to see people laughing but not to hear their laughter, or in a boatyard to see a glowing rivet struck with a hammer but not to hear the ring. And only after this, rain and the winds. More like those of winter than of summer, they lashed the estuaries. Thunderclouds streamed in from the ocean to bank against the mainland and seek entrance at the river. Wind raging now with an undoing voice.

At this time, especially as the heavy weather had not yet reached New

Brunswick, Thomas was no more unsettled by his wife's absence than if she had gone to a spa.

She had said to him when he had mentioned that Rhodë, while admittedly a sensible woman, was nevertheless a devout Christian, that views of this kind could cost him his job. And in that connection he remembered that he must knock together a homily for tomorrow's service.

But more immediately present to his mind were the questions what was being done about the hidden boxes and when he was going to hear from Norfolk, from Commander Fulford, as the man on the telephone had turned out to be called, or whether. And with that thought, the telephone rang. When he answered, Sarah's disembodied voice asked him to hold for a long distance call.

When the circuit had been completed and he had been told to "Go ahead, please," he ventured only: "Thomas Strikestraw."

And the brisk reply came back: "No names, if you don't mind. I spoke with you the day before yesterday. Do you know who I am?"

"I do."

"When we have finished speaking I will ask you to take down a number then to telephone me at that number in a quarter-hour from now. Will that be convenient? Shall I give you some time to think of a place?"

"That will not be inconvenient; but I don't know what you mean by 'place.' "

"I want you to move to a different telephone. Don't use your own."

"Oh. No. I have a place in mind that I think will do."

"Good. If you will give me the time, I'll synchronize my watch with yours."

"Very gracious of you." And Thomas gave Commander Fulford the time.

A pause. A soft sigh. Then: "Very well. I'll be expecting your call at nine forty-three. I can't offer you to have the charges reversed; I'll be at a pay station. Here are three numbers. Take down all three; use the one corresponding to the alphabetical rank of the letter that is your son's middle initial." Thomas did not see why nine forty-five wouldn't have done as well. But he wrote down the number and they said Goodbye. He did not say to himself: Stranger Things Have Happened. For far stranger things had happened only within the previous not-so-many hours.

He looked in on Rhodë. "Is everything under control here?" he asked cheerfully, and Rhodë nodded and smiled. "Then I am going to see Mrs. Lucas."

Thomas's visits to their close friend Alenda Lucas were weekly, usually on Thursdays, and had a specific purpose. Every so often Grace accompanied him. This was one of the two means employed by them all for keeping the meetings from seeming clandestine and scandalizing the townsfolk. The other was the unspoken rule that Alenda and Thomas should not be inside the house at the same time, on those occasions when he went alone. Today's call, on a Saturday, was a departure.

Alenda had seen Thomas approaching and had come partway down the verandah steps to meet him. They kissed each other on the cheek. "I missed our regular visit; I hope you are well. How is Grace?"

"Grace has gone away for a few days. Was there anything particular you thought I should know, by the way?"

"No. Smooth sailing, so far as I can tell."

"I've come to use your telephone. At nine forty-three. Will that be all right?"

"I believe nine forty-three is still available. You know where the monster lurks. Wisty is off today. The whole place is yours! But please do bring some *eau minérale* when you're done, and coffee. It's ready in the butler's pantry. I'll wait out here, of course."

Thomas went into the drawing room (At Alenda's house you really could not escape calling it that) and sat down before the telephone apparatus. It was just like his own. But here it was not the only ugly thing in the room. For the Lucases had maintained their wealth right through the second half of the Nineteenth Century.

Waiting for nine forty-three, Thomas thought about his hostess and friend. He had been frustrated in every attempt he had ever made to classify her. (He was destined never to do so.) She had been reared by British gentlefolk on a sugar-cane plantation on the Island of Barbados—Alenda spelled it "Barbadoes"—and somewhere had met and had been married to the son of a family who for many generations had lived in New Brunswick. A legend claimed that a very early ancestress—a Lucas one; not one of Alenda's kindred—had been there when the White Man had first arrived.

Alenda herself was tall and slender. She dressed most often in black but never without attaching some very conspicuous color-saturated accessory to whatever she was wearing. The three friends were about of an age. Lucas, who had met untimely death through accidental drowning, had been spared long enough to father a son, William, who was now growing toward manhood in the Township. Alenda had brought a dowry, eventually, and the Lucas money was intact. If this did not amount quite to great wealth, it amounted at least to great ease.

Thomas proposed next to let his eye roam over the drawing-room. But the first thing it fell upon was a clock in a Baroque case made of *or moulu*, and this clock told nine forty-three.

When he came onto the line, Commander Fulford said: "We have not heard from your son."

"You should not expect to."

"Why? Do you know where he is?"

"I do not know as of this moment. How much do you want me to say over the wire?"

"Not much, and I may have to interrupt you. However, when did you see him last?"

"Around seven o'clock last Wednesday evening. But he was seen much later by someone else."

"How much later?"

"Past midnight."

"Indoors, or outdoors?"

"Out-of-doors."

"Now, listen carefully, because this will seem a strange question: Was there any...cargo about? Do you know of anything like that?"

The strangeness of his question was lost amid a labyrinth of strangenesses. "Yes, there was."

"Excellent!"

"I'm glad it seems so to you."

"Do you know where it is?"

"Where what is?"

"The cargo, as I'll call it."

"I know approximately where it *was*, but just now, no, I am not certain."

"Then listen carefully."

"I assure you I have been listening most carefully."

"First, try to locate it if you can—the cargo. And second, tell no one about any of this. Now, will you be at your...usual place tomorrow? I don't mean at home."

"Yes."

"Good. I will meet you there."

"It may be that a number of people already know. Possibly a rather large number."

"If so, it can't be helped. Do all you can to keep secret all aspects of the matter. Tomorrow, then." And he rang off. Thomas was irritated by the man's manner, but he reckoned his irritation in with pride and tried to put it away. That the location of some boxes should be considered of greater consequence than Robert's destiny seemed intolerable, even though such boxes should contain the bones of all the Apostles. Thomas reminded himself, at that point, that all of this was taking place in time of war, that the good of the many had to be considered first. He would see how things stood once it was known what the boxes held. If that were to become known.

"Something is wrong," Alenda said when Thomas returned to the verandah, "I can see that. Let me know—now or at any time—whether I can help."

"I didn't do as you asked. I can't stay."

As he walked homeward, Thomas observed the sky to darken. Then the storm, having found the River's mouth, and thus a pathway inland, smote the Town. But if Heaven had to be bent, or Hell raised, Thomas felt he must find Harry Weston at once.

At this same time, downriver, Grace, who had remained seated upon the park bench while all others hurried to cover, fleetingly thought that if seen she would be likely to be taken for a madwoman—and she would not have argued the point—but she sat with her face to the dashing rain, to feel it pelting her, to see the lightning flash, to have her senses scorched and wrung. For this was rain in its own madness, driven by the gale to strafe the land. And she knew that within this surge and whorl crouched some calamity of dot and dash, and that out upon or perhaps beneath the black sea was her one son, single whelp of her litter. She imagined the atmosphere to thicken and swarm with illegible signals that seemed to come from nowhere, yet from every direction, charged, at once—from cat's cradles of wires, arrays still more complicated, stretched among towers at ocean's edge. Grace supposed she might be sensing these herself, faintly as she tasted the minute concentration in the air of sodium, ionized by sunbeams, from the briny waters of her lowlands. Well, no sun shone now, and now she had gone completely mad. There could be no more doubt of it.

And in the depths of the ocean, too, she thought as she began at last to move away, there reverberated clangor and ringing. There, too, were flashes and blasts, with roll and yaw of dread. Nothing made fast. Nothing to make her fast. Grace went inside and to bed, and gratefully to sleep. She dreamt of skies clearing overnight, and the purified radiance of a midsummer morning after a thunderstorm.

Harry Weston said to Thomas: "All life has lost its direction because of the War. I can't keep on living as I am now. We can have nothing without fighting for it and winning it back. I think about nothing but about being called up, and then when I do go, I won't be myself anymore—just part of some battalion herd."

"You may find relief in giving up your individual identity for a while."

"Why do you say that?"

"Because individuality can be a kind of enslavement. It separates—obviously. Sure as families used to be separated in the days of the slave trade."

"I don't know about all that. But I do know that if I could go on with my life as it has been, then I would. But I can't."

"This is the second time this morning I've had to think consciously of things in general, rather than of things in particular."

All this had taken its beginning from the priest's observation that, while his wife had lost direction in her life and had abandoned herself to the loss, he had himself in the same circumstance persisted in trying to resolve it by reacquiring direction. He was—whether he acknowledged it or not—carrying out orders from a superior officer. It is what men do in wartime.

"At any rate, Harry, to go back to where we began, apparently Robert's superiors know something about what has happened; I mean about all of it." And he went on to recount his communications with those at the Naval Base. "And the Commander is particularly concerned that no one else know about it. He's coming here tomorrow. I'll want you to join us if you can. I wish there weren't so many other people involved."

"There aren't," Harry said. "I didn't go to the Coast Guard about it."

"But I thought I had talked you into going,"

"In a way, you had. It seemed right to me, too. But you had said it put Bob…I think you said 'probably in a bad light,' and I thought about that, and about what people might try to make of it. And then I wasn't willing to go; I've known Bob all my life, I suppose, and I'm not prepared to believe he's done anything wrong, not unless he tells me so himself. And even then I'd wonder."

There was a little space before Thomas could continue. "What about all those friends of yours? What did you tell them?"

"Nothing. They didn't ask. They were actually my brother Courty's friends. What I told them to do is what they would have been doing anyway—just in a different place. Most of them have only now graduated from high school, and the rest will in another year. If there is another year."

"There will be."

"Not for all of them. They don't know whether to enlist—those who're eligible. Some had planned to go to college, but now they're not sure why. Anyhow, I just told them I needed people at that spot all day, and I set them up with refreshments. Of a kind."

" 'Wine that maketh glad the heart of man'?"

"More like 'malt that does more than Milton can to justify God's ways to man'—sorry about the sacrilege, Canon."

"There is no sacrilege," Thomas said under his breath. But Harry heard him.

"So do you mean to say that, besides the men involved Wednesday night, you and I are likely to be the only ones to know?"

"We are definitely the only ones."

"In that case, those boxes and whatever is inside them are still hidden in the dunes?"

"They are definitely still there, and I know now who the other man was. The one I could only almost identify: It was Albert Sculpin." That man's name, in its original form, was Albrecht Seeraben.

Grace had awakened upon the Sunday morning to find that her dream had been a seductive lie. Rain had stopped hours before. The sound of the wind, no longer laden with water, was an unabating roar, fierce, steady. The sand that formed a rim of shore in front of the motor hotel had reverted to powder, as though it had long lain in a desert, and was borne now in fine streamers within the wind. The sticky brine clinging to the windowpanes caught and held it, so that just as Grace looked out, the last patch of the desolate scene outside was blotted away.

She kept a journal, in which she made infrequent entries. More often, when she took it into her hands, she resolved to destroy it presently, and then she would put it away again, unextended but intact. Now, though, she wrote: "I feel as though I have been sitting in a theater, watching my future being played. I know I ought to have gone up onstage and taken my part. But now—Is there Now?—the curtain has come down. I'm sitting in the dark. I'm maddened by a storm I dreamt had gone away, and the path before me really is overgrown and overshadowed." Then she resolved once more to destroy the little volume, but instead she put it away.

Harry Weston had gone on Thursday evening to assess the activity of the picnic detachment. Just beyond the Intracoastal Waterway, a delivery truck stood parked on the shoulder of the tar-and-gravel pavement, which was liquefying in the great heat down into the soft sand. He passed without slowing but noticed two men slouched in the cab.

The party was only now breaking up, even though most of this "shift" had been there since early afternoon. It was eight o'clock. A little after eight, in fact. Courty was among those who had remained.

Courty, who at a glance might be taken for his older brother, left in Harry's car. This ruse, which targeted the two in the truck, was scarcely necessary. But Harry had begun to warm to the element of adventure in the affair. He went again into the dunes, again to keep watch. The delivery truck soon appeared, driving upon hard sand eastward and northward, very slowly, then back again. That was all.

On Friday, Harry sent numerous citizens of New Brunswick and Southport to Oak Island to see the beached whale. A press photographer came from Wilmington. But nobody could find the whale.

That night, he went again, in a borrowed car. The delivery truck was there again. So Harry parked out of sight and encamped beneath the beacon range, and presently he began to lie rather low. The sand was agreeably warm. The sky was half full of light. In it, the moon and Evening Star shone in silvery beams. Harry gazed at them through a lattice of sea-oats stalks.

If the sun rises in the morning, the sea oats will be seen in their ripeness—in their summer gold. Darkness fell and the delivery truck came.

At his post, Harry watched the truck move past. It came to a stop a hundred yards away. The occupants evidently judged that they had reached the site they were looking for. Harry judged so as well. Yet a quarter-hour, dragging its heels, went by before the men got out. The driver was not equipped in any apparent way; the passenger carried a border-spade. They went quickly into the dunes, stealthily, just as though the truck were not blantantly advertising their presence. *It is possible these men don't possess great mental gifts.*

Then the one with the spade began to dig, carefully, too, as though disaster could be the issue of his work. Harry watched. Then both figures grew abruptly still. It was clear that they had been alerted by something farther along the narrow strand, narrower than before by, on the one hand, the passage of two days, on the other, by a four-hour anticipation of the tidal phase. Because they stood where the shore starts to curve back to the northeast toward Fort Caswell, they were able to see what Harry could not yet. They crouched down out of anyone's sight. But the handle of the shovel they left standing up like a sentinel. *Definitely not great minds.*

Eventually Harry could see and hear what had interrupted and alarmed the two men: An uncertainly swaying yellow light, and the sound of a kind of singing. The breezes were light and the song was unmistakable, though not sung quite true. It was the hymn "O Jesus, I Have Promised," from that remarkable era during which sentimentality was widely introduced into Christian worship. There are only three stanzas, but the singer ran through them mercilessly, over and over. Furthermore, he was bestowing unique interpretations upon each, resorting every once in a while to *Sprachstimme*, and swinging a kerosene lantern in vaguely accompanying rhythm, except where florid ornament in song might have resulted in spillage and self-incineration.

The singer and bearer of light was Duzey Blanding, who had established himself as town drunk after a conspicuously promising career in engineering had been tragically cut short.

It is well known that some people when drunk nearly out of their senses may nevertheless be uncannily observant. Thus Duzey, when he had come abreast of it, made straight for the jutting handle of the border spade—which Harry himself had already lost sight of in the gloom and distance—remarkably, unmindful of the truck, just as its two occupants had seemed to be, earlier.

He stopped, then altered his course in order to satisfy his curiosity. He had abandoned hymnody. The lantern no longer swung. Harry quickly moved closer, in anticipation. The two men behind the dunes sensed that they were about to be exposed in the very last way they might have imagined. One of them reached up stealthily for the spade, which was after all what had first posed threat of discovery. But the abrupt disappearance of it made no impression upon Duzey, whose memory was now running in five-second instalments. Furtively, the traitor shoveled a thin layer of sand into the excavation, then knelt to pack it firm with his hands. The other crouched under the crest of the dunes, waiting to see how close the interloper would come and whether he were himself going to have to take action.

But Harry moved first. He usually made his plans on the fly. "Duzey! Hey, Duzey!" he shouted. Duzey turned to peer into the last of the twilight. "It's me, Harry Weston." Duzey held up a hand to shade his eyes against the darkness.

"Big Harry or Little Harry?"

"Little Harry." The drunkster had forgotten about the spade and still gave no sign of having taken in the imposing presence of the truck. In order to confirm Little Harry's identity, he raised the lantern until the burning wick was at eye-level, with the result that he was temporarily blinded by the flame.

Nevertheless, he hailed Harry cordially: "Hey, there, Brother Harry! How're you doing? How're your folks? How about a little nip?" Harry was definitely not ready for a little nip, but did not say not. He came up and took Duzey by the arm, turning him away, yet not leading him from near the dune-line. He intended for their conversation to be overheard. The first elements of his plan had fallen together.

In the manner of town drunks everywhere, at least then and in that region, Duzey was dressed in faded denim overalls and a plaid shirt. Likewise, he carried his bottle twisted into a brown paper bag. But Duzey Blanding's clothes were immaculate and the bottle was not of a typical shape, bulging broadly at the base. For he had an income, a fine old house, and two live-in servants. And he drank only Cognac, of which he must have amassed a great store, for he drank it as liberally after 1939 as he had done before then.

Harry reconsidered the drink, rarely as he drank and little as he relished Cognac in its strength. But he had decided that a quick pull would not be too disagreeable, and he felt it might help to authenticate the slurring of speech and ataxia of gait that he now planned to adopt, in order to seem a credible companion to Duzey. But he bore in mind that the man whom he was trying to recognize might just as well recognize him. The thing must not be overplayed, nor undercalculated.

He began: "See that truck?"

Duzey repeated his process of scrutiny, but was somehow able to see the truck anyway, looming just a couple of yards away.

"Whose is it, I wonder?"

Duzey circled the vehicle, holding aloft the blinding lantern. "There's nobody in it."

"Where could they have gone?" Harry saw that the use of the hypothetical "they" posed no lapse in logic as far as Duzey was concerned.

"Maybe for a walk on the sand?"

"Did you meet anybody in the direction you came from?"

"No; did you?"

"No. I didn't either. And no footprints." Harry paused, he hoped dramatically and ominously. Then: "What if they went for a nighttime swim, got out of their depth...." Duzey's thoughts were muddled so that he could think about a maximum of one thing at a time. But he was still able to take this particular prompt.

"...and drowned!"

"Or something even worse may have happened." Harry held back again, battling an impulse to lead. Duzey was keeping up, though.

"Should we call for help?"

"Yes, and I think we'd better be quick about it."

"Right!" Duzey said warmly, borne now himself upon an agreeable tide of adventure. Both men, after all, were Little Boys Emeriti.

"And another thing; I'd better copy down the license-tag number so they can trace the truck. That could be helpful to the Rescue Squad."

"Or to the Police. We'd better get a move on!"

So they set off back toward the road, and made a meandering, halting progress. Before long, Harry heard the sound of the truck's motor, as first it came up behind them and to their left and then edged past them. The headlights were not burning. Duzey didn't notice the truck but continued to peer intently into the shadows ahead and to struggle to keep going, although he had already forgotten exactly what goal it was he was struggling to reach.

When finally the truck got to the roadway and had turned onto it, it suddenly picked up speed, the headlights came on, and soon it was gone.

Harry, in laying Duzey to rest within a wind-carved declivity, judged the cache secure for one more night, but he took Duzey's lantern and went back to see over it.

Multiple hand-prints appeared in the compacted sand. Several of the right-sided ones exhibited absence of the fourth and fifth fingers. This finding taught Harry why the other man had seemed familiar.

Grace had decided that it was pointless to remain so confined, even though the cyclone was churning with increasing fury off Cape Fear, seeming undecided whether to deal its heaviest blows here or to move on to the northeast. She repacked her suitcase and left the motor hotel. She was careless of the gusting wind that made her car veer, of rain squalls that kept her from seeing ahead clearly; when, under these influences, she several times either saw the center line appear upon her right or conversely drove briefly off the pavement, she merely reflected that nobody else was likely to be on the roads in such heavy weather on a Sunday morning, that she was not likely to do harm, unless to herself—not a very compelling consideration to her at this point. Except for Thomas. But him she had momentarily forgotten.

And then gradually she forgot almost everything real, and found herself again entering the realm of rêverie, this a familiar one. It was perceived in separate frames, each a little like a Hokusai woodcut, especially in respect to composition. Separations between colors and forms, though, were less distinct. Each successive scene was in her mind's eye set off by a decorated border, a different one for each, each differently conceived. Grace herself was strolling within a Japanese garden.

She wore a kimono. The season was late—with which the weather outside at this moment accorded. A few turned leaves lay about the walkways, scattered, and stalky chrysanthemums drooped onto patches of lawn, displaying still a few flowers, but mostly incoronated upon the earth with their own fallen petals, now so close to the end of the year and possibly, Grace thought, to the end of time, at least for herself.

Before her, a path was ending. At the edge of a lily pond, it became a series of stepping stones of irregular shapes running out into the dark pool, but only part way across, then there were no others. Having reached the last of them, Grace felt that the next step would be into the water and into a world beneath its surface in which she would have a surer place. By now, she was inexplicably carrying a basket of flowers, sprinkling them onto the stones and into the pool. And within this frame, whose border was touched with bits of silver leaf, whose lines more loosely drawn, whose colors more poignant and richer, even if appearing to have a quill's tip of India ink mixed in, she heard music in a minor key—was it the "Flower Duet?" Next, she realized that the flower-petals in her basket were ones only of paper and that this was an enactment, and that she herself was singing. But there was no answering second voice. From the last stone she stepped into thin air, prepared to be swallowed up beneath the black surface.

Nevertheless, some Japanese garden pools, although dark and in appearance deep, are actually quite shallow. And the one in Grace's vision was shallow indeed: Having leapt from the last of the stepping stones she found that she stood in a depth that barely covered her bound feet and ankles. She looked down and saw floating about her a margin of her silks, the ivory, vermillion, and green of lichen saturated and blurred. She began to laugh, lightly at first, then heartily.

Then the scene disappeared and she found herself sitting behind the steering wheel of Robert's car. Only she was still laughing merrily. And somewhere within her was produced a sporangium of joy—of joy once more. She switched on the fog-lights—she had forgotten to do that. And she made the windshield wipers go faster. In an especially heavy rain squall, she pulled the car off the road to wait for better visibility.

Thomas, rain soaked, arrived at home after devoting nearly all Saturday morning and a great share of the afternoon to conference with Harry Weston. He felt he ought to make at least tentative arrangements against the possibility of having to invite Commander Fulford for luncheon next day, and he knew he must compose a homily. But when he saw upon his desk a letter from Bunny Singleton, both other considerations were displaced. He picked it up, noting an unaccustomed thickness to it, opened it, read it. And this is what it said:

Collingwood Hall, Fauquier County, Virginia

My Dear Tommy,

I hope this finds you and Grace both well, and in as good spirits as may be. These really are trying times. Industry is booming all over the Country, yet you can't find a nut or a bolt at the hardware store! [*When had Bunny ever been inside a hardware store!*] We are trying to learn to live with the idea that we'll see dear Anne no more. Everyone has been very kind, of course, and of course we are grateful for their attentions, knowing that they are well-meant. However, we sometimes grow to feel that all this 'sympathy' just prolongs the realization and deepens the sense of loss!

We have our lives to get on with, after all, and it seems it would be better to put this tragedy behind us and to forge ahead. Some good many months ago, long before that terrible day, we booked places on a little cruise, first to the Bahamas, then on to Cuba and South America. (You have to book quite a long time in advance of sailing if you expect to get the best staterooms!) Of course that's off now—things being the way they are. There's no safety on the seas! Libby is terribly disappointed, and of course so am I. It would have been coming up in just a few months—they schedule these things for after the peak of the hurricane-season. Imagine calling such a thing 'peak of the season!' Ha, ha! It's really too bad, because I think it's 'Just what the doctor would have ordered,' at this point, and Libby agrees.

Well, all of us must be prepared to make sacrifices in times like these. So instead we're going to spend August and September at a delightful inn we know in Camden (Maine, that is; they have one in South Carolina, too—Isn't that odd?).

Anyway, this brings me to my main reason for writing. Little Edward is five months old now—or six, I forget—and growing like a weed—happy and healthy as can be, and *no* trouble. We've of course devoted ourselves to him completely. Libby has gone to the trouble and expense of outfitting a charming nursery, and we've had a nanny for him here around-the-clock, since the day he came out of the hospital (dear Anne died one week, to the day, after he was born, and of course neither of us will ever get over it).

But—especially now that we're going away—we really do need to make other arrangements, and Libby—God bless her!—has come up with what we think is the perfect solution: He can come and live with you—Edward can, I mean.

Consider this: With you and Grace, he'd grow up in a household where he'd have the same name as everybody else. Eventually, hopefully, he would have a father there, too, as well as a grandfather, which is so important to a little boy as he grows up, we think; don't you. Then, too, we are in and out so much, whereas your work [struck through] calling [struck through] clerical duties keep you pretty close to home, I imagine, so he'd have a steady sort of family life.

And there's another thing: We've never reared a boy—just the two girls (and the horses, of course. Ha, ha!). So we have no idea what a growing boy needs. But the two of you *have* reared a boy, and very ably, too, and would know just what to be on watch for.

Needless to say—or I certainly hope it's needless—we'd want to contribute to his upkeep. And later on, he would inherit from us, in his mother's stead. Talk it over with Grace (Give her our love!) and let me know what you think. I may write to Bob, too—or even ring him up since we're at least in the same Commonwealth—while I wait to hear back.

And, Tommy, *do please* remember us in your prayers. We're having a terrible time with the horses and may even have to reduce our stable. *Both* my stableboys have quit me and enlisted in the *Army*! They're brothers, and it will be a fine thing for their poor mother—she does most of the baking for Libby's parties—if they're both sent overseas and killed, which they probably will be. Sent overseas, I mean.

With warmest regards, yours,

Bunny Singleton

After reading this, Thomas found it once again necessary to remind himself that, for himself, to be uncharitable was to be also unprofessional. But the content pleased him immensely, the more because he thought it would please his wife, for he loved her. He abandoned the luncheon plan and applied himself to the homily.

The wind, which Rhodë maintained was the Breath of God, cannot be said to have guarded that night the mysterious boxes buried on Oak Island—in fact, it uncovered them to a depth of two-to-four inches. But its ferocity prevented anybody's retrieving them. And when morning came, there they lay, their brightwork glinting in the sunlight. They would presently be guarded by two fully-armed members of the Shore Patrol.

Grace arrived at home that morning between the two church services. "I'm relieved," Thomas said, "that you're safely back. I hope this storm moves away."

"It seems a little early for it, but I have seen them in early June." She stood on tiptoe to kiss him. "The rain is almost over up here, but that awful, steady wind has begun."

"Of course, if the storm moves from here, then that probably means the poor people on Ocracoke and Hatteras will get it—as usual. We can't really hope for that. I had a long letter from Bunny, by the way."

"A letter from Bunny, a long one? Are you sure it's authentic?"

"Yes, and you may read it if you want to, though I don't recommend it. They want to send little Edward to live with us." The sporangium, lying alone on the clouded heath of Grace's soul, burst open and let loose seeds and sparks of deep happiness. She turned anxiously to Thomas.

"Have you had time to think how you feel about it?" she asked him.

"Only to this extent: That I want to get through the day today, then telephone up there and ask them how soon they can have him ready." Wind blew every cloud from that heath, and every scattered seed took root, and every broadcast spark took fire.

On Sunday, July 12, 1942, in Christ Church, the Reverend Canon Thomas Grantly Strikestraw climbed into the pulpit and on his way took note of the dazzling whites of a Naval Commander among the congregation. He turned toward the altar, then:

"In the name + of the Father, and of the Son, and of the Holy Ghost."
"Amen."
"Dear People of God, I propose to speak to you today about war. For although the Church Year affords at this and at every season better and higher things for us to contemplate, yet today our own Country, and many of the countries from which our forefathers came, from some of which we draw the wealth of our customs as well as much of our own histories, are locked in mortal combat, so that from among this very flock there may be those—And let our prayer be that they be none or few—whom we shall see no more." Tightly grasping the sides of the pulpit, Thomas gazed out blindly. But this lasted only a moment and passed off unnoticed.

"We as a nation have entered this conflict at foreign provocation, presumably for the sake of right, and for the preservation of freedom and of all the other assets which have made the life of the United States of America so widely admired, not to say envied.

"I shall of course not mention those who have expected to have from it profit of any kind. For they are beneath our consideration.

"What I shall, with your indulgence, consider is whether war itself is to be regarded as wrong, as right, or as being apart from any such question. The Holy Scriptures bear plentiful witness to the waging of war, to its tragedies, as well, sometimes, as to its triumphs. When interpreting those sacred accounts, we are obliged to reflect carefully and indulgently upon the many and sometimes vast differences between life as led at the times of their composition—Let us not lose sight of the fact that all of them were written by man, and within time—and life as led by ourselves.

"Even so, I believe you will find in these writings that war is roughly comparable to pestilence and famine, natural as earthquake, wind, and fire.

"The twentieth chapter of Deuteronomy is devoted to instruction for making war properly—and apparently thoroughly, to the extent that if a besieged and duly captured town be distant, Israel is to put every man therein to the sword; but if the town seized be nearer by, and automatically more notoriously heathen, then the life of no one and of nothing in it is to be spared.

"Further, at the outset of battle the priest is to address the troops, assuring them that their God—and here I bid you pause to consider that their God, the God of Abraham, the God Who is the God of Judaism and of Islam, is also our God, in Whose house we propose now to be and Whose altar, standing now before us, awaits a holy, not an unholy, Sacrifice—'is he that goeth with [them], to fight for [them] against [their] enemies, to save [them].'

"Nor is our Maker's very Hand in the work of carnage elsewhere minimized, in, as an example, the First Book of Chronicles: 'God directing the battle, the greater part [of the enemy] had been killed.'

"Again, the Psalms, sacred not only to Christianity and to Judaism but also to Islam, virtually bristle, if I may say so, with references to the enemies of the Psalmist, presumably to be equated with those of Israel and her God. The concern is ever that they be overcome, usually with disaster accompanying defeat.

"There is one flicker of light: In the forty-sixth Psalm, at the ninth verse: '…all over the world he puts an end to wars, he breaks the bow, he snaps the spear, he gives shields to the flames.' But this poem has a refrain: [Yahweh Sabboth (an expression that Thomas did not speak, but substituted for)] The Lord of Hosts is on our side, our citadel, the God of Jacob.'

"Now I ask that we all be particularly reflective before and during consideration of the phenomenon of the transforming of swords and spears on the one hand, and, on the other, of ploughshares and pruning-hooks. For they are interchangeable to a disturbing extent. We are mostly, I think, more accustomed to hear of the former being beaten into the latter. For this is what is mentioned in Isaiah, the Second Chapter at the fourth verse, and quoted frequently throughout ages longing for peace. Less familiar to many of us is the passage from the Prophet Joel, at Chapter Three, beginning from the tenth verse, where we find an exhortation to battle beginning with the converse recommendation, that is, that ploughshares be made swords; pruning-hooks, spears.

"We must, I imagine, suppose that a scarcity of iron made the interconversion occasionally actually necessary, or that out of some like consideration there had sprung up an apposite saying, upon which both the corresponding sources drew.

"In the New Testament our Blessed Lord Himself lumps together war, rumor of war, famine, and earthquake—signs of the end of the world and of His own return in glory—which He discloses to His disciples in familiar passages from the Synoptic Gospels.

"But it is with the falseness of these signs—not with the error of war—that Jesus seems to be concerned. And so far as I am aware, He is not accounted to have spoken of war but one other time: In the fourteenth chapter of the

Gospel according to St. Luke, where He uses unpreparedness for warfare as an example, among others, of unpreparedness for discipleship.

"Behind and above me there appear, graved and gilded, the Commandments by which—they having been handed on to us from our parent-religion Judaism—we believe our Maker has intended for us to live. Of itself, war does not break them all, but it certainly breaks—and blatantly so—the Sixth and the Tenth, and war, in particular civil war, can reliably be imagined to lead to the breaking of the other Eight. Yet variously amongst the Holy Scriptures war seems reckoned less as a transgression than as a calamity.

"Recalling that at the time of my embarkation upon the Priesthood I vowed to uphold all these writings, now before you all I stand repentant of that error, as I find it to be, for I acknowledge that my vocation did not upon the occasion of my ordination cease to evolve.

"Let me attempt to make two points, and then I shall have finished [The common and to children present unwittingly tantalizing and cruel declaration]:

"Either war is natural and inevitable, though calamitous; we may in this case engage in it, when sufficiently provoked, with untroubled hearts, just as under the law of the polity we may with impunity commit homicide in self-defense, or in defense of another.

"Or war is the gravest offense against our Creator and Savior, and the world He intends, that can be imagined, if all the Law and Prophets hang upon these two commandments: Thou shalt love the Lord thy God with all thy heart, soul, and mind; and thy neighbor as thyself.

"But unchallenged stands the claim that among the first works of the Deity was the fashioning of the Cosmos—a Greek word meaning 'order' and used by us to signify the Universe—out of Chaos.

" In Plato, The *Timaeus*: '...fire, water, earth and air bore some traces of their proper nature, but were in the disorganized state to be expected of anything which god has not touched, and his first step when he set about reducing them to order was to give them a definite pattern of shape and number.'

"War brings about—I may say that its chief characteristic is the purpose of bringing about—disorder, a disorder which in some instances approaches, on a limited scale, that of the primal Chaos. Since this is the case, I believe we ought to enter upon warfare with our hearts filled always with penitence of the deepest order, bearing in mind especially that each of us has, by implication, no matter how small a part in it—remembering the well-known words of Milton's, that 'They also serve who only stand and wait,' applying them in a penitential sense, with our heads bowed as in anticipation of judgement.

"Now unto + God the Father, God the Son, and God the Holy Ghost be ascribed as is most justly due all might, majesty, dominion, power, and glory, both now and forevermore."

" *Amen.*"

The remainder of the service required of the congregation some thought, some response, a little physical activity, and—probably most important— some time, so that to the majority the several unorthodox remarks that Thomas had let fall in the course of this homily were lost. But they were not lost to Joe Watkins, ever-vigilant.

As the people were leaving the church, Thomas duly met Commander Fulford, whom he asked to wait until all of the congregation had left. And when they had, "Where," the officer asked, "can we talk privately?"

"Will my study at home be satisfactory?"

"I'd rather not leave the church, if possible, until I leave for good." In this Thomas heard an ominous note. As usual, some of the ladies of the Altar Guild were moving about the sanctuary, completing their ministrations and preparing to take the altar flowers to shut-in members of the parish. Thomas approached one of these ladies.

"Lucille, could you come up to the door?" In a moment she did, and Thomas said: "Lucille, this is Commander Fulsome. Commander, Mrs. Watkins. Could you show him into the sacristy. I must wait here for Harry Weston." The two went back into the church. When he could do so discreetly, Thomas removed his vestments, and soon Harry arrived and they joined the Commander. Not all three could sit down at one time, so all three stood.

Outside, Joe Watkins had helped Lucille his wife into their car and as he walked around to the driver's side she appeared to be settling herself, but was in fact steeling herself for two perils inevitable on the short trip home.

The first of these was that Joe, having discovered early in his driving career that once a car has been turned into a parking-place diagonal to the curb, which was the way prevalent there at that time, to back out one had only to retrace the original curve. So his approach was to start the motor, shift the gears into reverse, then let out the clutch-pedal while maintaining a deathlock on the steering wheel. Just those simple steps. That is to say, his maneuver did not include consulting the rear-view mirror. But this tribulation at any rate was quickly over, quickly decided. The other difficulty—more protracted—was the withstanding of Joe's critique of the homily of the day, which began with deceptive impassiveness.

While Lucille—they having got whole out into the light Sunday-morning traffic—was waiting for whatever might now come, the three men in the sacristy asked and answered each other in lowered but not conspiratorial voices. Commander Fulford, anchored by repeated exposure, was not borne along on any wave of sense of intrigue. He was addressing a problem relating to his work.

When Harry repeated the account of the comings and goings on Oak Island the previous Wednesday night and afterward, the Commander betrayed surprise at no point. He did interrupt several times in order to put questions. He seemed particularly concerned to get exact directions to Albert Sculpin's house and initially asked for a detailed description of the man himself, but he abandoned this after being reminded about the missing fingers, a reliable distinguishing mark. He thanked Harry, and commended him on the various forms his ingenuity had taken. He admonished Harry that he was legally enjoined from saying anything about the affair to anyone. Then he dismissed him as he might have a subaltern. They shook hands, then Harry left, nodding briefly toward Thomas, saying simply, "Canon."

Thomas had found Commander Fulford to be very agreeable in person. He was a pleasant-looking man in early middle life. There was not the slightest thing unseemly in his manner. He was direct in speech, but the effect, without the intermediary of telephone lines, was of straightforwardness rather than of curtness. They spoke again about the men on the beach, the boxes, Albert Sculpin. The Commander wanted to know everything Thomas could tell him about the man and his family, his occupation.

Thomas knew very little to say in reply: Albert had a wife—Trudy, Thomas thought her name was. They had lived in New Brunswick for almost five years. He worked as an automobile-mechanic's assistant, she in the post office. There was some thought that they had children who lived elsewhere. "I believe I know, at least in general, where they live," Commander Fulford muttered.

The Watkinses were heading home. Joe had begun by saying that the homily had been "interesting," then "a little bit out of the way, here and there. Obviously he doesn't think we should be in the War. And maybe not; war *is* a terrible thing. But what does he expect us to do? Sit around while all our foreign and home naval bases are bombed? Air bases? Army installations?

"Does he really want our children to end up speaking German east of the Mississippi and Japanese west of it? And what does it have to do with religion, anyway?" Lucille estimated that they were already two-thirds of the way home, and Joe was heated, yes, but by no means apoplectic. Not yet. "I don't believe all that stuff comes out of the Bible, either. I think he just thought it up. He does a lot of thinking-up, if you ask me, and will you look at the kind of thing it leads to!" At least Joe was keeping one hand on the steering wheel.

"And are we supposed to spend our Sunday mornings listening to *philosophy*!" The car had come to rest in front of their house, a tidy bungalow.

Lucille, as both of her husband's were now airborne, had her left hand discreetly on the steering wheel. With the other she had long since been clutching the arm rest. "And the *Jews*! I'm used to the Jews. We're all used to the Jews by now, but the *Islams*! What do *they* have to do with anything?"

"Moslems."

"Moslems, then. They're all Hindus, and they worship graven Buddhas!"

She bustled him onto the comfortable screened porch and made him lie down on the glider. *What I really need,* she thought, *are some green pastures and still waters.* As she went inside to get him a glass of iced tea, and a Miltown capsule which she meant to dissolve in it, he shouted after her: "All the upper-class British are Nazi sympathizers! Everybody knows that!"

Oh, Sabbath Rest!

When officer and priest were left alone in the sacristy, awful was the weight that hung above them as the bells' in the tower, just as if they had been standing inside the ringing-room—the weight of what must be said and yet could not be. After a while, the Commander began. He was looking out through one of two tall, narrow windows perpendicular to each other across an outside corner. His back was to Thomas, to the little high-ceilinged room in general. "Those same legal constraints...." He stopped here, or here his voice broke. Thomas was not sure which. At any rate, he began again, seeking another path. "I have no son, no child.... It is impossible for me to know what you must feel."

Thomas thought it time to relieve him; for it was their mutual duty to find a way to the completion. "Please know, Commander, that there are no circumstances under which I would wish you to...surpass the bounds of your duty."

This had provided the necessary interval, although when the Commander turned to face Thomas his eyes appeared full of seven seas of tears. But his voice was quite steady, and he did not allow tears to spill over: "If I were free to do so, there are many details connected to this incident, beyond the ones you already know, which I could tell you, and probably a great many questions I could answer."

"As I said,...."

"But your estimation of these events is probably sufficiently close to the truth so that—I hope—the information I have, you do not need; certainly much of it is irrelevant right now, to you, even if interesting."

"Thank you," Thomas said.

Like a bell rope, for a moment the great weight had gone well up into the vault of the room where for a moment it remained poised. But unless the bell has been set upon her stay, that suspense is fleeting. When she is pulled away and the immense throat speaks, a cycle begins, during which the rope, with its jaunty-looking sally, descends again, quite to the floor of the chamber. And likewise the burden descended square onto the men's shoulders.

"You will be wondering about your son's...honor," the Commander said. Now he looked directly into Thomas's eyes, evidently waiting for a response. And he was awaiting a particular response.

"Yes," Thomas answered, "there is that question." And at this the officer smiled broadly and with satisfaction, his military bearing now dissolved into grateful relaxation. He walked across the floor and placed his hands upon Thomas's shoulders, still looking directly into his eyes, as though to imply something of great importance to them both.

"*No*, Sir," he said. "There is *not* that question. And now I must go."

II

"When you were still in Heaven, an angel found you
crying. He touched you there and said, 'Shhh...'."
A physician to his grandson, who had enquired
about the philtrum of the lip, c. 1947

L ATE OCTOBER DAYS had taken to closing early, so even before suppertime,
to the rich, the rice-bearing, the deer-breeding earth below, the heavens
displayed the semaphores of night, as each acquired its silent fire. Bat
flown, owl poised.

Not quite within the Crossroads, which was a place unofficially limited by
the distances in any of the four directions at which the pavement of crushed
oystershells ran out, were parked two battered school busses—each vintage-
marked by the light value to which its paintwork had faded, by the advance
of the frontlines of rust—but under oaks that held their great dark boughs
across the face of the chandlery, two- tenths of a mile farther up the road,
northeast of the intersection. And even though the gathering crowd were not
actually furtive, coming quietly and in small groups to attend the dinner
being prepared for them, nothing much that autumn evening was being done

quite out in the open, if by "out in the open" be meant in the open places and not in the hideaways of the gracious world, and beneath honorable eyes.

Permission, for example, for this use of the school busses had not been sought and would not have been granted. Woody Paget's solution to this kind of problem was not to ask but rather to take and use, to say nothing, and expect to hear nothing, about it. But war or none, he intended to remain industrious in ingratiating himself with the populace; on that night, with a particular part of it.

Either he was far-seeing. Or he was fearful. But he knew that after the War Between the States, during what is known quaintly as "Reconstruction," far more Colored people cast votes than White. He knew, too, that when the Federal military presence had once been withdrawn, White Southerners had straightway initiated a series of measures—mostly restrictions upon eligibility for voter-registration—which by the turn of the Century had had the effect of disenfranchising Negroes. But the matter was in ferment again.

Paget had read a speech someone had made exhorting Negroes to register and to vote (for Franklin Roosevelt), and he had been favorably impressed by the arguments it contained, for they seemed to him much sounder than others; they represented Colored people not as victims of a long era of repression, but as individuals with a right equal to that of any other, which nevertheless they were themselves allowing to lie unexercised, as it were, in the dust. Woody had doubted at the time, and subsequently, that many Negroes had listened to and grasped this point. But to himself it seemed to go straight to what underlay their dissatisfaction. Millions were becoming eligible to vote; yet they remained unregistered. The discrepancy, though, would not last forever.

One had only to read, to listen, to open one's eyes to see. Woody Paget proposed to be ready when the unforeseeable day arose.

The dinner was going to be held as usual, and as usual at the Renezon Club. This landmark, built of cinderblock and painted white, except for blue window- and door-casings, was well away from the Crossroads. In fact no one knew for sure whether it were even in Peell County, the part of the congressional district which might one day become important to continued fulfillment of Woody Paget's ambitions. It shouldn't have mattered. And really, it didn't. Except that an anticipatory phase of the electoral process was going to take place there. If it came to that, though, then the project itself was no closer to being licit than the situation of the place where it was to occur.

Every so often, now that the proceedings were getting underway, Woody himself—short, wide-set, bald, to a degree bestial-looking, and just then quite red in the face—was sauntering along, grasping a waxed paper cup in one hand and, gesturing with the other, greeting those who were coming together, urging them to get aboard and refresh themselves before departure.

That most of those being courted in this way were not literate would have been surprising in one of South Carolina's more populous and more prosperous counties; Orangeburg, for example, where at that time in order to foster racial segregation, White boys of a certain age would upon a particular evening be brought to the lighted Courthouse in order to register to vote. And one of the things each must do—with his father beside him and his father's friends around him (who were of course the fathers of his own friends)—was to read a brief but complicated passage from the Constitution of the United States, of all remarkable instruments, proving the expected literacy and thus eligibility.

But Woody Paget welcomed with a view to coming days dark skin and illiteracy both, and oftenest in combination. He looked forward. He wanted to be sure of an unfragmented constituency, and he wanted what it could bring him. He had never lifted his eyes above the appurtenances and perquisites of membership in the Lower House of the State Legislature and so always congratulated himself inwardly upon the modesty of his aspirations. There were unspoken advantages connected to it; they were what he really craved.

A few of the District's old-timers needed no urging from the Congressman in order to begin revelry. And as the crowds inside the busses became increasingly derepressed, more and more of those standing about outside decided to go in.

Woody worked the Crossroads assiduously, and the floozy who was at the time married to him—for one or other always was, it seemed—did what she could.

Three young Colored girls who were friends together had walked down, just for a look. None had any intention of attending the dinner at the Renezon Club, which was as well, because their families thought Woody Paget was "trash," and these young girls would have paid harsh penalties at home if word of their taking part had reached their people. Still, they wanted to see who *was* going along, what these reprobates were wearing, how they were all behaving. And, of course, they wanted to catch a glimpse of Congressman Paget and of his current consort.

Of these young women, all of whom were eighteen years old, the loveliest was called Lilia (pronounced Lily) Belle Gadsden. She had an older sister who was married, noted for her own good looks. And though they were remarkably alike, it was apparent that Lilia Belle would be the fairest flower of her family. The sisters shared dark golden-brown skin, the classic Nubian features, eyes large and almond-shaped, set above high cheekbones. The irises—for theirs was only a faintly nuanced jog in the continuum of human beauty, in fact of beauty taken generally—were not light brown, in no way hazel, but at once clear green and clear blue, as if pigmented with mystic ore mined from an ages-old lode, at the headwaters of the Nile. And the sisters were voluptuous of frame, the elder of course more so than the younger. Lilia Belle did all she could to conceal this. But in the lower river-basins of South Carolina, October weather is warm weather—and sometimes hot.

This is all to show that the elements of disaster lay to hand. No, nothing much that evening was taking place out in the open. Not that it was a night of roaming spirits, whom blue-painted windowsills could forfend. Or any sort of Witches' Sabbath or Druidic Samhain. Instead, on this night the ill-craft would not come from dwellers in another, unseen world but from what in the deep well of man's being is least good—or close to it.

Woody Paget's eye fell upon Lilia Belle. And he deeply offended two men in whose affairs he was feigning lively interest when he broke from them abruptly and walked straight over to the three girls and stopped face-to-face with the one of his choice. "What's your name, Darling? Or do I already know it and just not recognize you, got up so prettily? Are you coming to dinner with us? I surely do hope so; now that I've laid eyes on you it doesn't seem at all worth having it without you." Paget by this time bore resemblance, unaccountably, to a turkey-gobbler. "And what did you say your name is?"

"I didn't say, Congressman," Lilia Belle answered in a very low voice, looking down at the ground under her feet. *Toothsome, I believe is what this is called.* Paget was unconscious of it but he took her reply as somehow a challenge. Plainly, for example, her manners were better than his.

"Well, say it, then. I asked you. Now say it!" Her two friends stepped back a way.

"It's Lilia Belle Gadsden," she answered finally, hardly above whispering. If her name had been Ashfield, the name of so many of her relatives, or Araby, her married sister's name, then Woody Paget would have left her as suddenly as he had come to her. For either name would have connected the girl to Woodleigh. And Paget usually considered Woodleigh and the Ashfields as potentially the seat and agents of his own eventual undoing. But in the District every time you turned a corner you met a Gadsden.

Woody was aware that he had become entranced by the girl's eyes. He had stopped with her so long that the Floozy, unshepherded, had got out of her depth, and the embarkation would have become disorganized, except that now it was moving along under its own momentum. And the two hired drivers were making themselves useful.

Woody had taken Lilia Belle by the arm and was coaxing her roughly toward the chandlery, where the busses were filling. As he half-dragged her across the road, bits of shell worked their way beneath the straps of the girl's new pink sandals. Woody, with the softness of Lilia Belle's upper arm in his hand, was now looking her over less modestly, away from her face, so that he broke out of his trance, yet not into his right senses.

He was forgetting himself, and forgetting fatally. The faraway Hag stirred and awakened. With the silver scissors open, she lunged. An oystershell cut Lilia Belle's heel, and now Woody saw, as he allowed his gaze to fall slowly and systematically, a drop of blood, a dove's, killed in the field.

To those standing about or walking toward the busses, seeing all this, what was happening was not clear.

Most of them were behaving at least a little cautiously, for they were carrying not completely unburdened consciences themselves and were bent upon being not too much noticed—if they could get away with it, not noticed at all.

Paget was able to drag Lilia Belle across the road and into the dry, tall autumn grasses standing in the vacant lot between the Post Office and the Hardware Store. In the latter place, Sarah Hawkins, young wife of the proprietor, had remained after closing to balance the accounts. Looking out through the window before her, this is what she saw: Woody tore Lilia Belle's clothing, then his own. He shoved her. She stumbled a few steps backward and fell, and at once he was upon her. Like a hyena, Mrs. Hawkins thought, oddly, for she did not know exactly what a hyena was. But the name seemed appropriately loathsome.

As she emerged with a pitchfork, the pricetag still tied with a scarlet string about its neck and fluttering as she hastened, Paget had already, in porcine filth, begun the furious violation. Just now he realized that Lilia Belle was yet a virgin; and it caused him pain. It also caused her pain. Blue-chip pain, too. And he scooped it all up, both hers and his own, and cashed all of it in for heightened pleasure. For he knew every sort of moneychanger.

Sarah Hawkins had got near. She raised the brand-new pitchfork and with all her strength, which was augmented by outrage, by rage, by invigorating disgust, brought the rounded backs of the prongs down upon Woody Paget, striking him between the shoulder blades. When the blow fell, Paget had just struck the girl across her exquisite face with the back of his hand; she was resisting him. A small rent opened in the child's upper lip, at the left angle of the mouth; a second scarlet drop welled from it. Paget had been about to turn this also to his swine-lust when Mrs. Hawkins' assault rendered him closer to senselessness than he had been before. And now mindful of the capital nature of Paget's offense and (correctly) transposing her stance into that inculpability before the Law that shields one who kills in order to defend, she turned the handle of the pitchfork halfway round—taking up the slack in the red twine attaching the tag—and prepared to plunge the prongs themselves (They were so clean and shiny and sharp!) into the offender. But just then he desisted.

Mrs. Hawkins was simultaneously relieved and partway disappointed—the tines were so sharp and bright!

The Sheriff and a police sergeant had got there by then—for they had stationed themselves not far off—and now were pulling Paget away. When the Law arrived, the busses left. Surprisingly few of the passengers suspected that anything was amiss. Or extraordinarily amiss. They were taken to the dinner; Paget was taken to jail, which was in Ashfield, the County Seat.

Seamlessly, Mrs. Hawkins was transformed from ferocity to gentleness and cure. She held Lilia Belle until a Colored woman came to relieve her. Then she went back into the Hardware Store to fetch water and a towel, with which she began to comfort and cleanse. No male person thought it right to come near.

Lavinia Ashfield and Lilia Belle's sister Mary Alice Araby arrived. Their husbands were still in the fields and had not yet heard of the abomination. Mary Alice went to kneel beside her sister, who was calm now, looking straight up into the violet lake that the sky at its central height had become. A slight diminution in the family-likeness had occurred, except that even in deep dusk the two pairs of eyes defied comparison to anything but to each other, or to a couple of identical, unaccountable gemstones.

"How badly do you think you've been injured, Lilia Belle?" Lavinia Ashfield asked gently. And then, turning, "What do you think, Mrs. Hawkins?"

"The…he cut her lip. I can't guess at…the other. I expect the Doctor will have to see about that, Mrs. Ashfield ."

"Well, you've been her only help; I want to thank you on behalf of my family and, I know, of hers."

"Yes, Miss Sarah," Mary Alice added. "We do all thank you very kindly."

Lilia Belle had left off staring upward and turned to look at her sister; she tried to smile, but the expression ebbed from her face even as it was beginning to form. Then she turned to Lavinia, who had continued to stand and to keep watch. "I can get up now, Miss Lavinia." They helped her to her feet. She turned to Mrs. Hawkins and said, in a voice more modest than feeble, "God bless you for your kindness, Miss Sarah." After she had stood they noted the dark stains on her clothing.

As the other three were about to get into Lavinia Ashfield's car, Sarah Hawkins called out: "I reckon Woody Paget's life's not worth much right now!"

And, her own included, to everyone's surprise (for it was unlike her) Lavinia answered: "Was it ever?"

But at one time it had been.

Waiting at the Renezon Club when the guests arrived, in addition to what may be called the caterers, was a preacher of dubious stamp, or so he seemed. The clothes? The demeanor, slightly unctuous? Or was it that somehow he just looked like a fraud? He had been signed on by Paget as a sort of Master of Ceremonies—of such ceremonies as there were to be.

But the diners were entering the hall and seating themselves along the three tables with evident diffidence. The Preacher had the very remedy: "Brothers and Sisters," he said in a loud and somehow put-on voice, "let us all rise "—most were still standing anyway—"and give thanks for this good food and fellowship; let us now sing 'Praise God from Whom all blessings flow'!"

There is nothing to equal joining lustily in the Doxology or in some other familiar strain to banish misgiving and conduce to conviviality. There was also the comfortable feeling that the protective effect of the blue trimwork was being augmented. So afterward, everyone sat down with smiles upon their faces and with emboldened hunger and thirst.

Besides, no one knew exactly what had happened back at the Crossroads or with certainty that anything had. So the servers filed among the tables covered with bright paper tablecloths, carrying pitchers of iced tea and of beer (never too much, though, because the guests must be able to remember what they had been given and what would one day be expected in return). Platters of barbecued pork, baskets of fried chicken, and all the things that go with them. And as often as wanted.

Then the Preacher, who had come all the way from Thunderbolt, Georgia, and must before long return there, climbed onto a small platform festooned with decorations aimed at stimulating patriotism and advantage for the deprived. He extolled Woody Paget's record, which was shameful, his principles, of which there were no longer any, and his vision for the future. In this last essay, the Thunderbolt Preacher's cast fell fully wide of the mark. But he struck it squarely when he added that "The Congressman so much regrets not being able to be here among all of us this evening."

Finally, as each guest left the hall he was given a silver dollar and a facsimile of an official ballot, marked. For those who wished to try their hands at it, available also were printed passages from the Constitution, for memorization (for Woody Paget had been confident that in the fullness of time he could control which passages would be employed in the literacy-testing process—if, indeed, this process itself should survive).

The caterers were long gone. As the crowd were filing out, short work had been made of table-clearing.

All the kitchen cleaning had been accomplished during the last stages of the dinner and the address by the Preacher from Thunderbolt. And the hired help had packaged the leftover food in waxed paper bags to be dispensed along with the ballots and the pieces of silver.

The presumptive voters-to-be, now initiated and prepared for the rite which would take place none knew when, began climbing back into the busses. As the last of them stepped outside the Renezon Club, the Preacher turned to put out the lights; Paget's wife, who with him had been bidding Farewell, now said: "My husband has been taken to the County...Seat, and I have no idea how to get there from here. From anywhere, so far as that goes. Can you direct me?"

And as the Hall went suddenly dark, the Preacher answered: "No, Ma'am, I can't. I've heard of it—It's called Ashfield. All of us down my way have heard about it, and the word is it's a pretty town—fine, big courthouse and so on. We've heard about it all right, but nobody has ever been there." With these words, he closed and locked the doors.

As he started to move off, Mrs. Paget called after him: "Why has nobody ever been there?"

"Because nobody lives there, Ma'am. Good night!"

"Good night. Thank you, and be sure to drive carefully; it's so dark."

"I will, Ma'am. But don't you worry: When I crank up this old crate, it just goes of its own accord right back to Thunderbolt, Georgia!" He had got far enough away by now so that his voice sounded like the moan of a ghost must sound: "—kind of the way Ashfield goes of its own accord. But nobody knows where it's going..."—Now the voice was no more than the breezes of night in the pines, could have been taken for them—"...because none of us has ever been there."

The dimly lighted busses had filled and the two drivers stood up stiffly from empty nail kegs upon which they had been sitting, apparently since their first arrival. One stubbed out a cigarette upon the earth.

Rita Paget went up and addressed the other: "Can you tell me how to get to Ashfield, please?"

" 'Ashfield' or 'Ashfields'?"

"What is the difference?"

" 'Ashfields' is the real name of the Crossroads. It started out a long time ago as 'Ashfield's Crossing.' The railroad crossing. From back when country crossings used to be named for the most prominent landholders nearby. 'Ashfield' is the name of the Peell County Seat. It's a town. But you won't find anything there at this time of night, except streets and buildings. If you need anything, you ought to...."

"No, Ashfield—the town—is where I want to go." She held for a moment, while trying to decide how much to say. "My husband was taken there earlier." And she needn't have said more. To the driver the thing was clear. He knew of many instances before this of people being taken to Ashfield at odd hours.

"At the end of this lane, where we all turned right on the way here, off the pavement…"

"Yes?"

"…and where we'll now turn left on the way back…"

"I'm following you." Understanding in a dark and alien land; the unfolding was so clear. Clear even in the dark; her way was nearly visible already. Because she must have *somewhere to go,* she knew she could find a way there.

"…You'll want to turn right. And this road will lead you onto a better road—it won't cross—and if you'll bear right at the stop sign, that better road will take you straight into town. It could be dark; I don't remember ever having seen any streetlights; but then I don't recall ever going there at night. See, Ma'am, no people live there." After this, the drivers boarded and drove the busses away.

Rita Paget got into her car. It was parked at some distance from the clubhouse, facing it across a clearing. She looked out for a moment before switching on the headlights. It was the dark of the moon. Unbroken to the eye the land stretched back into the pine forest and encompassed, along with the somber treetops, the shingled roof of the building, leaving a soft, dark field, not so fully committed to the absence of light as black is, but rather like an etching in which a large region of the copper has been subjected to acid. The ink is held, then in the printing process released in a sometimes wonderfully and softly irregular manner, avoiding uniformity without at the same time suggesting shape or pattern. The building was just a faintly gleaming rectangle of drowned white, floating within this eclipsed field of vision. The shape grew inexact toward its edges, where it imitated twine of jute pulled tight. Straight, yet not sharply distinct from its ground.

As Rita looked, she thought of a grave marker. And then she asked herself a question of a kind not usually considered to weigh upon the minds of floozies: *Am I thinking of it as a tombstone because it looks like one—because it doesn't. Or is it really a burial-place, and does it then look like one because it is one?* When it comes to floozies, one is seldom on very solid ground.

Rita drove into downtown Ashfield. Or, more correctly, into Ashfield, which was only a downtown. There *were* streetlights, and they were burning. It seemed ordinary enough; to be sure, no one was abroad, but it was very late, and so who should have been? The Courthouse dominated the town for a number of reasons, the main one being that it stood upon a large block of land that took the place of what in its absence would have been the principal intersection. *Like those squares in Savannah they go on so much about.*

So Rita drove around the Courthouse and noticed in her first circuit a lighted sign above a half-glazed door in the basement storey. It read "Sheriff, County Police." The upper half of the door and windows to either side were also lighted. There was a walkway. She drove around again and parked.

Through the glass in the door she saw a young man in uniform—not a service one—seated at a desk; she liked his looks, because she thought he seemed resolute—probably only in her imagination. She stepped inside. The man in uniform stood when she entered. *I've never seen a sheriff—if that's who he is—do that before.*

And Rita had seen other sheriffs.

"Yes, Ma'am?" he said courteously but directly. Rita liked that, too. *So many of these Southern men seem to let their words drool out.* Alas for Southern manhood! Rita thought, and had often thought, that their speech was like toothpaste oozing out of its tube. Fortunately for her store of metaphor, she had never paid any attention to the way Southern women spoke.

But of course she didn't know the right *Southerners, women or men, bless her little heart. Anybody could have told you that.*

At any rate, the man's behavior (He was from New Jersey and a Marine) was a perhaps small but nonetheless real sign of respect coming at the end of a day otherwise empty of such things.

"I'm Rita Paget," she said simply. "I would like to see my husband, if that's possible."

"It is, Ma'am, but you'll find him in a bad way, I'm afraid."

"How, in a bad way?"

"Well, he's drunk, for one thing, or just now starting to come out of it. I don't know whether you know about that?" Rita knew. "And he's dirty and...a little bloody—Do you know what happened, I mean late this afternoon? Over at the Crossroads?"

"Yes, I do know. I was there. Not right there, but there."

When she said this, the Sheriff looked at her with sorrow. "Will you sit down, Ma'am? Could I get you a cup of coffee? Or anything? We've tried to let him clean himself up some, but he doesn't seem interested. I'll take you back when you're ready. There's and armed officer guarding the Congressman, and he will have to stay."

"I'll go now."

Through another door was a corridor small in each dimension. The right-hand wall dissolved into what seemed to be a forest of painted upright bars. Woody was wandering somewhere among them. On a faldstool halfway down the corridor a police sergeant was sitting, but rose when they entered. His revolver was unholstered. The Sheriff gave a sign; the sergeant moved away two paces from the door to Woody's cell. Rita stepped up to the door and whispered: "Woody, Sweetie, try not to worry. Think of Who You Are. We'll get the best defense. We'll get you out of this."

"Thanks, Honey." They kissed through the cagework of bars. Rita, so corporeally fastidious, had never expected to do a thing like that—have her face touch things God-knew-who-else had touched. And with what? They kissed, and kissed again. "But I doubt it. Four people saw me do what I did, and each of them saw the others see me do it. Does that make any sense? No one of them can risk lying; they can't be sure some other one of themselves won't tell the truth. And there's the girl—and probably by now the Doctor. And not all of them are friends of mine."

"That's just how you feel tonight. Things'll seem better in the morning."

"In the morning, they're coming to take me to Columbia."

"For what, Darling, Sweetie? Aren't problems like this supposed to be taken care of in the county where they happen?"

"Do you know that what I did is a capital offense?"

"What's a 'capital offense'?"

"One they can put you to death for. Now, listen: You've got to do a couple of things for me, and there's not much time. Some of them will seem natural enough; others are things you're not supposed to do. And they'll be keeping a sharp eye out."

Electric light was not in those days, or there anyway, ubiquitous, so that as Lavinia and the two sisters drove farther and farther from the Crossroads they drove eventually into complete darkness, other than for the beams of the headlights. All three felt soothed by it; none had to face another. Mary Alice cradled Lilia Belle in her arms; Lavinia drove, and as she drove she thought. *An appalling situation. And rather appalling decisions must be made and actions taken.*

She glanced briefly into the rear-view mirror. The two women were evidently in control of themselves.

"Lilia Belle," she said, "I want to take you to my house for tonight. Is that all right? Mary Alice ought to stay, too, I think. That way, if anything should go wrong we'll have the telephone just to hand."

All of them had noticed ribbons or colored cloths portending some rite tacked to doorposts of darkened shanties as they had driven through the Crossroads community.

"Do it, Honey!"

"I'll do whatever you think best, Miss Lavinia. Just I don't want to be any more trouble than I have to be."

"You won't be any trouble at all."

"Thank you, Ma'am."

"Now, what I'd like—and the way we'll have it as soon as we can—is to have you and Mary Alice tucked up in Mr. Jack's and Miss Allie's big bed, with supper, or tea, or a little glass of wine—whatever you want. But first we're going to have to have Dr. McClure make a kind of examination, to make sure there's nothing that needs treatment. I'm sorry for that, but Mary Alice will stay right beside you, won't you, Mary Alice?"

"Yes, Ma'am; right by her."

"And Miss Alina or I may have to come in to help the Doctor. No men. Except Dr. McClure, and he doesn't count just for the reason that he *is* a doctor."

They drove on for nearly a mile, and finally Lilia Belle answered: "I have nothing to hide from anybody anymore."

"Honey, when this day has left you—now it will still be here tomorrow, and the next day—but when this day finally leaves you, you'll have everything. You'll have everything to give and everything to get! It will take a little longer to learn to accept, but not too long."

"I'm willing to do what I have to. I won't mind, either. You don't worry about me."

Finally the lights of Woodleigh appeared ahead. Drawing near, they could see that lamps were burning on the verandah, that two cars had been driven halfway round the big oval driveway before the house. One of them must be Dr. McClure's. The other belonged to the Joneses, who were Lavinia Ashfield's husband's sister and their brother-in-law. Instead of driving around to the back as usual, therefore, Lavinia pulled her car up behind the other two, and the three women went up the steps to the front door. Laurence Ashfield opened it for them. Alina Jones was the only other person in the front hallway. In an enfolding charge of green couture and hair like gold and copper spun together, Alina advanced and threw her arms about Lilia Belle and said: "Oh, Darling, the beast! I'm so sorry. I hate him and...I *hate* him! But everything is going to be just perfect for you—after you get over the shock and the wounding. And, as for him...."

"He doesn't matter, Miss Alina. Somebody else can deal with the Congressman."

"That's the spirit! That's our girl!"

Meantime, Lavinia kissed her husband. Then she said: "Is Miss Allie's and Mr. Jack's bed made up? The bathroom clean?"

Laurence looked uncertain; Alina said: "Everything's ready." They all met Dr. McClure and Mary Alice's husband Tommy Araby in the back hall. Lavinia worked silently to avoid the aggregation of people in any one place, since, one way or other, Lilia Belle would be bound to be at the center. She deputized almost everybody for something.

After the examination, during which Dr. McClure had needed nobody's help but Mary Alice's, he came out of the back bedroom peeling off his examining-gloves and in the process (intentionally) everting them and (unintentionally) shaking excess talcum powder all over himself and the old Heriz on the floor. "There was no laceration that needed closing, but it is clear that what we thought happened did in fact happen. There's a little bottle on the bedside table. It's sealed with a label, which I have timed, dated, and signed. Can anybody take it now to the hospital laboratory in Ashfield?" He looked around the back hall. Only Laurence and Tommy had returned. So McClure added: "I can tell you this: He may be a pig. But he is *not* a stallion. –Not nearly as much physical damage done as might have been."

Alina was just then coming out of the dining room carrying a small glass in each hand. "Carlysle! I can hardly believe I heard you say that! I'm surprised you even think about things like that! But I suppose all men do."

"I'm happy to know you think it beneath me, Alina. But you weren't supposed to hear it."

"Well, your mother would turn in her grave. And so would mine. Anyway, can I take these in, now?"

"What is it?"

"Sherry."

"Surely you have something stronger than that."

"They don't drink—at least these girls don't, do they, Tommy? I'll be lucky to get them to drink this. At that, I'll have to call it 'Sherry wine.' And, by the way, I'll take the specimen on my way home."

"No you shall not!" Laurence said. "It's not even on your way home. I don't want you driving all over the County at this time of night. And above all, not on this night. Where's Parker, by the way?"

"At home with John. I thought I could be of more use over here than he could."

"Anyway, I'll take the specimen."

Tommy stepped up. "Let me take it, Mr. Laurence. Lilia Belle is my family, and I want to do whatever I can. And this is not very much." So Alina, carrying the Sherry, went into the bedroom, came out with the specimen, and Tommy left gratefully on his mission. *The trouble with White folks is that you can't do much more with them than you can with Colored folks.* He felt that, after such a day, enough of either was enough. The road had been too long.

Carlysle McClure said Good Night and left.

The Sheriff, whose name was Merrimon Baker, had become increasingly concerned about Woody's progress from inebriation to sobriety. He had had already the alarming experience of having one drunken prisoner get the horrors while in custody. Woody was getting shaky. Sheriff Baker had already warned Mrs. Paget, if in a roundabout sort of way.

When she returned from his cell and asked whether she might get her husband "a little something to settle him down," the Sheriff at first put on a stern attitude, but then, in suspect haste, relented with a feigned reluctance.

"Well, Ma'am, this much is certain: We don't want worse trouble than we have already. I'll speak to Sergeant Wilson, and he'll find you a paper cup."

"Thank you...Sir." She had never before tried this and was pleased with herself about it. "He also wants things for writing. He wants to make a will."

"He doesn't have a will!"

"He wants to make another one."

"Why just now?"

"I don't know. But he's Hell-bent on it. If you'll excuse my choice of words."

Sheriff Baker thought over this. No prisoner of his had asked before for writing-materials. He thought through the Regulations. How could he make it work? He'd make it work, for he liked the lady. (He liked, too, some indefinite thing about the Congressman. God alone knew what.) "Here's what we'll have to do about that: He'll have to put his hands through the bars and let us put the cuffs on him again. Wilson can hold up a clipboard with paper. I think a will has to be witnessed by three people. Congressman Paget will know."

"I'll just step out to the car for a minute."

"And I'd better go and have a word with Wilson."

At Woodleigh, Mary Alice put her head out from the back bedroom door. "Mr. Laurence," she called out softly, "Mr. Laurence?"

Laurence came back from the front of the house. He had his finger in a book to mark his place. On its cover, once he had appeared with it, Mary Alice noted only the letters P L O T. Then three fingers. But she tried not to worry. Laurence said: "Is she all right?"

"Yes, Sir. But we are wondering about the dogs." She meant a group of homeless strays whom Laurence habitually befriended, had them vaccinated as each new one turned up; thereafter he fed them twice a day and allowed them to sleep in the downstairs hall. Lavinia's spaniels slept upstairs, usually with the Ashfields, though sometimes they had to be sent out into the hallway for the night. The two packs had nothing to do with each other, generally, which was a mercy, given the nature of their rare meetings together.

"Oh, Mary Alice, I've fed them; it's not at all cold, so I've told them to sleep in the back garden for tonight."

The young woman couldn't help smiling a little. "Lilia Belle feels she's putting them out of their place. She's unhappy about it, and wonders Could you please let them in?"

"Certainly, then, Mary Alice, if that's what you and she want. But there is no need."

"Lilia Belle never wants to drive anything from its place."

"Then I'll let them in. I can tell you, though, that Miss Lavinia doesn't necessarily consider this 'their place.' "

"No, Sir. But they do." She hesitated, and then said: "I will say there seem to be a lot more of them now than there used to be."

"Oh,well, they're wanderers. They come and go. I suppose some of them are lost out there." He opened the back doors. There really were a lot of hounds bedded down on the grass around the garden pool.

"Come," he said, and they all began to rise and stretch, occasionally scratch, and then they formed up into a quite satisfactory column and started up onto the back verandah. "Well, good night, Mary Alice. And say Good Night for us to Lilia Belle, 'sweet dreams, and slumber's light'. Has she taken those pills?"

"Yes, Sir, she has, and I'll make sure she takes the rest as they fall due. Good night, Mr. Laurence." She closed the bedroom door quietly.

While the van of the "Pankeytown Hounds" were selecting their berths, even as more were coming along in, Lavinia came from the Kitchen House through the dining room bearing a big tray with a white Damask napkin spread over it. "For Heaven's sake, Rennie! Not tonight!"

"It is being done at Lilia Belle's request. Are you taking them supper?"

"Yes."

"Then please double-check about the medication. There's no telling what the…what Paget may be carrying. I'm going upstairs."

When Lavinia had set down the supper tray and come again into the hallway, as she threaded her way amongst all the Hounds, listening to the pantings and the guttural and almost subvocal growls, the repetitive slap against furniture or wall or bedfellow of a wagging tail, she found it agreeable and realized that she simply liked dogs. But then everybody at Woodleigh did. Lavnia preferred ones whose families she knew or had known.

She liked especially to have bred dam or sire herself. But, that aside, she liked dogs. They were a comfort. Not to the numerous cats, of course, who got on with them well enough though at bedtime sought the elevated surfaces of chests or tables, where they could be trusted among the Chinese porcelains and silver picture frames. Thinking these mostly congenial thoughts, Lavinia wondered at the same time what in Laurence's nature impelled him to allow a drove of curs—even though he did refer to them as "The Pankeytown Hounds"—into the house almost every night. One way or other, she suspected that it was likely a goodly impulse.

She had not got far upon her way to bed when she heard a scratching at the door. She returned. When she opened the doors she saw a little mongrel, whom she did not recognize, pawing at the framing of the screen door with an apologetic air. He was carefully avoiding the screening itself, which might be torn. Lavinia held open both doors and said: "Come inside, Little Stranger, with all the others!" The puppy went along in, moonking about until he found space.

Lavinia went upstairs. She said to Laurence: "May the spaniels stay in here? You can be sure that this is just the night when the whole bunch would decide to get into a row."

"Of course. But they'll do best on the floor, I think."

After he had drunk off three ounces of whiskey in a little water with a few cubes of ice, which had been handed him through the bars of his jail cell in a waxed-paper cup—but leaving a generous moiety for later, in case of need—Congressman Paget stood quite still with his eyes closed. He opened them after a moment and said: "Much better. Much better. In a few minutes I'll be ready to start." First, though, he lay down upon his cot. He lay there only for two or three minutes. The Sheriff sent in paper and a fountain pen newly filled with black ink. He considered that the gravity of the document demanded black.

Rita had brought in the cup and now was merely waiting. Woody arose and beckoned to her. They spoke together through the bars, inaudibly to the others. When they had finished, Rita returned to the outer office.

Paget had studied law and knew the formulae. After the usual preamble about soundness of mind and body and payment of just and lawful debt, these were the provisions of the Last Will and Testament of Charles Spottiswoode Paget: He had no sister, one brother. To him he left the sum of fifty dollars. The brother, Francis, was married and now had three sons (and little else). To each of them their uncle left ten thousand dollars and additionally, to the eldest, the Paget family graveyard "situate upon lands lying not far from the ruined mansion, which mansion, together with the said lands, known as Dodona, these lands and this house having first belonged to my ancestors but since lost to my family, the said graveyard, however, together with an easement of access to the west, having been always excluded from the various conveyances through which the surrounding property has or may have passed, and being presently in my own personal possession" (Here followed a full reference to the particular pages and books in the office of the Register of Mesne Conveyance in the Courthouse in Ashfield).

In October, 1943, ten thousand dollars amounted to considerable money; with *Akagi, Hiryu, Kaga, Soryu*, long since lying berthed at the bottom of the Pacific Ocean, to anyone foreseeing the post-War economic expansion, more considerable yet.

All the rest of his property "of whatsoever kind and wheresoever situate" he devised and bequeathed to his wife, Rita K. Paget.

Finally, he directed that his last wishes be carried out by any who should survive him. These were that his earthly remains be interred in the family cemetery already mentioned, "according to the rites and observances of the Protestant Episcopal Church in the United States of America." The last bit precatory only.

This instrument would be executed upon the following morning, by which time the Testator would have slept off his drunkenness. For he did not want the will to be vulnerable upon such grounds. Rita, as a beneficiary, could not serve as witness. So at this time the fountain pen was surrendered, the paper taken away, the handcuffs again removed. Congressman C. S. Paget drew his hands back through the bars into his cell and refused to rub the pain from his injured wrists.

Most wills probably tell a part of the story of the testator's life. At least when current. Select a sheet of new copper out of which you intend to fabricate some object. Not at any time during its manufacture did anyone mean it to become a mirror. Yet you will hardly be able to handle it without noticing the whole or a corner of your own face with great fidelity reflected from it. Not until through reaction with whatever touches it—during time—will it, in corrosion, hold close and guard what it has seen and knows.

That is the way with wills; drawn for the purpose of conveying property, they promulgate histories, when fresh; and some are complex and others, simple. One acting promptly can find nearly any gradation between.

Charles Paget's last will had this story to tell, at the time when he made it: The meager bequest to his brother reflected estrangement (and, incidentally protected the integrity of the instrument). No member of the Paget Family had ever spoken of what underlay that estrangement. Some, of course, did not know and would not. When the rift was new there had been speculation about the cause. But time went by, and people ceased to interest themselves in it.

Charles, or "Woody," his brother Francis, and their mother had all but hated the boys' father, who was violent and abusive. On an afternoon when this man was absent, Francis had got into a very bitter argument with his mother because he thought she ought to leave her husband, and he spoke to her as no son should his mother, using in the process an unpardonable epithet in making clear what he thought of her for staying. Then, before Woody could prevent it, he struck her. She fell backward against the iron stove, in which a fire blazed hotly, so that she sustained a limited third-degree burn, fracture of the right scapula and humerus, and deforming contusion to the last cervical and first thoracic vertebrae. Worst of all, there was enough damage done to the brachial nerve-plexus so that the poor woman was deprived of the greatest part of the use of her arm and hand. As Woody had knelt to help his mother, he had cursed his brother and warned him not to seek to see him again.

The next bit of history reflected in the Paget will was the nature of—and the nature of the accrual of—that part of the estate which Rita would receive, for the original family lands, as noted, had been lost. There would be some money for her—about what the nephews were to have—but Rita's great share was to be in land. If not on anybody's tongue after so many years, thoughts of Woody's land lived—if as no more than smoldering ash—in a lot of people's minds. For at that difficult time when so many had been in default, when creditors were so frequently foreclosing, Woody had had money from some uncertain source and had used it to buy the properties of many "off the block"—properties of strangers, of friends, and of his own brother. By that time Francis had married and had two little boys. He had built a comfortable but modest house upon a tract of ten acres, part of which lay along the Pon Pon, and some disputed marshland, not far from the Crossroads.

Everybody had expected that the land would be restored by deed to Francis. Even Francis had thought it would be. He had made himself expect this as a way of ending the estrangement. The father, after all, had died, opening the possibility of harmony within the family.

But old Mrs. Paget had gone to live with her elder son, married at that time to a precedent floozy. The death of the old lady's husband had not restored to her the use of the atrophied limb and nor had it replaced the loss of tissue about the right neck and shoulder, or reduced the deformity. Nor did it cause the deed of gift to materialize.

After a certain amount of time had passed with the Francis Pagets and their offspring still without a permanent home, most of the community around the Crossroads became scandalized. Transactions of that kind were understood to be legal, and owned to be from the creditors' point of view right; still, they were not regarded as quite honorable, for they amounted to one's feeding off another's misfortune. But one's own brother's! Some felt there must be a reason for it and tried to bring Woody forward upon the subject, but without success. Others supposed malice was at the bottom of it and were allowed to persist in this belief.

What within just a few years would go unnoticed, unremembered, was the provision concerning burial. But in the short term it came to be much talked-about. To begin with no one knew that the old cemetery, together with an easement to it, had remained in the Paget family. And nobody would have guessed that Woody might have thought at all of his own demise, nor sought Christian burial. They all wondered what it meant.

This is what it meant: On the day of the accident down at the River, when Woody was eleven years old, he sat with his mother in the kitchen. She had wrapped him in a blanket and had insisted upon fetching a kerosene-stove out of summer storage and lighting it and placing it near the lad. There was no need yet for a roaring blaze in the cast-iron cookstove.

"After he had got us to shore and the ambulance had taken Frank away, Mr. Branscombe put his arm around my shoulder as we were walking up the rise toward his car." Woody glanced at his mother to see whether she were listening—she had had her mind upon nothing much that whole afternoon beyond thankfulness that her sons had been spared. But she was listening. She had only then realized what a sweetness it was to be able to listen to her son's speaking. "He stopped at one place, and I could see that he was looking over to the old cemetery.

"Then he said to me, looking down and right at me: 'Your forefathers would be mightily proud of what you did today. Don't ever forget that. If those people lying over there had known of it *they* would never have forgotten it.' "

"I think that was a kind thing of him to say to you, don't you?"

"Yes." Earlier, just after the ordeal, the boy's thoughts had wandered somewhat. His mother waited now. She knew that his mind was rearranging itself, and the Lord knew it had suffered perturbation enough! "Were we important? I mean a long time ago?"

"The Pagets were. Your ancestors. I'm a Paget by marriage—not by blood."

The boy thought over this, then said: "Then you're not *really* a Paget? Because if not, then how can you be my mother?"

Shall I tell him that the "begetter is the parent?" No. The statement never seemed to me to have much justification. "I'm *really*, as you say, a McQueen. But when I married your father I took his name, and that's what made me Paget enough to be your mother."

This was the first intimation the boy had had that "blood" was supposed to be what made one what one was. A primitive notion, but widely held. Nobody, he thought as he scanned in his mind the lists of real people, and people from the Bible, and people from myth, had ever had a father without also having a mother. He had not been told about Athena's birth. But the idea—with its ramifications—led Woody in the end to ask to be laid to rest among his fathers.

The testamentary instrument, once drafted, was placed in the lockbox installed in the Sheriff's office for safekeeping of the personal belongings of prisoners.

It was the quickening of the light and not its intensity—for it was only half past four, just about the time Woody Paget's will was being laid inside the Sheriff's safe—along with the restiveness of some of the Pankeytown Hounds, that brought Laurence, whose side of the bed lay along two east-facing windows, from sound sleep into the realization that he was awake, in fact alive. Wearing a dressing gown but barefoot, he went down into the front hall, then through the broad paneled passage beneath the stair-landing, to the back. He spoke quietly to the pack, calling them all "Pups," in the manner of a country gentleman, which in a way he was.

Then he led them out into the back garden, where he would feed them and then send them off to do whatever it was they did in the course of a day. If he had known about him, if he had known to look and where, he would have noted that the little mongrel who on the evening before had come late to scratch at the doorframe, had slipped away.

"Peace be over all your house, Mistress."

"Thank you, Miss Izora; please come in," Lavinia said as she executed that potentially so awkward stance: Back to the jamb, one arm holding the screen door outward, the other, the door itself inward, at the same time nodding as the guest crossed the threshold. Southerners were often able to do this with an easy grace, having from early childhood come to terms with spring-loaded screen doors. Besides, Lavinia did a lot of things with easy grace. "And peace to all of us within its doors," she said, guessing at a suitable response.

The old woman had with her a cloth, a basin, and a bottle filled with water. "Lilia Belle is in Mr. Jack's and Miss Allie's room," Lavinia said. Miss Izora knew the house; she had worked for three generations of the Ashfield Family, but now, at eighty-one, had retired. She was beginning to be troubled with arthritis and the crystalline lenses of the eyes were opacifying.

Mary Alice came out and led her grandmother to the bedroom. "Will you need anything else, Miss Izora, or will you need any of us?" Lavinia asked.

"No, I thank you, Mistress." The old woman smiled and then turned and went into the bedroom. Mary Alice remained outside and closed the door after herself.

"She was bound and determined to do this, Miss Lavinia; I hope she won't do or say anything to upset Lilia Belle. And I hope she won't be in the way."

"Whatever she does will be out of a wish to make things better. Lilia Belle will understand that. It will be all right. And certainly, Mary Alice, she will be no trouble to anybody."

Soon there came from the closed room a kind of atonal crooning. Laurence came in from the front hall. "Is Tommy here?"

"He brought Miss Izora, but he hasn't come inside."

"Just so he's here. I must discuss with him what we should do."

"What you should do about what?"

"About last night. Mary Alice, I'm going to speak openly before you, as I always have. I think we all know each other's feelings and beliefs about things." The crooning continued. "By the way, I know why Miss Izora has come; oddly enough, that singing has nothing to do with the rite, or at least I don't think it has. I've been hearing it at different times—different kinds of times, too—all my life. You may know different, Mary Alice, but I believe it's part of a Colored woman's way of giving comfort.

"Well, now, about what's happened: A lot of Colored people are going to have been enraged, mostly against Paget, but...."

"You're right, Mr. Laurence; a lot of others...a lot of them will hold anything against anybody."

"A good way to put it. Since I let the Hounds out, I haven't been able to get back to sleep—I've been trying to think of all the possible alignments— of aggression, of defense. And, literally, there's no telling. But I think the Gadsdens—the Woodleigh ones, anyhow—and the Arabys and the Ashfields, Colored and White both, should stay at home for today, at least. Maybe once they get Paget to Columbia, once a little time has gone by, then there'll be less to worry about."

In the bedroom, Miss Izora, still crooning, sprinkled her young granddaughter, treated her with kindness and favor, weaving in now some chant of which the words were as unintelligible as the notes were unmelodic, then she poured water into the basin, using the cloth first to retrieve scattered drops. "This water, Honey, doesn't come from the earth—come not from river, not from dug well, not from spring. It is water from the clouds, clouds like the ones that wrapped themselves around the Lord Jesus and took Him up to Heaven.

"Clouds like the ones that are going to crowd around Him in glory when He comes again." She moistened the cloth well and then she bathed the child's brow and breast and hands, as one might anoint a sovereign. Miss Izora went on chanting a little longer. Then she declared: "Now you are pure again, Honey; pure from stain and pure from shame."

Lavinia, as she was about to climb the stairs, caught sight of a revolver lying on the card table in the front hall outside the doors to the east drawing room, and a rifle and one-over-one shotgun, both leaning against the chair rail where it followed the shallow recess of the sidelights. From the aspect of these pieces she took far more alarm than encouragement.

Charles Paget was uncertain whether he were asleep and dreaming, or awake and remembering. And indeed the distinction probably could not have been made; no, not even through electrencephalography. For the storm within his brain was of an unorganized violence not yet recorded and studied by medical persons.

It was of a kind too rare, too fleeting; a kind that consumed itself too soon to be observed methodically.

Woody was back with his mother in the kitchen, sitting warmly wrapped beside the kerosene-burning stove. "Those charts of Father's—are all the things you told me about blood and name in those?"

"Yes. They are called genealogical tables. Some people call them 'family trees.' "

"Why are they so important to Father? He's very careful about how he touches them, how he holds them; when he's not looking at them, he keeps them locked up."

"I don't believe your father has much else."

"He has us; we're not very important to him, though, I guess."

"He doesn't look at things, I think, Woody, as though they kept on. I don't know where he thinks the family began. But he seems to think it has ended with himself."

"But…."

"I know. There are you and Francis. And I know that somewhere in his heart he loves you both. But I think your father is so much disappointed in what the Paget Family has come to that he has lost any wish to look ahead."

"He ought to keep on, and keep on keeping on. Maybe he could make the family a thing to be proud of again."

"It makes me happy to know you see it that way. But to James, the family has become nothing but himself. And I don't think he feels able to try to be more than he is." Then she prepared a light meal for her son, which was supposed to mark the end of their talk.

But Woody recurred: "An actual tree in a field branches outward as it grows upwards."

" 'Upward.' Yes, it does."

"But a family tree goes downward. It branches outward only as it goes downward." Mrs. Paget did not at once reply, because a great number of possible comments upon what her son had said occurred to her at the same time. "Maybe real trees are made of branches up in the air; maybe family trees are just made of underground roots…just hidden, underground roots." He was speaking now dreamily. And it did occur to his mother to wonder for how long a time *his* brain had been deprived of sufficient oxygen. Yet she was his mother and so thought this:

With that image the child may have spoken the key to the whole hopeless riddle: From the (illustrious) ancestor and his consort does a family usually arise, or does it instead extend ever lower, deeper? Till the last scion—not a "scion" at all, but a rootlet—is literally laid within the earth? Poor James. Poor James.

"Congressman? I think you'd better get up now. There is breakfast for you when you're ready. Mrs. Paget will be here soon."

Charles Paget was now certainly awake; he did not even momentarily wonder whether "Mrs. Paget" were his mother or his wife. He knew the time, the place. He knew Necessity. The brainstorm, however, was not fully abated. "No breakfast." Then: "Thank you just the same."

"People have started coming into town."

"What's today?"

"Saturday. The stores are open for a half-day. In a few minutes we can have your will witnessed." Paget sat upon the brink of his cantilevered cot and did not say anything. "In a little while there'll be a notary. The County offices aren't open today, of course. Neither is the Bank. But Old Man Branscombe at the feed and seed store is a notary." Paget said nothing. "Years ago he was just about the only one anywhere near."

"What?"

"Old Mr. Branscombe used to be the only notary."

"Oh. Yes. I see."

"The people from Columbia," Sheriff Baker said on his way out, "are supposed to be here about ten o'clock."

Thinking of his father's blood, thinking of his mother's name, to negotiate with all possible solemnity the maw of the vast and splendid arroyo that lay before him—this had become Paget's resolve. He knew that for want of practice, for lack of exposure little enough solemnity would be possible. Fewer steps now than he had once thought were there to be taken; of those, a great proportion rough ones. Those rough ones a lot of people would be reckoning up: From free to bond, from lawgiver to pariah. But he sensed a wider and more mysterious separation than just these, an involucrum between himself and the world he had known.

He only could feel it. He only would know himself more honorable, for he was newly borne upon this course, hadn't yet the feel of it. He intended to do his best. For the lapses, he would not justify himself to himself, to man, or to God. Only do his best, from now.

It was lost upon nobody that more people had drifted into town than on a usual Saturday morning. A lot of them seemed there without very pressing business, if they had business at all. It is true that in Ashfield all the stores and services are grouped around Courthouse Square. But the gathering throng were mostly moving along the Courthouse side of the street.

At half past nine, Rita Paget arrived at the Sheriff's Office. Her Woody's will had been executed, witnessed, and the witnesses had appeared before Mr. Branscombe to declare that the Testator had appeared to be sound of mind and uncoërced, and that they, all together, had seen him sign the instrument, first along the margins of all the pages and finally upon the ceremonial line of final avowal. The Sheriff gave the will to Rita, next-of-kin. She was, moreover, by a long chalk primary beneficiary and had been named Executrix.

Rita was attending in her established role as floozy. And for cause. But she had already shed this calling inwardly, and like her husband, though without their having spoken about it between themselves, seemed to begin to be actuated by a higher—if but slightly higher—impulse, and one without name. However many times she might stumble, Rita K. Paget proposed to gather herself up and pursue her new course. She would accustom herself to it as she went. And she would arrive chosen at the finish as Rita K. Paget.

The hour had come. Into the street around Courthouse Square a van was driven. It resembled an armored car, with two exiguous windows on either side of the rear compartment, and those barred. In front, it bore two guards from the State Penitentiary.

The circulation of humanity about the Courthouse stopped. Those of one race avoided standing beside those of the other; on this day Black friends of White men stood separately. But all sought points of vantage. The van veered athwart the traffic lanes then backed to the curb. The guard who had been driving got out. He was armed; he carried a sheaf of printed forms. Some were on white paper, others on pink, the rest yellow. He went with these up the walkway and into the Sheriff's Office.

The other guard got down and walked around to the back of the van. He unlocked the double doors and opened them wide. A stir among the watching public. A partly obstructed view of the dim interior. Benches along either sidewall; a small glass allowing surveillance from the cab. A bar down the center of the floor, shackles, hasps—everything riveted. The second guard, himself wearing a holstered revolver, withdrew a rifle from the van. Among more than a few, there was an unsupported but inescapable sense—and inwardly they scolded themselves for it—that this officer would execute the Congressman's unsentence on the very steps of the Courthouse. A few small children lightly supposed that the crowd, including themselves, was to be fired upon. However, the second guard followed the first, but he stopped in front of the door to the office and jail. He turned, faced the crowd, the rifle held across his chest. No one would go in, none come out until the times appointed.

Absent from that morning's gathering of the curious, to the surprise of no one who noted it, were any Gadsdens (Woodleigh ones), Arabys, or Ashfields (White or Colored). It was true that most had stayed away in part out of fear of a disturbance. But that aside, Laurence and Lavinia Ashfield, like Mr. Jack and Miss Allie, had never set as an example the lending of their presences to any demeaning spectacle. They felt, and let the feeling be known, that seeking to look upon another's discomfiture was to degrade and humiliate oneself. (They also thought—and they wisely kept this thought to themselves—that most people who behaved so hadn't after all much degradation-distance left to go before reaching bottom.)

Not all of their friends were as scrupulous, and so beneath a blackjack oak—one of unfortunately many planted over the Courthouse Grounds—stood a small representation of what were thought and sometimes spoken of as "Plantation People." Some of their identities would have distressed the Ashfields acutely.

Sheriff Baker had tried—and had failed—to purge from the Congressman's departure any element of public spectacle. But when the office door was at last opened, anticipation alone had wrought already the heightening of general emotion. First out was the prison-guard who had carried the forms. He carried now a diminished sheaf of them—still white, pink, yellow.

Next came Sheriff Baker and Sergeant Wilson, walking side-by-side. That Paget was not only handcuffed and encinctured with a glinting chromium-plated chain but also fettered to it caused a delay. The delay built toward climax. For the onlookers—the ones who from where they stood could see anything at all—saw for the next several minutes only a door standing open and beyond it room receding into shadow.

Then Paget appeared with his escort—another County Police officer keeping a firm grip upon the crook of the prisoner's left elbow—darkly seen at first, then etched against the sunsplashed side of the Courthouse. He was wearing an inmate's loose, light clothing: Trousers and tunic barred horizontally with khaki and black.

The Paget name, adorned in the Mother Country with nobility—what would the Heralds make of this device?

At the seams along the sides of the tunic, the stripes did not meet with exact correspondence. To anyone who might have known how during the previous eighteen hours Paget had been revisiting his earlier life, the incongruence would perhaps have suggested a little boy's jacket buttoned askew.

The Colored folk who had expected to relish his humiliation were themselves ashamed. For the most part. The "Plantation People" began to wish they were almost anywhere else, but must keep their places.

Last in the little procession came the second prison guard. He carried the rifle, still across his chest; to bring it up and take aim would require seconds only. The crowd were sobered, alarmed in some cases. But now they must wait and watch what they had come to see.

Miss Izora, once she had completed her office, came out of the bedroom. After a little while her granddaughter followed her. Lavinia heard them and came to them in the back hall. "Do you feel like being up and about, Lilia Belle?"

"Yes, Ma'am. And the Lord bless you and Mr. Laurence for seeing about me and taking care of me."

"Oh, Darling, you're so welcome. Miss Izora and I have learned,"—she turned toward the old woman—"haven't we? …that an opportunity to help someone you care about is a gift, and one that doesn't come often. Or it may be we ought to be looking harder for opportunities. And you two girls are learning that too, I know."

Miss Izora said: "I leave you peace, Mistress." Then they all went out onto the back verandah. Tommy had backed his truck up to the steps, had let down the tailgate. In the bed of the truck, facing backward, stood a great old wicker armchair—the kind with rolled arms rising in a curve to form a high back.

Tommy helped Lilia Belle into the passenger seat and Miss Izora into the chair, he put up the tailgate, nodded to Lavinia and to his own wife, remaining because her work was in the house. Then he got into the driver's seat, engaged the motor, and pulled away slowly down the wide brick walkway that led to the Street and to Miss Izora's house, taking care not to crush any of the plantings on either side. He knew that some were precious to Miss Lavinia, but not which.

Mary Alice and Lavinia waved them out of sight, Miss Izora backward enthroned. "I wonder how long it will take people around here to forget your grandmother?"

"A long time, I believe, Miss Lavinia."

"A very long time."

"And they'll probably remember her as a foolish old woman, or not quite in her right mind."

"Do you mean because she seems to see more clearly as her eyesight fails? Or because she looks into the fireplace to see, even when there's no fire burning? All that is uncommon, Mary Alice, but as old as mankind. No, I think people will remember her as a sibyl. And if they don't they'll be wrong, won't they?"

"What is a 'Sibyl'?"

"Well, to be honest, I can't give you the exact meaning. But we can go into Mr. Laurence's library and look it up. And we should do that right away, or we shall forget about it."

"Did you know she won't touch a pair of scissors?"

As the guards and their prisoner drew near to the blackjack oak, a friend of Laurence's—a younger man, but one old enough to have acquired better judgment—called out: "Hey, Mr. Congressman! How was it…dipping your pen in ink?" If it had not already been silent, the crowd would have fallen silent then. But all movement ceased; people were too shocked or too afraid almost to draw breath.

Suddenly a group of Colored men, mostly young, erupted from the congregated folk and charged the man who had spoken those low words, the switchblades of their knives clicking open successively. The crack of a gunshot. They all saw the Sheriff, standing with his back against the prisoner, his revolver pointed straight up into the sky. At all this a lot of people gasped, and the remaining ones did, too, when they saw the guard with the rifle, butt to his shoulder, scanning the mob through the sights as he steadily brought the muzzle through the arc of a half-circle that positioned them all in felling range. The Colored men stood still. And one by one they dropped their blades and insinuated themselves back into the crowd from which they had first emerged.

Woody Paget and the man who had uttered the taunt stood now face-to-face. In a very low voice Woody said: "My ancestors were granted every hectare as much land as yours. And yours had black wenches they took whenever they wanted them. Where's the difference?" Then the policeman nudged him along, but over his shoulder he continued, still in a quiet voice: "They say there're a couple of drops of ink in *your* blood."

And then he was sorry he had said it. And this feeling was unfamiliar to him, for he had done many far worse things and not felt sorry. He was glad he was sorry now.

When they reached the back of the armored transport van, any configuration of a procession dissolved into an irregular little band of men, asking questions of each other, giving instructions. For Rita a time of intense vigilance was beginning; though she stood at the inner fringe of the crowd, yet she could not distinguish what the various ones of the men were saying. Their movements were all she had to gauge her own actions by. She watched.

The first guard turned to Sheriff Baker: "Have you patted him down?"

Sheriff Baker, with a turn of the head, referred this matter to Sergeant Wilson. His answer, in turn, must have been either equivocal or negative, for, "I'll do it myself," the guard said, and he turned to the prisoner. "Sir, will you please see whether you can get your wrists up over your head? Thank you."

So this *did* have yet to take place. Rita was ready, all but to pawing the earth. She had prepared. She had dealt with her hair so that it was at once resplendently blonde and maximally voluminous. And she had dressed most provocatively—but not so much so as to risk being put off the public streets of 1943.

"Now, please stand with your feet as far apart as possible." As if the request had been made of herself, Rita heard and, like her husband, complied, though also with some difficulty, as the agile ocelot, seeking the widest possible base from which to spring, may not find within the tree, her eyes fixed upon her quarry, a branch just where she requires it for her footing, softly slips, but without attracting premature attention. When she reveals herself, her prey must be frozen in astonishment.

The guard began to examine Woody's clothes and person for the presence of contraband. It was while he was upon his knees in the dust, palpating about the ankles and therefore almost at the end of his search that the silence—The second guard had thought it a good idea to keep his rifle close to the shoulder, ready, evident—was cloven by what at first and by many was taken for a locomotive whistle. But it was Rita, off the mark. She bolted toward the van, clutching a Mexican bag woven of straw, with bright flowers of dyed straw woven upon it. As she burst from the crowd at a run, she threw her lower legs just barely outward, a little to either side, in a fetching way that suggested simultaneously a skirt very binding about the knees and a lack of athleticisim, the latter much appreciated in women of that era. She could not have done better than to draw attention to her legs, which were among her most arresting features. Not that she wanted for others.

"Woody, Darling! Don't leave me! Don't let them take you away from me!" The officers of the Law tried to rally as she reached the prisoner. There was a bit of a crush, during which Woody felt the cold of a glass bottle being shoved down between his belly and the drawstring of his trousers. "*I* won't let them take you away!" And she pummeled some of the other men a bit, enough to prolong the distraction by some few seconds.

And that was all. It was over. Rita was escorted from the scene, by this time weeping copiously. And out of genuine sorrow. For she loved Woody truly—a great deal more than she had thought before. She recognized this now, and she wondered why. A long, long time ago, there were three old women who could have explained it to her.

Woody was coaxed into the back of the van. He sat down upon the passenger side bench. The guard removed the cuff from his left wrist and locked it to a heavy ring welded to the body of the truck. He unfettered his right ankle and clamped the shackle to the bar running along the floor. The guards boarded; the van pulled away; the crowd dispersed.

Presently Rita dried her eyes. No indeed. She did not comprehend her husband's occasional and so overmastering alcohol-hunger. But he had it sometimes, and she would feed it when she could, for she loved him. There seemed little else she could do, just then.

At sunset Lavinia and Laurence sat beside the lily pool in the back garden at Woodleigh. The water-garden in autumn undergoes an engrossing change, but you must look at and into it for longer than a few seconds. It is bittersweet—like many other autumnal changes. Mystical and beautiful. The splendor of the morning-colored lotus flower will have yielded to mummied pod and graying stalk, leaf curling at corroded margins. The lessening light has starved all algae. The depths are clear and dark, and there the fattened carp, in this climate still active, write sinuous loops in gold, copper, amber— then at greater depths, invisible in onyx, known from their faint cavitation.

They had been looking into the waters for whatever they might see there. Lavinia at last said: "I can see nothing but Death; I'm sorry."

"I can see it, too, of course. But the water also speaks Peace, I think."

Following a time of reflection upon this, Lavinia said: "Peace, apart from Death? I think so. But…."

"What?"

"So many people, I'm afraid…don't believe that, don't believe in that." They both continued to gaze at the pool. The summer-straight stalks—some of them—with loss of strength bent at acute angles. Like broken bones before reduction.

"There's no wonder…no wonder."

"No wonder?"

"No wonder so many people don't believe in that—in peace apart from death. When they're so weak and broken." In the stillness they were able to hear from a great distance a car coming up the lane on the other side of the house. And then their brother-in-law Parker Jones drove up and got out. He made a perfunctory effort to push the car door to, but it didn't catch, swung open again. And then he simply stood there, evidently preoccupied, evidently distressed. They hailed him; he walked across the shorn and redolent lawn to join them. But still he stood, still said nothing. Finally, "Paget is dead," he announced, and all were quiet. All was quiet. Woodleigh-quiet.

Then Lavinia asked: "What has happened?"

"He's killed himself." They could almost hear the sound, dropping in pitch, of Earth slowing in her rotation. "He cut his throat. They watched him at first. Halfway there they took him out to let him stretch his legs. They must have got complacent. He did it with a broken whiskey bottle." Parker was grimacing just barely, but repetitively and regularly, in solemn rhythm of grief. The others could see that his teeth were clenched. The contours of the jaw-muscles stood out.

"How dreadful!"

Parker tried for a while to stare out into nothingness, but it wasn't there. "Look, is it too early for a drink?"

Laurence glanced at the last bit of sun, burning, burning its way down into the far pine forest. "It's actually late for one!" He stood.

But Parker said: "Could you get them, Lavinia? Would you? And leave Laurence with me?"

Lavinia climbed up the steps onto the verandah and went into the house. Parker sat down. Laurence resumed looking into the lily pool. There was a queer little fountain arrangement. A tall and slender copper tube—grey-green now; no longer copper of carp, gone its mirror-sheen—arched up over a stelë of granite, mossy to a point, but still an obvious import to the coastal plain—and spilled clear water into a rough-hewn catch-basin of cypress wood. It redounded from there into the pool without splashing. "Water lilies," Laurence had said, "at least the kinds I like, don't want the water disturbed." And who does? So they grew cress, which thrives in moving water, in the catch-basin.

Parker let his gaze follow Laurence's but saw nothing. He said without any warning: "He knew to cut his throat. But that's all he knew." Laurence looked up from the depths of the shadowed water. "Apparently he just started cutting—if you could call it that. He kept on till he had injured himself fatally."

"What a terrible thing!"

"I'm so…sorrowful about it. I can't think what to do."

"Must you do anything? You didn't know him, did you?"

"No. I've never even seen him. I might have known him, though." Parker fell to weeping.

On the next day, which was Sunday, Rita went to the church. She did not go to Church. She merely went to the church, and when the service was over and the congregation had departed, she went up to the priest. "Father, I'm Rita Paget. I'm Catholic."

"Oh! Good morning, Mrs. Paget—that is, I wish it could be a good morning for you. I know what has happened, and I know it is not a good morning. Is there anything I can do that would be a help to you?"

"Will you bury my husband?"

"Oh yes. Now I see why you may have been concerned. You are a Roman Catholic?"

"More or less."

"Please don't worry further. I shall be glad to bury him."

"In consecrated ground?"

"It is the least I can do for him and for you."

"I thought there might be some...interdiction."

"Don't be concerned for another minute. There is no one to object; and I would do it anyway. Now, if he were to be buried in the churchyard—which belongs to the vestry—then I should have to ask permission of them. But I have been told he wanted to be buried in the family plot. That Ground was consecrated centuries ago and now is owned by your late husband's Estate."

"All that is exactly right. They told me news got around fast down here. I don't think Woody had even made that decision until the day before yesterday!"

"No, no. It's not that. Sheriff Baker has spoken to me about this—and *only* this—provision of the will. Your late husband asked him to. The Sheriff telephoned me after...what happened. He just wanted to clear the way for you."

"All this kindness...."

"Yes?"

"It's just that we aren't accustomed to it in Paramus."

"Paramus? We're getting ready?"

"It's a town in New Jersey. I grew up there."

"Well, back to the task at hand: Your husband had been baptized?"

"Yes, here, in this church."

"Then there will be an entry in the parish register; I shall need nothing else. Listen carefully to the service—not everything I say will come from the Order for the Burial of the Dead—and you will understand. That is, you will understand why there is no interdiction."

"Thank you, Father. It is a great relief!"

"We aren't meant to bear every burden. However...."

"Yes?"

"If you had come to be married, and either of you had been divorced—Now that I should have to refuse."

An obstacle which had not arisen before the path it might have obstructed had been swept clear.

On Monday Rita went to Savannah to a fashionable salon that she had been able to identify. It opened off the lobby of a grand hotel. A stylishly turned-out woman, about Rita's own age, was standing behind a small antique writing-desk, and when Rita approached she smiled self-deprecatingly and said: "Do please forgive me, Madam!" She scanned the leather bound ledger rather desperately. "For the life of me, I simply cannot recall your name."

"Don't worry; you don't know it."

"Haven't you an appointment?"

In time of war? An appointment to have one's hair rearranged? "I haven't. But I must ask you to take me right away. All this (with a vague gesture she indicated her person and trappings, from head to toe) has got to be undone."

"Madam?"

"Everything that's ever been done—hair, fingernails, toenails, the makeup on my face—I want you to undo. I haven't an idea what I really look like anymore."

"We work only by appointment, Madam," she said to Rita, who had begun to look about the empty salon. "I am very sorry; do you wish to schedule?"

"No, thank you; not unless you can reschedule my husband's funeral. Otherwise, I must be seen now or within a few minutes. You surely can't expect me to be present looking like a floozy." The receptionist did not possess great mental gifts herself; she would not have been expected to. Rita's directness—which was straight from Paramus—rattled her briefly. She said: "Then of course, Madam. And what name?"

"Rita Paget." Scandal! With it, instant comprehension, instant absorption!

"Of course! I'm so sorry not to have recognized you. Please follow me. One of our staff will be with you momentarily."

If she can rustle one up—if there are *more than one.* "Thank you very much. I'm sure you can imagine what all this must be like."

"*Of course,* I can, my Dear." And in this she was most truthful; she had done nothing since Saturday evening, when she had heard the news, but imagine various versions of "All this."

After her cosmetic transformation, Rita remained a much simplified but very handsome woman. She entered a boutique, where, with good guidance, she purchased widow's weeds.

On Tuesday, air and earth were apt for the burial. The earth's yet unexhausted vigor called out: "Proceed; I will enfold him." The sky, weary with heaviness of rain, whispered: "But make haste; close the grave. I will settle the soil about him."

A service in the church had been omitted; the distance from the burial-place was great. Pallbearers were the decedent's three nephews; to the surprise of many, his brother; some kind of politician who thought he was stooping to conquer; and Parker Jones, who had telephoned to Rita and "presumed to offer." The priest had assigned the crucifer a very beautiful but rickety processional Cross that had been given in memory of a Paget of old. Therefore the quiet splendor, cached as simple dignity, which the Church could still at that time bestow, was met.

To the burial formulae the priest had added, from the Office for the Dying, these words: "Acknowledge, we humbly beseech thee, a sheep of thine own fold, a lamb of thine own flock, a sinner of thine own redeeming."

When the rite had been completed, as the grave was being closed, when it no longer mattered how much tissue had been avulsed from the right anterior cervical triangle in Paget's determined quest for death, then three old men, all in black, hung back for a while, leaning against the cemetery gateposts, trying to see the again-past—unaware that it was hardly better charted than the already-future—and knowing that before long none of it would matter to any of themselves. One was Mr. Branscombe.

"I remember it better than yesterday—a whole lot better. Woody was a boy of ten or twelve. He and his little brother Francis—helped bear him to his rest today, still without seeing him, either today or for years gone—they went fishing in the river. Right down there"—he pointed with a skeletal forefinger. "Woody decided the take would be better on the other side of the stream; so he told Francis to sit and fish from the little pier. They've put up a bigger one now—bigger, and sound as a dollar. Anyhow, Woody told Francis to sit still, not even to stand up without calling to him first so he could keep watch over what he was doing. Then Woody swam across and cast in his little line over yonder."

This time there was unsteadiness in the knurled finger; Mr. Branscombe brought it down. "The little fool...."

"Which one?"

"Francis. He must have thought he had a nibble. He jumped up without thinking. Now Woody was watching, but from across the creek. As close as I can figure, Francis began to run around the pier, pulling on his line and paying no attention to anything else. He fell into the water.

"Woody jumped in off the bank at once. I think, if he had been on the little pier himself, he might have been able to pinpoint where his brother had gone under. He swam back across, it seems, and when he had got near, he started to dive. There's no telling how many dives he'd made when I heard him calling. He told me that every time he came up for breath he shouted for help. A good thing, too.

"I heard the little fellow calling for help, and already his voice was weak. By the time I got down there—" Here the old man's eyes brimmed with tears; he tried to point again, but the index finger swung rather wildly with tremor of intent. The other two took to opening and closing the gate, stretching, and coughing. Mr. Craven even thought he might have to expectorate, a thing he had seen done in company but had never done himself, just in order to take up time.

But it is the Fates who take up time, just as it is they who spin it out. We are prevented, though, when we seek the nature of the spool that takes up the Thread.

"He was, I'd say, half dead himself. I tried to hold him back—all of his strength was gone, I thought. But he pulled away and jumped in—it was more like he fell in—again. And he didn't come up, so I went in after him. He had gone limp by the time I had fished around and got hold of him. I thought he had drowned, that they had both drowned. But I got a hold on him and dragged him to shore. And he had a deathlock on his little brother that time. And you saw Francis today. He was in the hospital in Ashfield—It had just opened; really, the whole town had just opened, if you can say that—but he lived. His brother, though, was ready to lay...."

The old pale eyes, irises of faded blue blending to the dense pallor of the corneas, threatened again. Open. Closed. Open and closed. In many years the graveyard gate had known less exertion than upon this October afternoon. Mr. Craven, though, in the end, was spared the breaching of decorum.

"...Down his life. I've read about it in the Bible, and heard it read. But that's the only time I've seen it. For that, he brings honor to this earth." To this ash, to this dust. With that, Mr. Branscombe stumped away, and the others followed. As the autumn sun set, the dead were left to lie in peace among the dead.

Toward Thanksgiving time, Lilia Belle found that she was carrying a child.

III

"...the dread of something after death,
That undiscovered country from whose bourne
No traveler returns puzzles the will..."
Wm. Shakespeare: *The Tragedy of Hamlet, Prince of Denmark*, 3. 1. 80-2

"The passage had begun; and the ship, a fragment
detached from the earth, went on lonely and
swift like a small planet. Round her the abysses of
sky and sea met in an unattainable frontier."
Joseph Conrad: *The Nigger of the 'Narcissus'*, II

"A gone shipmate, like any other man, is gone forever;
and I never saw one of them again. But
at times the spring-flood of memory sets with force...."
J. Conrad: *ibid.*, V

THE DEAD MAN was rather put out. The bottom of the coffin was cold and hard; its sides, while not actually confining, nevertheless grazed the shoulders irritatingly. Odd that he could tell. That's how it was, though. Maybe he wasn't really dead?

No, he was dead, all right. He wasn't breathing; his heart wasn't beating; he could see nothing. Fleetingly, he wondered what respiration and heartbeat were, anyway. But certainly, he was dead.

He had heard talk about death—a few physiologic facts, some anecdotes, a lot of speculation. But none of it had prepared him for this. He had taken the first few steps only along an endless way of boredom. And now it seemed he couldn't hope even for the respite of suffocation or dehydration or starvation.

Then there came to him, upborn upon the breath of a sweeter lassitude, a further slowing of all process. *This*, he said to himself, with relief, *must be very death*.

Just at the last he asked himself what name would be left, through all those ages of ages, upon the gravestone above. Not that he cared a great deal, or had any idea why he might care at all. What, for that matter, he wondered, was in a name? Or what was a name? But he knew that people had them, that he must have—or have had—one himself.

Probably, after all, it didn't matter what it was or had been, yet he was plagued by a small, goading wish to know. Then it occurred to him how, through the engagement of the imagination, he might retrieve his name, and he began this work, summoning to himself imagined beings who *would* know his name, people who would have to have known him well, even if, the shades among, he did not remember them. But once it had come to him, he was satisfied, and surrendered to the somnolence closing over him, and said: *Fare Well, All Ye!*

There was darkness all around, except that from directly overhead a row of colored lights stretched in a perfectly straight line away before him to a distant vanishing-point. Between every two of these, the distance decreased, decreased, decreased so rhythmically that it was clear that they had all, or all that he could see before they were lost in distant gloom, been placed equidistantly. He knew that if he stood and walked along beside them with some sort of criterion, then he could show this to be true. How did he know? He would be the last to know how he knew. Holding all that he now possessed—that is, his name—tightly to himself, he capitulated and slept again.

Above where the Dead Man lay, the sun shone in strength, although from a shallow angle, so that the clouds in the still-quiet blue dawn sky were ambivalently rich in grey or red and edged in brightness in the east, while in the west heavier palisades, more dun, corralled their lifting vapor for death-dealing use, bringing to mind the spider who spins a winding-cloth about the living insect. The cocooned fly waits a span that seems eternal. But it is Eternity that finally offers him an escape from Time.

Light fog mantled the great swells. Off the crests of some, the morning breeze blew banners of spume, so that there were reported to the bridge and navigator "small seas." For a destroyer lay just a hundred yards off. Another, at the horizon, was steaming away toward out of sight.

From the bridge the Captain and his Lieutenant had come down to the starboard bowrail. Each man stared out across the brief surface that separated the two vessels, each held in the grip of restless care. But not of the same care.

The Lieutenant thought over, and then thought over again, the battle just finished: Of its complexity and sudden reversals, of the fear which kept dissolving into puzzlement. Shadowed clefts of complete uncertainty within fiery billowing of cannon fire, blindness of shattered pane, brine-spattered lens, smoke, confusion of orders. Vessels coming onto a course for one purpose, but ending by accomplishing another. And finally the German submarine, already surrendered by default and going down by the stern; first shelled; then, by a depth-charge sinking beside her, rolling beneath her, detonating at a nearly-impossible depth of four hundred feet, pressure-hull breached or deformed, blasted upward and through the ocean's surface (Probably her tanks had been deliberately blown as well); afterward sustaining further damage in a sporadic exchange of gunfire that had spared none of the already-decimated enemy crew....

"Why, Sir, was it necessary to fire upon them when they were already abandoning ship?"

"It was necessary because some of them had got to the deck-gun and were firing upon *Kallisto*. We had no choice. Admittedly, theirs was rather futile fire. But gunfire must be returned. We had no choice."

The Lieutenant tried very had to feel better about it. "Then, Sir, we were right?"

"Not right. Correct."

And now *Kallisto* was on her way, carrying the actual, the viable survivors, the ones who had abandoned the German submarine before she had first begun to sink. Scattered, the dead floated upon the increasingly turbid wash between the two vessels, which had drifted even closer apart, forming as they did so narrow a sluice for the North Atlantic current, in the deceiving composure of its surface, rushing rapid not far below. When the Lieutenant had last looked, there had been bodies, too, upon the grating of the U-boat's deck.

She was well awash. Now, when he looked again, the bodies were gone—
all of them, gone. He felt relief; there was no more uncertainty.

"Now," the Captain said, "Benbow really must be off, or we shall lose
the most important advantage of the whole engagement."

When the Dead Man awoke again, he realized that he was no such thing,
but a survivor. For this time his mind was quite clear—in fact, a nagging doubt
kept suggesting that it was far *too* clear, that it had been swept completely
clear. At any rate, he was conscious, without doubt, and the consciousness, if
it were like an unmarked slate, was at least one which he knew he could both
write upon legibly and from which he could read fluently. It was puzzling,
though, that at that moment there appeared upon it no character, not even
an enciphered one.

But the border around the slate was permanently if minimally lettered;
he knew that he was an adult male—a man—and that he had emerged
from some disaster. He knew also that he was aboard a submarine and that,
although he was not so familiar with this kind of craft as actually to belong
here, nevertheless it was not as unfamiliar to him as it would be to a civilian,
whatever a 'civilian' might be. *Cives, civis.* He looked up again at the colored
lights; and they were not multicolored. That's what "colored lights" ordinarily
meant, didn't it? These were all blue. Clear globes, and dimmer now, so that
the filaments could be traced; figures-of-eight truncated at the tops—or
infinity-symbols stood upright, incomplete, failing to connect. Dimmer, yes,
and now the lights began to flicker.

Without difficulty, the Survivor rose and stood and then took a few
tentative steps. Everything around him was like the row of lights, straight
in rank—receding, appearing to diminish. Bright steel bars, for an example,
which he believed must be the frames of bunks, dashes nearby shrinking
almost to dots in the distance; the great, dark cylinders suspended over
some of them; baled tubing and cables running in perfect parallel along
the inner hull, groups of them distinguished with precision by color—odd
shades of it, too: Bloody vermillion, ochre, black—bending now upward at
forty-five degrees (or a hundred thirty-five degrees, depending upon how you
looked at it), back again, some then continuing to run together, others, singly
or in bundles of one color, deviating to convey liquid, or gas, or electrical
current to some apparatus which War would soon decommission. All these
things seemed to hurry toward a vanishing-point. But there wasn't really a
vanishing-point, was there? The early perspective-painters themselves had
found that too-close adherence to that principle finally produced distortion,
because, once the converging/parallel lines are expunged, the observing eye

has virtually no chance of meeting the originally-conceived focal point, if drawing is accurate. There is no vanishing-point in the world of light.

Now, on the other hand, the Survivor began to wonder whether he couldn't just make out, far off down the length of the boat, a cluster at least of vanishing-points, one for each of the lines and rows of things which he could see retreating. They appeared in a shaft of sifted light. And it was then that he realized his mind was *not* quite clear. But, however crabbed, the slate had upon it now at least a few markings. And among them, rudimentary as they were, was some self-consistency.

For example, he had remembered that it was often useless to think about thought itself, and he gave all this up for the time being and started moving about the unknown vessel, in order to explore the hungering, ghostly resonances he had been throughout all this time hearing. He wandered here and there, recognizing various compartments, valves, and fittings. He found torpedo tubes, like enormous pressure-cookers laid upon their sides; he realized it was their weaponry itself which he had noted earlier, racked beneath the bunks.

He entered the control room, where above him the shaft of the periscope disappeared beside the main hatch to the conning tower. He scanned a panel of indicators, noted the depth-gauge, wondered about it. For in the center of this spare instrument—and spare, indeed, was the whole craft, clean and unadorned—was written in impossibly ornate, impossibly romantic Fraktur the word "Tieffenmesser". That did not puzzle him. He readily understood the *word*. It was merely the teeming and elegant flourishes of the writing that rang a discordant note.

German. And he realized that he had been thinking in English—to the extent that thought is in words rather than in images. This must mean that English was his native—or at least usual—language. With this thought there came an overwhelming sense of relief and of satisfaction, for which, however, he could think of no explanation. All the written indications disposed about the submarine were like this first one, and he could understand them all. It was only that the lovely Arabesques intertwining, both with each other, and even about and through themselves, seemed out of place here in this rectilinear, aseptic ambience. The scene was one of chaos, of course, but of German chaos—different from other sorts. And, yes, he was happy that, though comprehensible, to him this also was foreign.

"Here he is now, Sir."

"Oh, Benbow!" The three officers exchanged salutes. "Your ratings have got the launch ready?"

"Aye, Sir. But she is not very sound. She floats, which is something of course, but the swell has begun lobbing her against our hull. When they strike, the launch creaks."

"Creaks?"

"Actually, Sir, there is a component of splintering to the sound."

"Can she make it across to the submarine, do you think?"

"Sir, it is my hope that she can make it both across and back."

The Captain seemed very gloomy all of a sudden, but then he straightened himself and said: "We must make do with what we have."

"Aye, Sir."

"And you have remembered all that we want to take off her?"

"Aye, Sir."

Back inside the submarine, the sole survivor—as he thought himself to be—was making his last observations, for presently he was going to be interrupted. Not knowing this, he took some time scanning the navigator's chart. It had slipped from its table; the southwest corner—representing hundreds of square miles of ocean—had been torn away. The last position plotted upon it was fifty degrees nine minutes north latitude by twenty-four degrees twenty minutes west longitude. Nearby lay three other objects: A large packet of folded nautical charts, presumably showing other sectors of the Ocean, a zippered pouch made of shagreen and bearing, stamped in a metal leaf exhibiting the dismal luster of newly-unearthed Colonial-era pewterware he had seen in a reconstructed town somewhere, a primitive jointed cross, limbs broken, with stylized wings. He had seen this, too, before, but, he thought, not often. He opened the pouch and withdrew the flimsy sheets it contained.

These were loosely bound and overprinted in an unfamiliar and pale shade of pink. There were columns of pairs of letters. The columns were arranged in groups of three, nine, or twenty-seven. These letters were all printed in *Antiqua*, as Germans then denoted Roman lettering, instead of the strange, florid, and seductive *Fraktur*.

Curious above the rest, though, and to the Survivor arresting, was something else he had seen before. He thought. While this third bundle of leaves exhibited mostly numbers and letters, yet the few whole words were in English. Not only in English, which he had already conscripted for himself, but familiar. That is, he had seen them before and was certain of it. He thought it possible that he might have written—or copied, at least—these very pages. He scanned them carefully, unaware that a battered launch was even then bringing men from His Majesty's Ship *Roxburgh* to the place where he stood reading. As he glanced over the pages, he imagined some of the groups' becoming legible: It was as though the figures were attempting to attract his notice, to have him watch them arrange themselves by date—day and month only. Then, from against these, there seemed to emerge times of day, by minute and hour, all according to the twenty-four hour clock.

Little of all this had been, as we have seen, comprehensible. But the lesson, once recalled—not to pore and pore over all that lay confounded before one—reminded. He would come back to this, perhaps. Then, as might be, he would see it all in clearer light. There might somewhere be a key with the clarifying silhouette to its bit.

The only other written words in sight were those upon a letter in its envelope, addressed in a sweet, graceful hand. It was postmarked "Flensburg." The posting-date was illegible. This he replaced. *I hope he got out safe.*

Above, the boarding-party were approaching, reluctantly but without need of leave. The chop had got worse. The "component" of splintering, which their commander sub-Lieutenant Benbow had reported to his Captain, had become the dominant sound, even in a turbid flow of ocean. They crossed to the submarine, though, without especial catastrophe. Benbow was first aboard. He walked the length of her deck. Then he summoned the others.

Below, the surviving member of the final eruptive, cataractal, matter-melting, ear-cleaving and violently buoying blast had begun to ruminate about pronouns. He wondered why he kept referring to himself, in word or in image or in uninformed idea as he/I. He didn't know, really, not with certainty, what either meant. Then he remembered the Name, the name by which anybody anywhere would know him. And, remembering his name, he became much less anxious, because he had this small symbol onto which to batten everything else.

One of the ratings had come up to Benbow and had asked: "Sir, did you see that cloud of dust coming out of the hatch? For a second, I thought she was blowing up for sure."

"I did not see it myself, Coker, but I was told about it. Probably the ship was thrust to the surface from rather a great depth, possibly deforming her pressure-hull. And then the captain—If he were still in charge, still alive, for that matter—opened the main hatch without first bleeding off any compressed air through the…well, through whatever apparatus these craft have for the purpose, if any."

"Och, I saw such an almighty puff of dust. It seemed to carry up in a cloud anything not fixed down. Fifty feet into the air. That doesn't make our boarding more dangerous?"

"Not at all. By the time the column of dust had fallen back upon itself—And it was only dust; nothing of any weight—the pressures were equalized, as normally they'd have been in the first place. There was no real danger, even while it was taking place, and none of those who died, died because of it." *And suppose it had been, instead of a pillar of cloud, a pillar of fire!* It was discouraging that he so often failed his men in their own way of understanding! All he could hope for was that what he had meant had somehow penetrated what he had said.

The man known up to now only as "the Dead Man" or as "the Survivor," stood in the submarine's control room in a broad shaft of reedy dawnlight; he noted bits of chaff—the ones not blown high enough to be carried away upon the early breeze—all around himself upon the decking. Because the hatchway was above the control room, the chop, which had increased further, was now audible, lapping and lapping against the hull, and in complex harmony with it could be felt a moderate roll.

I must not, Survivor said to himself, *be any kind of seaman.* Then, from some from unrecognized injury or despair, or from fatigue, he crumpled, sitting, onto the deck beneath him. Remnants of the telling dust scattered, stencilling a perfect and identifiable shadow around him, settling into what he thought heralded the peace of another sleep. But then hailings came spilling down, coming nearer. Rousing, alerting.

"Hallo? Ist jemand an Bord?"

"Ja, ich, allerdings bin ich doch der Einzige."

"Bist du bewaffnet?"

"Nein, ich bin kein Frontkampfer." *I don't think.*

"Was machst du denn auf diesem Boot?"

"Das kann ich Ihnen leider nicht sagen."

"Sehen Sie mal...Nein, warten Sie, Ich komme 'runter." The man who had been speaking then appeared, climbing energetically down the ladder from the conning-tower. He was in uniform and with difficulty keeping his cap under his arm while he climbed. His sidearm remained holstered. The uniform was greatly embellished, and there appeared among the embellishments the letters R and N.

Pointing to these, Survivor said: "Das ist aber eine Erleichterung."

"Warum können Sie mir zum Teufel nicht sagen," the officer said, "warum Sie sich hier auf diesem Ding befinden? Ist es Ihnen vielleicht nicht aufgefallen, dass es sich hier um ein deutsches Kriegsschiff handelt? Verlassen? Dass wahrscheinlich Sprengstoff vorhanden ist, der das ganze Boot versenken kann? Wartest du darauf, ins Jenseits abgeschossen zu werden?"

"Verzeihen Sie mir, aber ich habe nicht verstanden, was Sie gesagt haben. Davon abgesehen, kann ich Ihnen nicht sagen, warum ich hier bin, weil ich selber nicht weiss, was ich hier zu suchen habe."

"Quatsch! Warum tun Sie, als ob Sie erleichtert wären, als Sie die Buchstaben an meiner Uniform sahen?"

"Erstens, mache ich Ihnen nichts vor. Ich vermute, sie stehen für Royal Navy." Now, the words "Royal" and "Navy" rolled from his tongue with more fluency and authority than anything he had said in German. The British officer had been leery from the start, but now he became quite confused.

"Sprechen Sie Englisch?"

"Ganz gut, glaube ich."

Seeing a possibility for communication less labored, at least for himself, the Sub-lieutenant repeated, more deliberately and in English: "Do you speak English?"

"Yes. I just said I do."

"Well, you must have said so in German."

"You asked in German."

"You are from a country where English is spoken?"

"I believe so."

"But you don't know?"

"Not with certainty."

"Is there anything you *do* know?" for by now sarcasm was leaching through British phlegm. "Your name, rank, serial number?"

"I certainly do not know any serial number. If I hold rank, I don't know what rank. But I do know my name," he ended triumphantly.

"Well?"

"It's Doe. John Doe."

Hostility was by now palpable between "John Doe" and the boarding-party, but everyone, although expecting to go down with the enemy ship or to be scattered like chaff themselves by scuttling-charges, was still trying to maintain a degree of civility. After all, they spoke one language. But it was awkward, for the sub-Lieutenant was treating John Doe somewhat as a prisoner of war.

John had been sent topside, and two ratings had been detailed to "keep him company." The rest had been summoned below in order to try to discover and disarm charges and to fetch back to the captain all documents, particularly any enciphered ones matched by copies in clear.

The sub-Lieutenant himself went up. "We have nearly everything, and we appear to have found an encryption apparatus. That should make the Old Man happy."

"What about charges, Sir?" Coker asked, who after all had seen with his own two eyes the Pillar of Cloud and was expecting its Biblical counterpart at any moment.

"If there are any, we can't find them. Now please help Mr. Doe into the launch," and having seen the ocean, and the vessel that was supposed to bear them through it, he turned back to summon the rest of his party to come up without delay. But Coker called after him: "Sir, we can't put him into the launch. She's sinking. But Benbow had reached the end of that day's tether, and he said:

"I don't care. Put him in anyway. He has made me cross! And get aboard yourselves."

Only because the two vessels had drifted so close together did John, the unforeseen guest, and the party with their all-important gleanings, reach *Roxburgh*. A little apologetically, the Captain had said in thanking the Commander of the boarding-party and his men for a task courageously and successfully accomplished, that he had never meant there to be any question of the supreme importance of their own lives and safety. It was only that in wartime a few cartons of papers, a strange-looking piece of electrical gear could sometimes serve an even higher cause. Everybody, including the Captain, was immediately and profoundly dissatisfied with this remark.

Not that it was not quite right. It was only that it had been better left unsaid. For no one aboard had been in any doubt of it.

After this, the Captain turned and crossed the deck to the place where John Doe stood, flanked by his "companions," who saluted the Captain. John saluted simultaneously, to everybody's surprise. He himself had no idea why he had done it—it just happened automatically. Privately, the party believed that all of them were being mocked. But the Captain, who had seen the submarine blasted to the surface apparently by depth charges in concert with the crew's attempt to surface rather than sink and drown, who had been told by sub-Lieutenant Benbow that she had been either deep enough or otherwise subjected to pressure so mighty that her decking-plates had overlapped each other slightly, like shingles, was prepared to be more generous. "Welcome aboard, Mr. John Doe, is it."

"Thank you, Sir. Yes. John Doe is my name." The Captain was convinced that there was no mockery in this. "I imagine you need some attention right now, but I shall look forward to speaking with you later."

And they saluted, in spite of John Doe's having no cap to wear.

John was taken to sick-bay and asked to change from his clothes into a hospital gown. He did this and then sat upon the end of an examination table for a while. A steward entered, took the clothing from the chair where it had been left, and went out again. Presently a medical corpsman came in and performed a kind of physical examination. He considered all the joints, limbs, and digits. He looked—sometimes using a light and magnifying lens—all over the surface of John's body. He took samples of the hair and fingernails, and finally he drew off from a vein in the forearm a small sample of blood in a frosted glass syringe with a violet-colored glass plunger.

It crossed John's mind that perhaps he ought not to be submitting to all this. But then he could think of no especial reason why not. The corpsman said Goodbye, which was all he had said throughout, and he left the examining-cubicle. Presently the steward returned with the clothing, folded and stacked, replaced it upon the chair, and told John that he might now get dressed again. He added that he would wait just outside.

After three brief interviews, each with a different interviewer, John was taken to the Captain, by whom he continued to be treated courteously. "You are claiming that your name is John Doe?" he asked gently.

"Sir, it is. And it is about all I can definitely say of myself. Aboard the submarine, everyone seemed a little irritated, or perhaps they seemed skeptical, when I told them my name. Is there something about me that everybody knows but me?"

"I do not believe there is anything like that. I think, you know, the boarding-party were terribly on edge. Please don't take their reactions too much to heart. However, since you seem to remember so little else about yourself, perhaps you would tell me how you came to recall your name."

"Certainly, Sir. But, did they tell you about my thinking I was dead?"

"They did not," the Captain replied. He was more than slightly disappointed; he had believed he had upon his hands a case of amnesia, which might have been interesting, possibly absorbingly so; but now he feared he had simply got hold of an ordinary lunatic, which would be merely tedious.

"I may have forgotten to mention it to them. But I did think so."

"Think which? That you were dead, or that you had mentioned it?"

"That I was dead. I had been aware of nothing, and then I seemed to come to myself. It was not striking—no, very much muzzed. I felt something hard and cold at my back, and at the sides. I thought I was inside a coffin, so therefore I thought I must be dead. And besides, I could neither see nor hear anything. And even though at that time I wasn't very clear in my mind about heartbeat, breathing—about what they were, exactly—then my heart was not beating and I was not breathing. I'm sure of it. But now, come to think of it, I must have been wrong, mustn't I have? But, believing all that at the time, it was reasonable to think I was dead, don't you think so, Sir." The lunacy-theory gained in preponderance.

"Oh, yes, certainly, I should think."

"I did wonder, right at the last—or at what I thought was the last—what letters and numbers would have been cut into the tombstone above me. I tried then to remember my name and age. I couldn't. Then I thought that, if by looking back I couldn't know them, at least I could try by looking forward."

"Did you feel that you could prognosticate?"

"Do you never feel that you can?"

"No, I have never felt so."

"But prognostication is surely a more general thing than reading the precise text of the future. Say, for instance, Sir, that you have made plans to meet someone you…are very eager to meet."

"Yes?"

"Beforehand, you will think about the meeting, how it will turn out, and so forth."

"Yes, but that would only be my imagining it."

"But you are imagining into the future."

"That's just it—I'd only be imagining. It could turn out either better or worse than I should have supposed."

"Or, possibly, exactly as you had supposed."

"But there would be very little chance of that."

"Small chance, I agree, Sir, but nevertheless real. When your resources are limited, you must take chances, I think. For me there was no past, and little if any present. Imagination into the future, inaccurate as it might be, was all I had."

No, he is not a lunatic. He lost his footing, but as he regains it, his thoughts seem sound. "What, then, did you decide to do?"

"I decided to imagine a group of people looking at me, to see who I had been."

"People who knew you?"

"I imagined them to know. I couldn't actually remember any people who knew me. But these people in my imagination looked closely, then they spoke together, and I realized they recognized me in some sense. So I concentrated as intently as I could, to try to hear what they were saying. And finally, one of them pronounced: 'This is John Doe,' and another of them wrote it down in a small notebook."

"But then you awoke?"

"No. Then I went to sleep—that's to say, sleep as opposed to death, or whatever kind of delirium I had taken for death. It was a very comforting feeling, to leave an unnatural for a natural state, even though I was still…I suppose I should say 'obtunded'."

"And did you then awaken."

"Yes. Then I awoke."

"And you continued of course to believe your name was John Doe, for you told Mr. Benbow that it was."

"Yes. And it is. But what is so curious about it? Am I a notorious outlaw? Am I a rich and famous American, thought lost overboard from an ocean liner?" For he had become understandably agitated. But from the outset, the Captain had tended to be well-disposed toward this stranger. He had immediately liked his look and liked his manner. Though he had in passing thought him a madman, he now wished to understand and to help him. The small difference between their ages did not permit him to take a fatherly approach. He decided to treat him as a wounded comrade.

"There is nothing alarming or even very unusual in your name. And ocean liners are not crossing at this time. But tell me, were your father's people—were they called 'Doe'?"

John thought over this for a bit. Then for a bit longer. He said at last: "I don't remember any of my father's people." He said it as though he were admitting to some terrible congenital defect.

"Do you remember your father?"

John said: "I have no memory of my father." And this statement was evidently an admission of guilt.

HMS Roxburgh ran silently out of a fog bank into a vast mead of silvery light, upon a still, green ocean. A group of four men stood near the rail at her port bow. There a very remarkable thing happened:

The men were the Captain, his Lieutenant, sub-lieutenant Benbow, and Mr. John Doe. First, the Captain spoke to John: "Will you tell us where you think we are, and anything else you think we might be interested to learn?"

John replied: "I will try. Could one of you tell me what time it is?"

"Sixteen-hundred hours, two minutes."

"Thank you. I'm afraid I shall not be able to make much use of the two minutes." He was looking across and up at the sun, an indistinct but bright disk, very luminous, not golden, though, moon-colored instead. A puzzling thought came to him then: That it looked like an errant drop of solder might, fallen onto a firmament chill with altitude. "We are heading east by northeast. About…I think six, yes it would be about six hours ago, in the enemy submarine, I saw the navigator's last noted position plotted on a chart. Since then I've noted little sustained wind; I have no way of knowing the extent of drift during those hours when we stood off each other—we and the submarine—but I do not think we can be south of the fiftieth parallel, or west of longitude twenty-five degrees and possibly thirty minutes. We seem to be making for northern Great Britain, I presume for Scapa Flow."

All the officers were astonished, the Captain less so than the others. "May I," John continued, "have the use of someone's glasses?" Benbow handed him his own pair. Through them he began to peer ahead, then abruptly he would take them away and look directly into the sea. He did this four times. Then he leaned across the bowrail and looked straight down along the side of the hull. He stood up straight and turned to the others and said: "And we are making about fourteen knots. Of course all this is just guesswork—an impression. No more than that."

"You are quite a seaman!" the Captain said. The others joined in with reserved congratulation, before the sub-Lieutenant slipped away to the bridge to confirm their true speed and position.

"Then," John said, smiling for the first time since his retrieval, "you're not going to throw me into the drink?"

John was sent to refresh himself and to rest. On the way to his cabin, he wondered about the imagery he had found in the northern sun. He went through it again, to himself: *An errant drop of solder, fallen upon a firmament chill with altitude.* Where could this have come from? It was accurate. It evoked for him the appearance of the sun, at the time when he had first said it. Or had he said it? He hoped not, for when he took the phrase apart, none of the words singly conveyed any sense to him. At the time, though, definite emotion had been produced by the sequence of them.

The others were gathered in the wardroom. "He's definitely not German," the German-speaking officer assigned to interview the subject for this determination pronounced.

"He certainly deceived me," Benbow said.

"But not me," the other man, who had spent many years in Germany, answered. "His German is good, but not quite *echt*. And though he is familiar with German ways, his familiarity does not amount to intimacy."

The Captain said: "I think English is his native language," and to this there was general assent. "But I don't think he's actually English."

"No, I really do not think so, but I have to say I have considered the possibility."

"Then that leaves the United States. But his accent and diction certainly don't call them to mind. At least, not from what I know."

"But how much is that? The accents vary."

"What about the Dominions Beyond the Seas?"

"But which one? No, I don't think he comes from any of them."

"What about you, Herksheimer? Do you consider his English to be '*echt*'?"

"I am not the one to ask about that. It may be, though, that he is of the older aristocracy; their speech is often a law unto itself."

"But are you the one to ask about *that*?"

"His clothing is all American, and all new, with the exception of the pullover, which has no label and is quite well worn."

"How do you know?"

"The yarn about the cuffs is frayed; the elbows have been rubbed nearly through."

"But you believe the rest is new."

"It seems to be. There are no signs of wear. And the trousers, which are made of denim and dyed with indigo, seem not to have been washed, not even once."

"Well, then. But are we agreed that he is genuinely amnesic?" No one answered right away, for no one wanted to seem to the others to have been gulled, in case any of them thought John were an imposter. However, everyone, even Benbow, had by now begun to take the man at his word. And so to this question also there was ultimately general agreement.

"So that if he is a spy," the Captain said, "you all believe he has forgotten that, too."

Put this way, the matter became weightier. But concurrence was ultimately extracted from every man on this point as well.

"Does he seem to any of us familiar with the popular culture of any particular country?"

"Well, as I've said already, certainly not with that of Germany."

"And clearly not with England's."

"His clothing could be American without his being American himself. I can think of a dozen reasons for the American clothing, I suppose. And he hardly squares with my idea of a typical 'Yank'."

"And not the Dominions?" Nobody thought so.

"If we didn't have to maintain radio silence we could enquire of the Admiralty itself, or any of the Intelligence branches."

"Time for that soon enough. At least we have the machine and the papers. And those could win the War!"

"Really, they could, you know."

At Scapa Flow, where hard stone is forever being abraded by bitter sands and striving wind, by the striving and striving of etching wind, inhospitable vain bulwarks against the sea waited to embrace them all.

The Captain had completed his explanation of the use of the name John Doe to the man who thought it was his own. "It must be clear to you by now—although at first I'm sure nothing was clear—that you have been deprived of your memory of most things."

John made no answer to this.

"And now, with this revelation, I must seem to you to have taken away—

or, worse, to have taken back—the one very important thing you felt you *had* recalled to mind."

Still, John said not a word. This was not out of pique. He was afraid of saying anything at all because by now he was no longer sure that he could trust the apparent meaning of any word that presented itself for utterance.

The Captain went on: "I do not claim to know much about amnesia, and I have had little experience of it. In fact, though, anybody who is badly knocked about is confused at least for some minutes. And a friend of mine who was involved in a car-crash—this was years ago—could remember nothing at all for a time, but by the end of a fortnight or so he was entirely clear about his whole prior life, so far as he or anybody else could tell."

Then John spoke deliberately, because he had concluded that if he could understand the Captain's words, then probably his own words could be depended upon not to be wholly misunderstood: "But it has been a day, and I have remembered nothing, as it turns out."

"But even at the first, you had the presence of mind to know you could not think, so to say, into the past and so you tried—very ingeniously, it strikes me—to think into the future."

"But the attempt ended in failure."

"Oh, not entirely!"

"Why do you say not?"

"Because you thought of precisely the name we should have given you if we had found you dead, like some of those German sailors, and floating face-down within the swell." Then, following a pause: "Unless you had carried some identification. By any chance, do you know why you didn't?"

"I may have left what I had in one of my pockets."

"No. We went through your clothing carefully. There was nothing in any of the pockets."

"Oh, these are not my clothes! I hadn't realized you thought they were."

"You have been wearing them, after all."

"Yes, but they're not mine."

"And you feel quite sure of that."

"Oh, perfectly sure. I don't wear clothes like these."

"If they're not your clothes, then that must account for the absence of any identification. But I do wonder why you're wearing them."

"I wonder myself. And I'm sure it makes you ask yourself why I am at large aboard your ship—you having no idea who I am."

"Soon, perhaps, when we've docked, we'll learn more."

"Or perhaps not." By this hour, the sun after them had slid lower in heaven, as it sank filling the world below the clouds with the fool's-gold of evening. The breeze had wrought itself up to a low gale out of the northeast.

John went out again onto the deck to watch and listen and draw breath. It was all so familiar, seemed so momentous without his grasping why, and here he stood in someone else's clothes! The wavelets wrapped sea-green coils about decandescing ingots of evening brightness, before the wind came to dismantle the fragile work of light and water.

Scapa Flow stretched out her jetties, the Naval Station ready to consume, in bulk, improbably precious cargoes brought over the seas in careful parcels: Encryption and decryption, code and clear, things remembered or forgotten. For the little worlds of ships came home to her to be taken up into the whole world of mankind and his doing, his undoing.

Now John waited in a larger and slightly more comfortably furnished cubicle, where there were chairs, a desk, a photographic portrait of the King. A man in uniform beneath a long white smock had come in briefly. He had not sat down, but had said: "Good morning! Are you feeling well? I'm delighted to hear it! I am going now to see the Captain and learn from him all I can, so that I won't have to weary you by having you recite yet again all the events of yesterday."

And if I chose not to do it, then how would you "have me recite" them?

"But I did want to tell you this one thing before I disappear...."

No, please! Disappear.

"... because it will give you courage."

!

"Loss of memory can be brought on either by the tremendous kind of shock you have sustained, or by the emotional necessity to forget, or by some combination of those two things. Whatever the case, though, with rest and care, with careful treatment, we can in all likelihood help you to remember. And then we can restore you to your rightful place in the world!" With this presumptuous observation, he opened the door to leave. John caught a glimpse in the corridor outside of the goodly Captain and longed to have a word with him. The medical officer, for such the man was, of sorts, then said: "And of course that is what we all want, isn't it? I shall rejoin you within the hour, at the very most." And out of the room he popped, not the same kind of 'pop' as that of the proverbial weasel. But if a weasel were to pop out of a room, that was how he would do it, John felt sure. The whole time he wore a kind of mechanical rat-smile that John had seen already.

Before the door was fully shut, John heard the Captain say to the medical officer: "Nothing from the Admiralty, nothing from any Intelligence branch."

So John sat alone once again waiting to be interviewed. This time, though, he knew the wait would be long. He also knew something about the eventual interview: That it was likely to outline "care" and to detail "treatment" that awaited him in order that he be helped to remember all that he had forgotten. And at that under the supervision of a rodent-therapist whom instinctively he found loathsome. Probably with a rat-pack of helpers, barely convinced of the rectitude and value of their method, yet convinced, to assist him in his conclusions and prescribed regimen. What, then, was the right thing for him to do now?

First, should he entrust his future to someone whom he knew he could never trust, because he knew nearly viscerally that the man with the rat-smile did not really trust himself, but was possibly a minor charlatan content with the meager duties to which he had been relegated—the contentment in itself disturbing. If only he had looked and acted glum! Or betrayed uncertainty. But John knew that the man, so tightly bound and shielded in his sureness about "what they all wanted" had ceased to reflect or to repent.

And second—since his inner promptings (and where might they have come from?) coaxed away from all this—did he wish at all to recover his memory, even supposing this were possible? Had he fallen from a high place, to which it would be agreeable or advantageous for him to return? Or had he now risen free of some unpleasant situation, or some menacing one?

The clock above King George's picture must not be working. John didn't know through what time-zones he had passed, how many hours or even minutes had crept by. But the clock must have stopped. Or ticked one time only since the doctor had gone away…ticked a single second away. Then, surely, it had stopped. The King, though, looked just as he ought to look. And it was a great mercy he had ascended the Throne—but why shouldn't he have?

Back, though, to the decisions he must make before letting his thoughts wander to monarchies and so on. Should he consult his own wishes only in deciding whether to return to the land of lost content or discontent?

What of his responsibilities—say, to an invalid grandmother somewhere waiting and hoping? There was someone whom he had wished to ask about this, someone who was with him in the room even then, unseen. Well, no use to add this to the uncertainty actually present to his mind, and even that uncertainty nearly engulfed in a whole forgotten past, wholly forgotten. So, instead of asking or wondering, he decided merely to cogitate, hopefully to excogitate.

Or was this too much like the process by which he had arrived at the name that was not after all his own? But he sat and thought about his responsibilities, which was no easy thing, since he wasn't aware of any. He sat and thought, until he realized that the clock had begun to tick forward again.

Then he found that he had decided, and that King George the Good, as he was coming to be known, John believed, had given Royal Assent. For some verses came back to him, and he felt that they were so well known that almost anybody would recognize them. And anyone who did so would automatically ratify his decision: "…and makes us rather bear those ills we have/ Than fly to others that we know not of."

Whatever force had cost him his memory would absolve him of abandoned duties, would compensate him for lost wealth or honor. He would keep what he knew he had, how little soever that might be, and go forward. And so he arose from his chair and walked away.

The Naval Station—at least the part to which John had been taken—consisted of an irregular grouping of plain buildings, huddling together against the scouring wind. July. But it was "airish." Who used to say that of chilly weather—"Right airish today, isn't it?" John walked along as though he had somewhere to go. He felt that before, he must usually in fact have had somewhere to go. Now he passed a structure with windows set high in the walls, almost under the eaves. They were open, and he could hear water spilling down. He walked on, however, around to the other side, having checked an impulse to turn and retrace some of his steps. That would have made him appear diffident. He realized that he had made this choice because it would make him appear the more resolute. It was just that he wasn't sure why he should wish to appear resolute. But he surmised that the depths of his memory were sending him promptings and checks over a vast and possibly otherwise unbridgeable chasm.

He entered the building and found that, as he had suspected, it was used for bathing. In the space where he found himself was a row of vertical compartments. Not lockers. No doors. A shelf at the top of each, a meaningless number above this. There was clothing hanging within some of these niches. Before them was a row of benches.

Two officers entered, and John noticed that they were carrying fresh towels. One also had a small duffle.

That settled it, then. He had no towel. There could be no camouflaging shower, but as the two others had sat down nearby, John did start to unbutton his shirt. They looked at him and both nodded. One said: "Off *Roxburgh?*"

"Yes."

"Well, it's known all over the base she killed a U-boat. Good show! But everybody has been told not to try to talk to you chaps about the op."

"No." The two were undressing also. John noted that the one who had spoken to him was of about his own stature and frame. When they had gone into the showers, then John made his selection: The taller officer's khaki twills (the other's were whites), shirt and necktie, which was black, all free of insignia. These things he now put on, leaving the tunic, which was so crowded with bars and stripes and colored ribbons that it must surely have told the full history of the owner's adult life to anyone able to read from it. Perhaps, he thought, I should have had one of those—then I'd know. But he was a decisive man, it seemed, and he found that he did not want to know.

When John sat down again upon the bench to lace and tie his own—but even these were not his own—shoes, two distressing things occurred: The first was the appearance, still dripping from the shower, of another man. But he only nodded and went past. The second was his sitting down upon some bulky thing in the hip pocket of the appropriated trousers. He stood and found it to be a rather large sheaf of banknotes. He riffled through them, and in doing so realized he would need money—a little, at least. At that time, one still gave Crowns and Pounds and Guineas. He removed a five-pound note and placed the rest upon the shelf at the top of the compartment (The note was never missed by its owner, who didn't remember the exact amount of his winnings at cards the night before).

John felt some kind of regret at having taken the five pounds. He couldn't think why—so much was left over—but it comforted him a little that he did regret it. He kept his pullover.

IV

"Hail holy Light, offspring of Heav'n first-born…."
John Milton: *Paradise Lost,* 3. 1

"I CAN TELL you nothing, Father," Robert answered Thomas, who had asked about goings-on in the North Atlantic.

"Well what *can't* you tell me, then?"

"That's another story. We may not be belligerents, but we are definitely not neutral. British ships have been putting in for stores at Hampton Roads almost since the beginning. Other things have happened. A British aircraft carrier came into drydock at Norfolk after she had been bombed. She was there for weeks. People aren't blind. They certainly aren't mute. It would be better if a lot of them were!"

"How are the supermen taking it?"

"Keeping up the pretense. Scrupulously treating our vessels as neutral—so far. That Merkin-mouth is still so great a fool as to think we can be kept out of the War in Europe. But as far as I'm concerned we have never been neutral, and, frankly, not since the invasion of Poland."

"When we do enter the War, will we do it because they're wrong?"

"That, and because we'll have to defend ourselves. They will not stop invading, seizing. Eventually we would have to stand up to the whole gang alone."

"Thomas sighed. "Well, God keep us from wrong."

"In the meantime, God keep us, period." And the two men had continued their walk at evening along the esplanade.

"Good morning, Darling." Robert had come out onto the verandah, where his mother was sitting. "What would you like for breakfast?"

"Good morning, Mother." He bent down to kiss her. "Black coffee. Triple strength. One cup. If you please."

"But Rhodë is here and can prepare anything you want. And she would be so pleased if you were to ask her!"

"No use going through it again, Mother. I do not have breakfast."

"But breakfast is the most important meal of the day." Her son had sat down upon the railing, with his eyes closed, hands on his knees. She could see that he was deliberately Being Patient. She went inside to order the coffee. When she returned, she said: "I should like to talk to you about Anne, if you'll put up with me."

"Anne, in all her aspects, is my favorite subject."

"One of mine, too. But I want to ask something in particular and I don't want it to make you cross." For she could see that his expression was becoming clouded-over, and suddenly, like summer sky in the thunderous heat of afternoon.

She's not supposed to know.

"Anyway, it's this: Have you ever wondered—or do you know—whether she is their *adoptive* child?"

"Bunny's and Libby's?" He laughed loudly and heartily. And for some little time afterward unsuppressed chuckling kept returning, echoing his amusement. "You're afraid of the genes!"

"No, no of course it's not that. But she is unlike them—unlike Margaret, too." Grace went on, feebly: "It's just that her coloring is different. That is all I meant, really."

"No, Mother; she is *entirely* different. What makes this so ridiculous is that I wondered the same thing, once I'd met them all.

"And while I can't *know* who her father is, Bunny is supposed to be. And Libby complains constantly about having had to endure suffocating heat along with the late stages of pregnancy before poor Anne, who obviously is not one bit to blame, was finally born at the end of August."

"It's a pity the others are such fools."

"Mother!"

"Oh, I'm so sorry, Darling! I really did not mean that."

"No, they're decidedly fools. I'm just surprised to hear *you* say it."

"Well, I oughtn't to have said it. Anne could have sprung from a stock and a stone and still be adorable, and very fine."

An onlooker might have thought all of them were rehearsing a play. Grace got up and went into the house. Then Thomas appeared and held the screen door open for Rhodë, who made her entrance carrying a waiter with two silver coffee pots and two large cups made of paper-thin porcelain and bearing misty Japanese motifs. Thomas sat down beside his son, who got up to kiss him on the cheek. Rhodë poured coffee and served it. Exiit center.

"This," Robert said, "is a system guaranteed to chill a cup of coffee as quickly as possible." Each took a sip. Without speaking, they exchanged cups. "Silver, to begin with, has a very high specific heat. It extracts all warmth from the coffee. The nuisance is greater because the pot gets too hot to touch; that's why they isolate the handle with those little rings of ivory."

"Why not just drink it, before the phenomenon has a chance to progress?"

Son and father crossed again to the walk alongside the Great River. "When we were talking last evening about our position with respect to the European conflict…."

"The War."

"…neutrality, naval operations, and so on, you said the Germans treat our vessels as neutral. 'Scrupulously,' I think you said. Then you added, I think, 'For the most part.' "

"I don't remember exactly what I said, but that is how it is."

"The qualification; *does* it mean we're at war? Because a lot of people are hinting that we are, just without declaring it. But, come to say, I haven't heard it from anybody very highly placed."

"For months we've been sending a lot of supplies to the British—not just food and clothing; munitions, too, and weaponry. I think."

"But in British ships?"

"In ships that are British now."

"But we gave them to them?"

"Swapped them apparently, nominally in return for use of military bases in some of their possessions. Anyway, German submarines are sinking thousands of tons of our shipping. My CO doesn't know for sure. His immediate superiors don't know either, I believe. But word gets around."

"Are things no worse than that?"

Robert did not answer this without reflection. He contemplated the Great River flowing past, as through ages it had flowed. And he knew that he was seeing only the rippling divide between water and air. Oh, indeed, sunlight could pass down into the water, but so much of it was reflected beforehand that he was blinded by it and could not see into the depths. The fluid-friction, eddy and turbulence, were hidden. Waters from so many rivulets of time, now confounded into this resistless flood, were making for the sea ahead where origin would be forgotten.

"Poppy," Robert said, using a name he hadn't used perhaps in twenty years, "you're not supposed to know this, nor am I, nor is my CO, but we are moving gradually eastward, and they are coming farther west every day. We're patrolling off Iceland and Greenland regularly—beyond that, at times." Robert did not specify precisely in which direction, how far. "One of our destroyers reported laying down depth charges off Iceland.

" Inevitably, a German submarine eventually fired a torpedo at a freighter under our ensign. She sank. A couple of men from Norfolk were aboard, so that's another cat out of the bag.

"Everybody is talking about sightings and sinkings. Just not necessarily specifically—or even out loud. Add up all the rumors, and you've got enough torpedoes and depth charges going off in the North Atlantic at any given time to raise sea-level by an inch or two.

"But, yes, Father. We're at war."

These conversations had taken place, it seemed to Thomas, a very long time ago. That was because his Interlocutor had been taken from him. And because, in a way, four years *are* a long time. Now he ambled along that same esplanade holding his grandson's fat little paw and recollecting and wondering.

The winter before, this child was climbing the stairs inside the Strikestraw house. He wore a clean white nightshirt through which his infant form was shadowed; he carried a candle. This was held in an old brass stick, older, possibly, than the old house itself.

The little boy's grandmother watched him climb; she could see him through the French doors. At the tops of this pair, to the darkened dining room, from which Grace was watching, and of the matching pair across the hallway, opening into the library, the geometry ended a little prematurely, leaving, above the pointed arches formed by branching and interlacing of the muntin-bars, small triangles in a sawtooth row.

These spaces were filled by frosted plaques of colored glass, blue on this side of the hallway, amber across. Each had cut into it a six-pointed star. Two such stars, to be accurate, one from either side, congruent exactly. The centers transmitted nearly white light and must have been only microns thick.

Upward the child went. The candle's flame, just before disappearing, shone through one of the incised stars. Grace was overborne by the effulgence. Instantly, she realized that if she were to continue to be able to follow her little grandson's progress, she must close her eyes. Otherwise she ran the risk of losing sight of him.

So she did close them. And, yes, she could see him still—better, in a way, than before. He reached the top of the first flight, and as he turned onto the broad landing she saw that his candlestick had become a domed and many-paned lantern, which the boy held high. Twelve candles were set within it now, all alight at once. Again the child turned, now onto the second flight of stairs. The light became very bright and diffuse. From every space, from the slanted closet under the lower staircase, from corners behind doors which stood always open, too-high shelves, cupboards both too high and too low, the increasing light was driving—was driving still as for months, years it had been driving, ever since she and Thomas had fetched the boy home from Virginia—all shadow, all shade of sorrow out of the house and down to the river, where it rose with the mist and was carried away.

The desire of his grandmother's heart, she believed, was realized. Anyone who knew Grace, though, any of her friends who might have watched her flee, as she had earlier been driven to do, from insupportable grief, who might have seen her dashed upon the jagged headland of a storm that had seemed likely to obliterate, at first all light, then after it, the universe itself—hers, anyway—any such friend of Grace's could have looked upon her present joy only with misgiving. Because it was evident that she now felt that one lost could be substituted for by another—another sufficiently like the first, blood-issue of the first, even as though likeness to the father could drive away all likeness to the mother, as if the begetter were the parent, as if somehow it could all be played over from the start.

And for a time it worked. For the child strongly resembled his father Robert Strikestraw when at that early stage of life. And, he being a very young child, not much differentiation had taken place. He was a great deal like an embryonic cell, metabolizing, dividing, and waiting to disclose into which of the tissues it is going to develop. "Pluripotential," cells thought capable of evolution in any of a thousand ways. And to be sure, if at a dawning moment two of them be seen, even beneath what we now regard as the apocalyptic stare of the electron microscope, they may appear identical, yet during the developmental process one becomes an osteoclast, bone-breaker; the other a retinal cell, the physical body's Lucifer and bearer of light.

For things do not turn out against prognosis—not unless the prognosis has been faulty (and incompleteness is such a fault); the work of Destiny is not curbed.

Grace ought to have known better. She did know better. But her heart had sealed off her faculties in an alcove garnished with desperation and so made ready for festival. And we have seen her likewise imprisoned before.

Sure enough, just as at first she had out of diffidence concealed her joy, now, these many months later, she must admit that lapses had begun, had got longer, more frequent; so that now she had out of fear begun to conceal these. Those who might have known would also know that the concealment was mainly from herself.

For all the week after the child's first arrival, Rhodë had been constantly beside herself with delight, but without delusion. No patch of floor was swept, no cushion plumped, no meal quite fit to eat; so overjoyed were all to have him by. Rhodë was not in doubt, though, about who the boy Edward was. He was Miss Anne's and Mr. Robert's son, only son, only child, and always to be. For Miss Anne was gone—dead and gone—and now Mr. Robert was gone, too. Miss Grace had told her—and had told her not to say it, and she hadn't and wouldn't—that "Our boy is gone, and probably will not come back." Edward was not Robert. He was his son. And the rest of him came from Miss Anne. And that by itself was assurance that the Maker had an intention of filling the world with better and better people—things, too, as likely as not. Evil, Rhodë had by now secretly convinced herself, anyway, even if no one else, was a pitiable weakling, and in the end would be shown to be. One day, it would be clean gone. On what day, though? Well, the Maker would decide that.

Meanwhile, she had the joy of a small child again. And he *was* half Mr. Robert's. Nevertheless, after her week's undeclared holiday, she got back to diligent housekeeping, and when she did, then there was no other house in town so extravagantly burnished as to turn in its reflection back to the goodly Maker so uninterrupted a stream of thanksgiving, though it were silent as light.

Thomas was bemused; for here under his roof was a little lad who was very much as his father had been at that age, markedly, though, at the same time, quite another person. And that is why, although he was consistently attentive to and helpful with Little Edward (Soon they were going to have to stop calling him that), yet that is why he spoke to him always as though he were another adult—he adjusted the content of his speech, of course, but not the tone or the terms. For he felt sure that in time he would have this child as a companion; not only that, but even one who held the answers to secrets and riddles; who was in part his son; in part, even, himself; a companion, he was sure, who would ultimately help him make sense of all the dashes and dots now swarming in the atmosphere, or within his brain; of the pings and resoundings known within the depths of the sea. He must wait, of course, but the greatest rewards would be his.

He needed no replica of Robert. Robert he kept unchanged in his heart.

It is true that, for all his enlightened intentions, Thomas spent some days in allowing Edward to remind him palpably of Robert, but not necessarily of Robert at so tender an age. At this time, most of the things he could remember of his son were from much more recent months and years.

They had been walking together, he and Robert, again of so many times, along the little esplanade. They spoke of Anne. She and Robert had been married not long before to widespread rejoicing; not universal, of course, for there were many other men who had hoped to have Anne, and some few women who had hoped to have Robert.

Grace and Thomas had had a series of productive dust-up's over the form of the New Brunswick announcement-party (For there were to be two, one here and the other in Virginia, in order to minimize the need for travel, which was becoming more difficult every day). It was only because Thomas was rector. He did not feel he should plan this kind of thing without including the parishioners generally. Or, for that matter, have a band playing tunes that oughtn't to have sounded through a house in which a priest lived. They finally decided upon a three-pronged campaign: Through an announcement in the Church Bulletin and one made from the narthex immediately after the recessional hymn one Sunday, all were invited to "tea" on the day appointed, from four until six o'clock. The plan was to have India tea poured in the library, China tea across the hall in the dining room, and plenty of flowers instead of plenty of liquor. As a last-minute concession, a little chilled champagne was to be offered from an inconspicuous table in the hallway. Everybody came, as fortune would have it, and almost everybody congregated about the champagne table, not attracted to gleaming silver, steaming tea, and all the ritualistic accoutrements that go with it. Not even by the orchid-bowers set about, nor yet by the little pitchers of facultative rum on the tea tables, nor by candles burning in splendid, towering sticks.

Nevertheless, by six o'clock most of these guests had left—and had left satiated, since Thomas had providently ordered a good many extra cases of champagne—except for a few who decided to mingle with the fewer who had been invited for cocktails, from six until eight o'clock.

The father of the bride-elect was about to discover how fine a match had been made for his daughter. His head first entered the clouds when he learned from his hosts, the Howells—close friends of the Strikestraws who lived just three houses away down Front Street—that Thomas' mother had been English; yet Thomas' "Englishness" went back farther, to the Grantly great-grandfather, who had been an archdeacon in the Church of England. Next, after arriving for the beginning of festivity, he met Miss Mary Lou Schwenzfeier, one of the guests to tea. However, by now she was no longer Miss Mary Lou Schwenzfeier, but rather Miss Mary Lou Taliaferro. "Schwenzfeier" had never been anything but a snare to her. When the Saxe-Coburg and Gothas changed their name to Windsor, Mary Lou decided to fall back upon her mother's maiden name, the anomaly between spelling and pronunciation of course preserved.

Before making this move, she had sought guidance from Above as well as advice from her friends. "I don't care whether it *is* Austrian. The Austrians speak a kind of German, don't they? And they're no better!"

Bunny was entranced. And from that moment one sort of entrancement spilled over into another; he squired her about from then onward, paying homage and what looked a lot like court.

He accompanied her to the tea table (India, of course), where for himself he requested the much manlier potation of a shot of whiskey. He took it in one swallow.

Around half past six o'clock, the guests of honor and their hosts disappeared, two at a time, to change into evening clothes. For Grace felt that what could not be offered in sumptuousness could be compensated for by ceremony. First, though, she had a small, unexpected, but essential mission to accomplish: "Mary Lou, I know you don't much enjoy a drink—that's why we asked you for tea. But Bunny Singleton—that's Anne's father…."

"I know."

"…Has become greatly taken with you. Greatly. You've got to stay. Otherwise I don't know quite how we'll handle him."

"He has seemed attentive."

"He's smitten."

"But what about Mrs. Singleton?"

"Libby will be delighted to be rid of him; I'll explain it all to you later."

"But I'm not dressed for evening."

"I can fix that. Come upstairs with me when it's my turn." For the gentlemen were to change first.

Bunny came downstairs looking very much the part he had set himself to play. Robert, in dress uniform, caused a sensation. As Bunny glanced about, looking for Miss Mary Lou, he saw a gentleman who with his tuxedo was wearing a violet colored shirt-front and white clerical collar. It was Thomas. He had brushed his hair, a thing he normally did only once a week, and that at the unfortunate moment just before putting on his surplice for Sunday Service.

Bunny turned to a knowing-looking lady standing nearby: "Do you by any chance know why our host is wearing that purple shirt?"

Alenda Lucas answered: "Tommy is a Canon of the Diocese." And then she turned away. With this revelation, Bunny, who since late afternoon had been steadily ascending—head in the clouds first, walking on air next—completed his entry into the Nephelococcygia of Social Contentment.

Now the ladies began to return, Libby and Peggy leading the way, in *grandes robes de gala*. Mother and daughter, who looked a lot alike, were also dressed a lot alike: In columnar black, with slits in the cloth at their right legs. Libby was supposed to have wonderful legs, and this feature of couture confirmed it. The ladies looked away for fear of how high the slit might go. The gentlemen stole every possible glance, for the converse of the same reason. But you had to run your eyes on up along the line of Peggy's gown to appreciate the critical part of its cut: For her most memorable features were rigged farther aloft.

After she herself had changed, Grace took Mary Lou in hand. It could not have been simpler. Around her neck was a string of pearls. Grace had her remove these and stow them in safety. Then she hung in their place a necklace of amethysts and diamonds. There were not many of either, and the necklace as a whole was not very big. But the amethysts were big. And the diamonds, fewer, were great indeed. This did the trick, so the two ladies went downstairs. If Miss Mary Lou's transformation was lost on anyone else, it was definitely not lost on Bunny, in whose ear the gems kept whispering Ancient Splendor, Ancient Splendor. He became nearly unmanageable, but then nobody was trying to manage him. For the guests who had been invited to drink cocktails had begun to take their acceptances seriously. So all went well.

Neither Libby nor Peggy had ever been able to grasp what Robert saw in Anne. They did not discuss it between themselves, however, because each lady believed in secret that he was mesmerized by herself, not by sister or daughter. He was immensely decorative—especially on this evening—which was what interested them the most. But not at all flirtatious. This produced a small, gnawing doubt in each.

Anne, on her part, had dressed simply for evening, and she had removed all ornament besides her engagement ring. She was a young woman sensible of the purposes of things, open to the possible meanings of things not seen, nor even known. For this reason her life sometimes seemed to her a loosely linked progression of symbolisms. It made others wonder whether she were shy or haughty, though she was neither of these.

Anne did not "make an entrance" downstairs that evening. She was not a "figure." She merely became a presence among the others, causing them, as one by one they noticed her, to catch their breath. Beautiful, spectacularly serene.

Then Bob saw her. The crowd fell back as he made his way to her. The sounds of revelry were shuttered somewhat. The couple exchanged a kiss. There was a rippling murmur. Then no one could withhold discrete applause.

It cannot be denied that Miss Mary Lou enjoyed Bunny's fascination with herself, though she found it inexplicable. She had changed her name, to be sure, but she had never been invited to do it by the usual means. She drank a glass of Champagne and said she might drink another with supper.

Then people began to propose toasts, to Thomas' chagrin. Rhodë, no mean figure herself—since the subject of fine-looking women has been set afoot—once she and the people who had been got in to help her had the house completely filled with the seductive bouquets of a superb supper, stepped into the dining room. She stopped just inside, standing by the doorway. Grace went up to her to enquire about the preparations, mainly to tell her how wonderful everything smelt. Then she saw the little folded note in Rhodë's hand. "Rhodë! You've prepared a toast, or a good wish, haven't you? It will mean more to them than all the rest. Come, now, into the library and read it!"

"I couldn't, Miss Grace. I wanted you to look at it, and, if you think it's all right, I would like to ask you to read it for me."

Within a few minutes Grace, dabbing at her eyes with her handkerchief, was making her way through the press into the library. "Everyone! Listen, please!

" 'Miss Anne and Mr. Robert, the Almighty made each one of you in Heaven. And when the day comes, He is going to make your marriage in Heaven, too. May He bless you both forever. Love from Rhododactylë Harmon.' " At this, a full-voiced cheer went up. Rhodë heard it and hurried out onto the back porch to hide her tears.

Now Grace looked at her watch. With the utmost cordiality she went from one to another of the "Cocktails" guests saying: "Are you *sure* you won't stay for supper?" In this way, she achieved the leavetakings and departures of a large proportion of them.

After that, beginning at eight o'clock, a "fork supper" was served to the families and their closest friends.

It had been then, Grace being about to introduce the Hammonds to Libby and Bunny, and to Peggy, that Thomas had approached saying, both superfluously and unfortunately: "Helen and John Hammond, these are Anne's parents and sister, the Simpletons."

But worse things had happened. Worse things, as a matter of fact, were going to. Besides, Grace thought privately that he had meant to do it. And the truth is that he could but hardly have been blamed.

When the guests had all left, Robert removed everything merely decorative from his uniform. There was a great deal of it. Then he crouched among the fixtures in the downstairs bathroom. He closed the shutoff valve in the cold water supply to the washbasin. For the tap itself was fixed open. But Thomas, before the party had begun, had said of the profligate stream: "Not to arrange it this way would be the same as failing to break all the glasses after a fateful toast."

That night, when Bunny laid his head upon his pillow in the Howells' comfortable spare room, he felt a pang of sorrow for those who had little, who had to make do with that little. But prelacy! English blood! Ancestors in Colonial Virginia!—Those were the kinds of things from which was formed the bedrock of a consequential life!

The wedding, with as many of the usual trappings as could be managed, took place in Richmond, stylish for a world on the threshold of war, with as guests all the Right People. That meant Libby's family, so many as could be coaxed into being present, their friends, and her friends, and a few people invited by Bunny. A few only. No one asked questions, especially not now, when uppermost in everybody's mind hung the question: *Will there be any more fashionable marriages?*

The very closest of the Strikestraws' family and friends had been present, but it had been made clear that gasoline rations must not be squandered upon pageantry. Other little shortages and unavailabilities must be respected, too.

Thomas recalled all this, recalled a later confession of his son's as they had gone solemnly along the farther sidewalk on their accustomed stroll after dinner.

"Father," Bob had said, "There is something I feel I must tell you. Anne and I have agreed not to speak any more about it, and there is no one else for me to talk to."

"Tell me what the matter is."

"It's about Anne."

"I assumed it would be."

"Why?"

"Because I don't think anything that did not have to do with her could be cloaked in so much solemnity."

"She has a child."

"What!"

"I knew you'd be dismayed."

"I'm not. But clearly you are."

"Anne, of all people, made the well-known single mistake. Or she says so. And I believe her."

"Is she in circumstances that may have compelled her to tell you about it…or are you the father?"

"I am not the father of the little child; she had no reason to tell me, except that she is more honorable than to have me not know."

"That squares with my impression of the girl. But have you bitterness against her for it?"

"It's not possible for me to have bitterness against her for anything, because I love her. If it had been Peggy, of course nobody would have been surprised."

"Could I ask: Has anybody been surprised, as it is?"

"Nobody knows about it. Almost nobody. She went to Bunny."

"Not to her mother?"

"To Libby!

"If I had had a sister, in the same trouble, she would have gone first to Mother, then to you both."

They walked along beside each other in detonated silence, for they were son and father. And then Robert added: "For Anne to have gone to Libby about it would have amounted to her taking out a full page in the *Times*. Anyway, Bunny got for Anne the 'Best Obstetrician in Virginia,' which means…."

"…The best obstetrician in the World," the two men recited together.

Robert went on: "Then he got hold of The Best Lawyer in Virginia—same implication—who arranged for an adoption. He knows the family, or at any rate Who They Are. So Bunny was satisfied."

"If Bunny is satisfied, then the whole world ought to be!" They had laughed a little.

"Anne knows nothing. She wanted not to be told. She considers separation from her child to be her due burden."

"Poor child! She is due no burden."

"I agree that she is not." They walked on for a bit, and ultimately Robert said: "Thank you for not asking whether she knows who the father is."

"Anne! 'Misled by moonlight and the rose?' I'm sure she knows not only who the father is, but even the date and probably the time of conception."

"She says so, and I believe her."

"The poor girl! Well, you and she must have a child together and let the rest of the world slide down its ways and end where it will."

"We're going to. In February, I think."

For Anne Singleton, later Anne Singleton Strikestraw, deceased; for Lilia Belle Gadsen, decedent as all of us are decedent; for all in their perplexity, with the Poet Auden now we ask: Joseph, Mary, pray.

The violence done to Lilia Belle in the process of her conceiving a child we have seen already; and we shall in due time see the sorrow in which she bore him.

Anne did violence of a sort to herself, for she sought many ways in which to expiate her error, even though her father-in-law later declared to his son that she was due no burden of guilt. In general, she meant to reject all gratification of bearing a child, of having a child. During the last five months of her pregnancy, she asked them with whom she was lodging and boarding to help her lose track of time, and when her confinement came she requested liberal doses of opioids, directed that her window-shade be kept closed, that no one say to her: "Good evening," or "Good morning." She did not want to know and be obliged to remember the child's birthday.

Queenly enough to command, Anne commanded that she be told nothing about her child, that she not be shown it, although as things turned out there did occur what could be considered a small ambiguous divulgence in this respect. For when labor had become established, it was apparent to the obstetrician that the birth was going to be unimpeded and hasty. Anne was taken to the delivery room and a form of light anaesthesia, used commonly in those days, known as "Twilight Sleep," was administered.

The child was delivered with the anticipated ease and dispatch, Anne knowing neither the day nor the hour. Afterward, she became sentient enough to hear one of the nurses exclaim: "Lord! Look at all that brown hair!"

"Be quiet," the obstetrician muttered, completing his work.

But the nurse continued: "I don't think I've ever seen a White newborn with so much long brown hair!"

And then one of her fellows broke in: "Now if she had been Colored…."

At this the obstetrician, about to draw the needle-carrier through a last loop of silk, turned to them and said: "Get out…both of you get out, and *at once!* And come back when you've decided you can keep your mouths shut."

(The one who had said "she," had meant the mother.)

Anne subsided into the twilight of her sleep. She awoke when the doctor came into her room. A nurse was with him. She let up the window-shade, then withdrew. The doctor sat down upon a corner of the foot of the bed—a practice so maddening to patients, but doctors, who find it convenient in any case, seem determined to feel it strengthens the bond in between. He said: "Anne, you have given birth to a wonderful, healthy child. You have been the means of bringing new life. I think you ought to derive some thankfulness from it." They looked directly at each other for a few moments, and then the doctor got up and went to the door. Before going out, he turned back toward her and said: "Not all women are able to conceive and bear; you are. Go back to sleep, now, and dream about that."

Earlier in the year of Bob's disappearance, in the year when on the morning of the first day of his unaccountable absence nothing was said, earlier, that is, in 1942, when many Americans were not sure what to make of their Country's being at war, some good time after Anne's death, not in childbirth but one week afterward and as a direct result of it, just in the spring, in the chill promise of late March, Robert Strikestraw had come down from Norfolk to Wilmington to visit his parents. It had not proved feasible for him to bring with him his little son (christened Edward Grantly—the Singletons were still trying to put a good face upon their disappointment).

New Brunswick watched over the Great Watercourse along whose bank she lay, languid, upon a bluff—high enough so that one could look directly across onto the superstructures of the largest freighters that passed to or from the Port of Wilmington.

Two-and-a-half centuries before, the citizenry of Brunswick Town had looked from the same embankment down onto the fleet below, but in the years between, the scale of many things, relative to each other, had changed.

Now a few dwellings, a handful of stores craned upward, or looked precipitately down upon each other, built as they were upon incomprehensible Confederate earthworks. Farther to the north, where the little bluff slipped down to the level of the riverbank and woods adjacent; and farther to the south, where under the eminence of the bluff the land lay the same, later, ordinary commercial buildings and dwellings stood. The old Courthouse, Christ Church, and the modestly august houses, mostly along Front Street, on its height, a few others, scattered along Next Street, reminded of Colonial precedence.

Languid were the Town and River, and estuarial creeks, wreathed in stretches of tawny marshland—all tangentially gilded and warmed by the encamping sun. The water by contrast was turned to harsh, steely blue where the breeze abraded it, leaving it an unscathed indigo scattered in sheltered places.

Thomas and Robert had gone out onto the front verandah. They observed and commented upon the meager fishing-fleet, looking now probably to its last days.

Rhodë had stayed on to "see about" dinner, and Robert had visited with her in kitchen and butler's pantry while she prepared and served it. All the time they were together, continual peals of laughter rang out through the house. We could wonder whether there were so much cause for mirth in the whole world—particularly in that world, and then. But almost a quarter-century of camaraderie had accrued in those recesses—It had never been contained, not even when the Bishop came for luncheon after his annual visitations at the Church. Their laughter, like the six-pointed stars incised into the frosted glass plaques of the French doors, had always added welcome sparkle to solemnity.

"Well, Son, I don't imagine either of us will live again through so much change in so short time."

"No. I wonder whether we could withstand it, if so much should come again."

"Life seems, at times, fragile, then, in other circumstances, it seems ineradicable." And Thomas added: "Losing Anne without having Little Edward to fill some of the emptiness would seem intolerable."

"It seems intolerable anyway."

"Yes…it seems almost so, even to me. Of course, I love her very deeply myself—so short, such a miserly short time! And already people are enduring—and for four years have been doing—the destruction of their whole families, most of their friends, their homes, work, even loves, I suspect.…"

"And any prospect upon the future—I mean by that: Many of those who are left alive surely can't see through it all to anything real, anything of order or benefit, to come." The season and hour had brought chill. They went inside.

No candle burned that evening; "candlelight" struck an almost unpatriotic chord. Since the weather had got a little bleak, a fire had been lighted; it was time to start using up that season's firewood. Tomorrow Robert and his father would cut the roses back. Pruning was already overdue. Early narcissus had begun to push up out of the earth.

Grace came into the room, and they rose. She said: "If this is 'men-talk' I'll go back out."

"Please sit with us, Mother. The one thing I still have from before is Us—the three of us.

"Besides, there are things I want to talk about."

"My Goodness, that sounds serious!" She put a small log onto the fire, and then sat down beside her son.

"Nearly everything *is* serious now." There was brief silence. The house subsided and groaned as it sank just the few millimeters. "None of us has ever found being serious much fun."

"We've had fun watching Mr. MacAlpine be serious."

"Yes, but we can't laugh at even him anymore—not after what has happened." They did laugh, though, but not much, and not out of mirth, nor yet out of desperation. "And so," Bob went on, "we have to accept the circumstances we're in; we must study them closely and lose not even one day. Then we deal with things in the best ways we can think of."

And that, Thomas reflected, *is what made your ancestors in Jamestown, or their friends, resort to consuming human flesh.*

"What are people down here saying about the War?"

"That depends upon where their sons are being sent," Grace said.

"But what do you know of the War—right here?"

"There is no war right here."

"There is."

In those times, every claim was being met by counterclaim; not one from one band of like-minded persons, the other from another. But the man who maintained that a fiery light seen in the night sky, out over the ocean, was the explosion of a merchant ship torpedoed by a German submarine would be the same to say the blackened beach or iridescent serpentine gullies and unexplained trails of petroleum in an estuary were due to nothing more ominous than to leakage from storage tanks at Fort Caswell.

But there was no petroleum stored at Fort Caswell. Any there at first had months ago been moved inland to safety.

Men were at war within themselves. Many wondered all the time what they themselves were thinking and did not even recognize their natural faces in a glass. For war had indeed brought man closer to Chaos, as Thomas Strikestraw had forewarned.

"Miss Grace! The Police are here!"

"What!"

"The Police." Rhodë held out her wrists as though to be handcuffed. Grace took this in.

"What do they want? Did they say? Is there a whole lot of them?"

"Just two; one large, one medium. They want to see the Canon."

"Have you let them into the house?"

"Miss Grace! Those people have come to the *front door!* "

"I don't believe that is unusual anymore, Rhodë. However, you were certainly right not to let them in. I will go down and tell Father Thomas." She went downstairs and found Thomas in his study. "Tom, the Police have come here."

"Where are they?"

"On the front steps, apparently. Rhodë wouldn't let them in."

"Good for her!" But he went out to see them. "Good morning," he said.

The "large" peacekeeper turned out to be New Brunswick's Chief-of-Police, the other, his sergeant. The Chief spoke first: "We are sorry to trouble you, Mr. Strikestraw. We wondered whether you could come with us down to the Station?"

"Of course," Thomas answered, "Just let me get my coat and hat." Since he both slept the sleep and woke the watch of the just, he assumed that the policemen were in need of some kind of clerical service.

The three men walked toward the Police Station. As they went, Thomas asked: "Can I be of use in any way?" The two policemen looked anxious and glanced at each other. The medium deferred to the large.

"Duzey Blanding found a dead man ashore on Oak Island last night. We went out to get him this morning."

"Do you know who he was?"

"No, Sir," the Chief said.

"We've asked several people to see whether they could identify him, Canon, but nobody recognizes him," the sergeant said.

Canon? Thomas looked again and more closely at the younger man. "I'm sorry, Son; I didn't quite make out your name, I think?"

"Bill Lucas, Canon."

"William! I haven't seen you for such a long time. There's no wonder I didn't recognize you! I hope you've been well?"

"Very well, thank you, Sir. I'm afraid I haven't been coming to Church a whole lot."

"Well, I keep up with you through your mother."

"She tells me a lot about you, too, Sir."

I'll bet she does.

But now they had arrived at the station, situated between the bus terminal and the Living Fountain Assembly of the Saved, a storefront converted to a place of worship. Its windows had been opacified after being embellished with many a lurid religious symbol and slogan, the latter apparently standing in for Scriptural passages, which Thomas was pretty sure they were not.

But from that moment, without his sensing it, a seed was planted in the priest's mind. And that seed came eventually to stupefying germination, an account not yet due.

Indicating the Assembly, the Chief said: "The competition, eh, Mr. Canon!" Then they went into the station and along a hallway to the little morgue at the back of the building.

"You said, Chief, that Duzey found the body last night?"

"We think so, Sir. They opened the front door here when the watch changed—It turned out Duzey was outside propped against the railing, asleep, or...."

"…Or. I think, then, the body must have been left by yesterday afternoon's tide. I heard it was supposed to be exceptionally high. Duzey took you there?"

"Once we'd brought him round. Actually, we took him. I think you're right about the evening full tide."

At this Thomas entered the morgue, where the dead body lay upon a table at the far end of the room, before a large void filled with textured glass block. He went over and drew back the sheet that covered it, to reveal the head and shoulders. Except for pallor, the mortal part of this man appeared entirely normal. If the eyes had been closed, Thomas would likely have felt himself interrupting only sleep. They were open, though. The corneas were clouded. Beneath them the pupils could not be distinguished.

Thomas then rummaged in his coat pocket and took out a Prayer Book and a purple stole, which he kissed perfunctorily then placed about his neck. He opened the book, beckoned to William Lucas, and then the two men read responsively for several minutes. The Chief had no clear idea what this was about, but he began to doubt that the Living Fountain Assembly of the Saved was in fact the competition.

Then Thomas made the sign of the Cross over the dead man, anointed the forehead with Chrism, and snapped the Prayer Book shut. "Well, first things first. Now."

"The Coroner has been here."

Thomas closed the eyes already closed to the light of life, and replaced the sheet. The Holy Oil soaked through in a small grey-clear patch. "What did he have to say?"

"He completed the Death Certificate and left us a copy for our file here. And he made these notes, if you would like to read them."

The Coroner's notes began with official numerical designations of the remains for the Precinct and for Brunswick County, and specified the place, time, and manner of discovery and retrieval. After that, it continued clear and almost matter-of-fact:

The body is that of a Caucasoid male, probably between twenty and twenty-five years of age, well developed and well nourished. Vital signs are absent. The palpated tissues are extremely cold, certainly colder than ambient air and almost certainly colder than the shallow coastal waters. There is no external sign of trauma, and the integument bears no noteworthy distinguishing mark. Percussion-note over the lungfields is normal in timbre, indicating that death occurred before immersion. The neck has been broken, suggesting unspecified shock of some intensity but taking place at a distance from the subject, there being lack of burns or of other lesions (as noted above).

While death has not been of natural causes, neither is there anything about the subject to suggest so-called "foul play," beyond the abomination of war. Thus, I shall omit a formal post-mortem examination.

[signed] Benjamin W. Hanby, M.D.,Coroner, Brunswick County, North Carolina.

Thomas read this and thought over it. "I have a suggestion," he said. "The face would be easily recognized by anybody who had known him. For later, you know. I think a photograph ought to be made." So arrangements were undertaken for this to be done. "But what do you need from me? To bury him?"

The policemen seemed relieved that the priest had himself made the suggestion. "Yes, Sir, that's what we want," the Chief said. "But we don't know where."

"That will give us no trouble. The northwestern corner of our churchyard— all of which is hallowed ground" (the Chief was unsure about this, too, but he was pretty sure that the Assembly of the Saved did not stand upon whatever 'hallowed ground' was) "—was set aside at the end of the Seventeenth Century, I think for burial of people who expected to die in England but got caught short over here. Use of it is still at the Rector's discretion." Sensing the Chief's uncertainty he added: "I'm the Rector."

"Who would have to pay for it?"

"Nothing would have to be paid for. Somebody must build a decent, sturdy box. The sexton can get men to help him open the grave."

"Now, I wonder, what can we know about this man? What was he wearing? Was there nothing about him to help us?"

"That pullover and pea-coat on the windowsill were his," William said, and all three went over to examine them.

"Pea-coat, wool pullover," the Chief was muttering. "It looks like what a merchant seaman would wear."

"Or," William said, "somebody wanting to pass for one."

"What do you mean by that, Lucas?"

"He must—the more I think about it—have been trying to look like somebody he wasn't. Because there is nothing…nothing at all."

"How do you mean, 'Nothing,' Son?"

"Everybody carries something—a billfold with papers inside, a keyring, identification bracelet…."

"Or an identification neck-chain—'dog tags'—anything like that."

Thomas had been looking carefully at the coat and sweater while he listened to the reasoning of the other two. And he noticed that the labels had been removed. He pointed this out, and said: "It is certain he did not want to be known, but to whom did he want to remain unknown?"

"I think what happened to this man is something that is not supposed to be happening—at least not according to what you read in the papers or hear over the radio," William said. "But the word is out that German submarines are sinking merchant tonnage hand-over-fist, right off our coast.

"I know a man who lives up in Rhodanthe, and he says the beaches are nearly always streaked with fuel-oil; nearly every day they find dead bodies, sometimes burned, sometimes burned almost to nothing, and sometimes…."

"Not complete?"

"Yes, Sir."

"Well, maybe I do know something about who this man is. Or was," the Chief said, "because I have a friend in the Navy, stationed at Norfolk—knows your son Robert, Mr.Canon, and speaks highly of him—who claims some British trawlers with their crews have been sent over here to help protect merchant shipping along the seaboard. They're specially equipped for anti-submarine offense."

"Sould he have told you that?"

"No, Sir. He shouldn't even have known about it himself. But why all the secrecy? Because there isn't really any secret, not to talk of. It's got to be more a question of whether you just know, or whisper to a few, or talk out loud to whoever's by.

"Anyway, these crews have been chasing and killing 'U-boats' for two years already. They're supposed to be here to show us how it's done. Maybe this man is off one of those vessels?"

"The crews wouldn't be in British naval uniform, though, I shouldn't think."

"I believe, Sir, they would try to have the vessels look like a fishing fleet and the men to look like fishermen." All three looked again at the sweater and at the coat. "These, I believe, are exactly the kind of thing the crew would wear." The others concurred.

Grace had decided to remain at home while Thomas conducted the funeral. He had not tried to persuade her to come with him. That would have been to ask her to confront her greatest fear, to withdraw from the warmth of the fire, to draw near to the coldness of death. And worse, of death in the icy deep. Few others stayed away, however. For Thomas had had it put about that the body of a drowned British sailor had been recovered and that everyone in town, to the extent possible, ought to be present at the burial. Rhodë, who belonged to one of the oldest, and barring none the largest family in New Brunswick, had been commissioned to let her people know that they were welcome too, and expected.

It was Friday afternoon. Bleak. A quarter past five, and men and women were getting off work. The sun, in setting, slipped beneath the canopy of miserable cloud, and bailed ample sheaves of rays of golden light diagonally down Church Street, to steep the churchyard in vanishing glory, as folk began to gather. The Colored people congregated to the north of the grave. The White folk came up from southward. The Jews, of whom there were few, came as well but stopped outside the low brick coping that marked out hallowed ground. The Pliskin men—This family were particular friends of Thomas's—wore their yarmulkes, however. The Sabbath was near.

William Lucas waited in the sacristy with Thomas while he prepared for the burial service. He was fretting, as he did always before a funeral. He felt a great pressure to have every rite and euphemia strictly observed. After all, you couldn't rehearse this the way you could a wedding. "There's just one God," he said under his breath, remembering what Mr. Pliskin had told him when that family had had a falling-out about a Christmas tree for the little children—but William heard him. "There's just God. Just God. The whole thing, all of it, is God." Then looking directly at William, he added in normal voice: "However, that's another and a very long story!" William wondered greatly at the words he had heard him say.

They were waiting for the designated hour of half past five o'clock. And they were waiting for Duzey Blanding, whom Thomas had got hold of and whom he had dared not to be present. "You found him, Duzey," he had said, "and you must see him to his rest. You come to the sacristy a little after five o'clock and we'll wish him Godspeed with a glass of your favorite tipple."

The number of those gathering outside was increasing rapidly. William watched them through the old, distorting panes. The rest of the police force were there in a body, the rescue squad, the firefighters, wearing either uniforms or identifying gear. Increasing rapidly. Civic and fraternal organizations were represented. Increasingly rapid. Clergy of the other denominations—these and anyone who had from them heard of the discovery of the body.

Rapidi.

Pressure built. Get it right. Get it right the first time. It mustn't encroach upon the Sabbath. There won't be but this one time.

Thomas and William were startled by a loud grating noise; but it was only Duzey, coming through the door from choir (because the "choir loft" wasn't really that) to sacristy. He had his lantern with him, and a bottle, wrapped in a brown paper bag. "I meant you to understand that I am providing the refreshments, Duzey," Thomas said, and he indicated a glass beaker amply filled with Cognac, which, set upon the sill of the deep window embrasure, caught and seemed to hold and second sunlight, amber now, only slightly less deeply so than the liquid itself. Duzey smiled softly. He took up the glass and began to sip at it. "Be quick about it, now."

"Oh, he'll keep, Father."

"He may, and he may not. Remember, both of you: We don't know where he's going, or when he's due there."

Leaving the church through the outside sacristy door, which was closest to the grave, the little procession began typically and ended oddly: William Lucas, in surplice and cassock, from beneath which the police-issue shoes glinted with each step he took, bore the processional Cross. Then Thomas, reading from the Prayer Book. The crowd stood apart to let them approach the coffin, which rested upon the ground over three sturdy ropes knotted tightly at the ends. Last came Duzey Blanding, carrying a lantern, and—scandalizing those who could see it—a bottle wrapped in a brown paper bag. They did not observe the absence of the characteristic bulge at the bottom.

Everyone seemed to listen carefully to the words of the service. They were unfamiliar to many.

"I am the resurrection and the life...," a formula which always brought about a deepening of solemnity, brought also now a sense of mystery, for inwardly everyone present knew that the priest and townsfolk did not know exactly what they were doing; they all simply knew that to do nothing would have been an impossibility.

Then, "...yet shall I see God...behold him face to face...."

And then, "The Lord gave, and the Lord hath taken away...."

Gave whom? Took away whom?

Before continuing, Thomas asked Toby Harmon, a cousin of Rhodë's, and his own friend James Howell to lead all the men and boys in casting boughs of evergreen into the open and empty grave. Sprigs of rosemary were included. And the Rite for the Burial of the Dead continued.

At last came the pleading, Byzantine in its extravagance and always unsettling, even to the Episcopalians, who had heard it a hundred times over: "Yet, O Lord God most holy, O lord most mighty, O holy and most merciful Savior...."

"...Lord most holy, O God most mighty, O holy and merciful Savior, Thou most worthy Judge eternal, suffer us not, at our last hour, to fall...."

When all had been said, all done, many came up to the grave, after six of the sturdiest men left in New Brunswick had lowered the coffin down onto the evergreens, and cast in handfuls of earth. This was a thing the Jews present recognized and so all of the men and even a few of the women, led by Talia Pliskin, came forward and did the same. For it was to them a recognizable part of Christianity's vast inheritance from Judaism. But they were late and hurried off.

Some of the women, particularly the young ones, dropped blossoms down upon the makeshift coffin—others kept back their offerings—such ones as can be found at the end of March: Flowering almond and quince, narcissus, 'sweet breath of spring,' which blooms even through clear encasing sleeves of ice—in order to place them over the grave once closed.

The sense had passed over and through them all that they could as well have been burying a father or brother, friend or lover, a son, a self....

"Good People," Thomas said from the head of the grave—And before him William Lucas stood stalwart, holding the shaft of the Cross as though it were that of a battle standard—"I bid you remember this our brother in your prayers, for he placed his life in danger, and has lost it, in a perhaps very small but nevertheless real measure for the protection of each one of us here, as well as for many more." *For you and for many.*

Then Duzey Blanding, since deep dusk had fallen, took his lantern to the foot of the grave, set it down, and took from the paper bag a large bottle of purified oil. He filled the lantern and set it alight. He adjusted the wick. Presently, everyone else went away.

Duzey withdrew a little distance into shadow. He stayed with the sailor all through the night, offering prayers of a kind and periodic toasts in farewell, in Godspeed; for, hours before the crowd had begun to gather, he had seen to his own provisioning. At intervals, he ambled over to the grave to replenish the lantern. He meant for it to guide the sailor's footsteps to whatever realm Thomas had had in mind, hopefully to have him arrive there by the time expected. To arrive there, and to carry out whatever duties should await him, to assume whatever good might there be stored up for him.

V

"Oh sleep that dreams and dream that never tires
Press from the petals of the lotus-flower
Something of this to keep, the essence of an hour!"
F. Scott Fitzgerald: *"Princeton—The Last Day,"* 7-9

WITHOUT LOOKING UP from printed page, without lifting pen from paper, John Ashfield and his son Laurence were able to converse both fluently and without compromise of mutual understanding. For, after all, they had been speaking and listening to each other for almost half a century. They were in the east room at Woodleigh when, all at once, Laurence found he must unburden himself.

"Father," he said, "I think you ought to know that some people are saying Parker is marrying Alina for her money."

"I think you may set your mind at rest, Rennie, in that regard."

"I have never thought it myself; it's just that some people are saying so. It was unlikely enough for me to hear about it. It's practically inconceivable that you might."

"Well, I thank you for letting me know. But we could have assumed such a thing in any case, don't you imagine?" For everybody in Peell County knew the Ashfields had a lot of money and had had it for a long time.

"I like Parker myself…I think." But brother and chosen brother-in-law were still eyeing each other, still circling slowly. "He's a little too good-looking…and maybe a little too smooth. And Alina is clearly off her head about him."

"I don't see why that should trouble you."

"Because it has never happened before now."

"Oh, yes it has. You were away at school for the worst of it."

"I didn't know."

"No. It was insupportable! Every other man or boy she met fell in love with her."

"Was she falling in love all the time herself?"

"Constantly. But always with the alternate boys—the every second one who had *not* fallen in love with her. For months at a time—or it seemed so—life was scarcely worth living around here. It shows you the futility of wealth. I could hardly have bought her a sister, yet that is the only thing, I think, that might have done any good. But it's over and done with now, thank God."

"And Parker is not marrying Alina for her money."

"But how can you know?"

"I know, because he has a lot more money of his own than any of these gossips knows. When you set out to marry Lavinia, I made some recommendations. Do you remember them?"

"I remember them clearly. I should. I actually kept a little memorandum with me for practice. You told me to ask Mr. Cloudsley for her hand. You said I must mention that Lavinia had consented. Then, I think, I was to give him an account of my obligations, my assets, and my expectations. You said he had a right to know that his daughter would be satisfactorily looked-after."

"Yes, and that is the only circumstance, I believe, under which it is appropriate to discuss money in a primarily social setting, but you would have to ask your mother about that. In any case, Parker invited me to meet him for lunch last Thursday in Savannah. Very exclusive. Very posh. He has the right kind of connections.

"I hope that is of only incidental importance. Your mother does not believe that lopsided marriages succeed; you and I know better, of course. It's why so many men have had mistresses—to make up for the boredom of 'balanced' marriages. Of some, that's to say.

"Parker was courteous enough to make the same kind of disclosures I recommended you make to Adam Cloudsley. To cut a long story short, they will be richer than anybody I know for miles around, with or without your sister's inheritance.

"Another thing: Parker wants to consolidate the lands. When those negotiations begin, you will hear a great deal more comment than you've heard up to now."

They were interrupted here by the arrival of Miss Allie and Alina. Miss Allie said, "Rennie, could you come with me? I want to know whether you can advise me about the crabapple. It is not doing well." So they went out.

Alina sat down close to Mr. Jack and asked: "Daddy, I wonder: Would you consider giving me Clear Creek as a wedding present?"

"I'll have the deeds prepared. What do you want it for?"

"We're going to live in it."

"Would Parker be able to conduct business from there?"

"He says he will have it arranged so that he can."

"Of course, I suppose he doesn't have to work."

"No. He does have to work. And he has to paint."

"Paint!"

"Yes. Paint."

"Hah! Well, but his work—you won't have to be going to New York all the time, I hope. I mean, if it were necessary for you to go there and live, then that would be one thing. But I have found that people who shuttle back and forth over long distances, or one of whom does—distance has a way of turning into a more implacable kind of divide, and absence doesn't make the heart grow fonder for long—are seldom content. Or they have often seemed to me not to be."

"I wouldn't be. I won't be, as a matter of fact; we're going to have to make periodic trips like that at first—at least, a few. After those, the road branches; we'll have to make a choice. In fact, I think I'll make my half of it right now! You help me decide."

"Now, Alina, it is none of my business."

"But, Daddy, listen to this and tell me what you think: Either we can spend rather a long time making sporadic trips north. Or, on the other hand, we can move to New York soon and live there for about a year. Parker would be able to make changes in the operation of his offices—I think he wants to 'deputize' a couple of people and then oversee their work till he's satisfied with it."

"Then what?"

"Then we'd come back to Clear Creek. And live happily ever after!"

"Will you be happy living in New York for a year?"

"I doubt it."

"And then later would Parker be content living in our rustic surroundings? Because they very much *are* rustic, you know."

"Ask him to tell you about Dublin."

"What does he know—particularly, that is—about Dublin?"

"New Hampshire."

"Dublin, New Hampshire? Is that where he grew up?"

"Yes."

"And it's not such a big place?"

"A little bigger than the Crossroads, I think. But a different kind of place."

"Well, of course it would be if it's in New Hampshire."

"But what do you think, Daddy? Oughtn't we to go for a year, then come back forever?"

"To me that seems the clear choice—just so long as it doesn't put anybody out."

When later that afternoon Mr. Jack had told Miss Allie about his conversation with their daughter, his wife had this to say: "I don't know, John, whether you have deserted your faculties or they have deserted you. Either way, I should have thought that you would know that the *last* thing *anyone* must do is to give advice to a couple about their marital arrangements." And that was all she said to him for the remainder of the evening, except, much later, for: "Good night, Dear."

Next morning she spoke about it to Alina while they were having breakfast together: "I cannot imagine what can have possessed your father yesterday afternoon. But he's getting old, and we must make allowances.

"I will say, though, that it makes me weary just thinking of your and Parker's traveling back and forth between here and New York for the rest of your days. In my mind it would be far wiser to go ahead up there and spend the 'year or so'—if I have understood that part correctly—then come back here and settle permanently. Or at least settle permanently somewhere. No marriage could flourish within the nomadic arrangement which, I believe, would be the other part of the alternative.

"Of course, the two of you will have to suit yourselves. *My* only misgiving has to do with whether Parker could be content here."

Patiently, Alina answered: "This was Parker's idea in the first place, Mama. He has adapted himself to the City but he doesn't really like it. He grew up in the country, too. Besides, do you want to know what I think is really and truly behind it all?"

"Only if you think I ought to know," Miss Allie said with a show of demurral.

"He has become devoted to you and Daddy. I think he feels a little as though you were his parents; his have been gone for such a long time!"

"Of course you're too young to be his parents—naturally he realizes that."

"Naturally. Your father, though, is a good bit older than I am."

Three—and-a-half years!

"Anyway, we'd be more than delighted to be his extended family— speaking of which, the Family needs extending; I hope you'll have children very soon, if the Lord allows it. I can't see why Lavinia hasn't had any. But I have decided to say nothing to her about it."

"I think it will be far better for you not to."

"I don't quite see why you say that. I'm sure Rennie would like an heir. Incidentally, do you think Parker appreciates Rennie's qualities quite as much as he should? There is more to Laurence than meets the eye."

"There is more to Laurence than meets the eye," Parker said when he returned from walking with him through the rice fields and seeing the trunks and dikes under construction or repair. "I'm looking forward to being his brother-in-law.

"And how are Allie and Jack taking to the idea of our living in the other house someday?"

"Clear Creek. Do you realize you are the only one who call them that? Except for their old friends?"

"They asked me to. I hope you know I wouldn't have taken that kind of liberty."

"They did? When?"

"Today. At lunchtime."

"Had you said anything to Mama about Rennie?"

"No. Is there something I should have said?"

"Of course not. I just wondered. They are taking very well to the idea. Though I think they wonder whether you'll be happy once we're living here permanently."

"They don't know I like you best in your natural setting? But all that aside, shouldn't you be planning your wedding, as well as how and when and where we're going to live afterward?"

"Actually, there's very little to plan."

"I was afraid there might not be much."

"What's that supposed to mean? As a matter of fact, we can have whatever sort of wedding we want—as great or as small."

"Oh. I took it to mean they're all more or less alike. Certainly they are in New York. And I've been to so many! The service will be at St. Peter's,

St. Thomas', Heavenly Rest—one of those, and a couple of others. Then the Waldorf, The Plaza, The St. Regis. Or you trek out to the Hamptons. After six months you can't remember anything, or anything much, to distinguish one from another."

"Down here," Alina said, "it is much the same. The service is held in some Colonial relic, where everybody either suffocates or freezes. Then you go to the appointed plantation house—your own, preferably, if you still have one, even if it is uninhabited and half in ruin. You see, the real point of marriage in the Low Country is to link the past to the future, not so much the bride to the bridegroom. Then it's just as you've said: Looking back, after a while, you can't tell one from another."

"In New York, you invite a couple of thousand of your most intimate friends."

"Here you just have the attendants and close relatives and friends at the service—that's all you can get into most of the old churches. And we, being a great deal more selective, never have more than five or six hundred at the reception. Sometimes there is drunkenness."

"I can't believe it!"

"But we may decide against the conventional kind. I mean, churches and so on."

"Why should we?"

"Just that since you aren't particularly religious…."

"If I were particularly religious, that is exactly the sort of wedding I'd try to avoid. Besides, even if not pious or devout, I think I probably qualify as God-fearing. For me, for anybody, to be irreligious—that, I think, would be a great error."

"What makes you say that?"

"I think it."

"Then, what makes you think it?"

"I'm not entirely sure; I've never gone all through it. Don't you usually think that anyone who declares: There is no God, probably makes a great error? For anyone to say: God lives, and I know it, is probably as great an error, and I think those people ought to share with professed atheists April first as their National Day. However, mankind has always been prone to belief in Deity, always inclined to worship. Sometimes I have thought it intrinsic to our species. And therefore I wonder whether it hasn't got some adaptive advantage. Suppose that advantage were Redemption?"

"Redemption from what? You've already told me you don't believe in any doctrine of original sin."

"And I don't. That would mean the Creator had allowed something to go wrong in the process of creation. I don't think that is a possibility."

"I thought everything was supposed to have fallen pretty much apart shortly *after* the Creation."

"But that's as much as to say the Creator built a system from defective parts."

"And you consider that an impossibility, too?"

"I do. Speaking of which...."

"Then I don't understand what you mean by 'redemption.' "

"I'm not so sure myself, as it turns out. Let me think some more, and then we can talk about it again later. But plan the wedding. The people I ask will come, so please get Allie to let me know how many. And have it just the way you want it. I don't intend to do you out of what you want. I don't intend ever to do you out of anything, if I can help it."

"If I, Alina, have thee, Parker, then anything else I may have or lack won't matter. Don't try to answer; I know you can't." Yet he found a way.

Soon mother and daughter sat down to plan the wedding, the latter aware and the former unaware that it had really been planned already. And six months after it had taken place, Alina and Parker remembered everything about it, while no one else remembered anything at all.

Immediately after Alina and Parker had settled into their lodgings in New York, she received a letter from her mother:

Saturday

My dearest child,

How much we miss you already! Yet we are happy that you have arrived safely and are glad that you find the apartment—if that is what it is—so satisfactory. Of course, living in an apartment is bound to be different from living in a house. For example, there are no grounds to keep up or anything of that kind. But then you didn't have to keep up the grounds when you lived here, either, did you?

Do not waste your time trying to find a church where the women do not wear dresses instead of suits; you won't find one in the City. But you need not, in my view, adopt the practice yourself; no, not even for one short year! You must remember Who You Are. And, little as I like to say it, who they are. Or aren't.

And please do remember, my darling Child, that you are unaccustomed to heights. The ground itself hardly rises down here. *Stay away from the parapets of the terraces!* If you look over, you may become vertiginous, lose your balance, and fall! Don't dismiss what I have to say. Such things have happened!

Lavinia came up today with the spaniels. I have never seen hounds behave so oddly. We had tea on the verandah, and the whole time they either trundled back and forth across the lawn with their noses to the ground or came up and stood on their hind legs to one or other of the windowsills or kept disappearing behind the house. Finally, it was Lavinia who realized what they were up to: They were looking for you!

Well, I can hardly wait—I'm ashamed to admit it!—for the day when they come to Woodleigh and find you here!

Except that you'll be at Clear Creek, won't you? But it comes to the same thing.

All my love, Mother

And soon afterward a letter came from Lavinia.

Woodleigh Cottage
May 5

Dearest Alina,

I hope you are becoming increasingly comfortable with life in the City— in fact, I'm almost sure you must be. I'm sorry you find the apartment so little to your liking, but I can certainly understand that! It's so important, to me at least, to be able to look out of the windows and see the trees— their trunks and branches and shade. Looking down upon their canopies can't be very inspiring.

Gardening on the terraces ought to be satisfying, except that there can be no turf nor sand nor furrow underfoot. But never mind; you'll be back here before you know it. And I, at least, understand that you are happiest wherever Parker is—terrain and vegetation aside. It's how I am about your brother!

Do you already have domestic help? If not, then I'm going to make a kind of recommendation. Do you remember Yukoneta Browne? She grew up near Green Sea but came here several years ago to be nearer to her relatives (she is Miss Izora's great grand-niece—like nearly everybody else!). Then she developed a longing for the Bright Lights and emigrated, we thought to 'Philly,' where she did settle at first.

But I've looked her up. After a few months she decided to go for broke and came on up to New York. She has a job, but she doesn't like it much. She would be available to you if you need her. I thought it might be a good thing for you to have one of our own people around. If it sounds workable to you and is acceptable to Parker, this is how you can reach her....

Much love from us both, Lavinia

P.S. Yukoneta is thought to be a little gruff in her manner at times.

Then Parker decided he'd better write to Laurence.

2 E. 70th St.
11 May 1937

Dear Laurence,

I hope all is going well down there, that contentment holds sway at Woodleigh, that peace lies over the Crossroads. And I want to thank you for overseeing the repairs to Clear Creek. When we walked through it, I remember, we agreed that it had never been neglected (neglect doesn't seem to be the Ashfield way). I hope you haven't found much else that needs doing, beyond what is on our first list. Please ask the contractors to bill me directly, unless you think it would be better otherwise. When the house is wholly intact inside and out, then we'll unleash Alina, and I very much hope Lavinia, upon it! The way in which she has arranged the Cottage I find very agreeable.

Now, I trust you can give me some advice about Alina. She is not enjoying New York—at least not so far. Without pushing it—I hope—I've taken her, really, everywhere: The opera, theater, to galleries, shops, and to a few parties, where I will say she has always been at the center of attention.

She says she is having a wonderful time. But she is not. I can tell. And if it goes too far and she leaves me—not that there has been any talk or sign of that—but if she should, I think I'd close down the whole operation. And I don't mean by that my businesses. No, the whole operation. Because I have never been this happy before—I'm not even sure I've ever been significantly happy. Now I am. And if I lose Alina, then all is lost, for me.

With warmest regards, Parker

On a Friday morning later that same month, Alina and Parker were having coffee in the sitting room; Yukoneta Browne was working her way round the room with the momentum of a battleship, dusting and polishing. Presently Parker would leave for his offices.

"Are you in a great hurry?" Alina asked him.

"I'm not at all in a hurry. Why?"

"Because I would like to discuss two things with you."

"Two, precisely?"

"Yes."

"Is either ominous?"

"What makes you wonder?"

" 'Two things precisely' makes it sound somehow like a docket."

"Well, neither is ominous, but each is important."

"What is the first thing?"

"Redemption. Do you remember? You said the tendency in mankind to worship might have an adaptive advantage, that that advantage might be redemption. But you hadn't yet decided the question, From what?"

"Oh, yes. The sailboat!" he said apparently inconsequentially. "As a boy I was taken to church an awful lot. And when I say 'awful....' Never mind." Yukoneta polished on inexorably. "The clergyman preached one day about redemption, and he used this story as an illustration—a rather poor one, as it turns out. But useful up to a point: A little boy had a toy sailboat, which he treasured, and one afternoon he was sailing it in a pond. A rain squall blew up, and the boat was lost. Weeks later the boy and his father saw it in the window of a store; it was for sale. The father said they must go in at once and buy it. The boy wanted to know why they had to buy it, since it was already his. The father explained that he had lost it and that now they must buy it back—redeem it, in other words. Unfortunately literal."

"Why do you think that?"

"I won't go much into it all right now. But, to cut a long story short, even resorting to Christian orthodoxy, we are taught that 'Nothing...can separate us from the love of God.' Now, I grant you it was Saint Paul who wrote it, and if there has ever been anybody more theologically suspect, then I'd like to know who that might be. But I don't think man's falling into a trap laid by the Almighty could bring about such separation. Not that I believe such a thing ever happened."

The swishing of the duster ceased. Yukoneta had not followed the argument of the little story very closely, but she knew her Blessed Savior had not stretched out His arms upon the Cross to redeem any toy sailboat. Parker, who as he had promised had given further thought to the whole matter, continued: "If you think about it you will discover a great many flaws. But for now, consider this: Was the sailboat in peril or otherwise likely to have been any worse off before its 'redemption'?" With resignation, Yukoneta resumed her labors; every so often, though, she cracked the polishing-cloth like a whip.

"No, I shouldn't think it would have been," Alina answered.

"And did any valid thing happen to cause the boat to cease to belong to the little boy?"

"Anything—like what, for example?"

"Height, depth, things present, things to come…for example."

Alina began to muse about this. Parker thought she might have abandoned the exchange. Even though in the whole of her life she had never once been known to abandon an exchange. Finally: "God's attitude does seem to…differ between the Old and New Testaments."

"Then how do we account for: 'They wither and perish, but naught changeth Thee,' and declarations of that sort? What is supposed to be so much less potent about Life or Angels than about a tree with a snake in it? And please don't talk to me about disobedience. God dangled the fruit before them then told them not to eat it. He set them up. It was entrapment.

"And suppose the toy sailboat, to recur, instead of ending up in the store window, had been retrieved by a different boy—one who was better able to take care of it and to make use of it. In that case, it would have been better off, and that is the sense in which I mean 'redeemed.' Imagine that the best thing for us is not 'vertical redemption,'—from the pit of Hell to the height of Heaven; but, instead, 'horizontal redemption'—from a place where we don't especially belong, sidewise to one where we are both happier and more useful, and finally to a place to which we are perfectly suited. A place just to our right or just to our left, just ahead, just behind. That may be the reality underlying what people so often and so loosely refer to as 'salvation'!"

"Hmph!" Yukoneta said; "Mr. Parker, you'd better *hope* redemption and salvation are straight up and down. Because you are going to end up going one of those two ways.'

"Then you'd better say a prayer for me, Connie."

"I'll be saying more than one."

"And I thank you for every one you say. Because those are just some thoughts of mine. And after all, who am I? Well, then, Alina, what is the second thing?" Yukoneta had by now worked around the room and had got to a silver ewer, which stood on a small chest of drawers.

"I want to have a baby."

"Then you must have one."

"I can't do it by myself."

"Neither one of you has got any manners," Yukoneta muttered. She gave a final slap of the cloth to the innocent ewer and proceeded out of the room, down through the hallways of the heathen.

"I'm late. I may as well just not go to the office today. I'll telephone to Mary Jane."

"For what?"

"Just to see whether she's having to handle anything difficult. And to have her start a discreet search for the best obstetrician in town."

Laurence, meanwhile, had answered Parker's letter:

> Woodleigh Cottage
> May 21, 1937

Dear Parker,

Let me say first what I think about Alina. You and I must be about the same age, around four or five years older than she. When we were children, Mother and Father occasionally left her in my care—for an afternoon, at most, of course. I always took that trust very seriously; and my program included a plan for diversion. I would take her down to the river to go boating or swimming or fishing. I took her around the old rice fields, explained how they had worked and how I meant to work them again. I even sat down with her once and drew measured plans for remodeling her dollhouse.

And she never refused any of my suggestions. Yet I could tell they weren't things she really wanted to do (Speaking of the dollhouse, *v. infra*). She just couldn't think up any substitute. Finally I realized that if I simply let her alone for a while, then she would find something to do herself. And this—whatever it might be—she would go at with real energy.

So I would advise you just to wait. She'll come up with something— shoplifting, for example!—and become quite absorbed.

About the house (yours): Don't you think now is the time to have it newly plumbed and wired? Central heat installed? And what about bathrooms? I drew up the plans for having the four added to Woodleigh—you may have noticed that they are contained in two I hope unobtrusive towers, each overlapping slightly one of the two rear corners of the house, with small loggias between—the remains of the upper and lower verandahs— at the level of each floor. Shall I send along a proposal for a similar arrangement at Clear Creek? It's an aspect of things we forgot to discuss in the confusion of the wedding preparations and your departure.

Bear in mind that I count on you to decline this offer if it does not seem satisfactory.

Poor old Miss Izora is nearly blind. Father has offered her cataract-surgery, but she is adamant in refusing. She says, "If they meddle with my eyesight, I may lose my vision."

Love, Rennie

P.S. I am coming to Philadelphia in a week or so. May I come up and pay you a short visit?

Alina judged it time to send word to her parents, especially to her mother:

New York City

Dearest Mama and Daddy,

You must all stop fretting over whether I'm happy here or not. Who am I supposed to be, after all? It is not necessary for *anyone* to be constantly happy, and it's a good thing, because it is also not possible. A country girl ought to take advantage of contact with the Great World, anyway.

Besides, it grows on you. I walk down (up?) to the Metropolitan every few days, or across to the Frick Collection Museum, opened just over a year ago. Every time I go, I fall in love with something else: A Tiepolo the size of a motion picture screen, a little piece of Hellenistic silver. Or, above all, a Vermeer (little window onto color and light and pearls)! I don't really know what these things are. But it doesn't matter, does it? I'm not collecting topics to impress people with—either at home or here; I just get more deeply lost in beauty almost every time I have another look.

Parker is invited to a lot of parties (He says it's in connection with business—he is certainly not a comely bachelor; not anymore!), but we don't go to many. He doesn't think I like them, and I *know* he doesn't. People are curious, though, about the Southerner he has married, apparently against all expectation! They try to hide it, for the most part, of course, but of course they fail. One woman didn't even try (I believe she'd had one too many, possibly two!).

She came hurtling across the room, dressed in a satin gown that was too tight and made her look like an eel that had been fished out of Swan Lake. She came up to me and said something in an exaggerated Southern drawl (entirely inaccurate, as usual). Several different responses came to mind. In the end, I just said, in Standard English (Did you know I could do that imitation?): "I beg your pardon?"

After that I felt sorry, because Parker told me she is a registered nurse. She married a rich man then was widowed. Twice a year, for a month at a time, she goes to some very poor place in the Balkans and works double shifts in a hospital there—just out of the goodness of her heart. (I certainly hope she won't go next year! To the Balkans, of all places!). But she telephoned the day after to apologize. We struck up quite a conversation. She is coming to lunch on Tuesday and Connie is going to give her some real Green Sea style cooking. (You can't imagine how hard it is to get okra here; you have to go all the way over to a place in Brooklyn—but the people are as nice as can be. We always spend an hour saying, "How do you [all] pronounce this or that?" And we laugh a lot. The okra is excellent, too. It comes from New Jersey, right straight through Manhattan.)

Well, the main reason I'm writing is to tell you the use I hope to put my year in New York to: We're going to have a baby. Or try to, if God gives us one. Connie has been very severe with us on that point! We absolutely love her; thank Lavinia again, please.

I know you knew we were expecting to see Rennie, on his trip north. But he called the day before he was to arrive to say that he wouldn't be able to come, after all. He sounded a bit strung out. We were both disappointed, especially Parker, for some reason.

All my dearest love, Alina

Later she sent this message by postal card:

NYC *No*, Mother. Read my letter again, and please pay particular attention to the ending. I am not expecting a child; I just hope I shall be (I am making no effort to prevent it). Dearest Love. Alina. P.S. Remind me to tell you about the ewer. L.A.

The old church out in the wilds of the County was empty. It was never locked, always open. Today its nooks and recesses gave the impression of a hundred little availabilities.

"God, O my God, my father on earth once told me I might have anything I wanted, but not everything I wanted. What am I to say to You Who have given me everything I have, if not everything I want?

"God, O my God, it may be that this last thing is one thing too many, is the Everything I want but cannot have. Yet it seems to me the Anything. And that is why I am asking you—grant me to conceive and bear a child. In order to avoid this feeling of selfishness, I could ask, or pretend to ask: Let me give my husband an heir. But I should then be a hypocrite, and You would not be deceived. The impulse is so strong in me!

"God, O my God! I will tell you how desperately I want to conceive and to bear a child, what price I would pay. What pain and sorrow I would willingly bear: To love and rear the child, and then, if it were Your will, to survive it, to look upon its death. That greatest of imaginable sorrows I would bear, in return for having this barrenness taken away. I have no right to invoke the affliction of untimely death upon any child, and least of all upon any of my own—or is there a difference, since all of them are Your children? For in that case, my sin is greater."

Clearly, I have reached the gates of madness, Lavinia said to herself, *to be thinking these thoughts!*

And she remembered the frenzied grief of Countess Rostova, in *War and Peace,* who is bereft of her adored son: "There was no healing the wound in the mother's heart. Petya's death had torn half her life away." Lavinia stood up from the altar rail and drove back to Woodleigh, terrified by the implication of her prayer, but, unable to help herself, now more ardent than when she had first begun it.

At this time, Mr. Jack's eyesight had been failing him, and it had got worse. Miss Allie had developed bronchitis just before the wedding, and it had got no better. Already, Laurence or Lavinia, or both, had decided several times to stay the night at Woodleigh, to watch and to perform little tasks which the elder Ashfields could manage only with undue hardship.

So one evening after the four of them had had supper together, Lavinia said: "I have a suggestion to make, probably a tactless one. I say 'tactless,' because of us all I ought to be the last to bring it up. But I wonder whether it isn't time for Rennie and me to move up here?"

"My dear Child," Miss Allie said, "I don't think you could do anything tactless, even if you tried to. What is tactless is that the three of us all know as well as you do that the time has come; out of I think truly cowardly reluctance each of us has hung back and allowed the burden of first speaking about it to fall upon you."

Mr. Jack said: "Yes, my Dear, that has been our plan from the beginning—a plan we conceived in the abstract, of course—but now it is, I agree, if you and Rennie are ready, time to implement it."

"Lavinia and I are prepared to come when you want us…either now or later on, and we'll happily do what's needed in the meantime."

"Come here now, dear Children, when we're no worse off than we are. I'm coughing a little and John is squinting. But you don't want to risk waiting until you have both to make a move and to deal with frank invalids all at once." When the move had been completed—and it had involved very little time or effort—Lavinia wrote to Alina.

Woodleigh
June 16th

Dearest Alina,

I've been out of touch a little longer than usual, mainly because we have moved to Woodleigh. Your mother and Father are really quite all right, but the four of us have decided that they need a little more watching over. Miss Izora still comes, but she is not able to help much herself. Her granddaughter Mary Alice Gadsden (since she has only about 90 granddaughters!) does the housecleaning, and does it very well.

So nothing has gone especially *wrong*—they just shouldn't be in the house alone any longer. We have left the Cottage furnished, so there is a place for you and Parker and the baby to move right into until you get Clear Creek just the way you want it.

Please let Parker know about this, and make sure the arrangement suits him.

Dearest love, to you both, Lavinia

Laurence had taken Lavinia to Savannah to see the obstetrician. She had seen him on other occasions, and, after questioning her at length and performing an examination, he had told her that everything seemed in order, that phenomena which she had noted in the past had actually been early miscarriages occurring without awareness of pregnancy ("Most women have several of these at one time or other," he had said), that they were proof of her and Rennie's mutual fertility. He wanted, next time she even suspected she might have conceived, to support the pregnancy with hormone treatments. So she had gone for one of these.

During the drive home she had abruptly told Rennie about her impious prayer. For what she had asked for herself, she now realized, she had asked for him as well, without having meant to. He would be parent as much as she. She may have brought down onto him the curse she was afraid of having summoned upon herself.

"I wish I could remember my exact words. I don't think I actually attempted to strike a bargain with the Almighty. But I may have."

"But look at the answer we got."

"Yes. Look at it! Just look at it!"

"I don't follow."

"If God has taken me at my word, then this baby may be His answer, His agreeance in the bargain." They drove on for a mile in silence, then Lavinia expressed her fear: "That would mean that I would have to keep my promise."

"No. The Creator does not bargain; He's in no position to. He's above accepting men's conditions. He can't be obligated. It's not possible."

They drove for another mile. Then, for the first time, Lavinia felt quickening of the foetus. But the joy of bearing new life was wholly marred. Hadn't it been Countess Rostova whose earliest recollection of her son Pyotr had been a "stirring somewhere beneath her heart"? Or had that been a different mother, another child? The book was so long! She must read it again.

"Why do you and Parker go on so much about God and impossibility?"

"I don't know what you mean. I have never heard Parker say a word about God. Except during the marriage service. And that was scripted, so to say."

"He does, though. Alina tells me about it."

"Well, I suppose he simply has enough sense to know what does and does not square with a reasonable concept of the perfect Being. And, so far as I'm concerned, much—if not most—of what is thought and said of Him is impossible. We are man, and He is God."

"Do you think you have one?"

"One what?"

"A reasonable concept of the perfect Being."

"Oh, certainly not one I've ever tried to think through. Remember, Lavinia: You are married to a very simple man."

"Yes, and that comment probably contradicts itself." They regained good humor and enjoyed the rest of the trip home. A lot of Southerners actually like summer's heat, though they grouse about it.

"If I were a bear, living in the Lowcountry, I'd hibernate during the summertime."

"But you're not a bear...not often." Thus, after they had returned to Woodleigh, Lavinia wrote to Alina. For she and Parker were going to have a baby, and only now did Lavinia feel equal to speaking of it at any length.

Woodleigh, July 12

Dearest Alina,

I haven't had the courage—no, the trustfulness—to say anything before. But I am going to have a baby, too. The moon has waxed and waned without a sign to the contrary. And yesterday morning I was wonderfully nauseated! It's still a little complicated, though, figuring out exactly when they're expected, isn't it? But the little cousins can grow up together and, I hope, become fast friends.

The reason I'm telling you first (For I am telling you first, except for Rennie, o.c.) is that your pregnancy, in a way that I don't pretend to understand, has had something to do with mine, rather like those couples who decide they can't have children themselves, finally adopt a child, and then immediately launch out on often nearly numberless pregnancies of their own.

I'm going to wait a week before saying anything to anybody down here—I really do want you to be the first to know!

All my love, Lavinia

The summer ran its course, at last reaching the goal of insufferable heat but also of treacherous storms. And in time kindly autumn brought its shift in the color and density of everything.

Laurence wrote to his sister:

Woodleigh
November 1, 1937

Dear Alina,

Mother is planning to come up there for your confinement ("It's expected; every mother does it"). Lavinia says she has packed, and now has repacked twice, apparently to suit the changes of season. There would be nothing too much wrong with this, if you were in, for instance, Beaufort. But I assure you she is not able, I don't think, to come all the way up there. She's not actually ailing—she's just stepped down another rung in the ladder of days, and she's not going to recover it. Can you shuffle the dates somehow, to ward her off? I'm not asking you to lie outright. Unless you have to.

Isn't it funny that we're becoming parents at the same time? I wish I could be as excited about it, though, as Lavinia is. But I'm not.

Best regards to Parker,

Love, Rennie

Then winter came, slinking up to the edge of the forests and looking out over the fields. Looking with a rapid and killing eye. To disguise his evil intent, he brought down sunlight upon the frost. All the glittering, though, deceived no one who had seen it before. In February there was dreadful news.

Laurence had been waiting for Lavinia at the obstetrician's office. The doctor himself eventually came out and took Laurence outside into the street. He said: The foetus—the baby—is dead." Laurence's mind dissolved into scraps of thought, fragments of unspeakable imagery, hovering outside himself, forming a somber cloud. Had Lavinia given birth in the examining room? And the baby proved not alive?

The doctor had anticipated the shock to the father, and so was prepared to continue, even before Laurence could think of anything to ask or say. "We must consider carefully before we decide what to tell her. The child, though dead, will probably be born in due time, but that will be around ten days from now. It is not possible for either of us to imagine what she would feel during that time, if she should be told." Laurence was still unable to speak. "You must not be here when she comes out into the waiting room. You must collect yourself, and you must decide. We will tell her that we expected her visit to take longer, that we recommended you go out for a quick lunch."

"All right," Laurence finally answered. "But at least tell her that there has been a complication, and that you want to discuss it with both of us. Will you do that?" The doctor nodded. "Thank you. In the meantime please think up some plausible threat to the outcome—something we can mention now—to prepare her. Because when the word comes, it is going to be very bad. Really, very bad, indeed."

For the younger Ashfields, once the Joneses following some delays had got home, Sundays were spent partly in watching over their little nephew, John—John Ashfield Jones—while the others attended Church.

Lavinia had no plans to go to Church anymore, and Laurence, who had never had any, beyond ones made for him, was delighted to stay behind and keep his wife company.

They were cheerful, loved amusing the tiny boy, and speculated a lot about whom he "took after." They thought maybe he resembled Mr. Jack (The effect cannot have been striking, because nobody else noticed it). They consulted Parker, who said John reminded him of his great uncle Joab, though not greatly.

It had been Parker who had insisted on the child's name. He had said: "There has been a long line of John Ashfields in this place; it is not up to any of us, I think, to interrupt that tradition." Alina had burst into tears at this and had hurried from the room. Then Lavinia had burst into tears herself and had abruptly abandoned them all. Everyone had to some extent or other been moved by Parker's generosity, his sensitivity in the appalling circumstances surrounding them all just then.

Later, in the spring, the three menfolk got together and developed a plan for jointure of the lands surrounding Woodleigh House to those about Clear Creek. At a glance, it might have appeared that Parker, who was to buy the bulk of the intervening property, was putting himself out of pocket for the sake of his wife's family. Except that her property, like his, would descend to their son. And unless something were to occur which nobody expected, Mr. Jack's and Miss Allie's property would go the same way, through their children.

They presented their plan to their ladies, rather as something already decided upon, because each man thought women tended to come up with extraneous emendations, especially at times when it was essential to keep complexity as much as possible at bay. In fact no one really saw that things could be arranged in any other way.

The transactions, when they began, would take place in Peell County, in the State of South Carolina. But on Parker's advice the three of them consulted a firm of attorneys in Savannah over the particulars. And while on one of their visits there, passing Lavinia's physician's office, Laurence wondered whether he might have a quick word and sent the others on ahead to lunch.

"I'm very grateful to you for seeing me without an appointment."

"You're quite welcome. But for me to see a gentleman *by* appointment— now that really would be remarkable."

"What I'd like to know, if you can tell me with reasonable certainty, is on what latest date you believe Lavinia was first pregnant."

While the doctor waited for an assistant to bring in the chart, he said: "I am keenly sorry that this has happened to you and to so lovely a lady, one who clearly would make a wonderful mother."

"Oddly enough, I don't think she really wants a child…I think she wants our child."

"Which is now not possible. Why do you say that, though, I wonder?"

"Because in all our nearly endless discussions she has shown no interest— none at all—in adoption."

"You'll probably be surprised to learn how common that feeling is. Well, here are some data for us to work with. Thank you, Miss Emerson." You could tell he didn't usually call her that. Then the doctor began to pore over the chart, riffling through it, first forward, then backward, muttering things like "LMP concluded on…estimate three to five weeks intrauterine…routine laboratory studies at this time…." Next, he took up a little calculating-device made of two overlain circular cards, grommeted together at their centers. The top one had two small apertures cut into it, revealing numbers beneath. He adjusted the circles.

Finally, he looked up at Laurence and said: "By dates and physical examination she was pregnant when I first saw her this last time around; probably she was so at least three weeks earlier. But she was certainly pregnant at the time of her visit. I know because I ordered a pregnancy test; the technique is cumbersome. But when the results finally came in, they were definitely positive."

Laurence considered this. "So as early as June 15 of last year...."

"Before that.

"Much before. At least three, and more likely, five weeks earlier."

"She was pregnant, then, toward the end of May?"

"Beyond the shadow of doubt, I should say."

"I'm sure you must wonder why I so much want to know."

"If you think it my business."

"Lavinia's great anguish now is not that she has lost the child; it's that she believes—or half believes—that in order to have conceived it she may have bargained with the Creator. And she suspects that the stillbirth was in retribution."

"Well, I am myself a Jew; we do not consider bargaining with God at all the thing. Probably because down through our history we have kept trying it, with typically calamitous results. But I have never been able to convince myself that the Sole Eternal Being deals in such petty ways with human beings as those in which they deal with each other."

"Amen, and amen."

"When does Mrs. Ashfield think the pact was sealed?"

"I don't know, but I soon will." Laurence rose to leave. "And, since you are Jewish...."

"A Jew."

"...a Jew, I hope I may say I trust you don't have relatives in Europe now."

"I have, but very distant ones. I don't even know them. Thank you."

"Yet they are there; God keep them."

"God keep them."

Dr. Weil declined any remuneration. Laurence left with "Miss Emerson" a large check to underwrite some of the Good Doctor's charity work.

"Lavinia, can you remember when it was you feel you tempted the Almighty about your bearing a child? That is, if you did at all?"

"I thought you were trying to discourage my thinking about that whole matter."

"I am. Wait, and you'll see that that's why I'm asking."

"Well, I think I can be specific. Because I noticed that the wreath of flowers for little Lizzie Smith's Christening had not been removed from the font; it was dried up, dead, so I took it away with me."

"When was the Christening?"

"Let me look at the card—it's still stuck in the mirror in the front hall, I think." When she returned, she said: "June 30th. I was there on the following, I think, Wednesday."

"Then I can assure you that by the time you prayed for it to come about, your pregnancy was already well established." He explained how he had reached this conclusion. "The Father did not answer your prayer, which you have considered so damning."

They were sitting together in a corner of the east front bedroom at Woodleigh, which they were preparing to occupy. They sat for rather a long time, saying nothing. Finally Laurence said: "Do you realize what this means?"

"It means that He had anticipated my prayer. Bypassing—and therefore I hope forgiving—my impiousness."

"And not having entered into your bargain, He did not require you to fulfill your promise. I'm telling you, Darling, hard as it is for us to get used to, God *is* God."

They sat still for several minutes more, then Lavinia looked up and said: "The dining table?"

"How not?" And so this rather imposing couple, the lovely, statuesque Lavinia, now with her accustomed smile back in place, and the sturdy, unwavering Laurence, grinning broadly, having gone downstairs, each with an arm around the other's waist and in their free hands brandishing respectively a punch ladle and a turkey spoon, skipped twice around the dining table. It was a way they had of honoring happiness. Lavinia had thought two circuits would do, but her husband tugged her along into a third.

They knew that one day they would be caught in this act. But today, not that day.

John Jones recalled his early childhood as sunniness in winter, shade from the sun in summertime. From the sunlight everything took color. The leaves, fronds, pine needles in the woods seemed a hundred kinds of green: The yellow-green of the ferns first to unfurl, emerald moss clinging in shadow, dusty liturgical green of the native holly; cave's-mouth green of the junipers people called "cedars" that looked like shadows.

Through these woods he and Parker would roam, enfolded, as they scouted about for somewhat rarer sights—lichen, partridgeberries. Often they would bring Uncle Laurence back to identify something they had seen but not recognized. Sometimes all three would have to resort to Laurence's library.

Then autumn brought color of its own: Bright yellow in small fan-shapes, golden yellow with flecks of rust and a few dark splotches—proving, John's father declared, that even gold was corruptible, then explaining to the lad what he meant by this—parchment-like yellow, very pale and translucent, so thin you would have thought it impossible that it could transmit so much light, yet still restrict it to color.

His father had told him that the bestowal of all this golden brightness was the way the sun paid the earth a visit before they must move apart, or earth turn her face away.

But, he added, the bareness of the woods coming afterward made it possible to find the evergreens and holly berries needed for Christmas. He did not, however, speak of the rest of wintertime. He did not live to see it, but died in what is anomalously called by many the "prime of life." He died of a sickness called "Hodgkin's lymphoma," obscene of name—a turgid word. John was very careful about this, because he meant at some later time to give more thought to that particular means of death. Then he had been eight years old. The War was over by the time Parker was engaged in his own final battle, which was the battle against fear, not sickness. In the course of his life he had found nothing to be afraid of. And he found nothing at its end, and was therefore victor.

John had been very sad for a long time before his father's death, and for a long time afterward. But what he could remember even from these days was in sunlight, in full color. Life had been intense, and John had been intent—upon helping his father to laugh, upon helping his mother to cry when he saw that that was what was needed.

For days he was absorbed in making a little box with a lid. He decorated it with paint, festively, he hoped, but with enough restraint to suit it to its purpose. He had gathered some treasures from their forest, some small things from among his possessions, and he had carved three symbolic figures, each from a different kind of wood that he considered right.

And one afternoon when they were alone in the splendid house he took the box, full of the things he had prepared and gave it to his father, "for your journey."

"Thank you, Johnny Boy. I wish I could stay longer, but I think I must be on my way soon."

"Well, then, Father, I'll see you at the end."

"Yes, after you've spent the full amount of time here. And in the meantime, at certain times, I shall be able to look back and see you."

"Are you sure? You're not just saying that because of Church, are you?"

"No. That is not one of my reasons for saying things. I say it because I think it's true."

"Will I be able to look ahead and see you? Ever?"

"I don't think so." A beckoning cool breeze parted the delicate, veil-like curtains before the open window. "But remember, I won't see anything you don't want me to see—that wouldn't be fair. Sometime, though, if you find yourself especially wishing that I were there, that's how you'll know I'm watching.

"And thank you for these provisions; I expect each thing will turn out to be exactly what I need somewhere along the way."

"Alina, it's about time for me to shove off. Get Little John to come in."

"Yes." She left the room, indented by every kind of alarm. Mightn't Parker die while she was gone? Should her son be at his father's deathbed, that is, at the time when death finally came? Could John withstand all this? Without drugs, would Parker have asked for him now? But could Parker in this extreme ask for anything, and she fail him? And so she fetched their son.

"John," Parker said in an evenly sustained voice, "The Back-and-forthness…."

"Yes, Sir."

"I think I can say that it is not a question of two hammers, but one of a single hammer and an anvil."

It could be nothing other than the morphine. Would she be able to explain this to John later?

"Thank you for telling me, Father. It is a very good thing for me to know, at last."

"Here, at the last. But now at least we know." His breathing ceased. Then it resumed. "Or, I think we know."

"Shall I stay with you, now, Father?"

"No, Son. Thank you just the same. I am going to sleep." John kissed Parker, and then he went out. He surprised Alina by beckoning her to follow him.

When they were outside in the hallway, John said: "I know you don't want to be gone for long. But I'm afraid you may not have known what we were talking about, and I wanted to tell you that I will explain it to you later."

His father's death was for John a time of deeply felt sorrow, but it was sorrow that he wanted to hold close for awhile. He loved Parker and treasured the times they had spent together; this very specific happiness had now been reversed.

John did not want the hours they might have spent together filled with the presence of anyone or with anything else. Everyone was surprised by the solemn determination with which the little boy parried every attempt to turn him aside from the recesses of the house, forest, his own quiet thoughts. It was in these recesses that he nurtured his sorrow, which was the obverse, now, of the love which had been made to turn its cherished face away. He remembered what he had been told about earth turning from the sun, moving away. Out of reach?

When in the intervals, though, he did present himself, he was calm and alert. He spoke about his father, but not to worrying excess—and not in contexts of angels, Heaven, joyful reunions. Instead of all this, he kept on nourishing his sorrow until, by degrees, it had swung round again, and Parker was with him again, whole and living, obverse and reverse in his memory. Then he usually found it pleasant to think of him. Sometimes, though, these recollections would bring on a burning about the eyes. Then he would say to himself: "I miss him so much only because I love him so much." John did not think that love could be checked in its progress. Not by anything. It had neither aorist nor imperfect.

One afternoon Alina was seated at the piano, playing pieces she had been taught at school. She rarely played except when she was sad. John heard and went and stood beside her until it was time to turn the page.

"Didn't you love Daddy a lot?" Alina's eyes brimmed with tears, but she smiled, as though the sun had broken through before the rain had ended.

She said, holding her head up and inhaling slowly, as though to savor some delightful aroma: "Oh…!" It was all she was able to say just then.

Next, John asked: "Do you remember seeing a little painted box he kept beside his bed?"

"Yes, I certainly do."

"Do you know what happened to it? It isn't there anymore."

"He took it with him, Darling. But," she added, "he told me that if you ever asked about it, I was to give you something he left behind. I don't think it's a present of any kind. Shall I get it for you now?"

"No," John answered, "not yet. Finish playing. And I have some things to do. Just whenever you get around to it." Better than Christmas! Better than one's birthday! He would go off somewhere and spend a little time in anticipation. And that night at bedtime, like those near-magical gifts bestowed by unseen hands because the seasons are mystically important, there upon his pillowcase lay a small parcel wrapped in plain paper and tied with jute cord. It looked like the packages that lie about post offices, going out or coming in.

A little card had been stuck underneath the taught twine. John drew it out, unfolded it, read it:

Don't get your hopes up, Johnny Boy. This is very little, and possibly nothing at all. Love,

Daddy

When he was ready for bed, he slipped the folded paper into the breast-pocket of his pyjama top. He had sometimes wondered why there was a breast-pocket to something you only slept in; now he understood that it was there for keeping things near your heart all night long. And he was lifted, almost, in an aura of sureness and happiness, of eyes open onto a world he hadn't known about and onto a life that was keeping pace beside the one he was accustomed to.

He got into bed, holding the gift, and turned out the bed lamp. If the gift were "little," well, didn't the best things come in small packages? If it were "nothing at all," then he knew better than that. At last he reached down and slid the parcel under the bed, to the spot where he was accustomed to finding his Easter baskets. He would not need Easter baskets anymore, although he would still enjoy their being there, if they should continue to arrive.

But he knew that his father's "nothing at all" might amount to anything or even to everything. In the morning, John knew, he must at last open the parcel. You couldn't anticipate things forever, although you might prefer to. No, he'd better get it over with. For it *could* be a disappointment. In that case the sooner he began to deal with it the better.

The gift, when next morning John opened it, proved to be a further object of anticipation: A small clear-glass bottle, stopped with a cork, the stopper and neck of the bottle sealed with dark wax—black? Purple?

Inside was an apparently square piece of paper. You could tell it had writing on it, but on the inside. It had been folded over once, and perpendicularly again, then pushed down into the bottle, where the second fold had sprung out to the sides. If you looked at it from the bottom, the edges of the paper described an equilateral triangle. One limb was missing, of course, but John was a lad who did not have to connect dots to read a figure.

It was beautiful, clear, mysterious if not sacred. The instructions for use were supplied by a tag held with thread around the bottle neck, partly sealed within the dark wax:

Open this if you really need your father; if not, don't.

VI

" '…You are courting death.' Now the courtship
was ended; the lovely lady had said 'Yes';
the elopement was decided on, the compartment on the train reserved."
Giuseppe Tomasi (Principe di Lampedusa): *The
Leopard*, VII (tr. Archibald Colquhoun)

A T SUNRISE ON the day after the slain sailor's funeral, Duzey Blanding raised his head. The lantern at the foot of the grave was guttering. Again. All night, he had kept a sort of vigil, replenishing the lamp at intervals with the purified oil, usually taking the opportunity of being awake to enjoy a bit of rare Cognac himself, until eventually he had slept.

Taking care not to trample the flowers and greens, he knelt and emptied his supply of oil into the little tank at the bottom of the lantern. Then the flame burned high again, but it was outshone by the sun.

"I'll make haste, now, Friend, because even if you can't see this light, it may be you'll know it's here. Maybe it can help to guide you. Anyway, Father Thomas was right; I don't know where you're going, or when they're looking for you to get there. But while I can, still, I'm going to the beach!"

Duzey hadn't much with him that morning, especially as he was going to leave the lantern behind, and the oil jar was empty. Somebody would show him the way to go home, when the time came. He walked down Church Street and turned right on Highmarket Street, toward Southport. He walked the whole way.

Everybody knew Duzey, and generally the better they knew him the more they liked him. Several motorists stopped to offer rides. But Duzey was enjoying the walk and the minor degree of sobriety he was permitting himself (*I have to take in some of the world's beauty; if I don't, then what will fill my daydreams?*). But there was plenty of time for little conversations, and Duzey was scrupulous about offering refreshment. At seven o'clock in the morning, as well as at any other hour. He walked on.

From Southport he took the ferry to Fort Fisher. The gentleman-tippler leaned against a pile of gear in a sunny corner of the deck and took a discreet amount of Cognac. Then the sunlight seemed to sparkle more brightly upon the water; the gulls cried with a truer-ringing note. He found that he had been sleeping only when awakened by the gentle concussion of the ferry against her berthing pilings astarboard, from which she caromed lightly onto those aport, this oscillation continuing in dampening, muffled violence that made the whole craft shiver subtly, until she could be made fast. Large, freshly abrupted splinters bobbed about her in the water.

Duzey disembarked and set out along the narrow tar-MacAdam roadway that ran northward along the barrier island. There were only a few houses in sight of this southernmost point. Here there were only widely scattered sand dunes, each with no or only sparse growth of sea oats—nothing yet organized into a chine of high dune. Duzey felt that nothing could hamper his gaze. He looked to the east, hoping to see the place where the *fines champagnes* was grown; he saw only sea bunkers, the submarine pens at l'Orient. He moved on.

Soon Sonny McCallum, who had crossed on the ferry with his small, once-red pickup truck, pulled up alongside Duzey. Sonny was seventeen years old, a drifter in the making. He had been told he ought to be in school, but he didn't bother much about it. He had been told also that he ought to be in the armed services, but he didn't bother much about that, either. "Good morning, Mr. Blanding!"

Duzey stopped, turned, peered. His vision was suddenly less acute; he could no longer see across the Ocean. But he could see, and that was bound to be a good sign. "Who's that? Oh, hello, Sonny. Headed my way?"

"Yes, Sir. There isn't but one way."

"Not unless we turn around and go back. And I can't do that, since I just told a dead man: 'I'm going to the beach.' "

"Jump in, then; I'll give you a lift." Duzey went around to the other side and got in.

"May I offer you a little pick-me-up, Son?"

Sonny made a show of hesitancy, of looking at his watch, of thinking over this offer, then said:

"Thank you very much, Mr. Blanding. I think I will. I'm taking a holiday today." It is not clear what made him think this day was different from any other day. He drank from the amber bottle. His mouth and throat caught sudden fire. He jumped out of the cab, grabbed a bottle of beer from an iced pail in the truck bed, and bit the cap off it. *How can that poor fellow stomach that stuff?* He wondered. *And why?* For he knew Duzey lived in a fine big house and had two servants who lived there with him. *His money must have run out.* The cool beer was a balm as he swallowed, even to his nose and windpipe, which had also been scalded. He climbed back in, and they drove off.

The Manager of the Lumina saw that his wife was right. And so now he was at the top of a ladder, his left arm crooked around the last of the sixteen lampposts, while he dismantled the lamp with his right hand and removed the bulb. It had all stemmed from her remarks at breakfast: "Henry, you've got to understand that those young couples who want to stroll out onto the Pier after dark don't want a blaze of electric light—they *want* the dark."

"But I had those lampposts put up particularly so they could see where they're going."

"They *know* where they're going!"

The Manager stirred his coffee, into which he had put two aspirin tablets and several lengths of cigarette ash. It had been brought to him with milk already added, and, to his wife's touch, cold. But he had continued to stir until the cup and ambient air would not accept any further heat from the liquid inside. "And they know, too, how long they might be gone. And that's why I'm opening the Pavilion two months early—because some of those boys in uniform don't have two more months." He tasted; the coffee had reached the ideal stage of repulsiveness.

"And you're good and kind to do it. But let them nestle with each other in the dark if they want to."

"You're right, Mildred. The trouble is, I have to keep that dim blue light burning at the end of the pier—Coast Guard regulations—and they're all on the same circuit."

"Why don't you just take the bulbs out of the rest, then?"

The Manager relished the appalling dregs of his coffee, got up and kissed his wife, and said: "I will. But there's a lot else to do. Would you see if you can get Billy and Jody to come down and help me?"

But Billy and Jody were out of range. So the Manager, working as quickly as he could, had reached the sixteenth and last lamp and had disabled it. And, yes, he saw Mildred's point. Because it was his point, too. He was a man with the good fortune of finding his greatest happiness in making other people feel content. That made happiness always and everywhere available to him. Now he climbed down and collapsed the ladder. He had checked the refreshment kiosk at the end of the pier, and all that was left for him here was to admire the entrance to the attraction, its *porte sublime*. For in it, he felt, his fanciful good ideas had reached their zenith: There was an archway with a painted sign, flanked by two palmettos. The sign, in letters against a background of sea, horizon, and sky rendered in a satisfyingly lurid spectrum, read: "Stairway to the Stars," after the popular song. The palmettos had been a probably unwarranted expense; they must be taken from their habitat at or near the desired height. They grow slowly and their days are longer than man's. But to the Manager's mind they were necessary for realization of the clear connection between "tropical" and "paradise."

Well, it was good that the pier was ready, for it would be the first to attract couples, who in new dresses, or slacks and patterned shirts—tails out—or, best of all, crisp uniforms, would stroll out just before sunset to be seen and to see each other, to establish a corporate sense of festivity, to leave land behind, to leave earth behind—so gravely troubled the earth.

The alarming events of winter, 1941/1942, had produced in the goodly Manager, as in so many others, the evolution of occupation into vocation. *I have to earn my living,* he observed to himself, *but in the process I can do more than that.* He could give to young people, some of whose lives were surely soon to be extinguished, those of others to sustain wounding which could heal only with deep scars and deformation, before these things happened, an illusion, at least, of happy revelry. And their very uncertainty about the future—normal and natural enough in middle life—had been moved decades closer, had freed them of many expected responsibilities, had made them susceptible, he hoped, to the magic he meant to work.

Duzey and Sonny had fallen into a merry camaraderie as, one by one, they reached and passed through the coastal communities below Wrightsville Beach. *Sky so blue, gulls so true.* Eventually, Sonny had to stop the truck; that is not the same as saying he parked it. He merely stopped it, and got out. The exhilaration the two men were feeling was normative to Duzey, who suggested that the truck be placed more out-of-the-way, but novel—not entirely novel, but relatively so—to Sonny, who felt that the truck had been very considerately situated. They crossed berm and dune and began staggering through the pocked, powdery white sand above the tide line; this leant an at least partial justification to the ataxia now insinuating itself into their gaits.

Footprints left in the Sands of Time are usually thought of as a lasting, if not long-lasting, record of the traveler through life. Up here, though, where Sonny and Duzey were lunging and lurching about, there had been so many travelers. So many footprints impressed upon so many foregoing ones, themselves soon to be overtrodden or wind-screeded. But while they lasted the little declivities served as refuge for shards of seashell, fragments of last year's marsh grass, desiccated by brine and sunlight, fallen into bits as its fabric gave way; these same cusps caught and held other spent things, stubs of cigarettes unfurling and spilling shredded tobacco, which later in the season, with yellowing, could be mistaken for the seeds of sea oats.

And like these things blown about by the winds then snared into unlooked-for rest, Sonny suddenly sat down—or discontinued standing. He eyed the crowded imprints; he assessed their momentarily trapped contents. If a cigarette paper, then why not a rolled-up portent from a Chinese fortune cookie? And if that, then why not a message intercepted? Maybe he ought to go to war, after all.

Duzey felt that here they were no better placed than they had left Sonny's truck, but he made no objection, especially since it was time again for a draught. The two men sat talking for a long while, to each other, but not to the same points. Yet neither noticed, and the sun achieved meridian passage and then began to color things differently.

Into the great Pavilion itself the Manager now entered, noting that a lot of the white paint on siding and railings had "chalked," as it usually did over the winter season. He had to climb three steps; the building as a whole was lifted above the sand on low pilings. The first floor was a single large room, with a refreshment bar at its southwest end, a small stage opposite. The middle was floored with hardwood, for dancing. There would be no musicians that evening, but instead a "jukebox," and this had at least the advantage of making available the latest tunes, and performed by the most celebrated bands and singers.

From a joist across the center of the room there hung a sphere covered with a thousand little mirrors. And trained upon it from each corner of the room was a spotlight with a disk made of gores of gelatine-paper in different colors. For dancing, the sphere and the disks could be made to rotate slowly. When the house lights were dimmed or—if the prevailing mood seemed to call for it—extinguished (It was only now that he came to think of it that Henry realized this was just a different application of the Mildred Principle), then numberless specks of multicolored light were spilt all over the room, speed of flight and diameter increasing with distance from the sphere, intensity conversely decreasing. They skimmed across floor and ceiling, floated upward or sank against the walls.

Perfect chaos was what the manager was after; none of the four lights was to splash the same color onto the glittering sphere at once. Choice! There must be every possible choice. No order and no predictability.

What the future would bring was to be known only after it had come. The labor was intense and involved. But just in time, Billy and Jody showed up.

The wind sang through the screening and with its song brought the sweet scent of wax myrtle, extracted by sunshine from the thick stand of immense shrubs growing all along the porch that on two sides enclosed the Elkins's little beach cottage—two sides, that is, of the one ample room. The rest of the house was made up of crannies, for sleeping, bathing, cooking, either tacked onto the outside at grade, or folded into odd spaces beneath gables above.

Sarah Elkin, lying upon a daybed on the porch, was congratulating herself for having taken this particular day off from her work at the New Brunswick telephone exchange. For the weather was warm and clear—a sea breeze had even become established, just these few days into spring. She rested now, completely at ease; her random thoughts were pushed to the borders of her consciousness, like furniture moved back against the walls to clear a floor for dancing. In fact, in the center of her mind a kind of dance had begun already, languorous steps in an undecipherable sequence.

Soon she decided to go inside and speak with her father. She hesitated, anticipating cold upon her bare feet. But when she had swung her legs off the couch, she found the bricks of the floor, laid directly in the sand in herringbone pattern, to be agreeably cool instead; the unseasonable warmth seemed to have saturated everything.

Mr. Elkin, who did not have the use of his legs, was sitting in his rolling-chair. A portable writing desk was before him; upon it lay a number of papers. Some were evidently quadrangles taken from nautical charts—and at that specialized ones; not the kind you can buy in any chandlery—and a single hardbound book.

When Sarah came into the room, her father quite casually rested his forearms over all these materials.

"Daddy," she said, "isn't this a gorgeous day?"

"It is. I wish it were part of a better year...although, maybe this is a year when we need a day like this the most."

"I've be lying out on the porch. The myrtles smell so delicious, and somewhere pine straw is warming in the sun—I smell that, too. I think I'm forgetting how to say 'Number, please.' "

"Yes, it's above all a redolent day. It seems I can distinguish a hundred things in the ocean breeze."

"Make me a list!"

"It would have to be expurgated."

Mr. Elkin, who had come to terms with his debility—and without coming perversely to priding himself upon it—was cheerful and alert. Sarah, now that nearly everything anybody said or did related to the War, had grown certain that her father must be having to face life at an additional remove from its center. She finally ventured this remark: "I hope it isn't becoming too awfully hard for you, Daddy—I mean having the War going on and your being able to do so little about it." Then: "I hope I haven't made it worse by saying what I've said?"

"You have never made anything worse for me, my Sweet Girl. I may, you know, be able in the end to do more about it than anyone would think." Sarah had come closer; he placed certain of the papers on top of the rest, leaning forward a little farther. "And it won't be through 'also serving by only standing and waiting.' To begin with, I can't stand!"

"Well, one thing is certain: *I* won't be surprised by *anything* you do. And, Oh! Where is Mama, do you know?"

"She's resting, I think. I'd rather we didn't bother her. Not unless it's important." Mrs. Elkin was not resting. She had left the house upon an errand that humiliated her. Her husband knew about it. He readily excused her.

"Oh, no. Nothing urgent. I just wondered. I'm pretending it's a summer's day. On summer's days you think idle thoughts and ask idle questions. But if you see Jill, please tell her I think the Lumina is open."

"I don't think it can be, not this early in the season."

"There was a lot going on there this morning."

And then father and daughter stopped to listen, for music from four blocks away could be heard, waxing in intensity and waning. Scratching upon a microphone. Somebody was trying to adjust a loud-speaker system. "You must be right, Darling. If you and Jill do go there, watch out for men in uniform!"

"Oh, we will. That's why we'll be going!"

I expected to be afraid, the Captain said to himself as he walked onto the bridge, *but I had not expected to be so much annoyed.* He gazed out onto a placid ocean, blue where the sun still shone upon it, a strange glassy violet where the surface lay in shadow beneath a cloud bank. *All these operations seem uncoördinated. I suppose all we can hope is for some intelligence to allow them to be directed toward their unifying destiny. If they have one, which seems to me improbable.*

Low light from astarboard struck the water, just touching the wavelets—there were no seas—with gold, a meshwork across the blue. The Captain remembered that the Emperor Nero was thought once to have fished with a golden net. The association was unpalatable.

He was annoyed for two reasons, principally: One was that the destroyer *Lemuel Weatherington,* which he commanded, should, he thought—and many others thought so, too—be protecting convoys to Great Britain. The men and supplies needed to win the War had to be got to where the war was being fought.

But he and his ship were at that time temporarily assigned to the Eastern Sea Frontier. She had sailed from Norfolk and was to join *USS Harker* to patrol regions off the North Carolina Capes. And after all, this was a place where great carnage had been inflicted by German submarines upon merchant shipping up and down the Eastern Seaboard. Bloody, and logistically disastrous itself. For if materiel could not reach New York and Halifax, then obviously it could not be convoyed across the North Atlantic.

The course that *Weatherington* had been ordered to steer was to the Captain the second, the more immediate annoyance. In daylight they had followed the hundred-fathom curve, offshore by a great many miles. But as night began to fall they must come close inshore. The Captain found a great deal of fault with a schedule that directed him to skirt Cape Fear in early evening.

Inland lay the city of Wilmington, over which there hung by night a cloud of dull yellow light, the summed light from all parts of the town. Farther downstream, New Brunswick yielded ample brightness of its own. And near the mouth of the Great River, almost at the brink of earth, the fishing-village of Southport shimmered and twinkled.

Dusk was hurrying along, shielding them to a degree. It was clear that they were being guided, and must be guided, dangerously close to the fields where the killer prowled, at the far edge of which stretched miles of perilously festive beaches; the young were making merry before tomorrow. Unbroken, luminous strands against which they must sail, targeted in silhouette. Through glasses, the Captain could distinguish features of these places, just faintly.

Duzey Blanding prodded Sonny, who had slipped into a shallow torpor. "See those lights down there?"

"Lights down there."

"It's the Pavilion! It's opened up already! Be quiet, listen," he demanded of his motionless friend, whose breathing itself could not be heard. "Do you hear the music?"

The loudspeaker system had been successfully adjusted, so that variations Duzey heard were due to small changes in force and set of the breeze. He could make out the melody, and he knew the words: "We'll hear the sound of violins / Away out where the blue begins...."

Sonny was becoming less inert. Finally, after refreshment, they started off toward the Lumina. They held to the margin of loose, dry, dragging powder at the base of the dunes, even though the tide had ebbed, leaving, closer to the water's edge, sand that was smooth and hard-packed. Duzey had become a little leery of the sea.

Jill Elkin breezed into the cottage. It was the way she had of entering and leaving. Breezing. "Daddy! The Lumina is opening tonight! Do you hear the music?"

"Sarah and I heard it a few minutes ago."

"Do you know where she is? May we go down there this evening?"

"Upstairs. Yes."

"Oh, thank you! Damn! I'll bet she's already started primping." The effusive child embraced and kissed her father, who called after her as she breezed out: "And please don't say 'Damn'." He was answered by brief music—either his daughter's voice receding, or the sighing of the ocean breeze.

Sarah and Jill had been frequenting the Lumina since they had been little girls. Each year, a different aspect of going there had seemed most important. At first, before their father's injury, they had been accompanied by their parents. Ice cream and spun sugar, then inflatable rafts to rent. Later, they had gone by themselves and watched youngsters several years older than themselves dance and even hold hands! The prize *frissons* of these excursions had been glimpses of boys and girls kissing on the darkened verandahs.

Sarah had particularly liked catching glimpses of Robert Strikestraw, whom she considered "dreamy." That was when she was too young to know that dreams were themselves not "dreamy," but in general enigmatic or harrowing. It all went sour the night they spotted Robert himself kissing a girl beneath a moonlit sky.

The wound had healed. And he older than she, in the first place. Too old to take notice of her. Then.

"I'm sick of being 'pretty'," Sarah commented to her sister as they were completing their relatively simple toilettes. "Being merely pretty, particularly in wartime, seems trivial and silly somehow. And shallow."

"Don't tell me you want to try being ugly."

"Of course not. What woman would?"

"You're a girl, not a woman."

"You might be surprised. But, no, what I want is to be 'striking looking.' "

"Well, you may as well give it up, because you're too pretty."

"I'd say 'Thank you,' if I thought for a minute you meant that as a compliment." Sarah inspected her reflection more closely, and at once more comprehensively. She stopped looking at her hair, at her cheeks, eyebrows, lips—she looked then at her eyes, just her eyes, and deeply. She stood up from the dressing table, carefully keeping her actual and reflected gazes still locked together. By some little movement, or trick of the light, she saw that she was at any rate going eventually to be striking looking.

"I did mean it as a compliment."

"Thank you, then. Let's go."

"Are you in a hurry?"

"Yes, I am."

Throughout the sisters' preening, which alternated with expressions of hopelessness regarding their ability to attract, nevertheless at their destination preparation was being made to receive them and all comers with every kind of entertainment. For now the Manager climbed to the second storey of the Pavilion to make ready the most sensational attraction of his establishment. There, bolted to a mount in the floor, was a full-size motion picture projector, its barrel of lenses pointed seaward, the whole assembly looking like a gun-emplacement. But it was immobile. And if you sighted along it, your gaze was stopped by a screen held upon pilings twenty yards out in the surf. "Movies" were shown every week at the Lumina, and for opening night, an irresistible offering was in store: "The last Days of Pompeii," starring Miss Dorothy Wilson. This spectacle had been preceded by its reputation.

The Captain of *Lemuel Weatherington*, hours earlier more annoyed than afraid, was at this time more dissatisfied than uneasy. Air-reconnaissance and -support had been promised for the patrol, but no covering aircraft had been either seen, heard, or contacted by radio since they had put to sea, and now that night was falling there was no longer use for any. By now, they did not have to wait much longer to be on station.

The mission was evidently one that could not be carried out in any real degree of safety. If he were to seek out German submarines to kill, obviously he had to go where they could be found, and go there blind, except for sonar, an infant technology. And here would be precisely where they might find him first, and at that, on their part, armed with maximum visual acuity. They could be presumed—if there were any, and there were—to be lying off those regions around Cape Lookout and Cape Fear and Cape Hatteras that could be counted upon to backlight merchant vessels, which were their primary targets. His vessel, too, would be as vulnerable, and more estimable a prey. Depth charges! Weapons useful only after the enemy had been suspected present, or stumbled upon, if not actually engaged. No foreknowledge, no knowing before becoming known.

Little light was left in the sky. Seamen aboard *Weatherington* could see glittering fringes begin to appear along the shorelines. They had spent a splendid day at sea; now was the time of lighting of lamps, the time when men wish most to be at home, or somewhere at fireside.

The destroyer was running steady, herself darkened in the darkness, gauges with indicators settled. Over the radio receiver came only a sound as from beehives heard across a still meadow. The watch changed.

Lights at the Lumina were dimmed. The reflectant screen, yet well out in the surf in spite of the ebb, shone suddenly with dazzling light. When the projector had ingested all of the clear leader-film that had allowed the screen to blaze so brightly, then there appeared some intersected and concentric circular patterns for use in focusing the lenses, then countdown numerals, starting at nine.

Those who noticed began to count with them in a chant which grew louder as more people realized what was about to take place and joined their own voices. Then came the title of the film, and names of the actors. Many settled where they were. Sonny and Duzey sat down on the upper verandah and put their legs through gaps in the railing. Some raced back from the pier. Others stayed there in the now deeper darkness, more perfect aloneness.

The moon rose, but her light was diffused by haze into a surrounding circle. Several in the throng were ship's navigators. Some of these noted independently that this phenomenon was not explicable from the meteorological data prevailing, according to principles known at that time and to those men.

Sarah and Jill arrived. Jill was distracted at once and breezed off among the crowd. Sarah was intent; she selected a vantage-point and waited, for the instant, oracular dance had continued at the center of her thoughts. Just as the lights were being dimmed, she had caught sight of a man who she was sure was Robert Strikestraw. She watched his face alternately brighten and grow shadowy in the variable light from the projector. She ignored the film. Jill, in the meantime, had got up with friends and was avidly following the story.

But Robert was of course not there. For all she knew with certainty, he might not be anywhere. And he was a Naval officer. The man she was watching was in Army uniform. And Robert remained too much older, wherever he was, she supposed, than to take notice of her. He had gone off to Norfolk, and from there, God knew where, probably without even knowing her name.

Now the Army officer had noticed Sarah, too, and got up to canvass his friends, acquaintances, uniformed men he didn't know but could address by rank. He was seeking an introduction to this strikingly beautiful young woman. He thought he might already know her but was not sure.

Duzey complained of a "funny feeling" in his abdomen or chest—he couldn't tell which. "How about a little nip," Sonny suggested. "That usually seems to buck you up."

"No," Duzey said, "I don't think I can swallow anything." Sonny untangled himself from the verandah railing and stood up. Everybody behind him started shouting for him to sit down again; they were by now engaged in the story, sympathetic to the characters. The cataclysm had been foreshadowed. But Sonny was weary of being inebriated, and young enough to be eager to have a look around for other diversions. And he was hungry. He squatted down beside Duzey, whose color was appalling—maybe that was due to the projection lamp?

"If you don't feel like eating anything, then how about something cool to drink? Or how about a 'snowball'?" (This was a paper cone of crushed ice flavored with fruit syrup.)

"Well, now, that sounds like something I could handle."

"Grape?"

"Cherry, please, if they have it. And ask them not to make it too cold."

"Coming up!" And Sonny wandered off toward the refreshment bar, wondering whether Duzey had any idea what might be involved in altering the freezing-point of water. He could have told you, the next day.

Duzey, who had had a wonderful day, carefully titrating his consumption of spirit, had begun to feel quite hideous. Then, without perceived nausea, retching, or other warning, and he having no control over it, from his mouth and nose passively there rose and spilled a small quantity of thin liquid. This fell onto some of the watchers below, who, thinking it the dregs from an overturned cup began to shout up mild abuse. But this was abortive, because by now the last hours, not days, of Pompeii were come.

By the time Sonny had reached the refreshment bar, he felt quite robust, everything considered. He fell to chatting with a fetching young woman. She seemed in no hurry to be away, and of course nor was he. If only he were in uniform! The playing-field would in that case be level, as some say. But even as it was, he seemed to be moving toward the goal. He ordered Duzey's snowball—cherry, and not too cold. The boy behind the counter was unfazed by the fastidiousness of the choice. The young woman declined refreshment. Recreation seemed more on her mind. Sonny ordered a sandwich for himself, and, when it was ready, he gave the boy a dollar and asked him to take the snowball over to Duzey. "You can't miss him; he's not at all the right color. I'll keep an eye on the stand, but everybody's watching the picture show."

Under the veiled moon, within her search area *USS Lemuel Weatherington* was making way unhampered. No enemy activity had been reported since nightfall. She had herself nothing to report. The Captain had decided to hold his course for five minutes longer and then to begin to zigzag, just to be on the safe side—just to ward off the feeling only now born within him that all that was, was ending. After all, their patrol was to last only a very short time longer. They sailed on. The ship's wake roiled; her bow-wave seethed.

In twenty seconds, the vessel was to be brought hard about to starboard, beginning her zigzag pattern…just an added precaution. Crew had been advised. The lookout aloft steadied himself for the turn, which would spin him through a broader and swifter arc, as inertia of motion bore the mast farther to port.

The fireman experienced a brief visitation of Panic fear: The pressure in number two boiler had risen abruptly. The point of the indicator needle was obscured beneath a splotch of water-borne rust, now dried, on the glass cover of the gauge. The fireman wiped it away with a fingertip. The pressure was certainly too high; he could think of no reason for it. Then suddenly the needle slipped counterclockwise and rested at normal.

Bells on the bridge. Bells in the engine room. Astern in the darkness the immense rudder obediently inched out of axial alignment. All those aboard felt the expected slight shift of things. Then on the bridge the staff experienced a sharper displacement—a movement of no great amplitude, only an abrupt jarring.

The Captain believed they had been struck by a torpedo. They had been. It penetrated the hull, port side, forward. The ship's magazine exploded.

The Captain had begun to issue an order, but all burden of authority fell away from him as the cells which had constituted his central nervous system now scattered in a hundred directions.

Aft, there came a second shock, a small percussion, but sparing nothing that was left of the vessel's fabric: Another explosion followed. In the fire-room, the indicator-needle within the pressure gauge, which had recently and mysteriously risen, now fell rapidly until checked by a small stop beneath the shallow dome of glass.

The ship was without power. Momentum would have carried her some distance, except that the original wound had left her bows deformed and splayed, so that the forwardmost part of the ship plowed into the sea like the shovel of an earthmover. The disturbances in structure began to multiply like harmonics of a taut string plucked but twice.

The men who had not been killed or rendered senseless at first tried to launch the boats, but these either had been destroyed or were jammed in their skids. Two inflatable rafts were set afloat, but no one was able to reach them. For none of the crew, even those wearing flotation vests, willingly entered the water.

Now! Here it was—the eruption of Mount Vesuvius! The omens from the loudspeakers that were mounted to the pilings in the surf, the ones that supported the screen, though diminished in fidelity by the immensity of volume entering from the soundtrack electrically and leaving acoustically, drew the attention of even Duzey, who was nearer to death than he or anyone else knew.

The Mountain appeared, darker yet against an already darkened sky. From its crater a dreadful cloud emanated and expanded furiously. The crowd were rapt. Flame appeared, streaks of fire, rivers of fire; the loudspeakers strained to give forth the crack and thunder. At this, Duzey with his final voluntary movement, raised his head. He thought he saw burning streamers reach out past the margins of the screen and become brilliantly colored, like fireworks. Then copious blood welled from his mouth.

The torpedo that had struck *Weatherington* aft had breached the oil tanks, bathing part of the afterdeck in burning fuel. More oil leaked from the rent tanks directly into the water and encircled what was left of the fantail, which had separated and begun to go down in a ring of fire.

The surviving crew, in life jackets, struggled for foothold, handhold, or any other means of keeping out of the water. But the rest of the ship was sinking, too, and fast.

Those at the Lumina who had been baptized in Duzey's blood sent for an ambulance and then set about doing what they could for the sick man. It was not much. They unfastened his shirt collar, fanned him, slapped his ashen cheeks to try to revive him. They patted his hand. They said he would be all right.

The film had snagged within the projector, so that a portion of it was exposed too long to the heat of the lamp. The screen went white—blinding white, with scorched and blistered edging—the image receding concentrically as the film melted.

Many ran down to the beach and scattered, trying to see more of the conflagration out at sea.

Duzey was taken away.

The midship section and mangled bows of *Weatherington*, sinking, took her men into the water. Beneath them, the depth charges in the fantail, which had started to go down seconds earlier, began reaching the successive depths at which they had been set to detonate. The shocks were transmitted through the water virtually undiminished. These armaments had made the ship an illicit fisher of men, who came dead to the surface.

At this time a vast lashing of water was thrown high into the air, visible in the moonlight to the crowd watching from the beach. At its base, a flash of silvery light. The Hell-colored flames were blown out by the blast. There came another. Then a volley. Finally all was quiet. There was no more light, no more movement. The thunderbursts had sent crests across and among light swells. But these dissipated quickly. All that had been, had ended. Secure finally and forever from Battle Stations.

Earlier, the Army officer who beneath his imposing uniform was only Hal Whitman from Wilmington, found someone who knew the girl he wanted to meet. "She is—or she was—the telephone operator in New Brunswick."

"Named Elkin?"

"Yes. You already know her?"

"Not exactly; but my aunt and uncle and cousins live next door to her."

"Well, I'll be happy to introduce you—or re-introduce you, or whatever you want. But we'd better wait until after Pompeii blows up."

"Pompeii doesn't blow up. It gets buried in hot ash."

"Well, something blows up, and everybody wants to see that part. But after that."

"Good. Thanks. But come let me show you where she's standing." But Sarah had moved, or left.

"If she's gone home, I'll wring your neck!"

"What have I got to do with it?"

"I don't know. Somebody must have had something to do with it. It can't have just happened."

"You mean she would've waited for—whatever it is—to blow up?"

She would have waited for me. "Mount Vesuvius."

"What?"

"Hold on. There she is."

And there she was. "Sarah, this is my friend Brother Whitman. Sarah Elkin."

She said Hello as they shook hands, then asked: "Are you a monk in disguise?"

"Just my sister's brother. My real name is Halbert. People who haven't known me as long as Junior has call me Hal."

Sarah turned to "Junior." "And you are younger than someone else, who is 'Senior'?" She was already disgusted with herself for being coquettish. Strikingly Beautiful women never resorted to coquettishness in order to conceal their real emotions. They were able to control, rather than conceal, them.

"I want you to dance with me; come downstairs."

"The music has been shut off."

"You can sing." So they danced, holding each other a lot closer than they would have expected to, just a little while before. They both sang, and they danced. The four spotlights had not been turned off, and the magic wheels of color and the faceted sphere on the ceiling joist rotated still. The specks of colored light whirled across the walls and floor and ceiling, until the rose-colored ones that matched the color of dawn-light were absorbed into the coming day and disappeared.

"Is there still time?"

"Yes, there is."

A slightly bent old man came to them across the dance floor. He said: "Children, I'm so sorry that you've been disappointed. I did all I could."

"Sir? Disappointed in what?"

"In the evening," he replied.

"But we haven't been disappointed at all!"

"The explosion. The ship." He turned to Hal. "Son, you know what those last thunderclaps were?"

"I'm afraid I do know, Sir. But that was the War. The evening here was wonderful."

Sarah said: "I felt I was at a beautiful party…even that it was being given in my honor."

"I felt the same; I heard a lot other people say so, too."

"I did, too."

"You really did?" The old man's eyes shone.

"Because of it, we've met each other, and we're going to be married."

"And that is a sure sign of a grand evening!"

Upstairs, the projectionist was cropping and splicing the film. Some discarded frames lay about his feet.

VII

"I'D RATHER YOU didn't read me a story tonight, Grandfather."

"Oh, certainly we can skip it—we should, in fact—if you're tired," Thomas answered hopefully.

"No, Sir, I'm not tired; I would like for you to make up a story out of nowhere...the way you do in Church."

"I don't make them up from nowhere."

"Well, people say you do."

I will not rise. I will not ask. I will not. "All right, then. Shall I make up one about...angels keeping watch?"

"I guess that would be about the best we could do...on short notice." Edward was yet a very young child, and, like most little children, precocious in some ways but quite backward in others. "But if you don't mind, could we *not* have them guarding me 'till morning bright'?"

Thomas launched out, blindly and preoccupied: "Well, then, I'll tell you

165

about sunrise-angels." Edward hadn't known about this association, so he was curious. "It's completely dark when all this starts." *Try arguing with that!*

"Are even the angels in complete darkness, Grandfather, before the sun rises?"

"Yes and no. It's completely dark, but not to them. This is how it happens: The sun is an enormous, fiery globe, round like an orange, not round like a plate. And it doesn't go out completely overnight. You've been allowed to blow out candles. The flame goes away, but the wick glows until it cools off."

"But it does cool off, and then it stops glowing."

"Well, the sun doesn't. It's too big, and when it's shining, the temperature inside it is so high that you or I could never imagine it."

"*You* couldn't imagine it?"

"No. Anyway, the sun is near the edge of a broad plain of polished tourmaline, the color of a peacock's feathers. But at the time we're talking about, the plain looks nearly black. And the sun looks like a jack-o-lantern—with no face, of course. A dull orange light comes from inside it." Thomas found himself being drawn into the account, at least to a point. Perhaps soon he would gain some real momentum. "Four angels—these ones are the kind we call 'Thrones'—are stationed around the sun, the same distance apart from each other. Keeping an eye out to be sure everything happens in the right way.

"Then, from far above comes another angel, an Archangel, carrying silver fire in one hand and in the other, the Command. Are you feeling sleepy yet? We could finish tomorrow night."

"No, Sir." Edward was not grasping all the details, but he liked the turn the whole story was taking. It was about angels—and he suspected God Himself would come into it—but it obviously was *not* a Bible story.

"Well, then, the silver fire we sometimes see at morning, and we call it the 'Morning Star' or the 'Daystar.' "

"I've heard of that. Can I see it, do you think?"

"You can, and the next time I see it burning clearly I'll show it to you. But you must not mind my having to wake you up very early."

"Oh, I won't. Go on, then."

I don't think I can take this much farther; when you start lying to children it can be hard to disentangle yourself.

"The Archangel alights on the plain of tourmaline with the fire and the Command, and he goes around to each of the Thrones, asking whether all is well, and giving to each one a fourth part of the fire. The Thrones relight the sun, which quickly gets much brighter; the orange turns to yellow and the yellow turns almost to white."

"Isn't the heat terrific?"

About like any other hydrogen bomb.

"Not to the angels, but, yes, it's quite terrific. Then the Archangel, in a very loud voice, reads the Command to the Sun: 'Burn, and run your course!' "

"I," Edward said, "have never heard the loud voice."

"We can't hear it."

"Why not? Especially if it's so loud."

"Angels hear things men don't hear; and they hear them differently, anyway. Well, at this command the sun begins to turn slowly—spin, not roll. And two little children-angels, there to help in the dawning, grind up violet chalk in a bowl, and when they have ground it to powder, they run a fine linen thread through it. *I wonder whether I may not be overdoing this? I'm beginning to think of it as real. It must be the color, the fire. So festive!* Then they take the thread, miles of it, each holding one end, to places where in the tourmaline plain...."

"What did you say 'tourmaline' is?"

"I didn't say." At last, though, Thomas had been able to see through to the end of his story. He could stop at the end, whether Edward were ready to go to sleep or not. "Far apart are set two markers. They are made of silver, then covered with gold. One of the children-angels kneels beside each marker. They stretch the violet thread tight across the *tourmaline* plain, then one of them plucks it...."

"Which one?"

"One, one day, and the other, the next." *A lesson in fair play.* " When plucked, the thread leaves a perfectly straight violet-colored mark."

"Does the thread ever pop?"

"This thread could be 'popped' only by the strength of...but never mind."

"I bet I know what you were going to say."

"At this time, the sun—still turning, you know—starts moving forward to the mark. It moves straight across, just at the precise center and at exactly the right speed."

"I bet you think I don't know what 'precise' means."

"Stop betting. It could ruin you." *Has this child no concept of bedtime, of being weary at the end of the day?*

"Who wrote the Command?"

"The Lawgiver."

"God?"

"The Creator."

"What's his name?"

"We do not know His name. He is King of the Universe, the Almighty."

"I know *that's* God. I've heard that much in Church. But then is it morning?"

"Nearly. The sun moves to the edge of the plain, which ends at the boundaries of night. That is when its complete splendor appears. Its rays fall on us, a few at first, then a great many. Then come the light and warmth that all living things have been waiting through the night for. And then we see."

After he had thought over it, Edward said: "You don't suppose it's all bunk, do you, Grandfather. I mean, we can see a little, even at night."

Thomas stood up. "Who's to say? 'The Twelve Dancing Princesses' is certainly all bunk. Good night, Edward."

"Good night, Grandfather."

Thomas, going downstairs, dreaded somewhat to see his dear Grace, who would be waiting for him in the library. He dreaded what he knew—approximately—she would say, and he dreaded to see again how enfeebled she had got over the past two—no, nearly three—years.

He went in, and there she waited; she always sat now in the chair where she had been sitting when he had deemed it time to tell her what he suspected about their son Robert, on a July day so long ago. She had overturned a specimen-vase with a rosebud in it. From *Rosa 'Désprez à fleurs jaunes,'* he thought he remembered. Turned it over while laying aside a magazine, her movements spasmodic with grief, after a day of dread. Of stone-heavy dread. For a particle of a second, like fleeting passages of desperate hope—of hopeless hope—the water droplets from the silver phial had held their integrity of sparkling brilliance, then suddenly disappeared, absorbed into the worn fabric of the carpet.

"Grace, Dear, I wish you would take a turn at bedtime-story patrol. Just so you could be reminded of the trickery involved in getting away," Thomas said lightly. "Of course the classical approach is to cause your subject to fall asleep."

"I know it is terribly hard with Edward."

"Not any more so, I think, than with any of them."

Grace looked at him in a faintly conspiratorial way, as though they shared a dusky secret about their grandson. "Edward really is not like his father, is he?"

"To the contrary, he seems to me very much like his father. Not exactly, of course. But then without the differences, there would be no memorial of Anne. Of dear Anne, too, remember, he's all that remains over." And then he realized his statement had been inaccurate. But surely he needn't go into all that with Grace.

"I know I've been very foolish. I thought having Edward would be like starting all over again with Bobbie." *"Bobbie!" The regression had been continuing, unremarked as an underground stream!* "But you can't start all over again, can you? We want to, sometimes; sometimes we try. All of us, I think, are afraid of the future—we have to be; we have to be on guard. I don't mean the War. That's almost over. And the last losses will be more tragic than the first. No. Other things, mostly normal and natural things. But, Thomas, I am more afraid—right now, as we're sitting here and talking—I'm more afraid of the past than I am of the future. I'm afraid it may already have undone me."

"What can I do? Tell me anything you can think of that I can do to help you."

But Grace said nothing. *No, Tom, I think my doom is sealed, has long been sealed...and I shall have nothing to show for my life and you will have nothing to show for all our years together.*

The study had been rearranged as their bedroom, because Grace could no longer climb the stairs without becoming exhausted. She had been taken to the doctor, of course, who could find no specific thing amiss. He had sent her to the hospital at Chapel Hill, but the doctor there concurred in his opinion, and sent her back. He recommended she drink a small glass of beer a half-hour before both lunch and dinner. "It stimulates the appetite; besides it offers in itself both fluid and nourishment." Grace promised she would make herself do this. But once at home, she found that she was unable to make herself do that or anything else, other than rising in the morning, dressing, sitting through the day, and finally retiring.

"The story I was just telling Edward—I started out making it up as I went along—pure fantasy. I thought he'd soon go to sleep. Especially since he seemed so skeptical; I thought he wasn't greatly interested."

"Oh I think skepticism represents one of the keenest forms of interest."

"Well, he was certainly wide awake when I left him. But, as I was saying, I couldn't see any way to end the story. And then I did see a possible resolution. I finally saw a way to bring it to a coherent close. Somewhat coherent. And now I wonder: If a story can be completed, mustn't that mean it has at least some truth in it?" Grace thought not; the story of her own life, when completed, would contain no truth.

Before they turned out the lights that evening, Thomas told her this: "If you were to make line drawings of Bob's and of Edward's characters on sheets of tracing-paper—If you could somehow do that—then superimpose one upon the other, against the light, you know the images would not be exactly congruent. Try, if you can, to see Edward's differences not as distortions but as embellishments. And love him for himself; I think he senses that you don't."

"Oh, no! No. My God, no!" And from the next morning she showered her grandson with heartfelt affection, even though the remedy had been put into effect too late to figure in her own recovery.

For a while yet, the War went on, and the folk kept dying. But one day news came that Germany had surrendered. Rejoicing burst forth everywhere and sought to fill every niche in which misery had previously been roosting. Those clefts left unfilled, however, were darker now than ever.

Bank tellers, postal clerks, everyone was excused from further work, as shouting, singing, bells ringing broke across the little City in waves of relief and thankfulness.

Thomas and their grandson went in to see Grace. She seemed to be drifting in a fragile sort of peace, dressed, but stretched out upon her bed. All the window shades were closed. "We're going down to the church to ring the bells. If other people join us, maybe we can ring some changes, or at least rounds. Do you need anything?"

"No, I have everything with me. Go and ring the bells. I'll listen from here." Each kissed her, and they went out. Edward wanted his father back, now war was over, but was afraid he wasn't going to have him. Thomas knew that while so many were rejoicing, others were sorrowing and rejoicing at once, and he wished fervently that his Grace could be among those last.

A crowd was building in the midst of town, which the church overlooked from a block away. The child and the man climbed to the ringing-chamber. Edward rang the treble, as fast as he could. Thomas rang the tenor in time with the beat of his own heart. And heavy was his heart as the tenor bell.

The effect of the peal was charming, rather Russian. Tinkling of the treble; far from the grim Russian wrath in Berlin. Soon others joined them. Edward was relieved first, then Thomas, who was not really a qualified ringer. They stayed for a while, as glorious, clangorous changes rang out, one upon another.

After leaving the church, they stopped for a time to exchange greetings among the ebullient throng, then they went home. Edward was sent in to the breakfast room for his supper. Thomas found Grace just as they had left her, but now entirely still.

"Thank Goodness Grandmother is dead," Edward later said to Rhodë, "or I'd have to have a rest after dinner." He was just a little boy, but he was in a hurry. He and his friend Bobby McCallum had built a keep the afternoon before in the back garden, and this morning Edward had decided to moat it in order to make it more secure. He had left the water running and had to go outside and see about it. He didn't want the moat to overfill.

Rhodë was so astounded by his remark that she hurried from the room without a reply. For young children can be very hard to understand. Edward regarded the loss of his grandmother with so profound a sorrow that he did not speak of it much, but in this instance he had finally seen some infinitesimal advantage arise out of it, and he had spoken his thoughts.

His room was at the back of the house, across the hallway from what was now his grandfather's room alone. In it was a large piece of furniture, which they called "the wardrobe." It served in place of a closet. It was closed by a pair of tall doors, and there was a tall mirror set into each door. There were two low drawers underneath. Edward was in a hurry, but he stopped and gazed for a moment when he caught sight of himself in one of these mirrors. *Is that really me?* Of course he knew that it was only his reflection he was seeing; that was not what he meant. He meant that which was reflected: *Is* that *really me?*

Within the keep, which was made of rosy old bricks from a dilapidated stable-house, Edward and Bobby meant to deposit objects with mystical properties. Every so often the boys would rummage through the mounds of dereliction behind the automobile mechanic's shop. Albert Sculpin had worked there once, but he didn't anymore. Back here, the boys selected those things that suited their needs. Then they would take their choices inside to be inspected by Mr. Brandenburg, the proprietor and mechanic. He would remove anything he thought he might be able to use and then send them off with a rich treasure, for he seemed never to take away any of the things they particularly prized.

Shock-absorbers and ophthalmoscopes of that period greatly resembled each other, outwardly. That instrument clearly held mystical properties. Otherwise why, when being examined with it, did Edward sit in a throne-like chair, have the lights put out, and then have a tiny bright beam—which at times turned to blue—shone floating before his eyes? Furthermore, the doctor had told him that with this device—and only by looking with it into the eyes—he could learn also about his brain, about his blood-vessels, other parts of his systems.

So some things did have these mystical properties. And Bobby and Edward were not fools enough not to realize what that meant: That other things hadn't. There must be a safe reliquary for the ones that did have.

Later on—days or weeks it may have been, for the summertime seemed only a slowly turning eddy in the flow of the year—Edward stopped again before the same mirror in his bedroom. The same, because it was one of only three in the whole house that came down low enough so that he could look into them without having to climb onto a chair; its pair, the one impaneled upon the other door of the wardrobe, had become badly tarnished and did not reflect clearly. (The third was in the front hallway downstairs; with time it had turned dusky blue, so that to look into it was unsettling. Thomas called it a pier glass or a looking glass. He recommended the latter expression to Edward, who was as ready to call a mirror a 'looking glass' as he would have been to take his books to school in a lady's handbag.)

Gazing again at his reflection, again he asked himself: "Is that really me?" This time he stretched out both hands and laid his palms to the cool glass. But no answer came to him. Then he withdrew his hands and placed them against his child-smooth cheeks. "Is this really me? Am I really somewhere inside here?" Then he moved his hands down to his breast, where he could feel his heart beating. Answer enough, at least for the time being. And with that, he was off to find Bobby (whose grandmother also was accommodatingly dead).

Another day both boys happened to be in the bedroom, sitting in chairs pulled up to a desk, grappling with some affair they had in hand. Bobby climbed down and went over to look at the mirrored doors. And so, for a third time, and so far as he ever consciously remembered afterward, for the last time, Edward, watching, had looked into the mirror—the still-shiny one—to look at and think about the reflection there and about the friend whose reflection it was. *Was Bobby really in there? Again, not in the mirror. But did Bobby think he was inside what he saw reflected? Were there really other people, with as much going on inside themselves as he felt went on inside himself? Or did it just seem to him that there were other people? How could he tell, for sure? Would he ever know?*

Bobby, though, was not looking at any reflection but at the mirrors themselves. "Why is this mirror so dark? Is it worn out from so many people looking at themselves in it?" For he knew it was old; nearly everything in his own house was at least a little bit newer than anything in Edward's house.

Bobby really did have a lot of good ideas and knew quite a lot about a lot of things. Edward, however, sensed some vague duty to know at least a little more.

"No. That mirror has got dark because when you open that door it faces out into the hallway, and it's shadowy in the hall. This other mirror faces the windows when you open the door it's attached to; it faces bright light."

"Are you sure that's why?"

"Yes; a mirror that just reflects shadows gets dark, but a mirror that reflects light stays bright."

Edward felt on fairly firm ground. The doctor, on the day they had talked about the ophthalmoscope, had told him that light is good for the eyes and makes it so they can work; he had even said that anybody who stayed in complete darkness long enough would lose his eyesight for good. It came to the same thing with mirrors, probably.

In fact, a cleaning woman long before had spilled a bottle of ammonia down the back of the wardrobe door. It had got in behind the dark mirror and spoiled it.

But it is hard to be absolutely sure about things, and nobody knows which of these explanations is the true one—if indeed either is.

When Thomas overheard his grandson say: "Thank Goodness Grandmother is dead...," he was wrung inwardly by pain with a kind of surprise that amounted almost to alarm. At that moment he would not have been able to respond, even if he had wished or been expected to. Before long, he reminded himself that these were the words of a child, that Edward could not possibly have meant them in the way in which he and Rhodë had at first understood them. So he held his peace. But after two days had gone by, he said next morning to Edward: "Son, I wish you would plan to be back here today at eleven o'clock, instead of at noon."

Edward answered: "Yes, Sir," and came in from playing at that designated hour. Bobby, purely as it happened of course, had come with him.

"Good morning, Bobby. I'm afraid you will have to excuse us until after lunch." The words were not entirely clear to him, but even so Bobby did grasp that he was expected to abandon his friend, and at once.

Earlier, Thomas had found Rhodë in the kitchen, flouring the pin, getting ready to roll out biscuits. "When you reach a stopping-place, Rhodë, please help Henry put all of the leaves into the dining-table and draw up all the chairs. Then if you will put two of the big candlesticks on the table—just anywhere. I'll position them and light the candles when the time comes. I'll go out and ask Henry to come inside after a little while."

"Yes, Sir. And, Father, will I need to prepare a special dinner? Do you want me to lay the table?"

"No. No, this has nothing to do with dining. But thank you. Edward and I will have our lunch in the breakfast room, as usual."

In apostrophe, a moment later, when Thomas had gone out, Rhodë said: "Miss Grace, come down and help me. Come down and *help* me! I'm afraid he's got so he misses you too much." But she and Henry did as they had been asked.

For Thomas had decided that the best approach would be to have the boy experience emptiness, loneliness, but not without light to guide. And if he learned that lesson only in a general way, it was as well.

When Edward was ushered into the dining room, he was puzzled, but unafraid, for his grandfather had never done anything to hurt him. It seemed twelve people were coming to dinner, with the table open to its full length and all the chairs close around it. Near each end of the table stood a tall silver candlestick, with a candle burning. They were off-axis.

"I want you to sit down, Edward, but at a particular place."

"Which place, Grandfather?"

"You must find it by lining up the two candle-flames. They will point to the place. When you have found it, I want you to sit there for a quarter-hour; that's a long time for a young lad. But you will have some time to think." And he went out. Edward went to the farther end of the table. He had to stand well up on tiptoe in order to see, and even then he was not tall enough to coälign the noonday flames. But he could get the nearer stick to eclipse the farther and assumed that would be as good. However, his line of vision fell between two chairs—just exactly halfway!

He had the presence of mind to try lining up the two candlesticks from the opposite position, before going back to his grandfather in premature perplexity. And this method worked. He sighted right along to the middle of the back of his grandfather's chair. He hurried to take his place in it, and he remembered to start thinking. *Does he want me to know that I will probably take his place here someday, for good? But he has already told me that.* Edward was in the difficult but not uncommon situation of having to decide what to think—to ascertain what he ought to be thinking about. He knew that some people at all times—and all people sometimes—are unable not to think; then it is hard for them to rest. This was not that.

He had been careful not to tear the faded yellow silk cover on the seat of the chair—he knew it was very old and fragile—careful, too, not to mar the lustrous wood. The surface of the table, including that of the removable leaves, was so highly polished that he could see in it a surprisingly undistorted reflection of the chandelier above. From the reflection he tried to count the prisms. His Grandfather had been right: A quarter-hour was a long time. Eighty-three. An odd number. (A prime number, too, though Edward knew nothing about that.) So, probably a wrong number. He looked up at the chandelier itself and counted eighty-six rock-crystals. That might be right. It was hard to be sure; some hung in the way of others. Well, but that was certainly not what he was supposed to be thinking about. He lowered his gaze.

As he did, his eyes fell upon the chair at the other end of the table, the one directly in front of him, but a long way away—his grandmother's chair. He almost saw her sitting in it, but the vision would not quite take shape. He forgot about thinking, then. He tried and tried to see his grandmother, but he could not. Because she was gone forever. He loved her. He knew he was supposed to see her again in Heaven one day. But he didn't especially believe it. He didn't think his grandfather really especially believed it, either, even though he had been the one to tell him so.

Thomas looked in and said: "Time for lunch now, Son."

Edward expected to be asked what he had thought about, but he was not asked. He said: "Grandmother's chair seemed so far away with the table all the way long. I wish we could make the distance shorter…have her closer to us.

"Was that a sort of game, Grandfather? Finding my place by lining up the candles?"

"In a way a game—at first. I think the way in is a game. I think the way out is looking for light beyond light…."

Edward said nothing more, but finished his lunch in silence, because he knew that Thomas was no longer speaking really to him. Not really.

There came a tap upon Thomas' study door. "Come in, please." It was Rhodë, with his afternoon drink. Such a pleasure! A small gallery tray holding a squat, richly cut decanter that contained four ounces of whisky, a silver pail of ice, tongs, a folded linen napkin, a beaker. Rhodë really was Grace's finest memorial. He would never, so long as she lived, sink into unkempt and untended widowhood.

"Father," she ventured, placing the tray upon the tooled black leather top of his desk (which she would not have done if the tray had not been footed), "I was about to go home…but what about the dining room?"

"Oh, all that was to reassure me that Edward is a good-hearted youngster. I am very grateful to you and Henry for setting it up. And do go ahead home, by all means—it's probably past time!"

"Thank you, Sir. I don't know what you set him to doing in there, and Henry and I are always glad to do whatever you need from us—we miss Miss Grace, and if we do, it pains me to think of how much you do, Father. But I could have told you Mr. Edward is a good-hearted—a golden-hearted—boy."

"I hope I never doubted it, and I am very much ashamed of it if I have. I didn't punish him, you know."

"No, Father. I know it's what he said that afternoon. It knocked me winding, and when I crossed the hall and realized you must have heard him, too, my blood went to water. But I knew even then it was just something in his head that an old Colored woman didn't understand."

"Nor an old White man. But watch what you say—we're the same age, I think!"

Rhodë laughed a little. This was intimacy of a kind. "But the dining room—do you want us to put it back as it was?"

"No use to go looking for extra work, any more than to go halfway to meet trouble. It'll be Thanksgiving before you know it, then you'd just have to drag all those things out again."

"Father, it's the thirtieth of August!"

"Still, never mind. Good night."

Now what, Miss Grace? The Canon needs to be guided and urged. What if he's getting into a bad way? You've got to help me help him. Because most of it is just not my place. And you're right here—not in any graveyard. We all talk about you every day. You're with us here. Of course, I've never had a man of my own around, so for all I know, this may not look as bad to you as it sometimes does to me. But, please, Miss Grace, stay close to us.

"Good night, Father."

Thomas settled with as much contentment as was possible for him without his Grace, to read over a few pages of a book George Elkin had leant him. In Nineteen thirty-nine, the Federal Government, either in an effort to simplify, to equalize, or, on the other hand to homogenate and to take under its own control the remnants of a great Country's far-flung and various resources, had placed—at least in legislative theory—all lighthouses, lightships, beacons, and other aids to navigators off the American coasts under the management and cure of the United States Coast Guard.

There had been hurriedly compiled, and in 1940 published, a work entitled "A Catalogue of Lighthouses and other Navigation Aids Placed by Congressional Act under Management of the United States Coast Guard: An Initial Essay." The title bespoke scholarly intent; the result would have been disappointing, except for the qualification "An Initial Essay."

Thomas wanted to craft, from the known principles of an old beacon-system, the heart of a homily…one that Edward could not claim he had made up from nowhere.

Toward the beginning of the section on the Cape Fear Lights he read:

The system for the guidance of navigation at the mouth of the Cape Fear River has become a very complex one, now, as we approach the middle of the Twentieth Century.

It began from the foundation of the First Light, as in modern times it has come to be known by its new custodians. To those, however, who over the past two-and-one-half centuries—and perhaps longer—have lived and wrought either in its shadow or within sight of it, it has always been known as the Old Light…Bowe Bells, as it were, of Brunswick County.

Then other beacons and ranges have come and sometimes gone, guiding or attempting to guide shipping over treacherous shoals and shifting bar to the towns of Southport and, farther upriver, to New Brunswick—an ancient settlement, first called Brunswick Town, and for a brief time, after 1720, the Colonial Capital—and, eventually, through a rather refractory channel to the City of Wilmington, in modern times principal port of the State of North Carolina.

The First Light stands about four miles south of the old Price's Creek range, upon an island to the eastern side of the mouth of the River, called Bewley Island; on a chart dating from 1694, this island is shown, and the name is spelled 'Beaulieu.' The architect of this Tower is unknown. No logistical details are recorded, either, at least not in the annals of the General Assembly. It must have stood for a very long time, for when already apparently no longer considered to be a recently-built structure, it was superseded by the first Bald Head Light, or Cape Fear Light, at a considerable distance south and slightly westward, this tower having itself been constructed at an early date, variously given as 1789 or 1794. Of the First Light no measured drawing, photograph, or copy of first-hand description is to hand at the time of this writing. It is generally reputed to be immense, and in form, unique.

The history of the development of the system as a whole—and there appears to be no period at which there was agreement regarding heights and hydrographic relationships amongst all the lights, beacons, lightships, and buoys which have been mentioned, or are even said to have been mentioned, in documents from the early days of the General Assembly, other surviving records, documents, or commentaries, of which some clearly attempt to make cases against others—is more complex than the system itself. Many early letters—though by no means all—their accounts in this respect being as various and mutually contradictory as in other records, may not be relied upon as useful for indication of fact.

Although the construction of the Cape Fear (Bald Head) Light must have begun, as noted above, and may even have been completed, at an earlier date, it was not first illuminated until 1795. There is the possibility, as there nearly always is, that vested interests of one sort or another bore upon the decision to build anew. The reasons given openly seem to have been, first, that the Old Light (or First Light) was inadequate as a seacoast beacon, as it could not be seen beyond the extensive and perilous shallows, which reach about twenty miles beyond the River's mouth, often concealed beneath a fair sea.

The other objection was that, supposedly through an anomaly—and it is difficult to imagine one that was intrinsic—the distance from which the

Light could be seen varied with the observer's position upon the lantern's circuit. But the discrepancy was clearly real: No fewer than four ships went aground and sank because of it.

The structure known as Bald Head Light and presently standing was built either in 1817 or 1818. It was deactivated in 1935 by the Lighthouse Bureau.

Later that evening Thomas was sitting in the library; Edward lay upon the floor. Thomas had found in the book about lighthouses the passage which he required. Edward was supposed to be reading, from a schoolbook, about the foundation of Rome. Naturally, and only because the task was one required of him, he found the topic of little interest. His thoughts were drifting this way and that, until suddenly a picture of the exuberantly beautiful lily pool on the south side of the house formed itself in his mind. In midsummer, full with its water lilies in intense and extravagant colors, enormous shell-pink lotus blossoms shedding sweet odor, floating plants—water hyacinth, water lettuce, duckweed, others—it seemed, certainly when compared with a photograph of a grizzled-looking quadruped of some kind giving suck through brazen dugs to two fat babies below, the subject of ineffable wonderment and splendor.

Yet to look at the pool from inside the house was difficult. In the dining room you had almost to put your face against the windowpane, turning your head far to the right. From the breakfast room, you had to do the converse. "Grandfather," Edward asked, "why do we put the windows in our houses evenly spaced all the way around? Is it because the four Thrones are evenly spaced around the sun at daybreak?"

Thomas wondered for a moment whether the boy had got into something; then he recognized the allusion. "Because we, as a people, like symmetry. It is a primitive form of balance. It produces a tidy effect upon the eye, and it frees the mind for whatever must be addressed at a given time."

"I'm not sure I understand that."

Thomas closed the volume, leaving a finger inside to mark his place. He looked straight at his grandson and said: "If you think about it for a while, you will probably understand every bit of it. But, so that you can get on with Romulus and Remus, let me see whether I can't put it another way. If you go out through the front door, and there is a window sixteen feet to your left, the right half of your world—just at that moment, of course—is going to seem a little bit empty. But then you look to the right and sixteen feet away is another window like the other. They make a kind of frame, with you in the middle. You feel equally supported from both sides, and you feel like walking straight out into the world to do whatever it is you want to or must do. How's that?"

"I believe I see what you mean. And if we had a window that looked right out over the lily pool, the spacing would be...would be not regular."

"Would be irregular."

"Still, it would be nice to have a good view of the lily pool. You said 'We as a people like symmetry'. Do you think there are any other people who would rather have the windows jumbled? But at least be able to see the best of the things outside?"

"First, let me point out that we enjoy seeing what is outside as much as any other people, though we prefer to go outside in order to see it. But, yes, there is a people who do things like poke round holes in their houses so as to be able to 'view the moon' at a particular time of year. And things of that sort"

"Who are they, Grandfather?"

But Thomas had reopened the book.

"Who did you say they are?"

"I didn't say." So after looking for a minute more at the picture of Romulus, Remus, and the she-Wolf, Edward asked again: "Who are the people who make holes in the wall just so they can see the moon?" Thomas looked up. He did not answer immediately. Then: "The God-damned Japanese."

Edward was thunderstruck. He pretended to read for a few minutes more, then kissed his grandfather goodnight and went up to bed. As he lay in the darkness, trying to think of an explanation for the occurrence of the impossible, he at last concluded: *Grandfather must have had a little stroke.*

The next day, at school, he said to his friend Bobby: "I think my grandfather must have had a little stroke last night." Bobby did not know exactly what a "stroke" was; neither, for that matter, did Edward.

But when Bobby saw Miss Bena Lucas at lunchtime, since she had been his second grade teacher and must know, Bobby said: "Edward's grandfather has had a stroke." Miss Bena was horrified!

"How," she asked, "do you know?"

"Edward told me himself." When she heard that, Miss Bena hurried off to the principal's office, where there was a telephone. First she rang the little hospital in New Brunswick, but they had not admitted any Thomas Strikestraw overnight. It must be graver even than she had imagined! She made another call, interjecting an enquiry of Sarah Elkin at the telephone exchange. But Sarah knew nothing. The stroke must have been so severe that the patient had had to be taken to the larger and better-equipped hospital in Wilmington, so Miss Bena asked Sarah to put her through. But Thomas was not there, either.

Knowing how fond her sister-in-law was of Thomas Strikestraw, Miss Bena hesitated to trouble her with the ominous news. But she did not hesitate long. "Alenda, this is Bena. Do you know anything about Thomas's condition, or where he is?"

"Do you have any reason to think his 'condition' has changed in any especial way?"

She hadn't heard yet, poor thing! "Oh, no, no! Nothing of that kind; just calling to say hello, to see if you are—and everyone is—all right," Miss Bena lied, with near-perfect implausibility.

"Nonsense, Bena. You've evidently telephoned for some particular reason, and I want to know what it is."

"Oh, Dear! The children! Bobby McCallum told me that Edward had told him…."

"Bena, when you have to use that many 'told's, then distortion of fact is bound to be in the works. Give me the telephone number there, and stay where you are. I'll let you know something presently." Alenda was a woman who began things at the beginning. She telephoned to Thomas.

In the evening, after supper, before going into his study to try to forge the homily he had in mind, Thomas said to his grandson, who had finally turned the page in his history book, the one with the bronze twins and the *lupa* on it, "Edward, did you say at school that I had had a stroke?"

"Yes, Sir."

"Do you mind telling me why you said that?"

"It's just something you sometimes say about old people."

On a lazy afternoon in New Brunswick the loose ends of the day were coming unraveled and Edward and Bobby were in a desultory way trying to tie them off, before it got to be too late. "Let's go to the tree house," Edward suggested. They got up and started to the back of the property, where a cluster of mature sweetgum trees rose into the air—where the year before, upon a framework of timbers through-bolted to the slenderest trees (Thomas had insisted upon this building-code), merely nailed to the thicker trunks, where these were contingent, they had laid a decking of clear pine boards. There were no walls, no roof. There was no ladder. You had to be able to climb one of the trees; this had kept out a good many undesirables.

When it came down to it, there was only a certain amount you could do with a tree house besides build it. You could have picnics in it. You could hide in it from your friends. You could in vain beseech your grandfather to be allowed to spend the night in it. And that was about all.

But once aloft, Edward had an inspiration. He had begun to have them rather often; Bobby seemed not to have many at all. "We can," he said, "discover and give names to stars!"

"How?"

"I will lie in a certain position on the flooring boards; to make sure I can lie exactly there at any other time, you make an outline all around me on the boards. Then I can draw your outline beside mine."

"Who's going to go and get a pencil?"

"I always have a pencil with me."

"All right. Then what?"

"Then each of us chooses a name—we'll get to make them up ourselves. Then we each pick out a limb above us, against the sky, that branches at a certain place, or two that cross, as we look straight up. We memorize it. Then at night, when the stars are out, we come back, get in position, and then give a name to the star that's nearest the branching-point."

Bobby's enthusiasm, though probably real, was limited. "Isn't that a lot of trouble to go to?"

"Not for naming a star! Pick a spot and lie down."

And so it was that on a clear night a week later the astronomy had added to it "Harropit" and "QZ-38."

Thomas was finding the symbolism for his homily on near and distant lights intractable. He had now grown to feel that a story that could *not* be finished held no truth. It was Saturday evening—late Saturday evening—so that time was growing short.

A Homily delivered by the Reverend Canon Thomas Grantly Strikestraw, in Christ Church:

"In the Name + of the Father, and of the Son, and of the Holy Ghost."

"Amen."

"Dear people of God, I propose to speak to you this morning about a journey, the journey that each of us is in the midst of making. Among noted teachers down through the ages, and, as I have no doubt, amongst some of yourselves, there is not perfect agreement about when life begins—in the extreme, whether it begins at all!—and when it ends. Preponderantly, we do not think it ends finally.

"Gestation ends in childbirth in life in the world we know; life ends in death. We do not know how death ends, but most of us think it does, and a convenient expression for that ending of death is 'Heaven.'

"A question not, I think, amply examined in the teaching of the Holy Catholic Church is: What is the nature of Heaven, and in particular, whether Heaven, too, is not itself another stage of transition. But certainly this is a question for those far advanced in their meditations, and the commoner concepts of the life to come are a great deal more straightforward, whether or not they ought to be.

"My old nurse, for example, described Heaven to me as a place where we would all float about on little pink clouds, drinking milk and honey. I hardly slept that night, from anxiety about the boredom and the monotony of the diet.

"Most people, I think, regard Heaven—and vaguely, at that—as being where the Almighty Father reigns, where His will is done, where otherwise we shall live very much as we do here, except with all wrongs put right.

"But of course no one knows. Some thinkers conceive of a realm of which you and I, in our present state, would in all likelihood recognize no feature.

"However, I want now to change course, and as it were to say, as we maritime folk do, 'Ready about!'."

And little Alice Barnes cried out in reflex: "Ready!"

"Excellent!" Thomas continued, "Helm to lee!" as Alice was escorted briskly out of the church by Mrs. Barnes. "For finding ourselves upon a journey, yet having little if any idea where we are going, we need a guide. Let our troublous circumstance be thought of as darkness, and we find that we need light to show us our course.

"A ship sailing down the Great River beside which we live, in order to escape the shadows of crowding structure or of dense overhanging growth, to make way through waning day or through night itself, in order to reach the ocean and then be always in the sun of a new kind of life, of voyaging unimpeded, must be guided by beacons, to be sure of escaping danger in form of underwater banks, wrecks of sunken ships, other shallows of harm.

"Hereabout, in order to be safe, the ship must run down a channel close to the western riverbank, but at the mouth of the river she must turn very hard to port and follow the channel as it runs northeast. Long ago, as many of you know, the way was shown by two beacons on shore (The familiar ruins of them are there still). One was closer to the River mouth, the other farther away. They were so situated that the helmsman, steering a course so as to keep the two beacons in a line with each other (for the one behind had been made taller, so that they both might be seen at once), would be able to keep his ship in safe waters.

"Furthermore, the farther beacon was at one time placed on a transverse railway, so that it could be moved, according to a contemporary account, 'to the right or left, to suit the changes in the channel.'

"This was midway through the Nineteenth Century, at a time when in Western Europe and in this Country engineering was already far advanced, so that this ingenious system was probably not thought very remarkable, though it still seems so to me. It was flawed, however, and as it proved, unable to mark the range over the bar, the two beacons—to return to the contemporary record—'being so near each other that considerable deviation from the true course [was] necessary to make them appear to separate.'

"We imagine our journey—just as a figure—to be across water. The darkness that surrounds us upon this journey is a figure of our imperfect knowledge. Not long after we set out, we see a lighthouse, tall, and blazing brightly, as the Old Light did, as Bald Head Light did afterward. And we set our course for it, using whatever resources we have or may acquire—the gifts and faculties and discernment that we all have, if in varying degrees.

"As we come closer, sometimes only after many years of voyaging, we begin to see that there is a stricter course which we must hold to. And there, just when we need them, is a pair of beacons, the farther one taller and brighter. We align their midnight flames. We arrive safely at the first and begin making for the second, keeping to our revised course as closely as we can.

"And now I shall say what I think must happen next: Lo and behold, another beacon appears beyond the second, and, aligning our course accordingly, if necessary, we reach various stages and we go on according to our best judgment, and in guidance other lights appear! And so, once launched, we quest our way. Each next light is taller, each blazes with mightier fire. Somewhere along the way, our right reckoning gradually turns to knowledge—partial at first—but finally our courses become wholly true, as what has been wholly Other becomes wholly known."

He turned toward the altar, lifted his hands. "And now unto God the Father, God the Son, and God the Holy Ghost be ascribed as is most justly due, all might, majesty, dominion, power, and glory, both now and forever."

"Amen."

Before the oblations, leaving the ushers and acolyte stranded, Thomas hurried down from the pulpit and out by way of the sacristy to try to forestall any retribution leveled at little Alice Barnes, and to tell her mother how charming her impulsive rejoinder had been and what a fine sailor she must be shaping into.

Joe Watkins said not a word all the way home from Church that Sunday. He stopped at an intersection, where the light was green. He sat and stared out through the windshield. The light changed two times. Lucille, seeing that no traffic was being hindered, relaxed her grip upon the arm rest. She did not know what Joe's silence meant. She definitely did not get as far as wondering what the homily had meant.

Edward and Bobby had graduated from high school in the spring. Edward would go—far away, as he considered—to college at the end of the summer.

He did not know what Bobby would do. He had not seen him or spoken with him often during the year past—No, longer than that. The children of New Brunswick, now grown into young people, had ventured from their neighborhoods, from their early ways, from their first comrades, and had regrouped according to other considerations—romantic attachments, new interests in common, and, often, into groupings corresponding to those of their parents or even of their grandparents.

So Edward had telephoned to Bobby to suggest an outing to Bewley Island, to look again at the vast fabric of the Old Light, to have a picnic in its shadow, maybe a swim. Maybe they would find old Mr. Benny Ormond, hear his story again—maybe a little more of it this time, better understand what more they might hear—for nobody had yet heard it all. Everybody agreed in this.

Each of them was prepared for the possibility that this would be a reliving and a leave-taking. They found themselves still at ease with each other, recurred here and there to the past they had spent so much of together, speculated without awkwardness about the future, even though each had come to understand that this future would be one thing for one of them, another for the other. Still, each was relieved to some extent when they met Mr. Benny, walking toward them down the narrow strand. His little cottage stood nearby, the only dwelling in that part of the wildwood.

Benny Ormond had resorted there to recollect himself after the Great War, but in the end had never gone back to living with his people in town. He became reclusive. He attended Church on the second Sunday in Advent, every year unfailingly, but not at any other time. His wartime experiences were believed to account for much of his eccentricity; it was largely a right opinion.

Bobby said: "Yes, but tell us again; we're older now and we can understand it better."

"When you do understand it, I hope you'll come back and explain it to me. But at least I can tell you what happened, whether it makes sense to me or not." The three men fell into step, walking together, up the hard sand and down, at the edge of the softly sounding sea. It was not the kind of story you sat down to listen to.

"The War was blight enough upon the earth; the influenza epidemic of 1918 made it a scourge of God, so people thought. The War was let loose upon mankind by his own hand. But the Plague—it was a plague if there ever has been a plague—was laid upon us by the hand of God!

"Half my Company and all my platoon were stricken with it. We were all put into the field hospital—but not all at the same time. Because as one bunch was being brought in, another was being sent out, and that's feet first, you understand. Most times. Finally, on my ward, there were only four of us left—patients, I mean to say; the old doctors and nurses were spared, for some reason. To carry out their work of mercy, I always have thought. Although, the young orderlies dropped like flies...like us.

"At first, the four of us seemed to be getting well. Because over all, a good many people actually did recover, but nothing to compare to the number that didn't. Then one relapsed, as they called it—the nurses.

It came time to turn out the lights, and I fell asleep. Next morning, all the curtains around his cot—he had been to my left—had been pulled back. The cot had been made up fresh and crisp, the way they do in the military.

"That afternoon, the other two out of the four had the inflammation in their lungs get worse; some corpsmen came in an ambulance and took them off to a bigger hospital where they thought they might be able to give them stronger treatment, or something of that kind.

"They brought me some broth, then, and I found I had an appetite for it. Then I ate some bread along with the broth. My strength started to come back. They let me walk around in the mud outside the tents. And eventually I got well. Three of us, I thought, out of all those hundreds. So they got me a berth on a troop-transport sailing back to America.

"But I found out from the driver who took me to the quay that the two men who had been taken away had died, one in the ambulance on the way and the other just a few minutes after they got where they were going. I boarded that ship and lay down on my bunk and I was shaken up, because I realized that I was the only one to have been spared. And I didn't see why."

Nobody said anything just then. They looked at the sand; Bobby kicked at a broken conch shell. They looked at the channels of sea- and river-water running alongside and around the Old Light, isolating them beneath, and watched as a breeze stirred its surface. They gazed up at the dark immensity of the Tower, as the sky clouded over above it. Edward, knowing all this must herald a rain squall since it was only mid-August, thought the atmosphere harbored undertones of November's grey and chill. And as he thought, a sprinkling of bright yellow hackberry leaves fluttered down ahead, some falling upon the sand, others alighting upon the water, troubled just into cats' paws. He finally said: "Well, Mr. Benny, if only one could make it, I'm glad it was you."

"Thank you, Son. So am I. But I do wonder about it. I wonder about it all the time. Because it happened again. Not the same thing. If you survived the influenza, you didn't get it again. But the same *kind* of thing happened.

"The transport, which sailed the afternoon of the day after I went on board, was making for the mouth of the Channel—the English Channel, I mean to say—and the North Atlantic. Halifax was going to be her first port-of-call. She struck a mine that the sweeps had missed. Some of us were on deck, and we saw it. It slid along the starboard hull without detonating, for some reason, but when it got amidships it exploded. The hull was breached, but not widely. Some crew and some troops were killed then and there. I swear to you; I swear to God I didn't take a scratch, yet I had been standing right above where the thing blew up." Under his breath he muttered to himself: "But I don't have to swear to God, because He knows. He knows. I know He knows. I know He did it."

Between them, Bobby and Edward were able to piece this and other soliloquies together later. And they wondered greatly at the words they had heard him say. Returning to his account, Benny Ormond continued: "The ship took on water, and soon she was riding lower. I heard later that the captain radioed for a tow. I guess that's what he was preparing for when he started bringing her about. But by the time he had done it, a breeze had come up and looked to be stiffening to a gale.

"It was November. Freezing cold. The sea was nearly ice. Seawater got to one of the boilers—at least one, anyhow. It exploded, not far from where the mine had detonated in the first place; that was the explosion that sank the ship. Water started to pour in on the starboard, so fast that there was not enough time for it to spread across the beam and get...."

"Equilibrated?"

"Evened out, that's it. And she listed badly. The order came to abandon ship. A lot of the men—troops, mostly—started putting the starboard boats over, counting on their swinging away from the hull. And they did. But it was a madhouse over on that side, with men swarming and struggling but not knowing what they were struggling to do. I decided to do whatever could be done on the port side; I knew it wouldn't be much. I had to browbeat some others into helping me. It looked like it would be impossible to get any boat free of her stays. Most of my bunch left, slipped off one by one—went around to starboard, and they paid for it, too." Benny began to mutter again: "Four of us. Seemed like the same four. All over again."

In his normal voice, he went on: "Lifeboat Six. Or, was it Seven? We struggled at the davits. Somehow she started to come free. We boarded her, and just then she slid down across the hull. The ship was away over by then, because we struck against—I could have sworn—her keel just as it broke the surface. One of us four was—You boys see, there were four again?—thrown from the boat, and we didn't see him again." Muttering: "One first, two left. Besides me."

Aloud: "The lifeboat crashed off the keel—if that's really what it was—

and ended up in the drink, but upright. More or less; she did quickly right herself, though. We were able to pull away—just in time to see the ship go almost all the way over. She crushed or drowned the men on the other side. I guess, just as they were thinking they'd get clear. We pulled. I don't even think all of us were pulling in the same direction. We were hoven away at first, but we began to be drawn back as the ship went down. By then, though, we had got ourselves straight, and we pulled all together. Finally the suction eased. It gave up its hold on us, and we were safe away.

"Did you boys really want to hear me tell all this over again? You've heard it before. I expect I've put in some details I've imagined. Probably left out some things I've forgotten. I'm an old man."

"I think you have been telling it to yourself, Sir, this time."

"Ben's crazy story. Crazy Ben's story. It's old. There's been another war. But this is what happened to me, and I don't know what it means." Muttering: "But I do know what it means. I'm sure I know."

Aloud: "We passed by several bodies and tried to get them aboard. But we couldn't. One of the other two of us—he was pretty far gone himself—fell overboard trying to pull a dead man in. Then he was gone, himself. The last one froze to death before I was rescued."

Once back in New Brunswick, Edward and Bobby came to an intersection which they must leave in different directions. They enacted a scene they had once upon a time seen in a film. They had elaborated it a good deal, of course. It represented a tragic leavetaking and ended with each saying: "This is it!" "This is it!" Now they realized that, for practical considerations, this probably really was it. Bobby went off to the left; Edward continued to Front Street. They were friends from childhood; they had never, therefore, learned to shake hands with each other.

Edward found nobody at home, and this suited him, for he had a small ritual to perform. He climbed into the tree house, then hoisted a two-inch paintbrush and a jar of India ink, which he had diluted. The outlines of two little boys could hardly be seen, with defects through some line segments; but Edward knew the two figures well. With quick strokes he painted in the forms, watching the ink all but vanish into the dry boards. He stood to look down on his work: Shadows cast—indirectly, it might be—by starlight.

VIII

"To suffer woes which Hope thinks infinite;
To forgive wrongs darker than Death or Night;
To defy Power which seems Omnipotent;
To love, and bear; to hope...."
P.B Shelley: *Prometheus Unbound*, 4. 570-573

MANY TIMES, WHEN a provisionally unwanted child is born, it meets with its mother's unexpected, undoubted, and unaccountable love. Explanations for this have been put forward: When she sees the child, the mother realizes she really did want it all along. Or the mother sees the newborn infant, and hears its cry; instinctively, she loves it and wishes to nourish it. That is supposed to be the way nature has of propagating the species. From farther fetched comes the idea, undoubtedly first propounded by fathers (or by men who thought they were), that the newborn babe calls to the mother's mind her love for her mate, which she then shares with her child. Like most subjects of speculation, this one leads to plausible ideas sometimes, and sometimes it doesn't.

Lilia Belle Gadsden approached the birth of her child with other concerns.

She did not place the yet unborn baby either in the category of 'wanted,' or in that of 'unwanted.'

Her religious beliefs were not fundamentalist, though outwardly she professed them to be. She suspected that those of her family weren't, either, although they, too, professed them to be. She did not consider that many people had given enough thought to those tenets even to be qualified to profess them, and she knew that she herself had not.

But there is one passage of Holy Scripture which she did accept, and literally: That men are born "not of blood, nor of the will of the flesh, nor of the will of man, but of God." For she understood the absolute reality of the second life within herself, and recognized it as the work of a mightier Hand than man's.

Yet she silently asked her God, every day, and every night she asked Him, why life was to be given out of such sorrow and hatred and wreckage as were now hers. But she did not demand an answer. She knew better than that. If an answer were to come, then it would come. As it fell out, she waited all her life for that answer. It never came.

The answer might not come, but the child would come. And then what to do? For it would belong to one of three sorts: A child obviously "of mixed blood," as the picturesque and ill-conceived expression of the time had it, welcome nowhere, the worst outcome of all. Or it might prove to be so much like its progenitor as to be taken for a white child; that would be the most perilous possibility. Or, by God's grace, it might prove exactly like a Colored baby. That would be safest and best—for it to seem to belong where it had been bestowed.

Between Thanksgiving and Christmas of 1943, Laurence had received a note of enquiry and then a visit from Rita Paget. When she arrived at Woodleigh, she seemed to Laurence to be in mourning, because she was very conservatively dressed and in her manner, most restrained. Of course, she *was* in mourning, and Laurence had to grapple for a long while afterward with his own failure to have expected this, with his preconceived belief that Mrs. Paget would not, or even could not, have been moved by her husband's death to this state.

"Good morning, Mrs. Paget."

"Mr. Ashfield." She gave him her hand.

"Besides offering you my condolence upon your husband's death, is there anything I can do?" They sat down in the east drawing room, where Laurence had started what he termed a "little blaze." Outside there was December's grey, cloud, cold, and rain. In wintry gusts, the movable window sashes rattled lightly. One could for some reason smell apples ripening somewhere.

"I hope there is. I have heard that the young woman whom my husband...."

"Lilia Belle Gadsden."

"Yes. I have heard—but I don't know whether to believe it—that she is going to have a child, as the result of...."

"Yes."

"She is?"

"Yes, she is." And to give her time to reset her composure he went on: "There are no plans, as it stands now, that I know of." Rita was not yet prepared to take up the conversation. "But please let me assure you that Lilia Belle and her child are provided for."

"But that is why I have come; I want to provide, myself, if there is a way."

"That is very gracious of you."

"I am not in a position to be gracious, I know. Although I have been surprised, and grateful, for the kindness many people here have shown me, I know I'll never get it right—about life in the South. I'm afraid now I won't ever get it right about life anywhere. But before I go back, I would like to do something for the child—that is, the girl—and her child."

"That's very generous of you, as I've said, and I'm sure whatever you want to do will be very much appreciated."

"I'm sure it won't be. And that is why I have come to you. So that the money, which is all I have to give, can go to them through you, even if the family would not want it, coming from me."

"Your feelings do you a lot of credit, Mrs. Paget." She felt an intense wish to ask him to call her "Rita," but she knew it would be presumptuous, since it might suggest to him that she wanted to use his Christian name, also. "The truth is, sometimes our notions of pride—and I think this kind of thing may be commoner down here—lead us to do things like that. I mean, not to accept gifts in the spirit in which they are offered. Codified behavior. But I think these particular people can be dealt with very reasonably. They are good, sensible folk."

"But you will help me? I really do not want them to know. You see, I have never had anything of my own. And so what I offer will really be coming from my husband...."

"But, coming through your hands, such a gift would have to be separated from any kind of bitterness."

So Rita Paget wrote out a check and handed it to Laurence. He was startled when he read the draught, and said: "This is most open-handed, to say the least. We shall have to establish a trust."

"That is the kind of thing I had hoped for, but I do not know how to go about it. Then, you will help me?"

"Of course. You are the grantor. 'Grantrix,' actually. But I don't think they use that anymore. All I need to know from you now is who you want the beneficiaries to be, and who you want the trustees to be."

"The beneficiaries…they are the ones for whom the money will be spent?"

"Yes."

"Then the mother and the child."

"And the 'trustee or trustees' decide when and for what in particular it is to be spent."

"I would like for you to have that position."

"Very well. But it is usual to have two trustees—sometimes more. That's so each can check up on the rest. To be sure the money will be spent properly."

"You decide."

"Well, I think you ought to consider yourself."

"No, I don't know enough about it. Besides, as I've said, I think the farther away I stay from this, the more good it will do." Inwardly, Laurence was dissenting increasingly from that idea.

They were surprised now by the entry of Lavinia and the Spaniels. Lavinia and the Spaniels were surprised in their turn. But when Laurence had made introductions, Lavinia walked over to Rita and took her hand in both of hers, saying: "My Dear, I am so sorry; I have been thinking of you constantly ever since the Trouble. If I can be of help in any way, let me know!" Then she went out with her hounds.

She is so kind to me, and she doesn't even know about the money. But it is probably not so much to them.

Laurence was by now smiling. "I do have to say this, Mrs. Paget, about trusts—I guess we're all to a point hypocrites; I am, I find—that although we need a second trustee to keep watch over the first, still it is best that we be able to give control to one, in case that need should arise, by making him able to fire the other. Be thinking about that. I will get a draft copy of the instrument to you as soon as I can have it drawn up."

"This amount of money probably will not last long, but it is all I have to give."

So Laurence explained to her about investment, interest, reinvestment, and the consequent munificence of her gift.

As Laurence was saying Goodbye and seeing Rita Paget out, Lavinia reappeared and invited her to stay for lunch.

During the weeks before her confinement, Lilia Belle had confided to her grandmother that she had misgivings about the child she was going to bear and what these misgivings were. Miss Izora had agreed with her estimates of the child's wellbeing under each circumstance, but had said: "It is going to be a Colored child." Lilia Belle didn't even think of saying: "How do you know?" Miss Izora always knew. There was too great a tale of examples to allow room for questioning. Still, she could not take comfort from that assurance. Her trust was not so great.

Miss Izora, though, had gone on to say: "But you stay close by, and you must come to me as soon as it starts. That way, all will go well."

"Mama," Lilia Belle said to her grandmother—she was holding onto the back of a wooden chair—"I think I've twisted my back."

"No, Daughter. It's starting. The baby is coming."

"It's in the wrong place, Mama. It's right in the middle of my back, down low."

"Tell me when it goes."

"It's going now."

"The baby is coming. Tell me when the pain comes back."

"It's coming back now."

"Has it moved around any? Around to the front?"

"No, Ma'am. It's just the same. And now it's going again."

"When it has gone away, come and lie down."

"Yes, Ma'am." When she had got herself settled upon the daybed in the living room, she thought at first that the pain had stopped. But it was only that the interval had got temporarily longer. Miss Izora placed a cool hand on the girl's protuberant belly and pressed in a very little. Presently, she felt the inexorable hardening of the uterus begin, but it was several seconds before Lilia Belle reported the return of discomfort. "It's coming back and it is moving to my sides, to the front."

"I can't see anybody in the lanes or anybody in the fields. There's no way to get word. But when the pain goes off, I'll tell you what I do see."

A few minutes later: "What do you see, Mama?"

"The baby; he's coming."

"A boy baby?"

"Yes, and a Colored baby. Black as night."

The baby was born, was named Benjamin, and there was unexpectedly great rejoicing. Lilia Belle had harbored no wish for herself that this child could fulfill. But she recognized him as a divine gift, no matter the circumstances of his conception. She gave him all the nourishment she could summon, and all the mother-love, for it was going to have to last him a lifetime.

Everybody had come. The women were seeing to the new mother. Parker and Laurence sat in rocking chairs on the front porch of Miss Izora's house on the "Street" running back from Woodleigh and smoked cigars, which both hated. But they felt like uncles. Tommy smoked, too, and talked with the White men, though he stood. He felt like a father. Colored relatives stood in the front yard, smiling and laughing soberly; groups of the women, now and then, would go around and enter the house through the back door.

At one point, Lavinia and Alina came out onto the porch. They didn't know it, but they had been sent away from the childbed; a rite in which they could have no part had to take place, but there was no resentment. Colored people did things one way; White people, another. There was no matter. Not there. And not then.

Miss Izora both saw visions and dreamed dreams. She saw the child's life, saw that it would be a good one. There would be trouble enough, but then all would be well.

Ben was born in August, 1944. Lilia Belle cared for him meticulously for two months, but all the time she was saying Goodbye, God keep you. Then, around the anniversary of the Trouble, she slipped away. She knew about the trust. She knew that many would come forward to care for her little boy. She left a note. It told of her love for her people. It told of her love for her son. It contained an explanation—which none of those she was leaving behind could entirely grasp. It ended: "Don't forget me. But don't come looking for me."

In secret, she boarded the northbound train. She had expected to sit up all night. But the conductor came to her just as the bright dome lights in the railroad car were being dimmed for the hours of sleep. "Come with me, Miss [He had said 'Miss' because he was himself a Negro]. Your accommodations have been changed." He took her to a "roomette," which had a washbasin of its own, a freshly made-up berth, a soft light that burned all night.

Rita Paget took Lilia Belle's place in the Pullman car. She had not been sleeping, anyway.

Lilia Belle's son Ben, spending his sixteenth year with his aunt and uncle, Mary Alice and Tommy Araby, as he had spent all his other years, had run away from home. He had left before daylight. He had been away all the previous day and night, and for most of that morning. The little children had been lied to; Mary Alice had been distraught and hadn't been able to come up to Woodleigh House to work. This had not happened before.

They had decided not to tell Miss Izora about it. Even so, halfway through the morning she had tapped on Mary Alice's door and whispered: "He's coming back, now, Daughter; he's on his way home; I can see him coming across the field." At midday he had arrived. But all was not well.

Looking for him, asking for him down at the Crossroads, Tommy had learned the cause of the trouble: Mr. Easterlin at the filling station, which was also the grocery store, had seen Andy Hawkins (the next-to-eldest son) pull up to the pumps—there were two, one for "high-test," the other for "regular" gasoline—with three other youngsters in his car, just as Ben Araby (for from the beginning he had been called by this name) was going out of the store, and had heard him shout: "Black Bastard!" The other boy in the car, whom Easterlin hadn't recognized, repeated the insult, and then one of the girls in the back seat had leaned out of the car and had screamed: "You probably don't even know who your *mother* is!" And then, giggling and howling, they had sped away.

Tommy was in great distress and had walked up to the house to ask Laurence's advice, who answered: "As to Ben, tell him we're thankful he has come home again, that he will occasionally hear that kind of thing, but only from that kind of people. I will go now and see what I can do about the Hawkins boy."

Then Laurence drove down to the Crossroads. First, he spoke with Mr. Easterlin, not in order to confirm the account, but to discover whether either of the girls had been recognized. The one who had shouted at Ben was exactly who Laurence had expected, so that that matter was already dealt with. After thanking Mr. Easterlin, he went out, past the Post Office, which was naturally closed at that time, and past the vacant lot, once so blasted, now green with lush weeds and sparkling with late snowdrops, two rows of them, ghost of a walkway, untrodden for so many springs upon so many others.

Nobody was in the Hardware Store but the proprietor, who said: "Good afternoon, Mr. Ashfield."

"Good afternoon, Mr. Hawkins."

"May I help you?"

"Yes, if you will. I am very sorry to trouble you with this at all, but particularly during business-hours."

"No trouble, Mr. Ashfield."

"I hope not. Is there anyone else here?"

"Just we two."

"I wonder whether you will ask your son Andy to come and see me, when he can find the time."

"Is there anything the matter?" The poor man grew pale, but with a resigned and familiar sort of pallor.

"Nothing at all for you to give another thought to. But please tell him that it is important, to an extent urgent.

The youth arrived just at suppertime. Mary Alice had got herself together early enough to serve midday dinner and so was there to answer the door. She had been coached and was ready.

"I'm here to see Mr. Ashfield," Andy Hawkins said, cockily as he could. But a glimpse through the sidelight of quiet, select grandeur and space, of mystic antiquity, had already taken some of the wind out of his sails. They were not very capacious sails, to begin with.

"Who shall I say is asking for him?"

"What?"

"Your name, please." Mary Alice was by any standard a magnificent looking woman. We have already taken note of her cat's-green eyes. These she now held unmoving. Staring directly into the setting sun, which made them paler. To Andy they seemed unseeing, like those of an otherwise lifelike statue, spawning in the boy the onset of fear.

Yet there exists a kind of impertinence, usually seen in persons of little breeding, that seems limitless: "Mr. Hawkins," he said in reply.

"I'll tell him," Mary Alice answered. "Go around to the back." And she closed the door.

Andy Hawkins was so startled by this that, without hesitation, he 'went around to the back.' It was Laurence himself who answered the back door, stepping directly outside. *Let him see what it feels like not to be allowed inside, not even through the back door.* He began: "I have been told that you called Ben Araby a 'bastard,' and publicly."

"He is a bastard."

"What, exactly, do you mean by that word?"

"Oh, I know what 'bastard' means; it's somebody without a father."

"Everybody has a father."

"All right; everybody has a father. But not everybody knows who his father is."

"Or another kind of 'bastard' may know who his father is, but know also that his father was never married to his mother; that is exactly the point I am coming to. But it can wait for a time. What do you imagine can be gained by calling someone in that position a 'bastard'?"

"Just a little fun, I guess."

"If that is your idea of 'fun,' then I hope you'll never have very much of it. But if a little 'fun' is to be gained, what is to be lost?"

"Nothing."

"What about your standing as a gentleman?"

"Who wants to be a 'gentleman'?"

"I ought to have foreseen that, in your case, it is an idle question." And with a kind of glee at once both reprehensible and excusable, Laurence saw Andy Hawkins' eyes narrow, as he felt the stripe. "But tell me this: What do you think is lost by the one who is called 'bastard'?"

"I don't care."

"Don't you? Well, we've established that you know what the term means, and that you don't care how it feels to be called it."

"That's right," he said, throwing his head back, folding his arms over his chest, a pure-and-simple fool.

"Come with me down into the garden; I don't want to be overheard." And starting down, turning, over his shoulder he added: "And you won't want me to be overheard." Laurence led the boy out onto the stretch of clipped lawn surrounding the lily pool, hedged with desperate box and overhung by flowering trees, among which was the crabapple that wasn't doing very well.

Since Laurence judged that by now the boy was merely going through motions, but was to a degree inwardly dismantled, he allowed himself to overdo things a bit. He began by glancing about furtively, and then he said: "Here are my recommendations to you…." But the boy had a little fight left in him, which made Laurence feel less caddish for going on, and sneered and began to slouch away into the dusk.

When he had got about ten yards off, Laurence called out after him, then came up slowly in the gloaming. Through the shadows his eyes glittered, in fact with mischief. Andy Hawkins stood this time. "You did not let me tell you what will happen if you don't follow my recommendations. Before God, I have never yet spoken about this to a soul, in all the—What is it?—twenty or so years since you were born. Not even to old Dr. Lambert. And he took the story of your birth, so far as I know, with him to the grave.

"But listen to my words; do as I say,"—now he was speaking in conspiratorial whisper, hoarse, as for the stage, almost as though he were performing a part in *Il Struggietore* (his opera, and definitely a work in progress)—"and do it no later than Easter Even. Otherwise, everybody for miles around will know who *your* real father is." Then, after sentences of instruction, the two parted.

Lavinia was already seated at the supper table, which had been set up in the west drawing room, and she had seen, first through the west windows and then through the south ones, Andy Hawkins cycling away through the twilight. Something about the way he was pedaling suggested…Was it panic? Undirected haste?

Laurence came in. He unfolded his napkin into his lap. "Sorry to keep you waiting," he said, "but it was rather important." He realized that the diabolic light probably still gleamed in his eyes, but he couldn't help it and it fretted him, because Lavinia was capable of being severe when she suspected that mischief had spilled over into malevolence.

At this time, Mary Alice entered the room looking entirely bland. From a decanter she poured a small glassful of chilled white wine for each of them, then said: "If that will be all, Miss Lavinia?"

"Of course, Mary Alice. Go and see to things at home. I'm sorry you've had such a trying day."

Mary Alice turned to Laurence: "How did I do, Mr. Laurence?"

"Splendidly, Mary Alice; and wait till I tell you how *I* did!"

On the Wednesday of Holy Week, Andy Hawkins cycled up to Woodleigh again. This time, he went to the back of the house and climbed the steps to the verandah. When he knocked at the door, Mary Alice answered, and said: "Good evening, Mr. Hawkins. Have you come to see Mr. Ashfield again?"

"Yes, I have. Is he at home?"

"He is. I'll fetch him. Won't you step inside?"

"No, thanks; I'll just wait out here."

Soon, Laurence appeared and said: "Good afternoon, Andy. What can I do for you?"

"Could we go back down into the garden?" They went down the stairs into the intoxicating afternoon. Bulbs of all kinds had pushed out of the earth and into bloom. The cherry-trees, flowering almonds, crabapples (except for the refractory one beside the steps), and dogwood were all covered with buds, some with blossoms. Was all this supposed to be going on at the same time?

"Yes," said the Faun of clear marble, as he poured water from a basin into the farther end of the lily pool; "It is how Spring mollifies us, just before her final outflanking manoeuvre and capture, how she prepares us to let life flow into ourselves anew."

"I did what you told me to do," Andy said, once they were out of any earshot and protected by an overarching rose, *Rosa fortuniana* it was, that shed white petals all around them.

"I heard you had."

"How?"

"I specified you were to make your apology with certain witnesses present—the same people who heard your insult."

"Well, I did say I was sorry. I was forced to say it. But I'll tell you this: I don't feel sorry."

"I can't exercise control over your feelings; only, and as it turns out, over some of your actions. You probably can't, yourself."

"Anyway, now that I've done it…all that you said you wanted…I think I deserve something in return."

"And what is that?"

"I want you to tell me who my real father is, and to promise not to tell anybody else."

"Your real father is Mr. George Hawkins, as far as I know, the father of you brothers and sisters."

The boy stood silent and unmoving. The Faun continued pouring water profligately, as though there might be an endless supply. Water, opposite, spilled too into the catch-basin of cress.

"If I thought or knew about anything irregular in you parentage, do you really think I would dishonor your mother, whom I have every cause to respect, by telling anybody about it?"

Laurence imagined that Andy wanted to call him, too, a "bastard." But it was obvious that he could not speak. He grabbed up his bicycle from where it lay upon the ground and was soon out of sight.

Two years passed by. One day, at evening, Tommy Araby, waiting on the back steps to the kitchen house, said to his wife's nephew: "Sit down here, Son, and listen while I tell you about your Mama."

"A whole lot of people have already told me about my Mama."

"Well, I'm going to tell you the truth about her. There was a man named Woody Paget...."

"This is one of the ones I've heard."

"Then be quiet, and hear it again. You're nearly a man now, and you will need to know the straight of it. He was White...but what Miss Lavinia and Mr. Laurence would call 'trash,' if they talked in that way. A long time ago, his people, who weren't 'trash,' owned a lot of land around The Ruin, and The Ruin was where they lived. In those days, according to what Mr. Laurence says, it was grander than Woodleigh and Clear Creek put together."

"Then he must have come a long way down."

"A long and a *very* long way down. He went into politics.

"And he had a lot of women-friends, some White and some Colored. And he married a woman from up North. They say he married her just about right off the bus. Your mother, now, was a beautiful young girl. One evening, when Paget was drunk, drunk half out of his mind...." Tommy really did not want to get on with it, so he started adding in details that didn't move the story forward. "Dr. Lambert explained it to me one time: To get on with living, we have to hide some thoughts—and some wants—far in the backs of our minds. But drunkenness, just as it makes us weak in other ways, it makes us too weak sometimes to keep those thoughts in their hiding places, and they get loose." Ben listened but did not say anything. Tommy went on doggedly, sorrowfully: "Anyway, he saw your mother and he took a liking to her that overcame him. Being drunk, he couldn't control himself. Or he didn't. He grabbed her arm, and he dragged her into a vacant lot—the one between the post-office and the hardware store. Then...he lay with her, by force, against her will." Tommy stopped there to try to see whether Ben understood what he meant.

"He raped her. That's what they say. Is that what you're talking about?" Tommy felt tremendous relief. His ordeal was over. The boy had known all along.

"Yes, Son. That's what I mean."

"How old was I when all that happened?"

Laurence waited by the river. Spring was getting on with her mastery of the world, dipping long and supple branches of river birch, with pale leaflets spiraling out of bud, into the silently welling water—preparation for her lustral rites.

Tommy had promised to send Ben to the little wharf about four o'clock; Laurence came on purpose with time to spare. He removed his shirt and sandals, and dived into the water, letting it buoy and bathe him, him too, as though he were one of those trailing branches and a part of all the things which, having slept, now drew actively again upon their life-accounts.

The boy came along, walked out onto the wharf. Laurence was in the river, his head and bare shoulders out of the water. What if he were naked? At that time it was supposed to be all right for men to be naked in each other's company, the motivating philosophy for this being obscure. What about station, age, race? But looking back at the pile of clothing, Ben Araby was relieved to see only sandals and shirt. And Laurence climbed then, decently clad in dripping khaki, up onto the dock. He shook hands, and this surprised Ben slightly. Laurence said: "I'm glad you've come; your uncle was very much worried by the talk the two of you had last evening. He was afraid he hadn't made his point."

"He didn't…Sir." Ben sat beside Laurence, looking sullen and pathetic. They let their legs hang over the edge of the boards. "But I can add forty-four and eighteen" (for in several months' time he was going to be eighteen).

"And so you realize that Woody Paget was your biologic father?" Ben was in fact adrift in some ways; he felt let adrift in every way—emotionally, socially, racially, physiologically. With the extremest tips of his toes grazing, just barely, the turf of childhood, he clung with only a feeble grip onto the sturdy vine and lifeline of manhood, in any case entirely certain of the dreadful fact of his parentage.

"Not 'biologic,' Mr. Laurence. Plain and simple, that man was my father."

"I don't know, Ben, about 'plain and simple.' He was not your father under the law. He was not your father because your mother ever chose him as a mate. Neither of you ever saw the other or heard the other's voice. You weren't even alive—not for one second—at the same time." But he sensed doubt, ephebic confusion sprung from incomplete knowledge, from calamities within the boy of meteorologic proportion, yet unseen.

"You've studied biology?"

"I've *taken* it—I don't know about studying it. I do know about what they call 'the facts of life,' if that's what you mean."

"That's what I mean—and you and I call it 'human reproductive biology'."

"We do?"

"Yes. Now we do. It sets us apart."

"Do I need to be set apart any more than I am already? The only thing left for me to be set apart from, Mr. Laurence, is from myself. Can that happen?"

"Yes, I think so. But only in certain kinds of crazy people. You're not crazy."

"How do you know I'm not?"

"Trust me." And Ben did trust him. That was the good thing about Mr. Laurence. You could trust him, even when you couldn't tell exactly what he was talking about. For he seemed not always to know, either, not exactly. Not always. But you could tell he was never trying to deceive you. Only to help, if he could. "But to go back to human reproductive biology, fertilization of the woman's cell by the man's cell doesn't happen right at the time of sexual intercourse, the way a lot of people think. You probably know that."

"I thought it did. I read a story—a famous one, too—about a man and a woman being together the way we're talking about…."

Laurence felt an access of courage. Ben had said: "We're talking." Laurence had been unsure whether that could happen.

"…And as soon as it was over she knew she was going to have a baby."

"In the story. And she *thought* she knew. An author gets to say things like that in order to make certain points. In real life, she could not have *known,* although she could have held right opinion. In fact, it takes hours for the male cell to reach the female one—I'm not sure how many, but a lot, I think.

"The reason I'm going into all this is to reassure you that by the time you were in any sense alive, Woody Paget had already taken his own life. There simply has been no crossover between you."

"He took it pretty well, Mr. Laurence. And you were right: By the time he had gone down to the river to talk to you he had figured it out for himself."

"Yes, he told me he had."

"But I hope he didn't say anything out of the way."

"Oh, no. Anyway, it wouldn't have mattered. An eighteenth-birthday candle will have a good many grains of gunpowder embedded in its tallow, you know."

Tommy thought over this. "Mine did."

"Mine did, too. And I wouldn't give anything for a one of them." He let his thoughts travel a small way. "And my sister's definitely did."

"Miss Alina? They say she made this countryside sparkle, when she was a girl."

"'Set fire to it' would be more accurate."

"But I've never heard of one mean or low thing she ever did or said."

"No. I think all she's ever wanted has been to make everybody else have as much fun as she's having."

"She did get down over Mr. Parker's passing, though."

"She did. She did because I don't think she had ever loved anybody that much, in that way. There have been times when I've doubted she'd recover. But it has begun."

Tommy felt awkward enough talking about White people to other White people; about White people in their right minds. Talking about ones in love was ground upon which he did not wish to tread.

"She's ready to go on with life by now?"

"She is. It has been a very long time. But she doesn't expect ever to get over Mr. Parker altogether. She wouldn't want to. She would consider it disloyal."

"She won't marry again? Because—well, Mr. Laurence, I reckon you know about this *Odyssey* they've given Ben to read over the summer?"

"Yes."

"Well, for years that woman had her own house full of men trying to talk her into getting married to them; you all wouldn't put up with that; but I expect there'll be a good-size pack of them—if you add them up—turning up, off and on, now she's happier, if she gives any sign of it."

"I can't speak for my sister, but I would think she'd be married again, to the right man. Her husband really is dead, after all. And Penelopë's wasn't." Then he said softly, to himself: "That poor old pup."

What pup? "Mary Alice would out-and-out kill me if she knew I was making so free as to talk about this—about things like this. But you don't mind it, do you, Mr. Laurence? You'd let me know if I got off base?"

"Not at all, Tommy. You are one of the few people I have to talk to; I mean people I can trust with my private thoughts."

"I thank you, Sir. What I was going to say is: There are bound to be some wrong men looking to marry Miss Alina."

"You mean because of her money. Those can save their breath and their time as well, because they wouldn't have access to it or be able to inherit it. Everything will go to Little John—and we've *got* to stop calling him that!"

Alina had asked Lavinia to come to Clear Creek for tea; but when she rang the little silver bell upon the tea table, Yukoneta came in with champagne.

On her way down the Magnolia Lane to the house, Lavinia had thought over all that had been done, all that was underway. With the Magnolia Lane—a hundred and forty-two trees, the *grandiflora,* of course—you really didn't need anything else in the grounds, yet a landscaping scheme was in place and had long since begun to have its anchoring, mystifying effect. And the house!—What a pleasurable struggle she and Alina had had with it, beginning nearly twenty years ago! Alina would reach for the example of water-patterned magenta silk, but Lavinia herself would then say something like: "Or you could use just unbleached linen, and let such-and-such have the spotlight." When the effect proved wonderful, she would always attribute it to Alina's "sure touch." Finally, this became a little conspiracy between them; Alina stopped protesting that the sure touch was Lavinia's, for ultimately she had developed one of her own.

And then there had been the matter of the pilasters in the ballroom, Laurence surprising everybody, as he did at never-long intervals, by presenting a solution.

"I have something I want to talk to you about, Lavinia. I need a favor."

"You know I'll be glad to do anything I can."

"This is a bit different. I am going to New York, shopping, and I need a chaperone."

"To go shopping?"

"I'm going shopping for a husband."

"What an excellent idea! Otherwise, some are going to come shopping for you."

"Can you make the time?"

"Certainly. But you aren't planning to go up there and just buy one... or are you?"

"No. A...um...situation exists. I'm going to explain the whole thing, but please don't say a word about it to Rennie. Some parts of it might infuriate him."

"The wise chaperone is firm, but thoroughly sympathetic and discreet."

"When we lived there, four—no five—men I met made proposals, and not of marriage. Two were married themselves."

"Good Gracious, Alina! How did you deal with *that*?"

"Well, it's actually not hard to deal with, as it turns out. I mean to say, if they're going to behave in such a way, it really hardly matters what you come back at them with. Doesn't that make sense?"

"Perfect sense, although I should never have thought of it," Lavinia answered admiringly.

"So I'd just say something like: 'You will get nothing from me, in any case. If you bring this up again, Parker will know of it, and you will lose his friendship.' And of course none of them wanted to lose Parker's friendship—and some couldn't afford to."

"But you don't mean to say you'd consider those men now!"

"Well, I'd like to see some of them again, just to find out how they make me feel. And, after all, you can't blame a man for trying."

Lavinia could blame a man for trying. But here she decided not to say so.

"I can see the disapproval," Alina said. "But one, in particular, was exceptionally decent afterward."

"Nonsense. We can be as close friends as we like, yet without seeing eye-to-eye on every single thing. I may like to hear about the exceptionally decent one, though, if you don't mind telling me."

"Not in the least. I rather liked him anyway. And he was a little drunk. But he sent flowers the next day—very splendid. The note said: 'From your many admirers, all of us sick with jealousy of Parker.' Then, on a part of the card that could be torn off was added: 'One of whom has been lacking in respect and deeply ashamed of behaving unworthily to a Wonderful Lady.' I wasn't holding much of a grudge, anyway; I knew who had sent the flowers and written the card. I knew it wasn't really a joint effort."

Now Alina rang the little silver bell again. Yukoneta entered after an unaccountably short interval. "Connie, I'm afraid we've let this wine get a little too warm. Would you bring us another bottle, please? Maybe you can use this in cooking."

Yukoneta said, "Yes, Miss Alina." And she went out with the "warm" bottle, which seemed to her to be at an ideal temperature. Cooking? Not with this! Mr. Parker would not have allowed it.

"But that's not what the champagne's for."

"What is it for?"

"Parker."

Under the circumstances it seemed natural enough to ask: "To say Goodbye?"

"Oh, I will never say Goodbye to Parker," Alina answered, and her eyes filled with tears, but the same smile reigned over them, just as it had done when she had been sitting at the piano, those so many years before.

Yukoneta had wondered all her life about White people. Now, continuing to listen at the door, a glass of vintage Champagne in her hand, she began to believe that Peell County White people might not be representative of White people in general. (She drew off a long and actually quite cool mouthful.) But then, whom did she know who was representative of Colored people in general?

"It began when he was a schoolboy. In an idle moment, the only kind he seems to have had; one day he drew a pencil point down along the wire loops of the spiral binding of his notebook, and it made a series of perfect scallops in the margin of the page."

"I've done that."

"Me too. Then he did it on each new page. He would embellish each scallop, maybe adding circles, with darts in between. He graduated to full-page designs. Still only lines and curves. Symmetrical, usually in both axes. Always elaborate. By the time he'd got to high school, though, he was committing—his word—irregularities. Shadings. Light-and-dark, and an effort at the illusion of the third dimension.

"By the time he went away to college he had developed an impulse to study drawing. And he went to a college that had a rather noted program in studio art. But he didn't want to associate with 'that crowd,' as he put it, so he found an instructor in the town. And his work gradually came to be greatly admired, within a small circle. A gallery gave him a show. Then they had a row because he wouldn't sell any of the drawings. I have them all. I want to give some to you and Rennie, and some to John. Then I want to get an expert opinion about the rest.

"But what I want us to toast this afternoon are his paintings. Nobody has ever seen them. Today I've hung them all over the house! Give us another glass, and let's go around and look at them." Alina rose; Lavinia poured out.

Yukoneta bolted. She didn't want to be caught eavesdropping; besides, that champagne would only be getting warmer (She had had to take the krater full of ice back with the fresh bottle). The two women walked through the house, while Alina discoursed upon her late husband's development as a painter, such as it had been. As Lavinia gazed upon each next enormous canvas, at them all framed in etiolated gilt mouldings, each radiating light and color into the space around it, Alina said: "He would not leave it at drawing, which he did well, but decided to paint. And when he tried it, which he did in seclusion, he was thrown off by the lag of the brush behind the movement of the wrist. And he was, he said, dissatisfied with the finish. When he began to work on that—and succeeded, I think—he found that all pictorial content had flown! And there had never been much."

"These are very, very beautiful!"

"But are they? Most of the ones we've looked at so far were done just before or during our year in New York. Connie kept asking, whenever she'd just cleaned the studio, questions such as: 'These things are "modern art," aren't they, Miss Alina?' And I would answer: 'I know nothing of it, Connie.' She would then say: 'No, Miss Alina, I think that's what they are, all right. Modern Art. And you know what that means.'

"One afternoon I looked in and offered him a Martini. He said: 'Yes, and of course there is color.' For a second I thought something must have happened to his brain, then I realized he was only preoccupied. Well, something *had* happened in his brain, or had failed to. Anyway, without lines and hachures, he couldn't see how to form a picture.

"I suggested he apply something pictorial over his color and finish. I suggested he try applying some abstraction, or even begin from the decorative motives of earlier days. He turned to me and said: 'No, Babe. You can't do that. You can't build something up and then just start sticking things onto it. If they are to come, then they will come, and they will probably have been there in embryonic form to begin with. You fare ahead; you cast about. You wait. Anyway' he said, 'these are in a way pictorial, because each one is an incident. Don't you think a painted incident is a picture? What make these into incidents are their frames. They stop them from going on, give them beginnings and endings. For more, I'll just wait.' And then, as it happened, he couldn't wait. But if he could have, he would have been shown the next stage. Or he thought so. And I think so."

They had by now returned to the tea table. Lavinia was overborne. It was as though Parker had made rough chalk glow like coals, or made dingy rust emit radiance of gemstones. The flat and dull had breathed and sung, yet apparently Parker had died in the belief that all he had made were rare surfaces of color. She filled their glasses again.

Raising hers, she said: "This time I don't care if it's downright hot! A toast to the *vernissage*! Alina, you must show these to the people who will be looking at the drawings. These paintings have completed what you and I started here, and Laurence. I mean the silver leaf, the sixteen tones!"

"That you like them has filled a want in my heart. Parker was afraid they might only be backgrounds. And that's how I've used them." So the sisters-in-law finished drinking the tepid Champagne, (Yukoneta had anticipated them) and Alina walked out with Lavinia to her car.

On an afternoon in late August, the school bus pulled up to the end of the lane. Ben got out. As the bus drew away and all fell silent about him, he felt an extraordinary affection for the world he dwelt in. Maybe because it had been at this time of year that he had first come into it. August. Heat. But July was always hotter. Not many people knew that, but it was so. It was just that everybody—every living thing—had already got so parched by the time August began.

But the boy, who now at age eighteen had still bred true as Negro, could sense the fingers of autumn softly exploring the stratosphere, pressing but lightly, scouting for places where summer's texture might first be torn through. Was he the only one to feel exhilarated in August? Maybe so. Who knew or cared? He removed his shoes, and, sure enough, the loose sand in the lane felt cool between his toes. He would have taken off his shirt, too, but then he had to pass before the big house. So he started homeward as he was.

As he approached, on the westward end of the verandah, the part he could see from farthest away, Ben indeed caught sight of Lavinia. She was tending her begonias. These were not pink or yellow macules with yellow-green leaves; these were magnificent, large and many-petalled, fluted pure white blossoms springing from rich green foliage. Everyone admired them. Everyone wanted to know Lavinia's secret for growing them.

She was just then divulging to any chance passerby her 'secret'—lopping them down to four inches with hedge pruners. The stems that fell over the railing she felt enriched the earth. The ones that fell onto the verandah floor she would sweep up later, and not leave them there for Mary Alice to see to. She caught sight of Ben as he started around the west side of the house, and she left off her pruning. She hailed him: "Hello, Ben! And happy birthday!"

"Thank you Ma'am!"

"Did Mr. Laurence get our little present to you?"

"Yes, Ma'am, he did, and it wasn't little, either. I thank you both very much!"

"You're most welcome. Many, many happy returns of the day, and I hope most of them will be as beautiful as this!"

They waved, Ben went on his way. When he had got past the kitchen house, then he removed his shirt. Coming closer to home, he wondered what kind of surprises he would find there. At school, during lunchtime, they had had a cake and had sung "Happy Birthday." He had been embarrassed, but it had made him feel—well, he didn't know how it had made him feel, but it had been an awkward, agreeable feeling. However, it was his own family's congratulations that he awaited most eagerly. And they *were* his own family now, for Mary Alice and Tommy had adopted him. And now little Haynesworth and Marigold were his real brother and sister. For now it was the law. And now his name really was 'Araby,' for that was the law, too.

All was quiet as he stepped up onto the porch. Were they going to spring out from behind curtains and furniture? Shout: "Surprise!" After all, it was his eighteenth birthday this time. He wasn't entirely sure what "majority" was. But proud he certainly was, and happy, to have achieved it. And his father had told him that it would mean more in years to come than it meant now, adding to the mystery and excitement.

He found, however, no paper streamers festooning the living room. He saw no wrapped packages, no candles, no birthday cake.

In fact, only Miss Izora was at home. She told him that Mary Alice had taken the afternoon off to go shopping for school clothes with Marigold in Yemasee. Haynesworth had gone into the rice fields with Tommy. Ben sat down and tried to complete his homework assignments for school, but kept looking up at every sound, at every movement outside the house.

As dusk fell, they heard the clatter of Tommy's truck coming near. He pulled up into the side yard, and everybody climbed out. *They've all come at one time, and they will have everything with them.* But of course they would all come at one time; the family owned only the truck, and Tommy and Haynesworth, Mary Alice and Marigold must all come home together, anyway. They came into the house, Marigold excited about her new dresses, Mary Alice worried about starting supper so late. Tommy and Haynesworth still talking about flooding of the rice fields, why it needed to be done, when the right time for it would be; Haynesworth didn't want to miss seeing it.

Ben stood up and started up the stairs. "Don't you want any supper, Honey?" Mary Alice called after him.

"No, Ma'am. I've already had something." He got into his night clothes, into bed, switched off the light.

Later, after everyone else had gone to bed and the house slept, Ben remained awake. Below him, he heard a series of scraping sounds. Then nothing, nothing you could be sure about. After that, noise upon the staircase. What was it?

It was a thing unbelievable, and it seemed to go on forever. It was something that hadn't happened in years and years. It was something nobody expected ever to happen again. Miss Izora was climbing the stairs! Fumbling about a bit, she finally came into his room, quietly. And quietly somehow she brought a low chair up to the bedside and sat down. Softly, she began to stroke Ben's head and to croon:

> "Run, tell Aunt Sammy,
> Run, tell Aunt Sammy,
> Run, tell Aunt Sammy
> The old grey goose is dead.
>
> The one she's been saving,
> The one she's been saving,
> The one she's been saving
> To make a feather bed."

IX

"When messages did begin to come through in clear, then
all secrets of the war really would begin to fade into history already."
The Lord Briggs, in an interview for television

"And surely your blood of your lives will I require; at the hand of
every beast will I require it, and at the hand of man; and at the hand
of every man's brother will I require the life of man."
Genesis 9. 5 *(AV)*

"…not content to rave with the Greeks themselves, they want to make
the prophets rave also; showing conclusively, that never even in sleep
have they caught a glimpse of Scripture's Divine nature."
Benedict de Spinoza: *A Theologico-Political
Treatise, preface* (tr. R.H.M.Elwes)

HALFWAY TO THE library at the front of the house, coming from his
study, Thomas Strikestraw lost his way. Lost, and in his own house.
No pane or railing, panel nor threshold familiar. A copse seemed
drawn all about him, heavy with vine and brake, with sapling-stems. Slivers

of sinking light smoldering among these. Ribbons of mourning, interlacing strips of ebbing hope. He held fast to himself. These bars of light and dark he would not allow to degenerate into pattern without image, columns of yes-or-no that took away life. Since the war, messages had been coming to him in clear. He had banished any more dashes and dots seen or heard in his world, unless decrypted. This was not a nowhere of one-and-naught. It mightn't be his home any longer, and familiar. But he insisted to himself that it be a *place*, a wood, a thicket. And there must be a path through it; somewhere to go, and thus a way to go there. But it was indistinct, unused, and overgrown.

He had the sensation of having moved between sleeping and waking, but he did not know whether toward or from, or which. He somehow came to himself. ...*Mi ritrovai*.... Little as he remembered of the Poem, that, clearly, was what had happened. He peered through the unreal but strictly enforced growth.

Summers and summers and winters and winters ago.

Edward's "little stroke." Was it this? No. Because he had "come to himself." With a stroke, it ought to have been the other way round. So he stopped where he was and waited; there is no way to tell how long. He was carrying the little silver gallery-tray, however, and when he became aware of this it occurred to him to continue with it—and the pathway opened a little to permit this—to sit on the verandah, while the air grew cooler and the sky quieter, and to decide what, if anything, to do—No, *what* to do, for surely there was something.

He placed the drinks-tray upon a low stool then sat down to watch the Great River comb its banks with low-rippling light. He thought for a while, and sure enough there came to him notions of two things—one he wanted to do, the other he thought he ought to do. He thought.

The next morning he telephoned to the Singletons in Virginia.

"Hello, Libby?"

"Yes?"

"This is Thomas Strikestraw."

"Oh, *Thomas*! How *are* you?" For she had shifted into her "social" tone and diction.

"Very well, thank you."

"How delightful to hear from you. And how is Little Edward?"

" 'Little Edward' is twenty-one years old, and by no means little anymore. But how are you? And Bunny?"

"Oh, we're both flourishing as usual. Bunny hunts less often now. All those years of riotous living have caught up with him, left him a little winded from time to time."

"Not his heart, I hope."

"No, nothing so serious as that!"

"Emphysema?"

"Oh, no. I wouldn't go *that* far. *I'm* just as always. Constantly on the go. Tennis matches all the time. Parties nearly every night. It's nice, though, to be able to fool yourself into thinking you're so much in demand...." Libby had long ago succeeded entirely in achieving that delusion. "...But it can be *very* wearing."

"I'm sure you're holding up beautifully. I wonder, is Bunny at home now, and could I have a word with him?"

Here there occurred an odd sort of pause. Something made Thomas think of a cornered animal anxiously looking for the likeliest direction for a dash unmauled. Then Libby said: "Um...yes he is at home; I'm not sure whether he's free to come to the telephone just this minute. Wait. Let me see." Another pause, suspect in its brevity. "Thomas?" Libby said, as though returning to the telephone.

"Yes?"

"May he call you back—say, in an hour or so?"

"Of course. I'm at home for the forenoon."

"All right, then. *Wonderful* to hear your voice!"

When the call came in, and Thomas had explained that there was an important matter he wanted to talk over, Bunny at first tried to persuade him that they hold the discussion over the telephone. He spoke in short bursts, sibilantly drawing in breath between. But Thomas insisted that they must meet face to face and further required that it be at a time when Libby would be out of the house.

"Any Thursday, then. That's her tennis morning."

"Next Thursday?"

"All right," Bunny gasped out. "I assume you can stay with us overnight?" Praying not, but obliged to ask, in order to foster the fiction of a normally-running household.

"Thanks all the same, Bunny. But I'll have to be on my way after our talk." *And you'll be glad enough to see my back! If you live to see it!*

As Thomas turned off the highway seven-and-a-half miles south of Warrenton, he calculated that this would be the fifth visit paid to their son's in-laws. He reflected, as he drove, upon the other four. Robert's engagement with Anne had been the occasion of the first. Then, Libby and Bunny had lived at Collingwood Hall, a big, very early eighteenth-century James River plantation house, circa 1935. It had earlier been the center of a lot of revelry—riding to hounds, dancing, drinking, other matters—centering around the two daughters, and friends, most of them male, from nearby schools; from colleges in some cases like Hampden-Sydney. There had been an ample stable. Anne had ridden a little; Peggy, a lot. Libby, who had practically grown up on horseback, had by now become indifferent toward the sport. Bunny was able after a fashion to sit a horse, avoided jumps wherever possible, and always managed to be limp as a rag—never relying solely upon the stirrup-cup—in case he were thrown. And this happened with trying frequency.

The second visit had been for the wedding itself, rather for some of the events surrounding it (the ceremony having been solemnized in Richmond). The third had been for Anne's funeral, which, tragically, had taken place a week after Edward's birth.

But the fourth of the visits which Grace and Thomas had made to Virginia had been purely for getting together with family relations and to fetch home their little grandson, though there had been rather a gigantic cocktail-party, to the side. By this time, the Singletons had retired to what they called "The Cottage." Thomas had been relieved when he learned they weren't going to call it the "Dower House," for by that time he felt he must be proof against almost anything.

And now, as he turned into the unplanted driveway, he caught sight of The Cottage once more. It was a studiedly humble-looking structure, consisting of a number of tenant-houses and accessory buildings brought together upon a single foundation of carefully-laid fieldstone, and further unified in appearance by siding of never-painted, weathered boards and battens. Three chimney-stacks rose above the roof-ridges. The whole stood in open pasture. It was picturesque beyond, almost, man's imagination.

When Thomas had first gone there with Grace twenty years before, she had remarked, somewhat uncharacteristically, as they had started up the drive: "This is a switch." For the Singletons were well-to-do and seemed when at Collingwood Hall to want that to be known generally and forthwith.

But once they had gone inside the rustic Cottage, the effect changed almost violently: The walls had been smoothed and painted in richly dark colors, rugs knotted in like colors and splendid patterns, drapery woven in them. Paintings glowed in heavy gilded frames. From polished wood, from bits of burnished glass or brass or silver, carefully marshaled gleamings conferred a further degree of opulence within the shadowy penetralia. As they were surrendering their hats and coats to the housekeeper, who was called Mrs. Murdoch, Thomas let slip this observation: "Well, it seems they still want you to know, but now they're content to have you know only if you've been invited inside."

"A step in the right direction," Grace had answered. And a little later on: "The furniture is too harmonious…even the little lapses into discord fit too well. These seem almost like public rooms." Support was lent to that view by the forty people who arrived for cocktails later on.

During that first evening, Thomas remembered, Libby had hurried up to Grace, just as she was about to sit down, and had said: "Oh, Grace, Darling! Please don't sit on Aunt Sophronia's ballroom chair; it's too fragile, even for you!" Then she had made a remarkable suggestion: "Come and join me on the 'Melrose Sofa;' it's sturdy enough to hold four or five of us…and almost big enough."

"Melrose?"

"Yes—one of Bunny's family places."

"Do you mean Melrose in Bedford County—the house that burned?"

"That's right." And she changed the subject, unaware that Grace knew far more about Melrose than she herself did.

Now Thomas stood before the weathered front door. He tried to absorb into himself all he could of the radiant morning. Then he knocked. The door was answered by a young servant, a lass with a shy, pretty smile. "I'm Thomas Strikestraw."

"Come in, please, Canon," the girl said. *Drilled.* "Mr. Singleton is waiting for you in the library."

"Thank you, My Dear," Thomas said, "and please tell me your name."

"It's Sally, Sir."

"Thank you, Sally. You know, you surprised me a little. I imagine I was expecting to see Mrs. Warbeck."

"Murdoch," Sally prompted. "No, Sir. Mrs. Murdoch is long gone."

"Of course. She probably passed on well before your time."

"I was two when she went to her reward, Canon, I think."

At this moment, Libby came from a passageway into the entrance hall. At first, Thomas did not recognize her. Sally stood back. Two decades before, Thomas remembered, Libby had had rich golden hair, but with some strands as pale as silver. The woman before him now said, "Thomas! How grand to see you!" and kissed him lightly on the cheek. "It has been too long! And now I have to go out to my boring tennis match."

Her hair was solid yellow. She wore tennis dress, with the shortest of skirts. Contrasting with all the white was a light blue sweater thrown onto her back, the sleeves over her shoulders, loosely wrapped together once upon her breast. The skin of her face was unnaturally pale, drawn tight as a drumhead across the facial bones. Now Thomas realized the duty of the sweater; it was just the same shade of the blue as Libby's eyes. But from the peripheries of the corneas, a cloudiness seemed to be advancing centripetally upon the pupils, one day, as soon as might be, however, dark and vacant, within them dancing the lucent prisms of lens-implants.

But by her voice, husky from the smoke of a hundred thousand cigarettes, Thomas recognized Libby easily. "It is so good to see you, too, Libby. I'm afraid my visit isn't very convenient. But there is something important I must talk over with Bunny—if he's up to it."

"Oh, he is! Definitely! I think he's breathing a little oxygen this morning—wants to be ready for Saturday if he can be.

"Well, anyhow, I'm away! We're counting on your staying for lunch." With that, she grasped the bright brass knob, part of a polished rimlatch of ancient design and baronial proportions, and opened the door, handsomely paneled inside, weathered outside, where the knob Libby held was answered by another of plain iron.

"I can't stay, thank you, Libby. I'm putting up with friends in Lynchburg, and they have made plans for the late afternoon."

"What a shame! Well, go in and see Bunny. He's been so looking forward to your visit." And she left them.

Thomas had not only heard that Libby Singleton had nice legs (It was a byword; but were "bywords" supposed to be actual utterances? Did people really say them? Or did they only float free in the mist of truth and swirling falsehood? And, was this kind of unbidden rumination a sign that he was going out of his mind?); he had seen for himself, thanks to a very long slit in the skirt of an evening gown she had worn at one of his son's two wartime engagement parties. The lineaments were still there, he thought as he followed Sally toward the library. But the subcutaneous tissue was now poorly organized, drooping a little over the knees, the skin lax, reticulated with wrinkles, excessively tanned. Dry.

Thomas said to Sally: "Mr. Singleton and I have some very important family matters to discuss. To tell you the truth, some of it is a little...awkward. While I'm sure a girl of your obvious breeding would never think of listening in—and I'm sure you would find it all extremely boring if you did!—still, we thought it would be best for you to take the rest of the morning off. We spoke about it over the telephone." He was surprised to find how naturally lying came as the years passed. Controlled lying, that is to say. Nine-tenths of the lies he told could not conceivably have an adverse effect upon anybody. One way or other, he really did not want the girl in the house in case he had actually to shoot Bunny.

So he winked as he gave her a ten-dollar bill, and he added: "Miss Libby doesn't know about this, so keep it a secret, and be sure to be back before she is!"

Beaming over the note and the conspiracy both, Sally tapped upon the library door, opened it, and said: "Mr. Singleton, here is Canon Strikestraw."

The library, at least, was greatly changed. Thomas remembered it as being over-furnished—sets of books in sumptuously somber bindings of leather, or what looked like it; a large armillary sphere, an enormous globe, heavy window-curtains of green velvet (deep red velvet?—at any rate, that sort of effect). Full of personages, too—"your great-grandfather's smoking-stand," "my Cousin Lillian's writing-desk," and so on.

Now, most of the furniture had been replaced by medical equipment. A folding screen of gros point needlework had been opened across the farther end of the room. Something bulbous at the bottom, sharp-edged at the top embossed one of its panels from behind. Eighteen inches of chrome-plated steel post rose above it, with hooks. No dark richness now. Window-curtains removed. The whole room flooded with daylight from two opposed exposures. One window with the lower sash raised, an oscillating electric fan on the sill. The *boiserie* revealed as faintly bogus—just knotty pine boards and stock mouldings, stained and varnished. No theatrical illusion remained to cast its spell.

Back and forth went the fan with deadly regularity. Bunny was seated beside the open window, his person unprepossessing as the room itself, although jauntily got up in tartan dressing-gown and chamois slippers, edged—therefore apparently lined—with fluffy white fleece, or what looked like it. He was wasted, skeletal hands gripping the handles to the wheelchair. Through once-transparent and now translucent tubing and mask, he was breathing oxygen from a green-painted cylinder fitted with chrome-plated brightwork. But needle-thin racemizations of corrosion spread like cobwebs, lifting an insidious filigree of the silvery overlay from the base metal beneath.

"Hello, Thomas," Bunny gasped. And the priest immediately took up the burden of conversation with a man whom he might nevertheless be about to murder. Or he thought so. Or thought he thought so. So irritating! This irresoluteness that had been with him since the afternoon when he had lost his way.

They drank coffee, which the gentle Sally had left with them; after a few minutes, through the window, Thomas could see her moving off along the driveway.

He could think now of several reasons for coming directly to the point, none for delay. "I know, Bunny, that Anne had a child, before she knew Robert."

You couldn't decide whether Bunny was dumbfounded or merely out of breath, but he said nothing, did not try to say anything for a time, then at once he found tongue and breath. "You don't know what you're saying. It's absurd. Who told you such a thing?"

"Robert did, and Anne had told him."

"The absurdity of the thing proves you wrong; if what you say *were* true, do you imagine that Anne would have told her future husband about it?"

"I don't know how clearly you remember Anne, or how well you supposed you knew her then. But Robert was the one person she would have been sure to tell."

"You're not making any sense, Thomas. It shows you're lying."

"I am probably doing much worse than lying, but I am not lying, as you know. And I know it. You haven't breath to waste, so we may as well get on with it." And sure enough, Bunny's agitation had increased his oxygen consumption; he was unable to speak, grasping for any firm thing he could reach in an attempt to lean forward, get himself up from his wheelchair. His breathing, through pursed lips tinged blue-grey, had become more rapid.

Thomas continued. "I know that the child was adopted at birth. I know that you know who the adoptive parents are; you know who the natural father is. I know that the father himself does not know he has this child, and I do not propose to tell him. But I do intend to find out for myself."

"You won't learn any of that from me."

"I will, because there is no other living person who knows all of it." And then, hardly believing what he was doing, Thomas went out into the entrance hall, to the closet where Sally had hung his coat, and from the right-hand pocket he withdrew a .38 calibre revolver. It had been in the house in New Brunswick for years. He had taken it down and cleaned it. He had fired it to make sure he could depend upon it. And upon himself. No license for it had ever been issued, so far as he knew. Thomas was certain it could not be traced. As though tracing it might make any difference, if he should fire it here, killing Bunny.

He went back into the library. Without a word, he showed the revolver to Bunny, broke it open, let him see that every chamber within the cylinder was charged. *Is this an* auto da fé? he wondered. *It has a definite Inquisitorial air about it.* He placed the muzzle in the declivity beneath Bunny's right ear, just behind the angle of the mandible. He was filled with pity when he realized how abnormally deep this depression in the flesh had become with the progression of sickness and its wasting. "Now you will tell me." But Thomas knew less about his adversary than he had believed.

"I will not."

"I will kill you."

"No, you will not. In any case, I am not afraid to die—what have I got to lose?"

"I am not afraid to kill you, as you may believe I am. I have nothing to lose, either."

"You have plenty to lose, and we both know it. But I have nothing, and for that reason, I am not afraid to die. I just don't want to have to suffocate in order to do it." Then, as some would say, Satan entered fully into Thomas's soul. For he saw that the means of coërcion he had planned to apply was in fact without force. But he discovered simultaneously another means, and one of certified potency. And one far more vile. He laid the revolver aside.

Hanging from the neck of the oxygen cylinder by a tarnished brass chain was a wrench, like a spoon in some ways, but with the curves reduced to angles, the bowl flattened, a hexagonal opening punched through it. As Thomas was fitting this over the valve cover, he saw from the pressure-gauge that the rate of flow was set very low. He believed this meant that the supplemental oxygen was, up to a point, of only psychological usefulness. He closed the valve. Bunny lurched forward, to the minor extent he could, but Thomas quickly moved the tank to beyond his reach. *Can I really have grown so despicable?*

This may have been his most malicious act, but realizing what he thought he knew about the administration of oxygen to patients with advanced emphysema, he knew that in fact he would hardly endanger—much less kill—the hollow, miserable man before him, and he realized that he did not want, and had not ever wanted, and had in no degree wanted to kill him.

But he ardently meant to discover the identity of his grandson's half-brother or -sister, even though he could not have given any compelling reason for wanting to know.

"Thomas! Don't do this!" Bunny screamed. But his voice was muffled by his clouded gag. He tore the mask off and began to shout for help.

"I have sent Sally away for the morning, Bunny. There is no one to hear you. You will tell me the name of the child's father and the names of the adoptive parents, all of which I know you know, remember. Then I shall turn the oxygen on again."

"I can't! For God's sake, turn it on. I gave my word as a gentleman that I would never reveal...." And there ensued a spectacle of coughing, gasping and choking, with wheezing, which would have been pitiful to witness, except that it was as empty as the man himself. "...any of those things."

"But you are under threat of death. That will release you from any obligation"

"A gentleman would die rather than break his word. Please, Thomas.

Look! My fingernail-beds are turning blue!" Thomas looked, and they were blue, the same blue as they had been while the oxygen had flowed.

Somehow, it occurred to Thomas, he was being led to a third and certain means of extorting confession, and he said: "What objection do you have to telling me? Who could suffer—and what could he suffer—as a result? Unless any one of them is somebody I know?"

"No. No, you couldn't know any of them. That's not it."

But Bunny had again unwittingly dealt Thomas a trump card, which he played at once. "I know perfectly well, Bunny, why you are so reluctant to tell me what I want to know. There can be only one real reason." Bunny said nothing. Thomas went on: "It is clear to me that the child was fathered by someone of not quite the right background. And, further, I am quite sure now that it was given up to people of—not to mince words—social unsuitability."

It worked like magic. "Oh, no. No,no. It is *nothing* like *that*! If that is what you believe, then it becomes my duty to tell you the names of the people involved. I owe it to my daughter's reputation! I owe it to her memory."

"Then shall I turn the oxygen back on?"

"Yes! Please, yes! I am about to go into a coma. And if I do—and die— then you'll never be able to find out. Because nobody else knows...." He let his voice fade to a broken whisper.

"I shall not do it until I have the names—as well as any other particulars you may know."

Bunny's voice grew stronger, and he told Thomas the names and where the bearers of them had lived, to the best of his knowledge, a quarter-century before. And, as Thomas had more-or-less expected, none of it meant anything to him at all.

"I'm sorry," Thomas said, after he had got the oxygen to bubbling merrily once more through the water in the humidification jar, "to have added this distress to all else you have to bear. But, you see, you and I are not connected by law only, we are linked also by blood—Edward is your grandson, and he is mine as well. I needed to know this."

"Eddie—a fine young man," Bunny said, appearing to relax, leaning back again into his wheelchair in the belief that he was now more comfortable.

"You think so?"

"Certainly."

"When have you last seen him?"

Bunny, of course, must hesitate, for he didn't really know the answer. "I believe...," and here he looked off into space, pretending to try to recall, in fact only trying to breathe, "...it was at Christmastime, no, autumn;

yes…autumn…hounds, you know…good pups…fine pups…fine English bitches….." And he lapsed into some unspecified state other than waking.

Thomas sat beside him for a time. Bunny roused himself. "Thomas, will you shoot me?

"No, Bunny."

"Please shoot me."

"No."

"Then, will you bless me?"

Thomas did have friends in Lynchburg, but he was not going to be staying the night with them. He had got what he had come for, and now he was going straight home with it, no matter the hour of his arrival there. He had left one place and not yet arrived at the other, limbo of the traveler, and neither itinerary nor schedule had been filed with those either at home or at destination. He had told Rhodë that he was going "for a few days' visit" with his fictitious sister- and brother-in-law in Aberdeen. There had never been mention of the surname. He was unreachable and free, in other words. He was on his way, encumbered by nobody's expectation.

But, although "on his way," he was mindful that, having lost his way several days earlier, he had not yet found it again. He had tried giving himself a mission; he had gone forth and fulfilled it; with its meaningless fruition, he was now returning. Yes. He was returning. He was on his way. Because he had a destination. Home. Still, there remained stubbornly that other sense in which he had lost his way and not yet found it back.

All I can do is try once more. I must give myself a task, and then complete it. It will have to be another journey, but this time a figurative one. And the task must have to do with my legitimate profession. I've been floundering. I imagine I have left my parishioners floundering, too, or some of them, or some of them to some extent. But do you see that? I'm still so irresolute. And it's not like me—or not supposed to be. And who in Hell do I think I'm talking to right this minute, after all? I'd better see a doctor. Or Alenda.

But soon after reaching home Thomas began to feel better about things. There came a time when one did lose one's way. That was all there was to it. If it were time now for him to resort to That Primal Sympathy, then he would do it. He would accept that the years had brought him low, and he would do it.

He was sitting at the desk in his study when Rhodë came in with coffee, all just as usual. He was tremendously glad to see her. The coffee smelled wonderful! When he had drunk a bit, and discovered that it tasted quite as good as it smelled—a thing usually considered impossible in the case of coffee—then all his misgivings and self-doubts dispersed for the moment with the vapor of the delicious brew.

They chatted together for a while. Rhodë's first cousin, Clash, had shingles and was in a lot of pain. Rhodë was skeptical of the regimen Clash *said* the doctor had prescribed for pain-relief. Thomas expressed sympathy, and willingness to be helpful if he could. He told her a little about his trip—road conditions, weather. How were Miss Grace's sister and her husband? Neither had a care in the world.

Rhodë had found Thomas hale, and she went out of the study thanking not only her Blessed Lord but also Miss Grace, to whom, as her worries about her surviving employer and spiritual guide had increased, she had begun to pray as some pray to saints.

Thomas, relishing the last of his coffee, wrote some names upon a sheet of his personal stationery, which he then folded and sealed inside an envelope. Upon this he wrote: "Edward," put it into the drawer above the kneehole, and forgot about it.

And he nearly forgot about the revolver. But he retrieved it from his topcoat pocket and placed it in the same drawer. He telephoned to Alenda to make sure their usual visit together could take place on the following Thursday. Then, with his heart missing an occasional beat, he set about the other thing he had thought of that afternoon upon the verandah—the one he felt he must do. He began to draft his homily for the Sunday service. For it was to be a special one.

And after an hour had passed, he went upstairs to rehearse the all-important lessons he had learned from Bunny Singleton's examples, the ones that would enable him to deliver the homily, once written, in the way he intended. He said all this to himself as he climbed the stairs, pronouncing the words subvocally. And when he got to "intended," he thought instead, "pretended." Something made him think of the slogans, couched in Scriptural language, blazoned over the storefront windows of the Living Fountain Assembly of the Saved, huddled beside the police station.

When he had reached the top of the stairs, Thomas paused, listened. Sure enough, Rhodë had gone into the kitchen; he could hear the clatter of pots and pans. So he walked down the hallway to his and Grace's bedroom, through it, and into the bathroom. There, he locked himself inside. He and his Grace had agreed long before never to do this. What if something should happen to one of them? The other could not get inside to help, at least, possibly not in time. But Grace was gone. And if he himself had "plenty to lose," as Bunny had put it, still, that abundance was at any rate now reduced by close to a half-century's worth.

So he went to the washbasin and ran the water—sound-camouflage.

Then, leaning forward a little, he made his first efforts at feigning respiratory disease. Naturally, he didn't want to reach the extremes that Bunny could; rather, had to. For in such a case he would be taken immediately to hospital. The first thing he tried was the "gasp." He simply drew breath sharply in, then held it. But he could see in the mirror that this only made him appear about to inflate a toy balloon. With recruitment of all the facial features, though, the effect was significantly improved upon.

Next, he tackled the "wheeze," which all people are able to produce if only they exhale forcibly enough. But that really did in Thomas' case look put-on. He left further work upon this sign until later. Last came the least difficult manifestation of trouble in the lungs, the "cough." It must seem spontaneous and irrefutable, however. The deliberate attempts led to genuine coughing, though, bringing Thomas close to active nausea, or "tussive emesis." He began to retch beyond control. But after he had drunk some water, he recovered, considering this session at an end. He wiped a light sweat from his forehead and unlocked and opened the door.

And there stood Rhodë, looking greatly concerned and a little alarmed. And a little suspicious. "Father," she said, "are you taking a cold? Or is there anything else the matter?"

"No, Rhodë, thank you," he replied, in some confusion. "I just had a tickle in my throat."

A tickle in his throat? That complaint was not consistent with the tumult Rhodë has just heard—and from downstairs. *And* above the crashing of kitchenware, one of the most distracting of all known dins. As she pondered this discrepancy, she looked at the man and saw that he had noted her doubt. She had very rarely seen him behaving furtively, and when she had, she had never had far to go in identifying the cause. She resolved to watch him very closely. He might be concealing a severe, a possibly unrecognized illness, one which, without treatment, could prove fatal. Or it might be his mind. His losing it, that was.

Away at their college in the North, Edward studying, Sandy, his roommate, musing, Sandy intoned: "Claire Cloudsley Elder; How do you think that sounds?"

"It sounds very good."

"It's coming out in Sunday's newspapers."

"You realize it won't say 'Claire Cloudsley Elder,' don't you?"

"It won't?"

"No."

"Why not?"

"Because it will say instead, Mr. and Mrs. So-and-so Elder announce the engagement of their daughter, Claire Cloudsley, to Mr. Alexander Caldwell Thomas...."

"Are you sure?"

"No."

"Then why do you say it?"

"Because I think it. But look, Sandy, I have to finish this translation before dinner."

"Sorry," Sandy said, sounding rebuffed.

So Edward added this: "I've asked my grandfather to have all our relatives and friends around Augusta to be on the lookout and cut out the announcement, so you'll have plenty of copies." Conciliation, Reassurance. Often needed with Sandy, who always felt better if he could think a lot of people were interested in the things he did. "Really?" he said. "Have you? That was good of you." Edward resumed his third round with *Pythia II*.

When the time had come for Edward to go away to college, he had been reluctant, but he did not say so. He did not want to leave his grandfather, who had never left him. And, although he had often been away from home, starting from an early age, and in some cases for long sojourns, still, he always knew then that he would be coming home to the house on Front Street. He would return there from college, too, but for vacations—not to stay. Or that was what going away to college usually implied.

He went, though, with a kind of purpose. From a lad, he had wondered whether he really existed, and he was a good deal more skeptical about whether other people really existed. Because he could not be them, too, and discover what that felt like. He knew not even to try. Ever since that day when as a lad he had touched his reflection in a mirror, held a chubby hand to his chest to feel his heart beating, he had wondered, at intervals, about this matter, half-heartedly questing about for an answer. At college, he might find time and context for whole-hearted searchings.

Early in his first year away, he had been sitting in a reading-room where quiet was enforced. Across the table there sat an upperclassman, one with whom Edward had very tentatively become friendly. (Edward was insecure in himself; nobody suspected this, because nobody could see any reason for it. But he was.) This man, knowing that Edward was thinking of pursuing the study of the Classics, scribbled a sentence in Latin from the book he was reading, and with a grin pushed it across the table to Edward, who read: "*Cogito, ergo sum.*" "I think, therefore I am"

Edward wrote, then, beneath it: "*Cogitas, ergo te esse cogitas*" ("You think, therefore you think you are"), and handed it back with an answering smile. Later, he had to clarify, but he had begun to feel that he was among at least some who (If they existed? If he himself did?) were asking themselves that kind of question, and, like himself, grappling with it, off and on, lazily and comfortably, without any anxiety or other distress. But for fun. And so he meant to apply himself to his studies in this way, but to elect very serious studies, and to be ready, in case congenial companions should emerge during the course of all this, to do it for fun. Bobby MacCallum would not have understood it—the impulse; not the material—Edward was pretty sure.

He and his roommate were congenial companions, but they did not talk late into the nights about metaphysical questions. Edward and Sandy, both Southerners, had been randomly assigned as roommates for the first year. Their incompatibilities and resulting standoffs soon became legendary, so that when in the spring they decided to share rooms again for the following academic year, there was widespread surprise, and some incredulity. But as Edward explained to his other friends, he and Sandy had spent a year figuring how to live together at close quarters, and there was no sense giving that up. By their last year, they were still together, although they belonged to different clubs, had different sets of friends, different interests, different tastes—except where Sandy found it necessary to follow Edward in his.

Rarely, he even brought himself to ask outright about matters of taste. In those days, only men attended their college. Ninety percent of them wore bluejeans to class, but with coat-and-tie, which meant a tweed coat, an Oxford cloth shirt, normally light blue with collars that buttoned, and any kind of necktie. Footgear was non-canonical, too—just whatever you pulled from under the bunk when the alarm clock sounded.

Sandy noticed that some wore bluejeans that had been ironed, shirts that had been ironed, or bluejeans or shirts that had been left rough-dry. While Edward remained oblivious to these nuances—if that is indeed what they were—Sandy had not only noticed, but for some while tried to identify a protocol governing the different combinations, for, as always, he wanted to do the very best thing possible in order to fit in—into what the British sometimes call "top hole." But having failed to reach any certainties, he gave in to himself and asked Edward what he should do.

When the enquiry came, Edward was grappling with another classical text. Without lifting his eyes, he answered: "Men don't wear bluejeans ironed; nobody ever wears an unironed shirt with a tie." Authoritativeness had conferred authority, upon that and numerous other occasions.

Another time, "Were you invited to join my club?" Sandy had asked, when the two were reading at home.

"Yes, I was, in fact," Edward answered. Study resumed.

After a few minutes, Sandy said: "I was invited to join your club."

"I would have expected so."

"Well, I was. And now I wonder whether I should have done it." Edward was a little cross with himself for having to refer so often to the lexicon, and now here was another word he must look up.

"Done what?" he answered abstractedly.

"I said, I was invited to join your club, and now I wonder whether I should have, after all."

Irreverently, Edward dog-eared the page in his Oxford Classical Text and laid it aside. "Aren't you happy where you are? I mean, since you had the choice, something must have caused you to make the one you did."

"Well, but you had the choice, too. What made you decide?"

"Oh, no one thing so much. The food is good. It's right across Washington Road, which is useful if you're running late."

"Is that all?"

"That's about all," Edward answered, just before setting off a stick of dynamite. Unwittingly, to be sure. "That, and the fact that some rather important men in Wilmington belonged to it"—he was by now restoring the turned-down page, delving back with pleasure into early Greek elegiac verse, tainted by the realization that he must yet again look up the next word—"two brothers and their cousin, friends of my grandfather's. I knew it would please him, since everybody down there thinks belonging to it is a form of apotheosis."

A silence fell—the kind of silence that follows a Wagnerian hammer-blow, whether there's an immediate note in the score or not. Because, as far as he himself knew, apotheosis was what Sandy wanted above all other things. He was wrong, of course. He thought of it as the completeness of "fitting-in." In fact, apotheosis brings total elevation above and separation from all usual things, one supposes, and he failed ungovernably to grasp the stout link between "exclusiveness" and "exclusion."

Although not thinking of it at the time, Edward knew this about Sandy, for it is nearly impossible to keep from someone whom you live with those things of which you are not quite proud. It is when your secrets most irrepressibly seek the light of day that your college roommate is likeliest to be on hand to detect the chink in your defense, through it to see what lies beyond, and to be more keenly alerted to it the more stringently you try to keep it concealed.

Apotheosis within his grasp—and he had let it go! Or, missed one chance. Perhaps he could manage to see his imminent marriage as a brilliant match, reaching his goal by that means.

Claire Cloudsley Elder—Yes, Elder, whether it would be in the newspaper or not—a very...well, imposing, a *socially* imposing name. And soon to be Mrs. Alexander Caldwell Thomas. Rather good-sounding itself, although being around Edward's friend von Babenhausen had sometimes made him feel a little concern about the baldness of "Thomas." (Edward had made friends with the amiable Babenhausen for the uncharacteristically hebephrenic purpose of someday taking him home and introducing him to everybody as "a Hamburger.")

Not long before the date set for Sandy's marriage, invitations to a hunt breakfast had come, one for each of them, since Edward was to be a groomsman and was therefore included in all the festivities:

> Mr. and Mrs. Laurence des C-L. Ashfield
> Crave the Pleasure of Your Company
> At a Hunt Breakfast
> In Honour of
> Miss Claire Cloudsley Elder
> *[There it was!]*
> And
> Mr. Alexander Caldwell Thomas
> Tuesday Evening, the twenty-second of November
> At Nine O'Clock
> Woodleigh House, Peell County, South Carolina

And to each of them also came informal, handwritten notes, one of invitation to the shoot itself, from Laurence, and the other from Lavinia, inviting them to stay with them at Woodleigh.

In New Brunswick, the day for the homily, rather for the reading of the "Parable of the Two Lamps," was approaching, and Thomas must at any cost keep Rhodë out of church. He called her into his study. "Rhodë," he began, as bravely as he could, "I have tried always—Grace and I both have—to avoid asking for your help on Sundays." Rhodë waited, for she knew already, as some say, that something was up. "If Grace were still with me, we *might* be able to carry this off by ourselves, but I doubt it. Simply put, I cannot postpone having a small luncheon party any longer. For various reasons, Sunday will be the day. Can you help me?"

"Certainly I will help you, Father," Rhodë answered. Thomas would have flattered her if he had had to. Not only must she be prevented from hearing the manifestations of respiratory disease over again, after an entirely symptom-free period. But it was also widely accepted that, if you required superb food and discreet service in the dining room, then Rhodë Harmon was your best hope. For with regard to the former, she was well ahead of her time; to the latter, charmingly behind it.

Rhodë knew Thomas' request had sprung from real need; she had no reason—or no definite reason—to question the timing. Further, she did not consider anybody else in New Brunswick, White or Colored ("Black," they were saying now) to be of—she might as well confront simple fact—*"quality"* enough to act as the Canon's housekeeper on an occasion of this kind. Except Miss Alenda, and she was bound to be one of the guests. And there was something else about her, too.

"I know the early service isn't your preference, but maybe you would want to attend that." For at the early service Thomas never preached.

"No, Father; on that day I think I'll do my duty just by being 'a servant of the servant of God.' "

The day and the hour had come. Thomas ascended the pulpit and, without turning toward the altar, substituted for the normal invocation of the Trinity: "Let the words of my mouth and the meditation of my heart...." It had for him a Sectarian ring, but, he must admit, he was about to become a protestant for a time (although not a Protestant).

"Dear people of God," he began as usual, "today...." *At what point shall I first run into trouble?* So he gave an introductory cough, skipping over a few syllables in the process. "...Parable of the Two Lamps. Less familiar than the Parable of the Prodigal Son..."—and at the word "prodigal" he gagged genuinely, although not markedly—"...or than that of the Barren Fig Tree, or even than that of the Gate in the Vineyard Wall...."

This last reference encouraged him a good deal because, though apocryphal, it was at least a real parable. And the Parable of the Two Lamps had never before been heard, nor read. Nor even written, for that matter, until four days earlier. It was a hoax, in fact, if you wanted to look at it that way. Thomas had faced this unpleasant thought square in the face—in his own face in the mirror above the washbasin, at least. He felt that to promulgate it was a right thing; that to attribute it—even by implication—to genuine sacred writ was fraudulent, possibly heretical. But it was in no way blasphemous. He had nothing to fear from heresy, but shrank from fraud as from a menacing beast, and from blasphemy as from something worse yet. He felt at the same time, however, that to withhold the story would be overwhelmingly wrong, for he had come to regard this lesson as a step upon the straight and true path. With the albeit false authority of Holy Scripture it would penetrate deeper into the minds of its hearers. Now this all took place during the time when Thomas had lost his way.

He thought he'd better get on with it. So he embarked upon the attribution, the part he had most dreaded: "The story is told in the Gospel ac..."—Here he coughed paroxysmally, ending with a terrible, stertorous intake of breath, and this was good for many lost syllables indeed. He continued then: "…'th chapter, verses f'…(a wheeze; a stifled cough, complementary gasp)…'ty-one."

Then he saw his Senior Warden, looking alarmed, sitting forward in his box-pew, with his hand on the back of the one ahead. For all Thomas knew, he might be about to rise, come forward to offer help.

So after a pause, he said: "May I beg your pardons for a moment." He went down and into the sacristy without having to pass in front of the altar and so to reverence it. He really did not feel he could do that just then. In refuge of the sacristy, he filled a small tumbler from a carafe of water which the ladies of the Altar Guild always set out for him, and carrying it, he started back into the church. Suddenly, Thomas Strikestraw realized that he need not avoid looking at or touching sacred objects. It was the light—from the fair linen, from the burnished brass, from the Office candles. He saw all this splendor as Light of Truth. The memorial asters and roses and lilies nodded their concurrence.

Once back in the pulpit, Thomas took a token sip of water to indicate why he had gone out. Those in the church who thought about it at all assumed that their Rector "had a bad throat," or even a "chest cold," whatever those maladies might be, and that the water had allayed the symptoms. William Lucas, sitting in the Lucas family pew, which Alenda had so seldom occupied, with his sweetheart, was the exception. For he remembered the afternoon of the burial of the slain sailor.

What had in truth put to rest Thomas's respiratory and other difficulties was this, as the brightness of the appurtenances of worship had reminded him: That from here forth he would be speaking the truth.

The Parable had been typed onto a sheet of paper—one side only, and one page only, doing away with the need for leafing—slipped carefully among texts actually known to the Council of Trent. Anticipation of this small heretical (and possibly, after all, blasphemous) act had given Thomas more than one sleepless night. But now he remembered his growing belief that any story, told in good faith, must have truth in it if it could be completed. And he acknowledged the Source of truth. He had never meant to give this spurious tale canonical status. After today, unless someone happened to remember it, it would be taken away, clean gone forever.

Studded across the page were question-marks in brackets following names, directions, places, geologies…all the accidental things …which Thomas had meant to test for plausibility. When he saw all the little symbols, when he realized his failures to proof the things they followed, he was not concerned, not anymore, because these had contributed nothing in the first place.

"There lived in a splendid house fast by the gates of a Great City, about a stone's cast from the spring of Benzrah-El, a certain rich man. Among his household were two stewards, whom he loved, both the one and the other. And he sought to try them for their worthiness. Accordingly, he sent for them at the going-down of the sun, and bespake them thus: 'I will give to each of you a lamp and to each a measure of oil. When darkness is come, fill and light the lamps and go forth out of this place, westward *[?]* toward Ephratah *[?]*, each filling his lamp from the jar, so long as the oil therein may last.'

"And, lo, servants came forth bearing the lamps and the measures of oil, for so they had been bidden. And one of the stewards said: 'Sire, are we to journey together, or apart?' The Goodman *[?]* of the house answered, saying: 'Neither together, nor yet apart, but so far distant, the one of you from the other, that each can see the light from the other's lamp, but dimly, shining in the darkness.'

"So the two, that is the stewards, went forth out of the house and parted from each other, as they had been bidden.

And they set their faces westward, toward Ephratah *[v. supra]*. And they went forth with their lamps into the darkness, outer darkness of the night, as their master had bidden them."

This seems to be going quite nicely. The repetitions lend a Biblical tone. The tone of the wrong Testament, possibly, but anyhow, Biblical.

"The stewards traveled through the darkness, their lamps lighting their ways. And they walked far enough apart, each from the other, as they had been bidden, so that each might see the other's lamp burning, dimly in the darkness. For when all is dark, even the feeble light of an oil lamp is visible; by day however, the Sun's light, falling upon the whole world, offers to the eye so many distinctions to be made that a lamp and its bearer may not be discerned.

Wording rings false? Too late, now.

"At the break of day, each one found that his jar was empty of oil, and that from his lamp had been consumed all that had been within it. And the lamp had gone out. And about that hour they were come to the edge of a desert.

"The first Steward sat down at the edge of the desert, and laid down his lamp, and beside it the empty jar. 'I shall rest, for I have done as my master bade me,' he said within himself, 'and surely now he will send to fetch me home.'

"The second Steward also set down his lamp and oil jar, saying to himself: 'I have done as my master bade me, but, seeing that it is day, I shall continue, and surely my master will send me tidings, if he would that I should cease from my journey. For if it were not so, he would have told me.'

"After the space of a watch *[?]*, the first Steward beheld afar off a servant of his master's, riding toward him and leading a donkey. The servant approached him and said, 'Sir, the Master bids me ask what you have found.'

" 'I have found that my master, before sending me into the darkness, and before that I should venture into the desert, has given me oil sufficient that I might have light unto my feet all through the darkness, so that by daybreak I might discover the marge of the desert before venturing into it, perhaps there to lose my life.'

"The servant replied: 'Here is a colt….' [Several prior words had been struck through, out of various considerations.] 'The master bids us ride together unto the courts of his house.' And so it was done.

"The second steward set out across the desert. Toward the going-down of the sun, he reached a well of water, and beside it trees, laden with fruit, and so he rested and refreshed himself.

"Now, within the well there dwelt two serpents, far advanced in years, beyond the accounting of man, and of goodly intent, full of knowledge and wisdom.

"As the Steward looked back, lo, he, also, saw one of his master's servants, riding toward him, leading a colt, as indeed the first Steward had seen. Just as before, the servant approached and asked: 'Sir, the Master bids me ask what you have found?'

"To him the Steward made reply, saying: 'My Master sent me into the darkness, but bearing light, a lamp unto my feet upon the journey. The oil was not spent until the dawn, when, by the light of the sun, I saw a desert. Needing no lamp nor oil to light the way, as it was day, I have crossed the desert and found refreshment ready to hand. For there dwelleth within this well two serpents, old, beyond the accounting of man, and of goodly intent. I had neither to search nor to ask nor to render payment, for all this was shown to me and offered freely.'

"Then, handing unto the Steward the reins of the colt, the servant said: 'My Lord, the Master bids you continue your quest.'

"But the Steward asked: 'How am I to know when I have reached the term of my journey and the object of my quest?'

" 'You have come nigh already to reaching this journey's end. But you are to continue. And in due time, you will come again to the Master's courts, fast by the gates of the Great City, the gate-towers of which you will discern long before you reach them.'

"Here endeth the Parable."

The end had been reached, the tale told. Thomas, who had found his way, hoped now only that he might never again have to hear any form of the verb "bid."

X

"Must the winter come so soon? Night after night
I hear the hungry deer wander weeping in the woods,…"
Samuel Barber: "Vanessa," (Libretto, G-C. Menotti)

"No more a fire in my veins hoarded away
It is Venus entire, ineluctably locked to her prey."
J-B. Racine: *Phèdre* (tr. JPT)

EDWARD, AS HE drove, noted the works of autumn: A dying-back of the outworn, a clearing-away of what had turned useless. Leaves, raked together from wherever they had fallen, smoldering now, gathered into small pyres around every steading. Life in retreat from the frontlines.

Wholesome grain in garner stored; ploughing-under and cleansing of the fields had begun.

Edward was on his way to Woodleigh; the extent to which he would leave there less a stranger than upon his arrival could only have been guessed at.

Because traveling southwestward, he had been gaining imperceptibly upon a declining sun. Not enough to make much difference. By the time he had reached the first borders of Peell County, angled light was intensifying color, deepening tone: The tawny broad marshlands and azure channels twisting among them, without shore or bank. Welling creeks and rivulets— Were they flowing at all? Estuarial and at flood? Even though Edward could not even smell the sea from where he had got to?

It was puzzling; or maybe just unfamiliar. No shores, no banks. Oxbows of water, glassy, mirror-like at their lilac-filmed surfaces, reflecting an air growing drowsy, with what looked like haze or dust thickening toward the nadir of the vault of the sky. *I come from tidewater country. But it isn't like this.*

As he drew nearer to Woodleigh, the directions he had been given became more intricate and less plausible. But he followed them, made the final right turn they specified, and found himself, not within an *allée* of majestic live oaks, but on a country lane, straight, level, edged with chance growth: Wax myrtle; *Juniperus virginiana,* known locally as Red Cedar; Chinese tallow tree (the only one with much color—a spectrum still including green); persimmon-hued sassafras; dogwood, rusty now; sumac of a species with small leaflets, uniformly the color of pigeons' blood…more. Parker and John could have both identified and described them all, and many besides.

After the promised three-quarters of a mile, the lane entered at a tangent into the eastern end of an elliptic drive, laid out long ago with two stobs and a line, overspread with uncounted layers of crushed oystershell. And there, centered on the farther long arc of the oval, stood Woodleigh House. There were no eminences in Peell County, yet the old house seemed to be standing on one.

Within The Circle—which was what they called the oval—randomly situated because not set there by design or labor of man, were the anticipated liveoaks. They were immense, all flying languid burgees of tangled Spanish moss, lifted at times upon the evening breeze. Some of the trees were centuries old—and had hindered the inscribing of the ellipse. Their lower limbs now spread so far, still maintaining such girth, that they bent again at last to the earth, touched it, then sprang again toward the sky.

On the right of the lane, the growth thinned then ceased, revealing a margin of land left fallow, and widening rice-fields beyond.

Here there was an area of worn turf where it appeared automobiles were sometimes left, though none was there now. Edward parked, got out of his car, and walked toward the house along the pavement of brick that skirted the driveway around The Circle, at once providing treadway and keeping the shards of shell in bounds.

A man was coming down the broad steps from the verandah. He held out his hand, and said: "I'm Laurence Ashfield; I believe you must be Edward."

"Yes, Sir." For the man was fit- and vigorous-looking enough, but close to, he appeared a decade older than from a distance. "Edward Strikestraw."

"We've been looking forward to having you stay with us. Are your bags in the trunk? Is it locked?"

"There are a duffle and a suit-cover; they're both in the back seat. Everything's open."

"Good." They started up the stairs together. "Ben will fetch your luggage, and Lavinia will show you to your room in a little while." Edward wondered idly who Ben and Lavinia were. "Nobody is here right this minute, I think. Maybe we can have a little visit, before anything happens."

"Is anything expected to happen?"

"Oh, no particular thing. No catastrophe, certainly. But there's bound to be some kind of interruption, before very much longer." This struck Edward as odd; not the uncertainty, but the frankness with which Mr. Ashfield spoke about it to himself, a stranger. The man obviously cherished his solitude, but seemed quite willing to share it. *Except that you can't share solitude, can you? Solitude shared is solitude abolished.* Laurence pulled a heavy rocking chair up next to his own. This produced a loud scraping sound. Edward was aware only then how quiet it was at Woodleigh. "I know you and Sandy are roommates; but you don't come from Augusta, too, do you?"

"I live in New Brunswick; it's near Wilmington."

"North Carolina?" Edward nodded. "What a beautiful region that is!"

"To me, a lot of it is very beautiful."

"Oh, it's true that if you go either too far inland or too far to the north the landscape gets a little scruffy. But the Cape and the River; the islands and shorelines! Those are unmatched."

"I feel almost like saying Thank you, but, then, they're not mine."

"Oh, yes. They are yours. And we ought all to look carefully at the beauty—or assess carefully the virtue—in what is ours—ours for a time. To admire is in a way to possess. Or, what do you think?"

"I have never asked myself about that. But now you ask, I have sometimes felt a little possessive of all that region."

"But, because it's beautiful?"

"Yes, Sir. I believe so. To a point, that's why."

"And, being away in the North, feeling a bit defensive?"

"Yes." He thought for a moment longer. "But not about the River itself; it couldn't be possessed, and it needs no defense."

"There's something…mystical about the Great River. When I was in school, I crossed it often. Inland. At Fayetteville. Each time, I felt I ought to be making the sign of the cross or pouring out a libation, or something of that kind." Laurence, who was God-fearing but not devout or pious, like his late brother-in-law Parker Jones, had never in his life made the sign of the cross, and never would. (The pouring of libations was entirely another thing.)

Edward felt this man was taking him on quite easily. It seemed essentially hospitable. It was very agreeable. Edward had long since wearied of having to *handle* people—behave, talk in a certain way to avoid tapping into an undercurrent of restricted ideology or simply one of general hostility.

"I live with my grandfather. Strikestraw, that is. Both my parents are gone—I never knew either of them."

"What a sorrow! What a pity." You could tell the news made him truly sorrowful. And you could see he mourned a little, in his heart, for Edward and for himself, as well. Perhaps it came down to the question whom the bell was tolling for. " We are the converse of you. We have no children. I don't know why, but it has never troubled me much. With my wife, it has been quite the other way around. It's a worn-out expression, of course, but we must 'play the hand we're dealt.' "

"Yes, we have to." Undisturbed silence followed for a time. "Sir, you mentioned having to cross the Cape Fear to get to your school; where did you go? I mean, if it's any of my business."

"Of course it's your business, or I would not have mentioned it. In Virginia; St Columba's."

"I went to school at home, in New Brunswick, but I had—have—a cousin who went to St. Columba's. I visited him there once. My other grandparents—not ones in common with the cousin, and he was—is—too distant a cousin, anyway—lived nearby. I should say, *live* near there. I seem to be trying to erase selected features from my past. It may be that I'm giving it up piecemeal, knowing that I'm going to have to give up the whole of boyhood before very much longer. And I'm going to miss it."

This young man must be very much at ease with himself—more so than I recall being. Ever. "When we first reach adulthood, I think, then we get an odd sort of feeling that our youth is over. It's not, though. Or, mine's not. It goes right along, keeping step beside us. Throughout all our life, I imagine. I imagine life must be cumulative."

"It would account for a lot of things."

"But, now, did you tell me your grandparents' name? The ones in Virginia?"

"Their name is Singleton. They're called Libby and Bunny. They live in the country, outside Warrenton."

"Good Lord! I'm not an educated man, Son, and I don't pretend to be, but all the same I'd hate for you to think I can't speak except in platitudes. Yet it really is a small world! I used to know them—your grandparents, and your aunts. No. One of them must be—have been—your mother. Which?"

"Anne. You knew her, too, then? Because I didn't. She died a week after I was born."

Edward was not fond of making this disclosure. When he must, he was accustomed to being offered condolence, and he didn't like that. Laurence Ashfield's reaction, though, was something entirely unexpected. He became quite solemn, quite still. He said nothing. He seemed to regard the loss as his own. But then his almost physical tautness dissolved, and he said: "Such a sorrow! What a thing to hear! No. I knew your mother, of course, but not very well. Nobody seemed to, really. Peggy—your Aunt Peggy—I did know well. Everybody did. But Anne liked to keep outside the lines; she watched the rest of us at play, fouling out, making fools of ourselves. She just watched. In fact, she watched so long it overcame me. She was very beautiful. I think I can see her in you. My recollection of her. But I expect I only think I do.

"Very suggestible! Me, I mean." They fell silent for another while. Laurence noticed Edward looking beyond the oaks, over the near ploughland, and across the rice fields, the broad marsh beyond them. He wondered whether the boy knew what he was seeing; whether, if he did, it might interest him. Maybe they would have a chance to talk about all that; maybe even go out into those fields, if there should be time.

Woodleigh House, abiding serenely in guard of her grove of ancient oaks, had never been one of those monuments most sought out by travelers, both because of its remoteness and because of its plainness. "Where," they would have wanted to know, "were the double porticoes and broken pediments, corbelled cornices, and quoins?"

The answer: Upon the kinds of houses that required them. But Woodleigh spoke with a quieter voice. Quieter and surer. For she was elder to all of the others, and had no need of giving loud commands. Depending upon which brick or plank or pane or peg you counted from, something of her had been standing there since the last decade of the Seventeenth Century. Two stories of plain board siding, butted, not lapped, rested upon an arcaded basement made up of many kinds of masonry—tabby to Portland cement—the unified form they made up had been stuccoed over at some point, and was due anytime now for a fresh coat of soft brick-dust slip.

The house exhibited a gentle but lively skyline, roof hipped, above it rising four tall chimneys, seeming to prompt, in whisper: *Lift up your hearts!*

The verandah, where Laurence was entertaining his young guest, was part of the first storey. It ran all across, with box-columns and picketed railing. Woodleigh seemed to be a simple farmhouse, which in a way, at first, it had been meant to be, but great.

Suddenly, Laurence laughed and said: "It would probably dumbfound your grandfather to know what, in the name of 'hunting' you are going to be subjected to tomorrow. He was a stickler for the right term, and he would...."

"Mr. Ashfield, I doubt whether my grandfather Singleton has ever been a 'stickler' for anything *but* terms. Hard of me as it must seem to hear it."

"No, Son. Still, I know the difference between 'hunting' and 'shooting,' and how important the distinction is to some people. We're calling tomorrow's outing a 'deer hunt.' And a very long time ago people in these parts did ride to hounds after deer."

By whatever name it was to be called, Laurence explained the characteristic features of the next day's quest for prey, leaving Edward to feel that the traditions of the Carolina Lowcountry were far other than those of the Virginia Blueridge.

"Not only that," Laurence concluded, "but even though it's how we do it here, on Blackwater and Coosaw Creek, yet some of my friends—grown men, and otherwise sensible—consider this way to be the 'real' way—to be what all people mean when they speak of 'hunting.' "

Laurence and Edward had spoken easily together and were inclined to like each other. They had spoken together, and now were silent, and comfortable in the silence. They heard, soon, a rumbling in the lane, growing louder. It was punctuated once by a sudden "thud." The rumbling was resumed. Into The Circle swung an open Jeep, with "Woodleigh Farm" neatly lettered in white upon the near-side door. The lady who was driving pulled up next to Edward's car. In back were a number of spaniels, who were eager to jump overboard but did not do so until the driver had come around and summoned them.

They sat upon the turf in a semicircle until given some voice-command by their mistress, from the verandah audible but unintelligible. As she and her hounds came toward the house, the men rose. The lady and her little pack came up the steps. "Lavinia," Laurence said, "here is Edward. Edward Strikestraw." Warmly she smiled and extended her hand. The spaniels sat again in a semicircle, this time upon the floorboards. Lavinia, tall, slender, was dressed in tweeds. There was also some touch of brilliant purple. Edward never succeeded in remembering what it had been. Imposing first, lovely second. The first Edward would sustain of a barrage of this. At first imposing, then, like Woodleigh House itself, lovely.

"Sandy has told us so many *impressive* things about you, Edward. Welcome to Woodleigh." *Sotto voce:* "I shall never forget the first time I was told that! I was standing just where you are."

"Well, Ma'am, now I'm afraid you'll find that nearly all of them are untrue!" Everybody laughed a little, and the spaniels all wagged their tails—to the extent to which an English Springer, in America where docking is legal, is able to do this.

"To the contrary, I think I can see already that they all are entirely true. Rennie, have you not sent for anything to drink?"

"No. We've been talking."

"Then you all wait here. I'll take care of it, get myself settled, and be back in a moment!" She left her hounds on the verandah.

Laurence stood up. "You may as well meet the Upstairs Pups."

"They're beautiful; and they must belong to a kindred."

"They do. How did you know?"

"Well, Sir...."

"Do, please, leave off the 'Sir;' that's if you can, and still feel comfortable'

"Anybody who knew about it, but not in depth, would say these are four English Springers, liver-and-white."

"Aren't they?"

"No. Not exactly. The true 'liver-color' has more yellow in it. The pups...."

"I wonder why we call them 'pups.' All of them have reached maturity; Proud Mary is an old lady."

"Well, but I think, Sir, that what are called 'dog-people' use it as an affectionate term. ...these pups' liver-color lacks some orange. They're actually chocolate-colored, and white. Some grandsire or granddam must have been white with black. That gives this color, and then it often breeds true. Not always, I think, but often."

"I wish Lavinia would come back. She would be so much interested in what you're saying. Anyhow, let me introduce you: Hattie Mae, come; Alecto, come!" These two obeyed. "Hannah Belle, Proud Mary, Come!" And they, too, eventually rose and welcomed Edward, who had knelt, holding out a hand to be sniffed at then licked.

Proud Mary hung back longest, but once the others had got out of her way, she came to all fours, ambled over to Edward, tentatively licked his proffered fingers, then his arms, and face, and hair.

"You really like them?" Laurence asked. "Because if you're just being gracious to them, I'll have them put up. Even if they are the Upstairs Pups."

!

"Oh, no, Sir! I can't imagine—I can't easily imagine—life without dogs. Ours at home, though, is on his last—on his assortment of last legs."

Edward patted Proud Mary, chucked her under the chin. Lavinia opened the screen door, just as Laurence was saying: "She's an affectionate old bitch."

"Shall I go back inside?" Lavinia said, her grey eyes sparkling. But she held open the door so that Mary Alice Araby, cook, housemaid, and one of Lavinia's true and most treasured friends could come through with a tray of iced water, hot black coffee, whiskey, and a siphon. Mary Alice set these things down, and the biped women went back inside.

On her way, Lavinia said: "We are very, very happy to have you with us, Edward. Please let me know when you want to go to your room; several young gentlemen will be staying with us. The girls will be at my sister's house." She let the screen door bang. Southern ladies often did; gentlemen, never. Why? It was the way it was.

"Her sister," Laurence said, "is in reality *my* sister. She lives at Clear Creek." After a moment's calculation he added: "That's another house. My great grand-uncle built it." Absently: "The only other big house just close around here is one *not* built by my family. It is far grander, but a ruin. In fact, that's what people call it: 'The Ruin.' The true name of it is 'Dodona;' I don't know why."

"Is there an oak—I mean a conspicuous oak—there?"

"Yes."

"Then that must be why."

"Alecto, Laurence said. "Is that a good name for a bitch?"

"It's an excellent name for one!"

"Just to look at the word, I can't tell whether it's masculine or feminine. But I thought I remembered that Alecto was one of the Eumenides."

"She was. A big, bad one, too."

"Weren't they the same as the Furies?"

"Yes, Sir, they were. May still be."

"It's at times like these I regret not having gone on with my education. Go easy on the *Sir,* now."

A young Black man, or a boy, had come from behind the house. Ben— that's who it was—waved first, and the other two waved in answer. He took out Edward's luggage, then went back inside. And now Lavinia came to show Edward to his room. Within, the house was more fully wrought, although not much more. The floors were of heart pine, highly polished; the dadoes, which skirted every wall, were of cypress, unpanelled, stripped of paint, and not polished, with unfinished plaster above. Or what looked like it.

Lavinia led Edward up a broad, shallow staircase, with a landing at a little over half its rise. Beneath, a paneled passage led from the front to the back hallway. You could look over one or other balustrade onto either space. It was like a small bridge. This architectural variation, Edward soon discovered, gave an immense psychological force to the difference between upstairs and downstairs. It was as though one must stop, think, be sure, before turning and continuing all the way up.

They turned, and then completed the ascent. Edward had the room on the southwest corner of the house. There were two tall windows on each outside wall. When his hostess had left him, he made a languid tour of these, looking down upon The Circle, its oaks and brick and oystershells. From the west windows he saw the forest, hardwoods, with a great many trees of very old growth.

Light through their screenwork of trunk and branch, in late afternoon, hazy and chromatic, told of the home of the owl, the place of streambed and running of deer.

Here he was, Edward, finally alone—which he considered his normal condition. Some of his friends scoffed at this. One even asked him why he thought he had a right to solitude. (He had answered never a word.) He walked several times along the two sides of the room, looking out through these windows at these sights. And then he realized that "sights," as such— and monuments—were lacking. It gave peace to the eye; the eye, to the mind. All in the quiet.

When he turned away from the windows, Edward saw that his duffle bag had been placed upon a folding luggage rack at the foot of one of the beds. Then, at the foot of the other, he recognized Sandy's suitcase (It was new. They had selected it together. It was important to Sandy, for it was to be his "honeymoon" suitcase—God alone knew what it was destined, on that occasion, to contain).

Well, so they were to be roommates here, too. That was all right. Sandy was neither a landmark nor a monument, and would not disturb the restfulness of the room. A fire had been laid, in case of chill.

November was readying everything, emboldening everything: Color, the curious warmth that breathes through the coming of winter to the Coastal Plain, imagination, expectation, appetite.

Here, in this choice room, there would be the privacy needed for Edward's tying Sandy's bowtie. For Sandy, although he had mastered many skills, had not mastered this one.

This first evening, everyone went to Clear Creek for cocktails with Alina and Bob Barrington. There were not many guests. Only half of the young people had arrived. The rest were expected the next morning, the day of the shoot itself. And the "outliers," as Mrs. Barrington and Lavinia Ashfield explained to Edward—the distant, older neighbors, many of whom had been friends of Mr. Jack and Miss Allie—had not been included, in order to spare them the journey on the eve of their having to make it again.

This house was more richly furnished—thicker Turkey carpets upon the floors, heavier drapery about the windows, more furniture per square yard of floorspace. But though rich, everything was select. There was nothing to suggest that either things, or ideas about things, had been too hurriedly acquired. The most characteristic feature of any given room was its paintings, which were not of a sort expected in a house designed, built, and otherwise furnished as Clear Creek was. These were very big, for the most part, and very strange, in every part. They neither depicted nor suggested anything. Not by form. Not even by color. They were all somehow refulgent. It was as though to remove any one of them would be to dim and flatten everything else around.

Edward asked Alina about them, and she seemed pleased to find he liked them. "My first husband painted those. But he said he never understood exactly where they were leading and would keep on with them until he made that discovery. His death took away any opportunity, and for years I stowed them, crated—assuming that if he thought they were incomplete, then they must be.

"But how much of this is a young man willing to listen to? I know I must be boring you."

"I will listen gladly to as much about them as you're willing to tell me." In fact, Edward was prepared to listen to Alina talk about the pictures, or about anything else.

"One day, when I was about to go and bring Bob down here to marry him, I got them out and got Connie—her real name's Yukoneta; she's the one serving drinks—to hold the ladder, and I hung them. If you can imagine that! Then I asked Lavinia to come and see them. She was affected by them. Really, very much affected. I could see it."

"Well, I can believe it easily. I know nothing of painting—therefore not even 'what I like.' But you can't imagine any of them taken away, can you?"

"No, you can't. Or, I can't." Hostess and guest had stopped beneath a painting, a particular one; it hung above the huntboard in the hallway. There seemed to issue from it an inexhaustible supply of light. The mirror—for Edward had still not been able to adopt the term "looking glass,"—hanging upon the opposite wall, once the two had moved from between, seemed to have to strain its physical property of reflectance in order to return all the light. According to the laws of physics, of course, the mirror could not have given back the light in its completeness. But physical laws sometimes add needless complication to simple truth, even though most often they bring simple truth out of needless complication.

"There is one other canvas I'd like to show you, possibly before all of you leave. Everybody says it is different from all these others."

"I should let you get back to the party; but I hope you will find time to show it to me later on."

The party ended. Back at Woodleigh, the household were preparing to go to bed. Lavinia and Laurence spoke about Edward. Neither had met him before, and each one had been favorably impressed. Laurence told her about Dodona, then about Alecto. "I do seem to remember a bit of a privately printed poem that ran: '...where Dodona's oaks yet wave.' I'd forgotten," Lavinia said. "We must look it up. He is studying the Classics, now. I think he plans to go to law school after graduation."

"Well, he certainly seems intellectually equipped to succeed. And I should think personally, although I don't know what the study or practice of law requires in that way. But if you ask him anything, either he knows how to answer or is not afraid to stop and think it over. If you say something to him, he listens to it."

"I think, Rennie, that he listens to you because he realizes that you actually *are* saying something to him. Much, if you ask me, is said to young men and women of his age that is scarcely worth listening to."

"And you think he knows the difference?"

" 'This Land is your land; this Land is my land...'?; 'If I had a hammer, I'd swing it in the morning...'? Knowing the difference doesn't take great power of discrimination. Though I think he may have such power."

"I can see that those are not closely-crafted ideas, if that's what you mean."

"That is what I mean. And, to a point, it's all right—on every generation floats a froth of lore thought characteristic of its members."

"It's certainly true that a lot of hubba-hubbering gets in the way of the serious ones. Of course I avoided offending, simply by not mixing with the serious ones!"

"I gather you still regard yourself as not serious."

"I do. And I look upon it all with tremendous relief."

"You think that, because you did not go to college, you are not serious; but let me tell you this: I did go, and there were no more than a handful of serious girls in my class."

"When it came time for me to go to college, I knew I was going to have you and the rice fields, and those were enough. I decided to spend some time merely having fun, while I waited to get a little older."

"Most of the people who do seek so-called higher educations aren't doing anything but 'waiting to get a little older,' either.

"But what about this: How many men of your place and present age sit around reading Plotinus? *Plotinus!* On Sunday afternoon, I found the book lying face down in your chair and thought I'd see what it's like."

"And what did you find it like?"

"Nothing. I spent forty-five minutes reading a very short paragraph, and at that I could hardly tell what he was getting at."

"It's a pity. He thought he was just interpreting Plato. (Hear me say, 'Just'!) But he was really a lot more subtle. Or contorted, whichever way you want to look at it. Anyhow, if you found him that troublesome, then you oughtn't do have bothered."

"Why do *you* bother?"

"I read him for fun."

"If you're planning to finish with one of your little grins, then you'd better hurry. I'm about to put out the light."

"We seem to have wandered from the point."

"I can quickly bring us back: Watch Sandy and Edward speaking together tomorrow; watch how Edward hangs on Sandy's every word!"

Downstairs, in the back hallway, the Pankeytown Hounds—they were different ones now, but like all of us, not very different in kind—growled softly now and then, wallowed about, struck their tails against door jambs and table legs. The house and household grew as quiet as they could be expected to grow upon such a night.

Tomorrow, they would have...*I can hardly believe my ears, Lavinia, when you speak in that way*...a wonderful evening's party, and, beforehand, a deer-hunt, a deer-shoot, whichever one might want to call it....

"Alina? This is Lavinia."

"I know. How are you?"

"Very well, thank you. All of us enjoyed tremendously being over there yesterday evening."

"We very much enjoyed having you." Then there followed a pause during which Woodleigh birds chirped through to Clear Creek and Clear Creek birds chirped through to Woodleigh, in welcome of so magnificent, so bright and cool a day.

"Do you think, possibly," Lavinia said at last, "that Connie could put on a brunch for the young people? I don't know how many girls you have there yet. But the boys are beginning to arrive here regularly; they're quite charming, of course, but they're getting underfoot."

"Connie can do anything. Send them over."

"Oh, thank you so much! I know I'll get flustered eventually, but now's entirely too early."

"Send them right along. And , Lavinia…."

"Yes?"

"This boy Edward…."

"Strikestraw."

"I showed him the ballroom—of course without calling it that. He was amazed about my Big Brother. But I took him there to show him the 'anomalous' painting."

"What did he think of it?"

"He seemed to like it quite a lot."

"And?"

"He said that in kind it was like the others, and seemed surprised that anyone saw any, as he put it, 'underlying' difference."

"Alina, here come more."

"We're ready and waiting."

Ready and waiting…and bedeviled. But she ought not to be. Probably nothing was amiss. When all these girls had got out, when Connie began straightening up after them, then surely it would turn up. She wouldn't fret over it anymore. Clothing, bedclothes, *chiffonerie* spread all about!

Her son was staying the two nights at Woodleigh, so that the bedrooms at Clear Creek—this one included—could be given over to the young ladies. If he had been staying at home, he would have occupied his rooms on the second floor of the Carriage House. His Spartan rooms, these given over, too.

But when he had been a boy, his had been the southwest bedroom—this room, from which something was now missing. When John—they had finally been able to stop calling him 'Little John,' now he was out of law school—had moved into the Carriage House he had had this request to make: "If you don't mind, Mother, no matter what use this room is put to eventually, please leave that little bottle in the windowsill."

And on the morning of the shoot, it had been gone. Or at least Alina had then first noticed it gone. None of the girls seemed to have seen it at all.

At the upper boat landing where the meet was to take place, Tommy Araby, with tractor and mower, had carved from the chest-high grasses a remarkably neat rectangle to accommodate easy circulation of battered Jeeps, pickup trucks, and boat trailers. The cut and fallen grasses would provide, for many, a vivid memory of that unforgettable afternoon, if not by their mown sweetness, then by their allergenic fire. The hunters were either at home in those regions, or wanderers there; staying and roaming, both, are in any case usually processes of alternating burn and balm.

At four o'clock, the guests and helpers began to arrive. Trucks backed down the ramp. The narrow little flat-bottomed boats of cypress, some very old, others new, all alike in fabric and design—except for notable variation in beam—began slipping out onto the shining water of the Creek. At first a few would be rafted together empty, but presently all, separated, carried their own hapless boatmen, whose duty it was to keep their craft milling about until the hunt could be organized and sent upon its way.

The elderly men arrived just in the way the younger ones did, except as passengers in their own conveyances. Colored men, who had been selected and hired according to their experience and skill, drove, and, once their sometimes rickety companions had got out and away, carried out backing and launching as easily as they might have driven straight ahead along a country road.

Everyone was dressed the same: Trousers and jackets in the clay-like orange of field khaki, lugged boots, shirts of Navy-blanket grey, usually very lightweight. It was warmer than was usual there, at that time of year, even at a quarter past four, beneath the westward-tumbling sun. Many of the gentlemen of all ages and both colors had taken off their jackets. A few of Sandy's friends—ones who considered that they had physiques to support it—so far forgot themselves as to take off their shirts as well.

But before the first could begin to preen, Laurence appeared among them, easy, smiling. He said a few words, and these young men all suddenly and simultaneously vanished into the grasses or the trees crowding the riverbank, to emerge in a moment entirely dressed, their canvas jackets concealing two distinct layers of sweat.

A half-hour had been allowed for organization. That is, no one who arrived after half past four could expect to take part. At twenty minutes past four, there entered the clearing a convertible sports-car, the top down. It was one manufactured by Mercedes-Benz, designated "190-SL," and it was at that time rather fabled. This one was driven by a young man who must be about Edward's age; probably, he thought, a friend of Sandy's whom he would meet later. Upon his pleasant face he seemed to wear constantly the approach of a smile. His hair was in brush-cut. That was all Edward could see from where he was standing. Then, as the young man got out of the car, Edward saw that he was above average height, and broadly built. But he moved easily. He went directly toward the river, hailing no one, but spoken to or patted upon the shoulder by all the older men he passed. He nodded or smiled or briefly clasped hands with each one.

Already, Edward had noticed that most people were outfitted with hip flasks, some of these quite splendid, of silver, of crystal with silver mounts; occasionally, there would be one in very contemporary design, in stainless steel, nickel finished. But the boy with the brush-cut hair seemed to have an ordinary Army surplus canteen in its canvas cover, worn upon his belt. It kept snaring the left side of his coat as he strode along.

Edward had been watching all the proceedings, all the people with interest and care. Now Laurence, with an elderly Black man, appeared beside him. "Edward, this is Uncle Ed." The old man found in the identity of their names cause for great mirth. "Unk, this is Mr. Edward Strikestraw. I'm going to leave it up to you to see he enjoys the afternoon. Is that good?"

"Yes, Sir, Mr. Laurence. Come on, Mr. Edward, so I can show you one of the boats and tell you how we do this thing."

"Edward!" Laurence shouted over a little distance. "You're the last boat— Please understand, it's meant as an honor." Edward waved. Laurence drifted off among the others, laying out the campaign, answering questions, accepting suggestions, exchanging greetings.

Soon, helpers appeared with the swampland equivalent of the stirrup cup: Shot glasses of bourbon handed around from the rusted lids of oil drums, over which, nevertheless, big linen napkins had been laid. Then Laurence said loudly, addressing them all: *"Bonne chasse! Bonne chance;"* Everyone drank. A tall man with a fixed smile ("Smile" comes closest to denoting the actual expression) and eyes of unsettling pallor and fixedness, before he drank, first poured a small amount of liquor onto the earth. Then they started down to the river and to the logjam of boats.

Setting forth wasn't easy. The embarkation point was a narrow rim of sandy beach that lay along the greater curvature of a bend in the river. "Right now, Mr. Edward," Uncle Ed said, "the trick is to get the right people into the right boats. There's already one in each—the ones with the red faces." And he found cause for mirth in this, too. The boatmen were in fact comical in their efforts to steer clear of each other while yet coming up in sequence for their parties "They'll mostly stay in their boats all evening. The other two—that's you and me—take turns driving the deer to the river. A lot of times, you see them already there, come down for a drink."

"How do you drive them?"

"It's easy, Mr. Edward. In fact, half the time I feel like a fool when I do it. You walk into the woods, quiet as you can be, for ten minutes or so. You stop and listen every once in a while."

"For what?"

"I never have known—just for whatever there is to hear, I reckon. Then, you turn around and come back, but this time you tread on dry sticks, brush up against pine boughs, make the leaves crackle. All that. And what is supposed to have happened is that you've got around behind some deer—or a deer. And I'll tell you a thing about that, Mr. Edward. When a stag and a doe are walking together, and they come to a clearing, the stag will stop at the edge. And he'll let the doe walk on. I who tell you this, I've seen it."

"Why does he do it, do you think?"

"So she'll be the one to get shot. Or, get shot first, anyway."

"The boat, all this time, is it just drifting? How do you know where to find it when you come back out of the woods?"

"You will find it right where you got out of it. If the shooter waiting in the boat sights any quarry, then he shouts and fires. Next time, after the boat drifts on along downstream some, you switch places. That is, it'll be my turn to try to drive the quarry, your turn to wait and hope to fire."

"How do you keep from getting shot yourself?"

"It just comes to you naturally. You'll pick it up in a hurry."

As the successive boats were boarded, Edward saw that most were outfitted with small trolling-motors. These were now cocked out of the water. They were suitably primitive, with cooling vanes, carburetion, components of ignition systems exposed. The boy with the brush cut, though, had taken his place in a very ancient-looking boat with an incongruously sleek motor. It was not larger than the others. But it seemed finely made and its works were concealed in an enameled steel cowl. It bore no manufacturer's mark. *This man must be working on having the best of everything.*

But that work was already done; for on that afternoon, he did in fact have the best of everything already.

Most of the boats carried paddles; nearly all, poles. In a few were oars. The brush-cut boy's boat was one of these, and so was Uncle Ed's.

When it came their turn to board, Edward was for some reason surprised to see that their boatman was the tall man with the fixed smile, if that were what it was, and white eyes. He introduced himself to Edward, then, with a single exception, said nothing more for the following two-and-a-half hours. "Mr. Szazarowski is our boatman," Uncle Ed explained, rolling his eyes all the way to the contrasting white peripheries of the sclerae. "He'll use the pole to push us on a little, maybe, and to steer around tree stumps and over waterlogs."

And about then such an obstacle loomed up; Mr. Szazarowski's work was hindered by the frail-looking motor clamped onto the transom. When they were past, the Boatman took out his flask, silently offered it to the others, who declined, then, before drinking from it himself, he poured a small amount of its contents overboard, saying: "Actaeon and Diana."

"There. Like that," Uncle Ed said, nearly in a whisper. "He'll just guide us downstream, if he doesn't guide us himself." Edward was puzzled, then understood. "Old Man River." As the little boats glided lazily upon the limpid water, the peaceable, jovial little mob from the landing broke up into individual groups of men smiling, saluting friends, and their friends. Laurence went back to Woodleigh.

Gradually the parties drifted farther apart. Edward, holding a borrowed rifle across his knees—he had rejected the use of deer-slugs or buckshot; he could not recall ever having fired a shotgun of any calibre or configuration—watched a late shaft of sunlight strike the water, bend in its course by a few degrees. Descending, it revealed the rich shades of amber that tannin, leached from the bark of trees growing at the stream's edge, it was said, lent to the water; it made the sand in the shallows glow like Rheingold.

A light riverwind had been blowing toward them at the start; it picked up a notch and set random leaves fluttering in little frenzies of holy madness. A few came free, fell onto the water, upon which they slipped away, outdistancing the stalkers, although borne upon the same current. *And the year is slipping away, too,* Edward thought.

And the years are slipping away, too, Uncle Ed said within himself.

"Now," Uncle Ed said. Mr. Szazarowski brought the boat to the right bank. "Mr. Edward, you go first into the woods." There was still plenty of light. Edward walked in as silently as he could, and out again, but as loudly, pulling back saplings then letting them go snapping, treading upon scrub palmetto to produce a satisfying clacking. No quarry was sighted. But Edward found making all the noise a lot of fun.

"Now let us go across, and I will get out on the other side." The Boatman, with his pole, pushed the boat backward, away from shore, and then they started forward, out across the river. By now, they had heard half a dozen shots from in the distance. When they had got to the left bank of the Creek, Uncle Ed got out and vanished into the darker wood. The other two waited, and while they did, they heard more shots, and a shout. Everything was quiet, then.

Edward loaded, waited. After a time the sounds of the swamp, of the evening's coming-on seemed to grow a little easier to distinguish from manmade sounds. They also seemed to grow more numerous, crowded more together. Edward was seized by the fear that he might suddenly become confused, do something foolish, disastrous, even. A branch cracked somewhere; the wind soughed in the pines.

Then came a brushing of scrub, and a doe appeared, in flight, but stopping at the water's edge. Edward took aim, fired, and she fell. When this happened, he was filled first with sudden sorrow, then with dread. *All right; we've played our parts. Stand up, now, and run away!*

Uncle Ed came out of the forest. "A fine shot, Mr. Eddie!" Edward got out of the boat to see what he had done; the Boatman came with him. He looked at the figure unmoving of beauty and grace. With her clear, dark eye, she looked up at him. He knew she could still see him and that, while she could, she wanted to study as closely as possible the man who had killed her.

Uncle Ed sat in the prow. Edward and Mr. Szazarowski had to climb in from abeam. Mr. Szazarowski had been placating lavishly the geniuses of hunt and river. He caught his boot heel between the inner gunwale and the slender shaft of the oar—going some way toward confirming Edward's view that oars were ominously awkward here upon this narrow stream. Proving it, the Boatman fell with a crash. Edward looked quickly around to see whether, at the sound, his doe, alarmed, hadn't stood and bolted.

So Edward punted out into the dark water; little flocks of duck settled on the surface nearby, then swam ahead, and alongside—black, mallard, wood duck. "Thanks for the compliment, Uncle Ed; I wish I'd missed."

The duck were now drifting most of the way, or most of the time, if to them those paths differed from each other. But every now and then you could see a small web of russet or black come nearly to the surface behind one or other, giving a lazy shove.

"Well, Brother Eddie, I know how you feel. I've felt it, too. Often and again I've felt it. They say we've got to keep them down, though."

"It is hard." They were in midstream, now, and the languid current bore them along. Among the duck, maple leaves came to rest. They were red, as of dried blood. Every one fell underside up, however, showing a glaucous surface without lustre. This was like the death that would have filmed over his doe's eyes by the time he saw her again. He knew that he would know her when they met.

"The deer weep; did you know that?"

"No. Do they really?

"Yes. Get Mr. Laurence to show you the skull of a deer. You can see the little dents where their tears run along. And do you want to know why they shed those tears all the time?"

"No."

"They do it because they know they have to be killed."

Edward thought over this. "I can see that. So beautiful and gentle, yet they must be killed."

The little bands of duck parted, then, and fell back. When ten yards astern, they flew away. The careful arrangement of the shooting-flotilla had collapsed, so that as darkness fell some of the boats were working the river and woodland almost in tandem; others had got entirely isolated.

Yet the pace of the party was steadily increasing as it drew to a close.

Volleys of gunfire were now heard; individual reports punctuated them. In the bows of more and more of the little craft, mantle lanterns had been lighted. Clouds of leaves were falling oftener now, but unseen except fleetingly in the lamplight, as the rising land breeze stripped the upper limbs in darkness; above the hunters the almost-bare tree branches declared the shoot over, as though by trying to deceive them into believing the forest exhausted of quarry, just as of sere foliage.

Abruptly, it was as though there were hounds, after all. Unseen but afield, howling through the forest like a winter's wind. Some only following spilt blood. Others locked with claw and riptooth onto their prey. An Actaeon whose luck had run out, in spite of all Mr. Szazarowski could do?

At the end of the shoot, shouting and lanternlight, now permissible, were bound to have increased. But the shouts were strident. Beams of light were rippling in chaos together with the sound. Edward's boat drew closer. He sensed Panic fear ahead. And then he saw it. The Jeeps and trucks and boat trailers had been brought down to the lower landing to retrieve hunters and watercraft. Now some of the men were apparently trying to maneuver the trucks so that headlight beams might be cast upon the cause and focus of confusion. Two, reversing in intersecting arcs, had their trailers snarled together; the temporarily witless drivers were continuously sounding their horns.

"Unk, put down the motor and get me over there."

"Yes, Sir, Brother Eddie!"

When a child, and facing something fearsome—a hypodermic injection, say—Edward had learned to distract his thought from fear by taking an interest in whatever was about to happen. Because he really did know that whatever it was, it was for his good. He really did know it. He had extended this process over the years, for avoidance of panic, or confusion, or delusion of any kind. And it had worked.

Thus, as they drew nearer, he overcame the fear all people have of being unequal to tasks about to be laid upon them by fixing his mind intently and systematically upon the scene looming ahead. "Take me right up to that boat, Unk." He jumped overboard, landing in four feet of water, with good footing, shouting at the same time: "Get back, you Goddamned idiots!"

A capsized boat was held by an oar from being righted. The oar had come unshipped, been drawn downward by the current, and had been driven into the sand just at Edward's feet, still fastened in the rowlock, the handle now protruding outboard and upward through the surface of the water.

Edward reached below the waterline and ran his hand along the shaft of the oar. Everything was jammed tight. When his fingers reached the rowlock, he felt carefully for the head of the pin. With grip-strength and might he didn't really have, he withdrew it. The oar came free of the gunwale, was at the same time buoyed violently upward and forced outward. And the boat was then free to be righted, seemed to try to right herself.

To the bewildered men on the other side, Edward, having evaded the trajectory of the oar, shouted: "Lift!" They lifted, together, more of them wading in to help, now that it was clearer what ought to be done, but some were impeded by the limbs of a fallen tree, waterlogged and immovable.

Bob Barrington had already left for Clear Creek. Tommy Araby went seeking him; they returned to the landing.

The boy with the brush-cut hair was stretched out upon the ramp. And he was still.

"He's dead, Bob; drowned." Hardly more than a whisper.

Then Bob saw the Strikestraw boy kneeling on the concrete ramp. "Dr. Barrington!" Edward shouted. "He's *not* dead. His heart is beating!" Then Edward turned back to the men standing near him, the only two or three who dared to, apparently. "Get his head *down*slope. Turn him over. Yes, I can see he's bleeding. He can survive bleeding. He can't survive drowning."

Dann Gadsden, a vast Colored man, had been told to press with his full weight on the boy's back, and had hesitated. But Edward, who normally exhibited restrained good manners, particularly toward Blacks in those uncertain times, ordered him: "And he can survive broken ribs, as well. *But not drowning.*"

Bob reached them. He, too, had had to accustom himself to look upon scenes like this one with detachment and calculation. But it was harder now, because of his deep emotional ties to the victim of disaster. He said to Tommy: "Get the oxygen from my workroom; the tank's painted green. There's one painted blue, too. But *leave that one where it is.* There should be tubing and a mask attached to the green one, but if they aren't, and you don't spot them lying about right off, then just bring the tank. There'll be a wrench slipped onto it; don't let that fall off and get left behind." Otherwise, he approved the measures Edward had taken.

A trickle of blood was indeed coming from somewhere. It ran down along the ramp. The river thirsted for it, though it did not wait. *You cannot bleed twice into the same river, for new waters are forever flowing on.* Then water gushed from the stricken boy's mouth. But this was passive, due to the pressure exerted by the gentle, hulking man astride the small of the back.

Bob placed a hand under the chin, lifted the head, smote the face on both sides. Immediately there came a cough, and more water. A soft murmur arose from the standers-by. Dann looked from Bob to Edward, then back again.

"Keep on!" More water. Another cough. The murmur grew to a babbling among the hunters. More water, this time flowing down after the blood and washing it into the stream. And it was gone, the river placated by it.

The boy lying on the ramp was coughing continuously now. Water flowed out, but less. Dann stood up, receiving many shouted congratulations and general applause, grinning broadly. The babbling increased to a shout. Movement of men, movement of light resumed. Bob and Edward turned the brush-cut boy (*He's got to have a name. Certainly, now, he's got to have a name*) over onto his back, for he had begun to breathe, and it was time to examine his wound. Blood seeped, but did not pour, around the shanks of buttons of polished bone. Dann Gadsden, by now completely integrated into the recovery effort, tore open the coat. Bob pulled out the shirttail.

Edward had thought the flesh would be soft, lax. But the flank muscles were firm with tone. Gratefully, Bob saw it was only normal tone. He called for vodka. At least seven flasks were handed forward. The stinging, when the physician poured alcohol onto the wound, further aroused the injured man. As central nervous activity returned, though, more oxygen would be required. A cuff on his cheek, gentle this time. "Josh! Breathe! Take deep breaths." It was too soon to expect Tommy back.

Bob thought the wound was probably superficial. But it would have to be probed. He pressed about upon Josh's belly and afterward felt further encouraged. He looked to Edward and to Dann and said: "Shall we get him into the truck?" Then Tommy arrived with the oxygen, and Josh was masked, then taken away.

A broad-beamed motor boat with a searchlight was dispatched back upriver to collect the kills. None of the successful marksmen had any slightest doubt about the *exact* place where his own trophy lay. Together they made up a kind of bill of lading.

The older men began to leave the dock. Three of them drove to Clear Creek; one of them knocked upon the door. Yukoneta answered. "Good evening, Gentlemen," she said, "Please step in. Doctor Bob isn't home, yet."

"We know," Mr. David Unthank replied.

"Miss Alina is upstairs with all those young girls. Do you want me to get her?"

"Yes, Connie, please. We must speak with her right away."

Yukoneta had gone unceremoniously to the foot of the staircase and bellowed: "Miss Alina! Folks to see you!" Then the second half of Mr. Unthank's answer sank in. She wheeled around. "Nothing is wrong is it?" Then she let out a terrible shriek, the way they do in Green Sea. "He's dead!"

she screamed. "Doctor Bob is dead!" Yukoneta, in the process of falling to the floor, yet caught herself upon the stair rail long enough to ask: "Was he shot?" and then she completed her collapse.

Alina appeared upon the staircase. "What is it?"

Mr. Henry Robeson spoke up. "Nothing has happened, my Dear, that should alarm you. Bob is not dead."

"Nobody is dead," Mr. Unthank said. Yukoneta began to pull herself to her elbow, to a sort of reclining position.

"But," put in Mr. Hall Smith, the third of the visitors, "Little Josh nearly drowned." Yukoneta relapsed onto the floor.

"There's no need to say that, Hall! Alina, he did have a close call. But he is perfectly all right. At least, I think he's going to be." At this, Yukoneta's usefulness for that evening came to a close. But she had laid on a mightily fine brunch earlier in the day on short notice, it must be recalled.

"They are on the way here now. In fact they should have arrived already."

"Bob is going to check him over. He has a scratch that only needs merthiolate on it."

"We hope, at any rate."

" It will need stitches, I'm sure. It may penetrate into the abdomen."

"For God's sake, Hall, do just keep quiet." And as they spoke, they heard the truck on its way up the Magnolia Lane. Whoever was driving took it directly around to the back of the house.

Here, beside a garden pool like the one at Woodleigh, and across a parking area covered in the ubiquitous crushed oyster shell and edged with a low brick coping, stood a very singular little building. Of uncertain date but earlier than the house itself, it was called the "Carriage House," notwithstanding that there was no place in it for even a single carriage. One of the rooms within its thick masonry walls, stuccoed over in the way of the region, was a fully equipped if small treatment room, Bob Barrington's "workroom."

Even though he had no plan to practice again, Bob had felt that having acquired the knowledge and skills of medicine he ought to be able to put them to use in case of need. As he and Edward went inside, supporting Josh between them, Alina came out and down from the back verandah, and joined them, staying close, not interfering, ready to do what she might. And of course she would have been nowhere else.

But Edward did not know it.

Around the dock at the lower landing, the observances were not quite over. When the crisis had ended well, when the elders had departed and sacred night was fully come, then the collegians, who had dutifully carried pocket flasks and with their fathers and uncles and other kinsmen and friends had drunk the distilled spirit, which must be sampled only, were ready for beer. Collegians drink beer, because it is a drink to be, as some say, "guzzled," and collegians—or at least men of that verdant time—are often guzzling life itself.

And so the men who had served shots of whiskey before the hunt, now, at its completion, served beer. This time they wore black trousers and white coats, for they must hurry back to Woodleigh for the start of the hunt breakfast. They handed shiny new pails—galvanized, with their crystallograins glittering in the light of torches—down to the grateful, joyful young men, who by turns brought their boats past the dock. In the pails were iced bottles of beer, with openers attached to bucket-handles by lengths of jute twine, for at that time the caps of beer bottles could not be twisted off. In the ordinary.

They took the torches, too, and moved just a few yards downriver, where the already-widening stream broadened further into a small lagoon, hemmed with the pond cypress, with some of very old growth, crenellating parts of the water's edge with their "knees." Here the young folk circled, made figures of eight, one after another, as fast as the toiling little trolling-motors would take them, and they drank and sang and shouted. And they waved their torches overhead, they dipped them into the water—how much immersion could they withstand, and yet flare up again?

And old nobles of Loire and Indre, at rest beneath wrought stone deep in parkland; and Teuton warriors, frozen among the charred planks of their funeral barges, within the abyssal declivities of their dark *fjorde*; and, farther abroad than these, lost in the rubble of their scattered cairns, men scarcely yet men; all these broke their sleep for a moment, listening to denizens of the New World, shouting in darkness, leading with fire, and marked with blood.

Alina came out onto the verandah that looked along the Magnolia Lane. There the three old gentlemen sat, wearing evening dress, and drinking whiskies. "You were right, of course, Mr. Unthank. Josh is perfectly sound—or soon will be." She was dressed for evening herself this time, and her radiant natural beauty had returned. She sat down with her guests, her filmy gown clinging about her lovely lap and legs. She had recalled, now, that the men were there by prior arrangement, to change, without going the long distances home and back. "Where did you change? Could you find any privacy?"

"First, Alina, I'm thankful for Little Josh's deliverance; next—and this is something I ought to have seen to years ago—please just call me David. There won't be too very many more opportunities." The other two asked to be included in this change of protocol.

"I've thought of you as 'David'—and 'Hall' and 'Henry'—for years anyway, so the transition will be no trouble at all. Besides, remember that I am growing old at exactly the same rate as yourselves."

"But, to answer your question, Alina, we changed in the Ballroom." For Henry Robeson had actually been to balls there, when the pilasters were gilded from ceiling to floor, before Alina had come into the world. "One of us would guard each of the doorways; the other would change."

"How many of those silly little girls are up there, anyway? They giggle constantly."

"Plenty, Hall. And they're not at all little. Wait till you see them!"

"I can't wait."

"And you won't have to, at least not much longer." Alina reached for Hall Smith's glass, said: "May I?" He surrendered it willingly, flushing a little at intimacy shared with a younger and beautiful woman. Alina drained the glass, caught her breath, and said, as she searched each face: "Now. What the Hell happened?" Robeson answered. All agreed that he had had the clearest prospect.

"The boats were coming in, and I was standing on the dock, watching. Josh's boat came along; he had the Ferrara boy—I forget his name...."

"Bardy."

"No wonder. And Michael Witherspoon. Those two, with him. Then I saw Little Josh turn his head, suddenly, toward the right bank—that's where we all were. That's the side the dock is on. But I think what he was doing was looking at a glass bottle. It had obviously come down with the current but had got caught in some branches poking up out of the water, near the shore."

"I saw them," Hall said. "They looked like the crooked fingers of the drowned skeleton of a giant."

"Of which we have so many hereabout!"

Alina had become very still. She asked: "What kind of bottle was it? What did it look like?"

"I was at some distance from it. I'd say, though, it was clear glass. It reflected lantern light brightly—there were no algae growing on it. You know how glass that's been submerged for a long time becomes slimy? But this was clean. It had some kind of cap or cork. And there must have been something inside it, because Josh kept staring, trying to manoeuvre their boat closer to it."

"Get on with it, Henry. This isn't the part Alina wants to know about."

"Oh, yes it is! It may be the most important part."

"Well, come to say, in a way it might be, because it's what made him turn the boat over. He was reaching for it, but they weren't quite close enough. I think the sunken tree was keeping the hull back. Josh seemed determined. He locked his legs under the thwart, and leaned out farther, as though he were desperate to get the bottle."

Alina bowed her head and brought her hands to her face. "Oh, no. No!"

David bent toward her and said softly: "I don't understand, my Dear." She shook her head, but said nothing more. So Henry continued.

"The boat listed a good deal, with Josh's weight; the other two leaned in the opposite direction, to try to keep them on an even keel. But Josh outbalanced them, and the boat took on a little water. The Witherspoon boy jumped overboard. Then Ferrara. Then the boat capsized. Josh made a lunge, I think at the bottle. Then he went under. And his legs were held by the thwart. They were carrying oars. The starboard one, which with the boat upside down was to port, out toward the stream bed, rammed into the sand on the river bottom. So that when people started wading in to right the boat again, she wouldn't go over.

"Then everybody got overexcited. The couple of men who went out into the river to try turning her from that side couldn't get the others to stop, so they were working against each other. Finally, the Strikestraw boy, whoever he is, came up and in a second, it seemed, released the oar somehow.

"But the bottle was carried off in the current."

Bob had decided that his patient could go to the hunt breakfast. That, after all, was where he himself would be, in case of complications. He drove the two younger men to Woodleigh so that they could change. As they went, Josh casually put out his hand. "I'm Josh Jones."

"Edward Strikestraw." Josh shook his hand firmly and politely, but winced when he did it.

"Edward. I'm sorry, but I didn't get the second name."

" 'Strikestraw,' " Edward said, smiling. "Nobody gets it the first time."

XI

"...a full and interesting content can put wings to the hour and the day;
yet it will lend to the general passage of time a weightiness, a breadth
and solidity which cause the eventful years to flow far more slowly than
those poor, bare empty ones over which the wind passes and they are gone."
Thomas Mann: *Der Zauberberg,* (tr. H. T. Lowe-Porter)

J OSH AND EDWARD had come down the back hallway at Woodleigh hoping
to escape notice. Josh's shirt had been cut away; the coat buttoned across
his chest was drenched with river water and his own blood. Edward,
though he wore his shirt still, for what it was worth, and though his canvasses
were less extensively stained in blood, was only slightly more presentable.
Scattered guests were already there, already swelling the sound of subdued
hilary with low, melodious voices or light, sweet laughter.

It was all right, though. For an hour, men in hunting gear would be
coming and going amongst what at that time were called "cocktail dresses,"
worn by most of the young women, evening gowns favored by the older ladies,
and the gentlemen's uniform black and white. And field khaki.

Turning to go up the first flight of stairs, they met Laurence, and he
detained Edward, while Josh went painfully onward and upward.

"I want to tell you a thing," Laurence said to Edward.

"Sir?"

"My wife is not a hypocritical woman."

"I can't imagine who might think she was, frankly."

"If we're lucky, this thing—our party—will spread into both front rooms, the hallways, the dining room, of course—that's where they'll put out a fork supper later on. The verandahs, and if the weather holds, the grounds. Seems stable. But hurricane season hasn't officially ended. However, you would know about that. The house is only twelve miles from the ocean."

"But what about hypocrisy?"

"Well, it's just that Lavinia insists on having the liquor served on the back verandah." Edward didn't say anything, so Laurence stumbled on: "Of course, once you get it, you're most welcome to take your highball into the house, or anywhere you like. We all do. It's just that single thing. I wanted you to know about it."

"But the waiters will be offering trays of champagne all during the evening and all through the house."

"Thank you, Sir. Nothing has been lacking; I'm sure nothing will be."

"I just wanted to point out that little…vagary. Make yourself completely at home! Actually, I want you to feel quite as much at home here as I do. A lot of other people have owned this house before me. A lot of our older guests were familiar with it before I was born." He hesitated, then: "A couple of people who will be here stood to inherit it at one time or other. Do, really, be at ease, and let me or somebody know whether you need anything."

What a goodly man; what a good man. Edward had known men to have to defend their wives' honor, but never before in quite this way. He went upstairs and to his room.

There was Sandy, a guest of honor, lying upon his bed, with his hands behind his head. The signs were all bad: He was grinning a little foolishly, as he asked, "Where have you been all this time?"; he wore his evening shirt, and the studs were in place, but his tie was simply slung about his neck; and he still wore his hunting trousers, which were variously tainted.

" 'Where have *you* been all this time?' seems more to the point."

In answer, Sandy closed his eyes and began to sing, a little boozily, Edward thought: "Rollin,' rollin,' rollin' on the rivaaah…."

"Are you drunk?" For Mrs. Ashfield expected Claire and Sandy to receive guests with her from nine until ten o'clock.

"No, I'm not drunk," Sandy said, leaping off the bed, as though to prove it. "I had a few brews down on the river, but so did everybody else."

"What about your clothes?"

"What about them?"

"You're only half dressed. It's a quarter past eight."

"Oh! I really didn't know it was that late. But don't worry. I'm more than half dressed. We wear our hunting trousers with the rest of the tuxedo." And sure enough, the second inspection registered carefully combed hair, cummerbund in place. The evening jacket was folded over the back of a chair. And then Edward remembered that Sandy couldn't tie a bowtie and was waiting for himself to do it.

Once he had, Sandy threw on his coat rather desperately and hurried out of the room. Edward shouted:

"You really aren't going to change your trousers?"

"I told you. We don't, at this kind of thing." Here was Sandy at his happiest: Having inside information about something. It enabled him the better to "fit in." It was a little pathetic, Edward felt.

"Well, I've got to." But Sandy was gone. *At least he's sober.* Edward went down the hall to the room he knew Josh Jones was occupying. He knocked upon the door.

"Come in, please." Edward went into the room. Two other men were there, getting changed, but Josh was sitting on the side of a bed. He had been looking at the floor before him, but he looked up as Edward entered.

Edward had been unsure about the extent of Josh's recovery. The man had nearly met death two hours earlier. He had been attended to medically. But it hadn't been enough. Edward's own inclination would have been to give him a sleeping draught and put him to bed. Not take him to a party that was going to last all night long. "Josh, are you up to this?"

"Oh, yes. Besides, I have to be."

"Why do you have to be?"

"Because of my girl. I've got to drive to Clear Creek—they're all staying over there—and call for her."

"Is she just somebody you were asked to call for, or do you know her?"

"She is my life. Now that I have one again."

"Anyway, I didn't come to give advice, but to ask for it."

"About what?"

"What to wear."

"It's black tie."

"I know. But Sandy left here a few minutes ago wearing evening clothes, all except for trousers and shoes. He kept on his hunting ones."

"Oh, well, Sandy would. He thinks it makes him part of the inner circle. And a lot of people do follow that custom. It's completely a local phenomenon, as far as I know. And honored in the breach."

"So plenty of the men just wear a 'tux' as usual?"

"Half, at least."

"Thanks, then. I hope…things will go well."

Edward turned to the mirror, when he had got through dressing, to tie his own tie. He ran his fingers through his hair. This did no good, but no harm. He started downstairs, with the diffidence of the outsider, slowly, to allow himself to be absorbed into the growing crowd of guests.

Lavinia was at her post now beside a round table in the middle of the front hallway. She seemed taller and even lovelier; Edward had seen her only in battered tweeds. The gown she wore tonight was violet-colored. It reached just to her ankles. It was very plain. The ankles were very slender.

But Mrs. Ashfield was much bespangled: Diamonds sparkled from her fingers and wrists and breast. And she seemed as much at home with them as with yesterday's walking-shoes. On the table was a generous cut-glass punch bowl full of flowers and dark green foliage, sheaves of autumn grasses springing out as water springs from a fountain. Edward would live to become an aficionado, but at this time he had no idea what sasanquas were—He saw just that they were beautiful pink or white flowers (There were no red ones yet), crumbling into the splendor increasing now all around him.

He went up to say Good Evening. Lavinia seemed to smile continuously, but kinetically. Her smile could subside to a baseline, one reach above simply a pleasant expression, or kindle to any degree of radiance, depending upon the intended object, or even mount to sweet music of laughter.

She greeted Edward warmly, murmuring a few words about his earlier heroism. Edward answered:

"It may, possibly, have been a low kind of expertise. It was not heroism; I was never in danger myself."

"Well, everybody is most grateful. Oh, and you look *so handsome!*" Women always seemed to say that to men in tuxedos. Laurence came up. She took him by his left elbow. "Even in a house *full* of handsome men." She looked fondly at her husband; for she loved him.

"What Edward did, Lavinia, was keep his head. That is often better than expertise. And always better than heroism, which is usually no more than folly, but from which another, or others, benefit." Then he took her by her own left elbow, bent closer, and said: "They've all just driven up. Claire and Sandy will be with you in a minute."

"Anyway, Edward, welcome to *my* party. I hope it will complement that thing Rennie had all of you involved in on the Creek this afternoon! And, by the way, he may speak like that about heroism; he's a hero, too. Decorated for Korea."

Now Mary Alice, uniformed, came up to them, with her by now notorious bland expression—carrying a silver tray full of glasses. "Champagne, Madam? Gentlemen?

Each of them took one. Laurence said: "Thank you, Miss." Mary Alice got away before all four of them burst into laughter over the unaccustomed rôles they were playing against each other. Edward withdrew to the foot of the stairs, leaned against the stair rail, and drank half his wine. Being a part of the festivity wouldn't be hard, since he was clearly going to be the man of the hour.

The first to greet him, very much to his surprise, was Miss Lucia Hamm, from New Brunswick. She turned out to be Claire Elder's great aunt. "Claire," she said conspiratorially, "is quite a catch for your friend. The *money* comes from the mother's side, of course. But on my nephew's side she is descended from William the Conqueror."

Which of us isn't?

Edward looked again at the scene before him. Only head-high from the floor, a grand, ancient-looking chandelier, apparently made of blackened brass or of bronze, without bangles, was suspended over the table, burning with what seemed like numberless candles (there were sixty-three; Laurence had had to climb a ladder to set and then again to light them all; there was a mechanism for lowering the whole fixture, but it didn't work). At intervals around the unadorned point from which the chandelier hung by a heavy wrought-iron hook were nine electric lights set into the ceiling, blazing downward through the candlelight. Was that why Mrs. Ashfield's diamonds sparkled so? And the facets and cut and polished edge of the punch bowl that held all the flowers? Possibly not, because the Champagne in Edward's glass sparkled a lot, too, the minute skeins of bubbles streaming upward to release God knew what kind of influenza at the surface, evidently potent, because Edward rather felt that he was sparkling a little himself.

Furthermore, a pier mirror, in the front corner of the entrance hall, which Edward could see but in which he could nevertheless not see himself, well out of the light—this mirror was sparkling, too. It was faceted in a way—beveled, at least—garlands and arabesques cut into its surface in a margin across the top. These were twinkling, too, and glittering. With light from within? Of course, some of the light came from within Edward.

Suddenly, Edward felt a lot odder than a half-glass of Champagne makes you feel. Something was going on.

Everyone was distracted, then, by a noisy crowd swarming in from the back hallway, young men and women arriving from Clear Creek. They were crowding into and spilling through the passage beneath the stair landing; Edward could see some of them in the mirror. And when they caught sight of their hostess standing with quiet dignity, they held back, became decibels less boisterous.

True to Uncle Ed's word, a young buck hesitated, allowing his doe to step alone into the clearing. Edward saw her in the glass, took reflexive aim, and dropped her with his first round.

However, he had no way of knowing it; there was never an outward sign.

This is what Edward saw: Watching the roisterers streaming into the front hall, he saw the first phalanx hesitate when they realized that Lavinia and Laurence were there. He recognized Josh. And he saw a uniquely winning girl, dressed in black, continue into the empty space before her without breaking her stride. As she went toward her hosts, her reflection came toward Edward. She was slender and sumptuous. Everyone knows what that means; the two characteristics do not, in special cases—as here—make war upon each other.

As she came up even with him, he now saw from the corner of his eye the shadow that she yet was. He still looked ahead into the glass—at her reflection, of course, but she wouldn't know for sure what he was looking at unless he gave in and glanced away. Then he saw that she seemed to have noticed him. In passing. Oh, certainly no more than in passing.

With an emotion close to fear, he looked from reflection to reflected. Her bright brown hair, seeming heavy as mail, lagged a little, so that she turned her face partly into its borders, as into the corner of a Japanese fan. Then the hair, in gaining the required angular momentum, swung back, turning with her, revealing her whole face. Not a glance, but a swift, serene survey. Had she smiled a little? She might have. It would be useful to know. Especially to know that she *had* smiled.

While the rest of the crowd newly arrived from Clear Creek followed her example, crowding around her and Lavinia and Laurence to fulfill their duty, Edward, astonishing himself, helpless to do otherwise, went to the pier mirror, "looking glass," anything his grandfather or anybody else might suggest he name it. For now he didn't know exactly what it was, to have given forth such loveliness. He grasped both sides of the carved and gilded frame, and looked as deeply as he could into the silvered surface. He stood there for several minutes. But he saw nothing he sought to see.

The Ashfields were alone again for the moment. Edward went back to them and said: "Who is that…umh…girl? The one wearing a black dress."

"Do you mean the knockout brunette?" Laurence asked.

"The one with manners?" said Lavinia, smiling a little ruefully.

"Mary Mountainstream," Laurence said, without waiting for confirmation. "From Augusta."

Edward thanked them and went away. "What now?" Lavinia said.

"Nothing. It's nothing to do with us."

"But it's everything to do with us!"

"Well, maybe so. But we're definitely nothing to do with *it*."

The younger guests seemed to file up and down the hallway all during the evening, smoking on the front verandah, getting drinks from the exiled bar, and, later, sampling a lavish buffet in the dining room, in contrast to the older guests, who seemed to have taken up stations: The tipplers on the back verandah, making conversation which didn't matter either then or subsequently; those with hearty appetites around the dining table, making little conversation at all; and the ruminating smokers, with burthensome thoughts to express and discuss, toward the front of the house, either on the verandah or standing under the great oaks inside The Circle.

There was a small orchestra on a portable platform set up upon the grass, playing the mellowest of tunes, whether fast ones or slow ones, new or old. The tips of the smokers' cigars and cigarettes could be seen alternately to flare and then to acquiesce in darkness, even though there were great white paper lanterns hanging from the branches of many of the trees.

Edward, as she was the honorée, sought Claire out for a dance. No one broke on him. He tried to talk as they danced. An obstacle arose. Claire couldn't make conversation, since she could neither speak nor listen, for looking about for people to smile at. She did this with the evident anxiety of the fading actress seeking the camera lens. When she determined upon a subject, and could get his attention, the smile appeared with startling abruptness. Like a bare lightbulb, controlled by a little chain. It was as though you could hear the string of tiny metal spheres actuating the switch, as each facial muscle hurried to take up its practiced deployment in time, before the object looked away.

When it was over, and the flurry of applause had died down, Edward thanked Claire for the favor of the dance, and added: "By the way, I know your Aunt Lucia. I have spoken to her, but I want you to give her this message: The Duke of Normandy was a lout. Goodnight."

Then, in a vague way, he migrated with the young, stopping often for bits of talk with men he had met upon the river, or with gentlemen who stopped him to thank and congratulate him. One said to him: "I heard Little Josh turned his boat over trying to reach a message in a bottle."

"That's how it began."

"A little too much to drink, ha?" The nudge, the wink.

"As far as I know, he had had nothing to drink. His flask had only water in it." For Edward had removed this at the landing. It was not an Army surplus canteen at all. The case was not of canvas, but some kind of leather—pigskin or ostrich skin? Edward had stuffed old newspaper into it; that is what his grandmother had taught him to do with wet shoes. The flask itself was of pewter. Engraved upon it were a complicated cypher and crest. The best of everything.

Mary Mountainstream. Mary Mountainstream, never smoking, drinking only a little whiskey, quiet, smiling often, was never far from the center of the party. And occasionally Edward caught sight of Josh, glad to see that he seemed comfortable and cheerful.

"Who is that boy who everybody says kept Josh from drowning?"

"His name is Edward Strikestraw. He comes from a town called New Brunswick. It's near Wilmington."

"I don't know it."

"Apparently it was settled very early on. It was the Colonial Capital for a time."

"Rennie used to know his grandfather in Virginia—hunt country. That was when he was in school up there, and afterward."

"The boy lives now with his other grandfather," Hall Smith put in. "His mother died right after he was born. And there was something...questionable about his father." Nobody took this up, leaving Hall to seem a gossip. Which he was.

" 'Hunt' and 'shoot.' They make a very careful, specifically very English distinction between the two things up there."

"If young Strikestraw is accustomed to fox hunting, then God knows what he made of our turnout today." After looking at the wristwatch: "Yesterday."

"What do *you* make of it? I mean, truthfully?"

"Well, it's our way. Our own way. Not borrowed from anywhere else."

"Where would you expect to borrow something like that? After all?"

"I don't know. But it's part of what makes us what we are."

"For better or worse."

Miss Lucia Hamm was trying to involve herself with these men, when her niece Claire Elder came up to her and said: "I have a message for you from Edward Strikestraw."

"Oh, my goodness! What could he have on his mind?"

"He asked me to tell you that the Duke of Normandy was a lout. Just that."

"I've never heard of any Duke of Normandy."

"Neither have I," the descendant of William the Conqueror replied.

By half past one, the crowd had thinned noticeably. Some of the girls had begun to ask their squires to take them back to Clear Creek. The thinning disclosed that Mary was there with Josh. When this dawned upon Edward, he was surprised. He felt unfounded resentment. Then, remembering what Josh had said to him about "his girl," he was thrown into a haywire of emotions. He went out onto the back verandah. Tommy was still faithfully tending bar. Edward asked for Scotch and a little soda-water, even knowing that morning was not far off, that the drink would not contribute to a bright-eyed awakening. But then, he wasn't planning to sleep.

When Mary had asked to be taken away, as she and Josh started down the brick steps leading into the back garden, she stopped where Edward was leaning against the iron railing, and she said to him: "Edward, I don't think you can possibly remember me. I'm Mary Mountainstream...."

"From Augusta."

She smiled quizzically. Edward wondered why. "I hope," she said, "that I'll see you again before we all leave. I'll remind you about our meeting before, unless you'll have been able to remember it in the meantime."

They all said Goodnight; Josh took Edward's hand and held it, saying: "I owe you my life. Thank you."

"You don't. You're welcome." Edward stood still for a while, wondering whether he were perhaps inhaling any of Mary's exhalation, grappling with a dilemma common among youth: The reconciliation of adoration and lust. *Her supple back—I can see so much of it! Her wonderful, night-dark hair.*

Mary and Josh drove through the dark night, on their way home. The afternoon and evening had been mild. But winter—or what passed for it in those lands—had begun a nearly inaudible chant within the distant woods. Stars were shining, and in Mary's eyes they cancelled any kind of darkness.

She thought of Edward, when as a lad he had spent a summer with his grandparents, near where she lived. She had fallen in love with him then, as far as she knew. But he evidently did not remember her, for if he had, he would not have thought she lived in Augusta. On the other hand, in order to know, he must have asked someone. That was propitious.

She knew more now, of course, than she had known as a lass, and she knew that somewhere along the way, when she had become fully capable of it, she had indeed fallen in love with Edward. But she had had to dismiss him from her thoughts. It had been a long time. She didn't know where he was, or even exactly who he was; he might have become entirely someone else, besides. *In love with a notion—so many have been.*

She had come up behind him in the entrance hall at Woodleigh, then, almost immediately, recognized him in reflection. His gaze, she thought, had been steady. He was not diffident. Not restless, like so many boys she knew.

She noted changes from boy to man: With satisfaction, a certain amplitude of limb and frame; with some regret, the loss of softness and childish sweetness in his face. But these had at least not been replaced by ugliness or by hardness.

All this time, she and Josh were rumbling along the road toward Clear Creek, with Ashfield-Jones land now on their left, wilder holdings on the right. Josh was fretted by her silence. Some wound in his side began to hurt him; he couldn't be sure whether it was the gash sustained upon the river, or a newer one. "You knew Edward Strikestraw when you were children?"

"Yes. And in twelve or fourteen years he has changed very little."

No! The note of satisfaction in her voice paralyzed the diaphragms—he couldn't breathe, or thought he couldn't. He didn't want to try. But he kept the car on course and recollected his strength and wits. They ran onto a much improved road with well kept acreage on both sides. But for Josh, darkness was overcoming the stars, overcoming everything. The pain originating in his flank grew more intense and less localized.

When they arrived at the great house, Mary stood on tiptoe to kiss Josh on the cheek and said Goodbye very sweetly, very kindly.

It was over at last. Edward sat in the same chair upon the verandah. All the events—whether touching, or exciting, or awkward, or astonishing—of this very long day were safe in a staging area of his thoughts, to be released and let pass in review at another time. Before him were ghostly limbs of the great oaks, flickering light in those of the paper lanterns that had lasted burning as long as this, stars casting their faint shadows. He was buoyed upon the stream of Sacred Night.

Lavinia stepped through the front door, scouting for possible lingering guests before helping Mary Alice outside with a large tea-cart, onto which they proposed to load glasses, ashtrays, napkins, other relics of revelry, so that lovely Woodleigh House might show a fit face to the morning.

She noticed Edward and went across to him. He stood. She said: "I hope you've been able to enjoy yourself—so many strange people! And of course it must seem to you that they all know each other. It's how I'd feel, I'm afraid. In fact, how I once felt here."

"Not at all, Ma'am. In fact, I've had a wonderful time. It has been a...a...a *beautiful* evening, a wonderful party. A grand day." He sat down a little abruptly, without being asked, as though beneath the weight of all that the day had held.

"I'm so glad."

Edward looked up at his elegant hostess, in whom he could see no sign of weariness. But that was in part because he wasn't even trying to see anything in much detail. "In a way, I wish I belonged here." He wondered what he had meant.

"Well, then, Edward, let's let it be agreed that you do belong here. You'll be welcome at any time. Never wait to be invited. But aren't you going up to bed yet?"

"Not yet, Ma'am. I feel I have to wait here, to see whether there really will be another day."

He didn't seem actually to be drunk, Lavinia thought. So she said: "I may know something about what you mean. I can remember days which I thought must be the world's last." She watched the flames dying down inside the paper lanterns. "Well, then, I'll say Goodnight."

Edward got back to his feet. "Goodnight, Ma'am. I won't be in the way here?"

"Not at all. Goodnight."

About four o'clock, having seen off those of their guests who appeared to intend to leave at all, Lavinia and Laurence climbed the broad staircase together. "What do you think?"

"About anything in particular?"

"No. Overall."

"Overall, it was a night of magic. Your parties always are."

"*Our* parties. Besides, with the friends we have—especially our young friends, and their friends—how could it have failed? And everyone looked so splendid!"

"They'd better," Laurence said with a chuckle, "coming to your house."

Lavinia laughed in her heart. "It's your house—if it's really anybody's. It seems to belong in small part to everybody." Dreamily, she added: "And to everything. To the spirits in the oaks…." Now they had reached the door to their bedroom. They stood quietly for a moment before going in. Lavinia continued: "And to those in the river-mists, and to those in the barred owls' calls. But what on earth am I rambling on about?"

Laurence held open the door and they went inside, for a few hours' sleep and to change for the day, for they had house-guests, and to some of these they must presently say Goodbye. Or, at least, that possibility existed.

"I want you to know that in all that time I drank three glasses of champagne—nothing else," Lavinia said and fell onto the bed.

The tuxedo, known for making many men look their best, does it in part by constraint. So with relief, Laurence loosened his necktie, unwrapped his cummerbund, and stepped out of his shoes. He sat down upon his side of their bed. "You weren't rambling. Woodleigh has become part of the land she stands in; tonight she was aglow. It was wonderful."

Drowsiness crept in with the silvery sunlight. Lavinia asked: "Do you truly not mind our not having children?"

"Truly, I don't. And if we had, they'd be leaving us about now, anyway."

"When I asked you how you thought the evening had gone, you asked whether I meant particularly or generally. Was that because you were thinking about something in particular?"

"It was."

"Did it have anything to do with Mary?"

"It had."

"Did you find her fetching?"

"Do you remember that expression of Mother's: 'Have your faculties deserted you, or have you deserted them'? "

"Yes."

"Well, then. I have not taken leave of my faculties. I found her quite fetching."

"She is coming back soon. She wants to have breakfast with me before many people are up and about."

"Oh, Lord." Laurence got up and poked at the fire. Then he lay down, took his bride's hand in his, and they slumbered.

Edward fell asleep before dawn, seated in his rocking chair. He awoke. He was still in evening clothes and thought he certainly must not be seen until dressed for daytime. It had got surprisingly cold.

Once upstairs and in his room, he looked again out of the south window closer to the middle of the house. There, to his left, in a luminence halfway between silver and gold, all of it scattered by mists rising from the woodland, doubtless from the River, blazed the Morning Star. How many people knew that it was really an archangel with The Fire to light the sun, and the Command: "Burn; and run your course"? *Then there* is *another day!* Edward was burning already. *And I shall run my course.*

He went for a shave and warm bath, and when he returned he found that someone had broken up and refueled the fire, which had been banked in the grate for the night. It had not been Sandy. He continued in sleep or in some, probably mixed, species of torpor.

Outside the window, the red sun had by now taken possession of the heavens, having crossed the line of violet chalk-dust, leaving behind the blue-green of the Tourmaline Plain.

Laurence came out onto the verandah with two cups of coffee; for, coming down the stair, he had noticed Edward sitting there alone.

"I wanted to see you again, Sir, if there's time before you have to start saying farewells," Edward said.

"I've already done that—as soon as I got up. Everyone is free to depart!" And he made an expansive gesture, spilling coffee from each cup. He gave one to Edward anyway. "Did you want to see me about anything in particular?" For Laurence would not have been surprised.

"No. Of course I wanted to say how much I have enjoyed my time here, and to thank you."

"Well, your being here has certainly been our pleasure. And Josh's deliverance! What time must you start out?"

"It doesn't make any particular difference; I'll just get there about six hours after I leave here. I ought to be there before tomorrow, for Thanksgiving."

"Would your grandfather be alone for the Day? Without you?"

"Oh, no. I don't think so. Sometimes there's quite a mob. There's a friend of ours—a lady—and I think Grandfather would be content if only she came, although he hasn't said anything yet."

"Love is in the air? It's wonderful for it to be—makes the air better to breathe, if you ask me—and it's wonderful to be able to have part in it." Edward looked at him uncertainly. "I'm still in love with my wife, believe it or not."

"I believe it. I think a lot of people are. In love with your wife." Edward was stunned, at first, that he had said this. But he was even more surprised that he did not feel especially uncomfortable, having said it. Laurence didn't appear to make anything of it, either, although he looked pleased. Then he had a little internal tug-of-war. But he won.

He asked, quite casually, as he supposed, "Are you in love? Or shouldn't I ask."

"Oh, ask. But to be honest, I don't know exactly what I'm in. I am definitely in some kind of peril."

"Sounds like love; anyway, it'll all shake down soon. And then you'll know." *And we'll probably all know.*

"Very soon, I think." *If "soon" means at no great remove from the present.* "But to change the subject…."

"Probably it needs changing, or one or both of us will get ourselves into a tight spot." But it was a subject Laurence was rather devoted to. And he said something that at first didn't seem to follow: "I want my ashes to be thrown into Blackwater. When the time for it comes, of course. Maybe they'll help feed the water plants or the fish or the waterfowl. A lot of fires will have burned those ashes!" He was looking into nowhere. And he kept looking. Presently he said: "However, you were about to say something else."

"I wouldn't ask this without your promise in advance to say No, unless it really suits your plans for the day. But have you got time to show me over the rice fields? I don't know how rice is cultivated; I've certainly never seen the process underway. I may not have the opportunity again."

"Lavinia hasn't warned you not to allow yourself to be taken on the Ricefield Tour?"

"No."

"She gets after me about entrapping people into it; actually, since it's my pride and joy, I can't think of anything I'd like better. And, then, I wonder... but you have a long drive ahead of you ."

"Not really very long. Anyway, starting later won't make it any longer."

"Would you like to drive over to Dodona. It's really not far."

"I'd like very much to see that place, too."

They had been into the rice fields. Edward was much absorbed, as he usually was in things new to him. Laurence had sensed genuine enthusiasm. He was now looking forward, as they drove along, to revisiting Dodona. The Ruin. Because he had with him a guide who could illuminate aspects of the structure, possibly of the place.

But out of nowhere a question about Edward himself arose in his mind, and he in his turn spoke it without reflection: "How was your father lost, Son—you did say in the War, didn't you?" And immediately he was alarmed at what he had done, because he didn't trust his memory and because of gossip he had overheard the evening before. "Overheard," because people did not gossip *to* Laurence.

Edward did not seem about to answer. Was the boy going to have to pretend he hadn't heard the question? Laurence started rummaging through his limited catalogue of Inane Things to Say, so that he could collude with this fiction as soon as he became convinced it was going on.

"He was a spy," Edward said then. "For our side, of course."

"Of course." A sign of loyalty. To a man he's never known.

"But at first, not everybody was sure of that. I mean, at first there was the other idea—and I'm afraid it was more for a period of time, really, than just 'at first;' and more than just an 'idea.' I think it was very difficult for my grandparents. But at that time, nothing could be admitted openly. I mean, not by the belligerents."

Laurence found he could breathe easily once more. It had been appalling, feeling tense in speaking to someone you were growing fond of. "What devastation for them, and for all of you! Can you…or, will you tell me about it?"

"I like to tell about it, but I don't often have anybody to tell it to."

Laurence pulled the car off the road. "We can't talk about this and an old Georgian house at the same time."

"Thank you.

" We don't know the actual beginning, and we don't know the end, really, at all. But he was a spy. He was a Naval officer. I don't know what cover story my father was given, but it was arranged that he pass on to the Germans false lists of convoys—complements, sailing dates and times, courses. One night he was to rendezvous with a landing party from a German U-boat. They lay right off our shores in those days. They actually succeeded in landing at least two other parties of saboteurs, one in New York, one in Florida.

"Two things went wrong on the night of my father's disappearance: First, the British made some changes at the last minute. And it's unbelievable, but these changes resulted in certain coïncidences of intent with the supposedly bogus schedules. My father's information had to be corrected—or, rather, 'decorrected'—and time was wasted. When he finally got the modified data, he arrived at the rendezvous point an hour late.

"One of the Intelligence services had identified a German couple who lived in New Brunswick. They had two children, living still in Germany. Because of the children, they could be compelled to coöperate in a German demolitions operation against America. The same that the other two landings were part of. But they accepted pay for what they did.

"What they were paid for was to transmit money and explosives from German submarines to saboteurs on American soil. My father's duty was to pass on the falsified logs at one of the *rendez-vous* points, but an hour before the part of the landing to do with commerce with the traitors was to take place.

The boats, right after the start of our part in the War, could come literally onto our shores without resistance because without detection. Sinkings of North Atlantic convoys were unbelievable at that time, apparently. So were sinkings of Merchant shipping—and by then it really was no longer 'commercial'—up and down the Eastern Seaboard. The Allies were getting pretty desperate.

"But to go back: When my father did get to the rendezvous point, the local German man arrived at the same time for his supplies and money, and blood-money, and he recognized my father and told the Germans he wasn't who they had thought. He was taken aboard the U-Boat, and it was sunk with all hands after three days, crossing the Ocean on its way back, apparently, to l'Orient. The ring was discovered before they could do any damage. The man from New Brunswick was hanged, along with four others. His wife was executed by firing squad, in a show of delicacy of feeling I can't help but share.

"It took five years to figure all this out. In the end it wasn't very important—except to us. In the meantime it was announced that my father had been lost in the service of his country. He was given the Navy Cross. Posthumously. That's about all there is. But that didn't lay it to rest for 'Rumor painted full of tongues.' I have felt a little sickened at what was done to those two people, whom everybody saw around town everyday. But I have a strange mental picture that takes it all away: Albert Sculpin—probably originally '*Seeraben*' or something of the kind—is about to go to bed; he looks out through his bedroom window; he sees lighted rooms in other windows all across town; he knows he and his *Frau* are taking pay in order to have the people inside them conquered, injured, or killed. "

Neither felt inclined to say anything for a while after this. Each sat in the car, relaxed, regretting nothing, windows open to another splendid day.

Laurence finally said: "You won't mind if I don't say anything in reply? Since there's nothing I can say?"

"Let's be on our way to Dodona."

Laurence was by this time driving over tracks only, where a road had onetime been, but ahead lay a vestige of the work of man: The *allée*. It was very broad and comparatively very short—the opposite of the Magnolia Lane at Clear Creek. Four live oaks on either side, spread far apart; within these, two parallel rows of tamarisks, known in those parts as sand-cypresses. Here Edward noted the first sign of upkeep. For the tamarisks, let go, would have suckered and spread over all, if they had not been doggedly pruned and otherwise kept in check, over, over, and over. He mentioned this.

"I was told, a long time ago, that great iron plates were sunk into the ground on the four sides of each of them. Josh told me he and his father found remnants of rust in straight lines in the soil around them."

"Josh Jones?"

"Yes. And look now at how they have got thickened and gnarled in their trunks, how the branches are held high. High, for sand-cypresses." Some of the grey-green feathering was left, but most of the branches bore none. There remained bits that had turned yellow, but most had fallen. All around grew broomstraw, as tall in their path now as everywhere else.

And now ahead, right in the middle of the way, there appeared an oak of unbelievable greatness, evident antiquity, and grace, possibly holy. Uncover one's head, or cover it? Put off the shoes from one's feet? The tree was wholly believably oracular. "We'd better get out of the car," Edward said.

"Certainly it's not as though we could continue driving."

"We'll go ahead on foot, then?"

"It is most...'awful,' to use Queen Caroline's expression—if it was Queen Caroline."

"Yes, and not 'artificial,' not to use her other one."

"Will you tell me why you said a 'conspicuous oak' might be associated with the name Dodona? I feel I ought to be bringing an offering." *And I feel you ought to be my son.*

"It's in the *Iliad*, I can't think where else. But the Oracle of Zeus sat beneath the tree, and interpreted the sound of the leaves rustling. And the interpretation was regarded as prophecy."

"But the people who built this place were Christians."

" 'Can't be helped,' as my grandfather would say."

"Would he? Really?"

"At every opportunity. He has a lot of nagging doubts about Christianity. Anyway, they may have been Christians, but they lived in an era when classical allusion was fashionable. It still is, actually. And they had this tree. I believe it would have been already fairly majestic two centuries ago. It all fits." *And I think it would have been good to talk about things like this with my father.*

"It's on an old map I have. What egregiousness, don't you think? A tree, one of many hundreds of thousands, yet specially indicated on a map. There's another one of these, on John's Island, up about Charleston. Tourist maps show it. This one is thought to be older, though."

"Do you know of the *arbre du Ténéré,* speaking of trees on maps?"

"I do, in fact. It appeared on a lot of maps, including some of a scale of 1:4,000,000."

"An acacia, green and blooming in the middle of the Sahara, in the middle of nowhere. They dug a well beside it down to, I think, thirty-five meters or deeper. They found the roots of the tree, reaching down to the water table at that level. I wish I could have seen it."

"I remember reading some of those things about it. I've thought ever since that it could be the Tree of the Knowledge of Good and Evil."

"A drunk truck-driver knocked it down."

"And that's why we can in many instances no longer form a clear distinction between good and evil." But they had got to the perimeter of the Oak of the Ruin Dodona. They passed under and through it, and each of them felt sure there were biddings among the boughs, letters upon the leaves, or some equivalent transformation to language from the whispering of foliage in the breezes. Certainly the Duke Senior could have heard it, and if he had, might have been able to understand the tongue of the tree.

Beyond was another foreshortened allée, axially aligned and corresponding

exactly with the first. Then the house. Everything deep in broomstraw grown
to uniform height, about thirty inches. The interior of the building, too, for
the roof was gone. Everything of wood was gone. Everything that had rested
upon wood had fallen. They waded inside. In a corner were stacked carefully
the dilapidate roofing slates.

Edward had seen, it seemed, the house before and recognized it. It was
nearly Palladian in design, for there was an important entrance upon each of
the four sides. "Why is it so white, I wonder?" he asked, watching, through
an upstairs window void, clouds blown across a blue sky.

"A motion picture company wanted to make a film here some years back.
They wanted to whitewash the structure. It was supposed to be ghostly, we
heard, with all the photography, or cinematography, I believe I ought to say,
done at dusk. The old man who owns the land and the building let them do
it. He needed the money. He is not prosperous. But nothing about any of his
property is untidy." He nodded toward the stacked rows of slates.

On the way back to Woodleigh, Edward said: "Thank you for both
sights—the forward-going fields and the nearly-gone house, so to say. Someone
should bring a compass here; the four fronts seem oriented in the cardinal
directions."

"You're most welcome; and I must thank you for an entirely new
perspective on Dodona. And, by the way, I don't think it's as 'nearly-gone' as
it seems. Josh has been talking about buying and restoring it. He's already had
an engineer come out to assess the soundness of the fabric."

"Really? He's an amazing guy. How well do you know him?"

"Know him? Oh, 'Jones.' I see. I've known him all his life. He's my
nephew." Edward was naturally surprised. "My sister's first husband was
named Jones. He's their boy."

Edward made some quick conjugations. "So Josh's father is the one who
painted the pictures at the Barringtons' house?"

"Yes."

"I guess I should have known about the connection."

"Unless somebody had told you, then you wouldn't have known about
it."

"Well, could I ask you something about him? It's perfectly…legitimate,
I think."

"You may; and by the way, I agree with you. He's an amazing boy, even
if it's I who say it"

"What I wonder about is this: Why does everybody call him "Little
Josh?" Because of all of us on the river yesterday, Black or White, I think he
was next to biggest."

"Well, there is an answer, I think, although I've never before tried to formulate it—just accepted the idea. If you go back, I believe you'll see that only the older men call him 'Little Josh.'

"I don't know how to say this except straight out: Someday he will inherit those old men's world. A big chunk of it, anyway. My family have owned a lot of land in Peell County, holding most of it through a good many generations. Now Alina Barrington, who is my sister, and I have inherited it. All of it will go in due course to Josh.

"Furthermore, in order to connect our two properties, Woodleigh and Clear Creek, Josh's father, my father, and I bought a good deal more acreage. My task has been to make it pay the taxes. But with the tremendous help from the overseers I've had—and have, thank God—I've been able to make it do a good deal more than that.

"This County has been those old gentlemen's world, and they're too frail to lay hold on a new one now. Josh is to them, I think, some kind of heir-apparent. Of course, when Parker—that's Jones—died, that put Josh a step closer. It's very rustic, very Southern. Really, very strange and hopeless.

"Because Josh can't live in their world, nor leave his lands behind in it. He will have to find a new world, and enter it along with his inheritance."

XII

"And through that cordage, threading with its call
One arc synoptic of all tides below—
Their labyrinthine mouths of history
Pouring reply as though all ships at sea
Complighted in one vibrant breath made cry,—
'Make thy love sure—to weave whose song we ply!'
—From black embankments, moveless soundings hailed,
So seven oceans answer from their dream."
Hart Crane: *The Bridge*, "Atlantis," 9-16

O N SUNDAY BEFORE Thanksgiving Day, 1963, in that season when for the planter in days gone by the year's work was largely done, when the effort had borne in plenteousness, when the subsiding hours enfolded a world seemed bound to exact gratitude from the hearts of men, if through nothing else than through visible splendor itself, Thomas Strikestraw found his way, as usual, to Alenda Lucas's verandah, in order to learn from her what sort of effect his preaching was having upon his flock. His pastoral duties were lauded everywhere, even within his own hearing, but his theological ukases were in some question. He had been to see the Bishop about it. Repeatedly.

"Thomas, before we discuss anything else," Alenda said, "I want you to look at this; my friend Mary MacDavid, who lives in Richmond, clipped it from the newspaper. I find it remarkable; really, quite remarkable. I wonder whether you do?"

Thomas took the slip of paper and read over it. First, across the top there had been penned: "Don't you know someone related to these people?" The text itself ran:

WARRENTON—Entered into eternal rest on November 14, James Hemphill Singleton, husband of the former Carroll Elizabeth Gilchrist, at his home in Fauquier County. Mr. Singleton was preceded in death by a daughter, Anne Huntingdon (the late Mrs. Robert Ardgower Strikestraw). He is survived by his widow, by a daughter, Margaret Chandler (Mrs. Singleton Hartweld), two brothers, Anton and Grigor Kubilsec, both of Paramus, New Jersey, and by a grandson.

"Good Gracious!" Thomas said when he had finished reading.

Once at home, his first deed was to write a letter of condolence to Libby. Her reply, which came back promptly, clarified much, although not all:

Collingwood Cottage, Monday

Dear Thomas,

Thank you so much for your gracious letter—for what you said in it, and for what you left out of it. I don't think anybody ever felt Bunny was really what he tried (so hard!) to seem; I didn't. But I did fall in love with him. I married him, of course over my family's strenuous objection. And in my way I loved him to the end.

On my wedding day—Not at all what that expression ordinarily brings to mind!—my father wrote a rather enormous check. Giving it to me he said: "This is your patrimony. I hope it will enable you to lie at least decently in the bed you've made for yourself." And it has.

After the check and those bitter words, nothing other than the usual greetings, wishes, and stock sentiments passed between us. But I knew I would not have the life I had expected. So I gave myself and my resources over to shaping for Bunny the life he had *never* expected, even though he had spent so much time and effort apparently preparing for it.

I always wanted to meet his brothers (They were his full brothers), but he would not allow it. It's the only thing he ever did to make me feel not completely his wife. There was a sister, too. Her name was (is?) Rita. I don't know where she is, or anything about her.

By the way, I've lost track of my Peggy, too. I think she is trying to return to the fold, a course I cannot elect for myself.

We must have seemed such *awful* fools. And of course Bunny was one. And I have ended one, playing along through all those years. Yet so many people—you and Grace, especially—have been so forebearing that I have few regrets.

Thank you again, Dear Thomas; and do please tell Grace, when you talk with her, as I now know you must.

All our love, Libby

Her letter brought sorrow and regret to Thomas's heart. But it also disclosed a goodness in Libby which he had not detected, and probably a deeper happiness than he had felt she might have had. And he was thankful, at once, and ashamed.

Autumn had already rolled out grey skies over the mouth of the Cape Fear River; she, with her apples scattering, would extend to the high air above Peell County soon enough. Still, in New Brunswick, nearly-bare branches seemed interleaved with flakes of parchment, persisting, persisting in many shades, each shade but a nuance of another; after rain had strung droplets along every eave and gable, then the evening sun came along and turned them to amethyst. Chrysanthemums clung to life; the *Camellia sasanqua* began to bloom in good earnest.

On the Sunday before Thanksgiving, Thomas delivered, in Christ Church, this homily:

"In the name + of the Father, and of the Son, and of the Holy Ghost."
"Amen."
"Dear People of God,
"By next Sunday we shall have observed the feast of Thanksgiving, and shall then enter upon the Season of Advent, during which we prepare for Christmastide. Today's world will not allow us observe it as a penitential season, which historically it is. However, we use purple as the liturgical color, and we omit from the service of Holy Communion the *Gloria in Excelsis*, as

we do in Lent, for it is an ancient hymn of ebullient praise—we keep it back, so to say, to make our celebration of Jesus' Birth the more joyous.

"The words from it that I hope each of us may make a part of our Thanksgiving meditations are these: "Wc praise thee, we bless thee, we worship thee, we glorify thee, *we give thanks to thee for thy great glory....*" To thank the Creator for all that the earth yields, and for all His gifts, is a natural and predictable response. For these things benefit us directly. To thank Him 'for His great glory' is quite another thing. For it is a glory that we do not apperceive.

"Once, when in seminary, I was sent a Christmas greeting card; on the front of it was a detail from a famous painting. It attempted to depict God the Father. It was a beautiful picture; I did not recognize it—It mustn't have been quite famous enough for that!—but if I were to trust my memory, to have to make a guess, then I should say it was from a picture of Tintoretto's. For it sparkled. The Deity was shown partly as the Ancient of Days, with long beard, the face of man, all borne upon billowing clouds. From these and from the Figure Itself there emanated manifold rays of light. Some may have been meant as lightning bolts. Such details need not occupy us this morning.

"The image was very moving, due to the skill, and without doubt to the inspiration, of the painter, in spite of the limitation incumbent upon him from the outset to employ only elements visible to the eyes of men. This, to represent what the human eye cannot behold. What the human mind cannot entirely comprehend.

"Soon after first looking at this, I met the Dean in a hallway. We spoke. We exchanged good wishes for Christmas and the New Year. Then I asked him whether he ever tried to imagine the majesty of the being of the Godhead. And he answered, very pleasantly, 'Certainly not, Tommy. It would be a waste of time.'

"Should any of us consider such an exercise a waste of time? Because it is, indeed, an exercise that cannot be fulfilled in its quest. Nevertheless, won't each of us, somewhere in the course of his lifetime, arrive at an impulse to know something of the nature of Him Who is the Underpinning of the universe?

"I think nearly all of us—No, all of us—will come to such a point. We will read treatises on the subject. Or we will discuss the matter in intimacy with just one other person, with one whose judgment we trust. Or we will meditate, possibly, like the Psalmist, day and night.

"And are we likely to find an answer? Not likely. Certainly not a very clear one, but perhaps one that will allow us to begin from what is practically assured: We may at all times and in all places, at the least, give thanks to God for His great glory. We do know that—that little. And it may be that it is all we—as we are—are meant to know.

"But what are we to make of those who believe they have somehow understood God's nature and know His will?

"My belief is that they err.

"If we consider that description of the Godhead, and the manner in which He is worshipped, given in the Book of Revelation, we shall note both confusion and *pro*fusion of images—which to me are not characteristics of authoritativeness. Reference to precious stones abounds—jasper, sardine stone, emerald, glass like unto crystal—all reflecting light. And of light there is a very great store to be reflected: A rainbow, lightenings, lamps of fire burning.

"Plainly said, the majesty of the being of God probably cannot be grasped, certainly not described. One must be satisfied with a series of inroads, approximations. Understanding this, the Jews, the first to worship the 'sole eternal Being,' Whom we recognize as the God of Abraham, that is, our God, execrated any graven image or other physical representation of the Deity. Muslims forbear in their art to depict the human figure, which they consider to mirror the image of God. The Jews believe to know His Name, but will not speak it, aware, I think, that at the last, it is not up to man to speak of God by name.

"Followers of Islam say simply: 'There is no God but God.' And in their Remembrance of God, they recite ninety-nine of His attributes. I wonder whether they are not withholding the hundredth for a time of greater wisdom, greater clarity of knowledge, more understanding within the heart?

"Going back, now, to the Book of Revelation, we find the basis of many of the expressions which occur in the hymn used for this morning's processional, where we name God as 'Almighty,' ' merciful and mighty,' 'having been, being, evermore to be,' 'alone holy,' 'perfect in power,' and finally and possibly most telling of all: 'One in three Persons.' Monotheism, or belief in and worship of one God, is a cornerstone of the Church's teaching—one to which we consider ourselves to hold fast. And yet, we do not even try to approach understanding except from any of three directions. A refinement of the process, used in worldly applications, that we call 'triangulation.'

"But what of possible reciprocity in our inability to know god? Some scholars maintain that the philosopher Aristotle believed that God was so supernal as to be not even aware of man, or of the Creation in general. For my part, I should not go so far as that, for any predication—almost any—is in a way a qualification or limitation, and he who proposes to qualify or limit the Godhead is…off-track, so to say.

"The two dozen elders who in the Book Revelation, and in that same hymn, 'cast down their golden crowns around a glassy sea,' end their praise by saying: 'For thou hast created all things, and for thy pleasure they are, and were created."

"I myself find that I do not—I cannot—believe that transcendent God could take actual pleasure in man or in the rest of the Creation, unless as a sort of toy. And neither God's greatness nor man's lesser but nevertheless real worth is consistent with such a notion.

"Howbeit, we give thanks to Thee for Thy great glory, O Lord God, heavenly King.

"Now unto God the Father...."

Nobody could ever recall with certainty at precisely what point in this homily Joe Watkins went berserk. Most thought it happened just after the words: "Understanding this, the Jews...." Joe had been provoked before. Two weeks earlier, to be exact (for one example). He declared to his wife Lucille, on that occasion, that he would *never,* under any circumstance, listen again to a sermon of Thomas Strikestraw's. He rejected the suggestion that they go to eight o'clock Communion, where there was no homily, on the ground that Sundays were supposed to be days of rest.

And gladness, Lucille thought, feeling, though, that somehow she had cast troubled waters upon oil.

But Joe regretted, the next Sunday, having sent Lucille off to Church by herself. And he had been unhappy about the way his stubbornness made him feel. Furthermore, he had great liking and respect for the Rector—out of the pulpit. He could put up with the occasional remark about the Jews, even if he didn't like them (without knowing any), and even about what he called the "Islams," even if he felt they were heathen (without so much as having seen one). So he relented, but his return to the flock coincided with the homily just cited, where, haplessly, Joe got it both coming and going, as some would put it.

Anyway, at whatever the phrase of detonation, he flushed all over—or at least in head and hands, which people could see. Wrath resurgent, he sprang to his feet and stumped out of the church without reverencing the altar. Lucille was horrified and embarrassed, so she whispered as loudly and to as general an audience as she dared that "Joe could not get his breath." And she hurried out after him.

When a few charitable friends left, too, to see whether they could be of help, Thomas, who from his training in the Army Reserve Corps (which he had joined during his seminary years in the hope of escaping at least some of the weekend retreats) knew more than a little about first aid, abandoned conduct of the service and followed.

By the time he had got out onto the portico, Joe was leaning against a white-painted pillar, gasping for air, face flaring red, vessels of the neck distended. "His heart's racing," Leila McLeod screamed when she saw Thomas, by way of handing on her scrap of clinical information to him whom she esteemed the mediator of divine help.

Thomas placed two fingers over the radial artery, once Joe had been coërced into letting the apostate priest take him by the forearm. The pulse was so rapid that it could not be counted reliably. Thomas had little *general* medical knowledge; he had been trained to help only the young and fit. But this was a disorder of the young and fit. This was "PAT"—paroxysmal atrial tachycardia. Carotid sinus pressure, which must be applied with caution, was the on-the-spot remedy. He remembered, though, that the rhythm disturbance was usually easily converted.

When Thomas placed his thumbs over these arterial formations, which overly the throat, with the other fingers of both hands wrapped around the neck, Joe fought back. The resulting spectacle, flailing coil of limbs, blur of grey flannel, fair linen, and a Canon's purple, so stupefied those gathered upon the porch that they did nothing but continue standing absolutely still.

There were no passersby, for everyone who approached, stopped. They stopped to wonder at what appeared to be two men, one in priestly attire, bent upon strangling each other—not a sight you saw everyday.

Additionally, before suffering too much shock at seeing him—seeing him review an already so shocking *tableau vivant*—we must make ready for the reappearance of Duzey Blanding, left presumably facing imminent death as the ambulance pulled away from the Lumina on that night fateful for *USS Lemuel Weatherington* and her crew and for Sarah Elkin and Hal Whitman.

For Duzey had survived. His liver-disease had been mercifully insidious, or he'd never have swung a lantern to the tune of "What a Friend we have in Jesus," at midnight on the beaches of Oak Island. But its slow progress did allow time for the veins in the lower esophagus and upper stomach to become dilated and friable.

On that night, these had ruptured and bled, making his presence among those out for an evening of diversion not agreeable. Barely alive as the ambulance had taken him from the Pavilion, he was curiously exactly so barely alive when they arrived at the hospital.

There, into his stomach was placed a largely unspeakable but cleverly designed apparatus called a Singstaken-Blakemore tube. This was actually three separate but concentric tubes, or chambers, of red rubber—a substance in itself often causing alarm—each separately accessible at the patient's mouth.

Innermost was a tube of rather small caliber, through which nutrients, iced water fortified with epinephrine, antacid—or, in fact, whatever the doctors ordered—could be instilled into the stomach.

Next ran a tube by means of which a balloon in the stomach could be inflated to secure the whole, when shortly afterward it was pulled upward with some force. To maintain this tension, the tube was attached to the face-guard of an ordinary football helmet, which of course the patient must wear until stabilized. "Stabilized" either through hemostasis and survival, or exsanguination and ignominious death inside such headgear, which had to be left in place for the prosector.

Finally, about these two was a long cylindrical tube, the esophageal one, and star of the Asklepian drama, which could be inflated to subject the oozing veins to stanching back-pressure, or deflated for periods, so as not to interfere with arterial blood-flow, essential, of course, to any favorable outcome.

Duzey was a docile patient and tolerated this well…better than an overworked night nurse who through error injected antacid into the balloon, rather than into the stomach itself. This was discovered by means of a radiogram, one of several made at intervals to confirm proper placement of the tube. The solids had settled out of the liquid part of the antacid and formed a cretaceous mass. To avoid surgery, aides and interns sat hourly, adding water, waiting, drawing off portions of the chalky material in the return. Meanwhile, the bleeding had stopped. The tube could be withdrawn.

As the resident physician was removing the football helmet, Duzey asked: "Is the game over, Doc?"

"The game is over, and we've won."

That is how he came to happen along, in time to see Thomas put an end to the fracas on the portico at the front of Christ Church by getting Joe Watkins in a headlock (which as a perhaps valuable concomitant subjected the carotid sinuses to plenty of pressure). Duzey had foregone attending Church that day, just as he had done for the previous twenty years. Through long experience, he had learned that things often appeared to himself in different guise from that in which they appeared to most other people. Still, he felt he had better fetch the police. They came, and brought to stillness and goodwill one of the strangest occurrences Christ Church, in all her years, had seen, though not the strangest, either past or to come.

Many years before all this, the season of Advent had brought to Christ Church Parish the unfolding of a remarkable spiritual phenomenon, and yet the rector had known nothing of it. It had to do with Benny Ormond's conviction that he would not see death, let alone corruption. The story he had told to Edward Strikestraw and Bobby McCallum, in the summer after they had finished school, had not been embroidered with retelling. Instead, it had been distilled to an almost journalistically accurate account—barring a few misapprehensions, due to one thing or other.

When Benny, from the Great War, had finally reached New Brunswick, his people decided—wrongly—that what he most needed after all his trials was solitude. What he needed in fact was perspective; he was not shaken by the strain, discomfort, or terrors associated with what had befallen him; he was a strong man in most ways, and reasonable, except for entertaining the prospect of immortality. If death was an "undiscovered country," then everlasting life here below was more mythical than Atlantis. For no one—no one whom one knows, at any rate—has experienced the latter, where the former is thought universal. And experience agreeth thereto.

A cousin owned a scrap of land and small house on Bewley Island. Benny was sent there for a couple of weeks to "get his thoughts together." And he did so. If he had been able to review these thoughts with another, then he might have carried them less far, been less tenacious of them. But as he poked about the coves and copses of isolation, poked about alone inside the Old Light, his ideas, too, like the later and standard stairways inside tall, East-coast lighthouses, curved upward and forward, then crossed on level above their own courses; up, forward again; again back across.

Benny relived sometimes the hour of his rescue from the madness of the winter sea. The one remaining soldier, besides himself, had let his oars slip from his hands.

"Pull, Buddy. Or we're lost for certain."

"I can't. My strength is gone."

"Then let's rest for awhile."

"I don't have strength even to rest." And the oars had slipped farther from the man's grasp, farther into the brine until, as the shafts widened toward just below the grips, they caught in the rowlocks.

Those blades in the water are going to interfere with my steering. Then Ben Ormond came as close as he had ever done, or ever would do, to laughing at himself. There was no steering to be done in that ungoverned sea.

"Come over here, Buddy. I'll hold you and keep you warm as long as I can. Trouble is, there's nothing to cover up with." He had tried, by lying low, to shield both of them against the weather. Then he thought the crew of any rescue craft might believe the boat abandoned. Then he didn't have to think about anything anymore. For his companion went down in death.

But now, here on Bewley Island, as winter lost its foothold, with no one else about to talk to, Benny had nothing to occupy the cogitating part of his mind but his Idea. His aunt, whom he took to church every Sunday, had left him a bible to read. But Benny did not read very fluently. And he was disinclined from laboring through genealogies; things that probably never happened, but if they had, then thousands of years ago. There was more evildoing than righteousness, it seemed to him, and the retributions, which were either divine or divinely underwritten, he found unsavory, occasionally ghastly.

And Church, if anything, was worse than Scripture. Benny did not grasp the significance of the Holy Sacrament (He had never attended confirmation class) and so did not know in what manner—outward or inward—to revere it. He didn't understand what took place in the sanctuary the rest of the time, or why some people genuflected or made the sign of the Cross, or why they did these things when they did. He felt about listening to preaching roughly as he did about reading the Bible. But he was glad enough to accompany his aunt, for she had been Mother to him.

The greater part of a Church Year went past. Then, on the second Sunday of Advent, 1921, Benny sat up and took notice. For the Gospel passage appointed for the day was from that according to Saint Luke, the twenty-first chapter, beginning at the twenty-fifth verse: "And there shall be signs in the sun and in the moon…." For the sun and the moon were his companions, and the waters issuing from the River, and the island to the southeast, where stood in dereliction the old, the great Tower, which, it was always told within the family, their ancestors had used to keep. "…Distress of nations…sea and waves roaring…men's hearts failing them for fear…." Nothing else could have been written to find in Benny Ormond's heart a so perfectly resonant chord. He continued to listen with careful attention. "…When ye see these things come to pass, know ye that the kingdom of God is nigh at hand. . .This generation shall not pass away…."

After this, Benny began to behave in such a way as to glean a reputation for real eccentricity. He continued to live in the cottage upon Bewley Island. He continued to take his aunt to church every Sunday. On one of these days, in going out of the church, he asked the rector whether the Tower of Babel had had a circular staircase, or merely a series of ladders. The rector said he thought Circular. Then Benny asked whether they had ascended clockwise, or counter, or whether it were known. The rector said he would attempt to find out, and the following Sunday said Clockwise.

Church seemed all downgrade after that. Before long, Old Lady Ormond died, and Benny stopped going to church. Except upon the second Sunday in Advent. He made small but regular purchases of lumber and ferried it across to his island. That was all people saw or knew of him. And he continued to believe that he would not see death. He gave little thought to the question who else besides himself would not see it, either. There seemed to him no sign, no criterion for this discrimination. And he didn't care, anyway. And the rector moved on, in time, without realizing that he had had in his cure a man destined to become a front-row spectator to the Day of Judgment.

A great deal of time passed, another war came and was won at dreadful cost. And much else happened. Benny Ormond's life, though, was not greatly affected by these things, until one day, when already he had got to be up in years, he noticed that a patch of skin upon his shoulder was raised slightly. And it itched. He thought little of it, however, until eventually he was forced to think more, because the condition progressed, spreading widely and itching and burning ever more viciously. He went to see the doctor, who had him try some salves, but these were not effective. He went to a specialist in Wilmington who dealt only in diseases of the skin. This physician removed a small sample of affected tissue to be looked at under the microscope, and prescribed a lotion and some tablets—but he cautioned that these would only relieve some of the discomfort, not necessarily cure the disease.

Benny went back a week later. The doctor said the affliction was called "mycosis fungoides." Then he explained as clearly as he could what the nature of it was, what it would lead to. Benny didn't even try to understand. He couldn't, anyway. And he was skeptical of the doctor's prognosis. Prognosis was a process which he did not believe applied to himself. He was told he must enter the hospital. Instead, he went home.

"...all the days of thy life."

"*Amen.*"

"Thank you, Father. I am trying to make my peace all around. With men—I never had much to do with any of them; I'm square with men, so far as I know. With myself, almost, I think. Now you've made my peace with God."

"No, Benny. You've made your peace with God. I've only put an official stamp on it...a holy bureaucrat. But—one further thing."

"What is it, Father?" Benny Ormond asked, turning to Thomas, with, for the first time a suggestion of fear, or of suspicion, in his thickly clouded eyes.

"You said you'd made peace with yourself. 'Almost.' Can I help you to finish the work? Then I'd feel I'd done my duty."

Benny hesitated for a long time, and Thomas didn't know how to interpret his silence. The old man was being given, among other drugs, strong sedatives; besides, he suffered from an illness not curable at that time, in so advanced a stage.

But Benny had neither died nor fallen asleep. He had merely been trying to decide where to begin. Translation of thought into words was a thing he was not good at. "You must have heard about my days in the Great War, the First World War, they call it, since there's been another one?"

The story was local legend, because it was unbelievable, yet true. After Benny had told it a few times, somebody or other had decided to see whether it could be corroborated. And it could be, and it was true, and then everybody was veritably amazed. Thereafter, knowing Private Benny Ormond's war story had become just a natural part of having lived in New Brunswick for any considerable length of time. Thus, "Yes," Thomas said, "I have, although I have no way of knowing how much of it I have heard."

"Well, it doesn't matter any more. I'm not going over it again. Not now, and not ever. Because what I made of it was wrong. That part I've never told anybody; yet that's the part that keeps me from being at peace."

"If you want to speak of it, I'm your man. My next obligation isn't until four o'clock tomorrow morning."

"What does a priest have to do at four o'clock in the morning? I mean, what, that he can foretell?"

"Put the turkey into the stove. Apparently Rhodë—you know Rhodë Harmon, don't you; or at least who she is?—feels she must roast two." For knowing Rhodë Harmon, or at least Who She Was, was equally a part of living for any considerable time in New Brunswick.

Benny fell silent again but did not remain so for as long. "I watched men die, and I watched men not die when I thought they were going to. But when I wasn't watching, when I was in the thick of all of it myself, a different thing happened. I kept surviving, and everybody who had come along with me kept dying. The odds weren't the same when it came to me. Anyway, I began to think they weren't.

"After I got home, I started going to Church with my Aunt Bertha. She brought me up. I couldn't have said No to anything she asked. But, Father, I have to admit I didn't get much out of it. Maybe because I didn't put much into it. Anyway, one Sunday I heard something out of the Bible that brought me up short. I thought it might have been written to me. It was…."

"I may know what it was."

"How?"

"Because you always come to Church on a particular day."

"You've noticed that, then?"

"How could I help it, once years had gone by? And, after all, Benny, you never come to Church *except* on that day."

"I expect that's not a very good thing?"

"Oh it's quite a good thing; and I don't concern myself with why people come to Church, or with when, or with why they stay away. It's not my place. But sometimes curiosity does get the better of me; remember I'm only an ordinary man—although you might not think it, seeing me dressed in all those paraphernalia at Sunday Service."

"So you know why I've always been there then?"

"I didn't mean to say that. Just that I may know what part of the Bible you thought could have been written for you—it possibly was, by the way, I think. Isn't it 'signs in the sun and the moon,' and 'this generation shall not pass away'?"

"How did you know?"

"I didn't know; but it's the only stirring part of that day's propers. Besides, I thought that 'distress of nations,' 'the sea and the waves roaring,' and the rest of it, might pertain to some of what I'd heard you'd endured."

"Well, you're right on the money. Since I had survived so much, so much that took away *everybody* else, I began to think…that maybe it meant…."

"What, Benny? Tell me. It doesn't matter."

"That I would live until Judgment Day—never die."

Thomas thought over this. "If you believe that part of the Scripture, somebody has to live until then. No, looking at the things that happened to you, and the way they happened, it seems to me reasonable for you to have reached that conclusion."

Although this observation seemed to have a decided calming effect upon the old man, still Thomas had noted that over all he had been getting more ill-at-ease. He decided this must be due in part to physical discomfort. He reached across and pressed the call-bell.

Presently there came a tap at the door, and a nurse in encouragingly clean and crisp uniform came in. After glancing at her patient, then she noticed his guest, whom she recognized. "Canon?" Thomas looked up in surprise. "I'm Sarah Elkin."

Thomas sprang to his feet at once. He looked at the woman, then kissed her impulsively on either cheek. He had not seen her nor spoken with her since the time of his son's disappearance. "Good Gracious, Sarah! You've become even lovelier! I should not have thought that possible." He looked at her identification badge, then added: "And you've apparently become Mrs. Whitman, too."

"I'll tell you all about that before you leave, Canon. Now, Mr. Ormond, what do you need? Oh, Dear! Your compresses are as dry as lightwood. You *must* let us know, Mr. Ormond, before they get like this. I know you don't like having them changed, but the longer we leave them, the worse it is taking them off." She examined carefully each section of folded gauze draped across the burning limbs and trunk. "Well, I think you get a little break this time. I'll put on a second layer to rehydrate these, then we'll wait for a little while. Your next injection is due in fifteen minutes; maybe you'll be sound asleep when I come back to put on the new dressings." She smiled brightly at Thomas on her way out.

"She's a sweet girl," Benny Ormond said. "She's very patient with me."

"She's a lovely woman. I've known her, at least slightly, since she was a little girl. I can't remember ever having seen her without a smile on her face."

"But she lost her husband in the Second War."

There the sentence hung, an unspangled banner, while each of the men tried and failed to think of some next comment that would not be vacuous. They both gazed for a while out through the window. Since it faced south, they could look down along the eastern bank of the River, to the islands at its mouth, spits of sandy shore, late afternoon sun lighting interfolded lines of forest, banks of cloud, circlets of gold about the clouds behind clouds, amethystine water, characteristic stamp of autumn upon the sea-pools of the Coastal Plain.

"Can you see the Light?" Bennie asked finally. But Thomas did not know right away what he meant, and so he let the silence—which was after all quite a reasonable thing—run for a while longer.

"The Old Light. Did you know you can see it from here?"

Now the door opened again, and Sarah Whitman brought in a basin of compresses, laid one of them efficiently upon each of the others, and went out.

"You can, if you know exactly where to look."

"I beg your pardon. What did you say?"

"I said, you can see the Old Light from here, if you know exactly where to look." Benny raised a hand to the window, and stretched out an osteophytic finger. Thomas came to the bedside to sight along it. At first, like a flame in a draft, it wavered. Then it held steady, respite of the compass needle aboard a ship on course. "Can you see just where I'm pointing?"

"Yes, but everything outside the window is very far off."

"But do you see a tree over yonder, taller than the rest?"

"I see it."

"To the right of it, can you see what looks like a great post, a little taller, it looks even from here, than the tall tree."

"Yes, I can see that, too."

"That is the Old Light."

"Is it, really? I thought your eyesight was supposed to be not so good."

"Father, I have looked at that tower so long, so many times, over so many years, from so many points…some far, some near…I think I could see it in the dark. Yes, I've looked at it when I could see it; I still do now, when I can't, anymore."

"It wouldn't surprise me if you *could* see it in the dark. But, Benny, I've been here a long time already. I'm sure I must be tiring you?"

"No. Stay a while longer if you can. I'll be getting everybody's plenty of rest soon." And as on cue, another nurse entered, holding high a hypodermic syringe. She was less winning than Sarah. She administered the treatment and went out.

Benny Ormond said: "That hurt, but I wouldn't let her know it." Thomas sat down again.

"I think often of the Old Light, of all that it must have looked down upon."

"When it had an eye to see. Did you know that my people, generations ago, used to be the keepers?"

"I didn't. You must have a particular fondness for it."

"I have. And I have a duty to it." The immense loops of gold had gone from encircling the clouds. The far junipers were no more now than dark shadow.

Benny's voice had got lower but oddly clearer. Was he seeing into the darkness already? Would he prophesy? "Father, do you remember the day I asked you about the Tower of Babel? About whether it had had a staircase, or just ladders?"

This was of course all new to Thomas, since Benny had asked it of an earlier rector. Thomas, though, imagined that the drug was casting the pall of timelessness across Benny's memory. He said nothing, but waited.

After a while, then, Benny went on: "You told me—But it wasn't you, was it?—that it had either a ramp or staircase that went around, clockwise as you went up and counterclockwise as you came down. I built mine the other way, just to be on the safe side." Thomas waited a little longer.

"Father?"

"Yes?"

"Because of that wrong notion I took so long a time ago, I haven't prepared for death."

"Besides leading your life, Benny, I don't think there's any particular way to prepare for death. I think it just takes us, when it's ready, and does with us whatever it is that it does. Like birth. We didn't prepare for that. Or, if we did, we don't remember it."

"Anyhow, it's too late."

"Why do you say so?"

"Because I'm dead already—just a ghost. I can't see people's faces, their expressions. So I don't know whether to speak, or not. Or what to say if I did. They don't seem to notice me anymore, either. And I'm burning in Hellfire right now, so I must be dead."

"When you are dead, Bennie, you won't burn any more. There'll be no flesh for fuel. And you will see clearly, because the diseased eyes will be gone."

"Then how will I see at all?"

"The Tower. You said you could see it in the dark. You will see in the dark. At first, just a light, but then, as you go toward it, beyond it you will see a brighter light, and you will go toward that, and on forth. Then in the last and brightest Light you will see everything. And you'll comprehend everything, I think. And clearly. 'Face-to-face,' the Prayer Book says, 'and not as a stranger.' "

"Will it take me long to get there?

"No time. The travel will take place in eternity, which occupies no time at all."

The drug took firm hold, then, and Benny died into the diminished, discontinuous death of sleep.

Thomas left the hospital room. It had become cool and quiet and dark. The light in the hall was soft, but desk lamps blazed in the nurses' station, where the staff were preparing to go off duty, to complete their notes in the patients' charts, to be ready to give report to the evening shift. Thomas found Sarah. As head nurse, she was not occupied like the others. She waited in a small alcove, which was her own. Anyway, she would work this night shift, in order to have a long Thanksgiving Vacation.

"Sarah," Thomas said quietly, deliberately. She looked up; her face held only the vestige of a smile. "I'm very sorry to hear your husband was lost."

"Thank you, Canon."

"Was he one of the New Brunswick Whitmans?"

"Yes, originally. Halbert. They had moved, though, to Wilmington. Our courtship was a little explosive. It lasted seventeen hours, then we were married. My family were naturally astonished, but they rallied round."

"When was he killed? And where? I mean, if it's all right for me to ask."

"Oh, of course. He was called up after three weeks. The troop transport was torpedoed the fifth day out, and he died in the explosion."

"But, Sarah! What a terrible thing for you, and what a waste of his life and strength." Sarah's thoughts seemed to be moving slowly off into somewhere else. Her smile returned complete.

"Nothing was wasted, Canon. You'll think me sentimental, if not insane. But for those weeks, time—and I'm not using the figure of speech—stood still. Entirely still. Believe it or not. I regret nothing. And I hope I'm not selfish in my satisfaction…no, not that; in my *stillness* about it all. When I said Goodbye to Hal, I told him to 'take care of himself.' He answered: 'Nothing can happen to me; I'm in Heaven.'

"All I wanted afterward was to be useful, so I studied nursing. The War was over, of course, before I got my cap. We have a daughter, and she has become a nurse, as well."

"How wonderful! A memorial. A comfort, I hope, and a joy. And where is she now?"

"Across the River, at New Hanover."

"I am quite embarrassed that I did not know about all this."

"You oughtn't to be, Canon—not for a minute. I know you had plenty to say grace over in your own parish. And there was your own loss. "

"Well, the Lord gave, and the Lord hath taken away."

"And blessed be the name of the Lord."

After leaving the hospital, Thomas was strongly inclined to go to visit the Old Light. On the other hand, he wanted to be at home when Edward arrived, who had telephoned earlier to say he'd be late, and why. But it was now seven o'clock, and he could've got there already. So Thomas drove back into town, and home.

Edward was not there, but Duzey Blanding, for some reason, was. "Rhodë let me in, Father. I came by to see whether you had any time to visit, but I ought to have called first. I know Edward will be here anytime."

"You know you're always welcome, Duzey. And I've started really to look forward to our chats. You seem to be the only one who can express…variant ideas, and hear them, without seeming to regard it all as…seditious. No need to telephone ahead. Really. Ever." But Edward came in just then, looking exhausted, and no wonder. After greetings, Duzey said: "I have a message for you, Edward; it's nothing important, though. When the telephone rang, Rhodë had already left." Then he turned to Thomas. "By the way, Canon, she asked me to ask you not to forget about 'Turkey Number One.' Does that make any sense?"

"Oh, alas, yes it does. And, Duzey, I hope you're planning to have Thanksgiving dinner with us…after Church. You may as well say Yes, because Mr. and Mrs. Simpson are coming to help Rhodë. They *said* they were sure it would be all right with you. I tried to find you, to ask. But I couldn't."

"When you were looking, I may not have known where I was myself. I've got to do better, work harder. I am slowly learning, at least, to enjoy being ful…nearly fully conscious.

"But it's certainly all right with me, if it is with them, to have Joe and Emily come and help out. And, thank you. I'd like very much to come, too."

"Virginia and Tuggs are coming…all the way from Laurinburg. They are bringing the children."

They had moved from the entrance hall into the library, where Edward collapsed into the big wingchair covered in cloth that depicted lychee fruit, looking as though he planned not to stir from it, but he asked: "Well, Duzey, anyway, what is the message?"

Duzey addressed Thomas again. "I would not have answered your telephone ordinarily, Canon. But after it had rung so many times, I thought the call might be important, so I picked up."

"What was the message, though?" Edward asked a little irritably, for he did intend to abandon the wingchair, and he wanted as soon as possible to have his supper—if there were to be any; there never seemed to be anything on hand for ordinary meals around the Holidays—and to get to bed.

"That's just it. There really was no *message*. The lady just said—in fact she said herself it wasn't important—to say she had called. She has to go to a dance this evening, but will try you again sometime later in the weekend." Edward suddenly came to General Quarters. He felt he was about to experience a surge of voltage or some like force.

"Who was she?"

" 'Mary.' And her last name is 'Mountainstream,' a surname I've never heard before today. But I had her spell it out for me."

Edward was on his feet; suddenly he looked rested and kempt. "How many times did you say the telephone rang?"

"I didn't say, and I don't know exactly, but a lot. It had rung nine times before I decided I ought to answer it. Then I had to get to it, so it rang some more. I thought it must be something urgent."

Edward took Duzey in a bear hug, lifting him off the floor. Duzey was not flustered, for, even since his brush with death, he had persisted in the habit of "taking a little something" once in a while, and this kept him calm. He said to Edward: "I didn't know you cared."

"The only thing that keeps that message from being urgent is that urgent things usually run their courses quickly. This won't."

Thomas and Duzey both thought they understood what underlay the revivification. After all, there wasn't but one thing that could. Duzey took his leave. Thomas said: "Thank you for coming by. Tomorrow we can have our talk after the Shouting and Tumult have died. It will give me something to look forward to. That's besides Turkey Number One."

"And, I guess, Turkey Number Two as well."

"If we get so far!"

When Thomas next saw his grandson, Edward had shaved a second time and changed his clothes. Something was going on. It would be clear soon enough. He said: "How was the deer hunt? Did you meet any people you liked?"

"I met a lot of people I like, and I like them a lot." He was approaching a full confession, by degrees it appeared. *Soon enough.*

"You must be exhausted; was the last part of the drive difficult? In the dark?"

"It would have been worse in daylight. At least by night I didn't have to *see* the road. As a whole."

"I don't imagine you've had anything to eat."

"No, Sir. And I was starving when I got here. But I'm not at all hungry now. Oh, and I've been meaning to ask you this: Will anybody be arriving tonight?"

"No."

"Thank God!"

"You may have heard me say that Virginia and her family are coming in the morning. Rhodë is distressed about the children."

"About what about them?"

"That they're coming."

"Oh. Well, you can hardly blame her."

"Not unless they've changed fairly radically. But they won't be spending the night."

"Thank God!"

"Edward, I try not to be priggish; but please avoid saying 'Thank God' so often within such a short space of time."

"Sorry, Grandfather."

"It's just that it would wound your Grandmother. She had come to be slightly pious. If you can remember."

"And I know she'll be among us tomorrow." He actually knew she would be. Both knew it.

"Rhodë thinks she's here permanently. I have actually heard her talking to her. And I rather think she sometimes prays to her."

"Good God!"

"I know it will take a little time to accustom yourself to being away from college. Now I wonder—since you seem refreshed—I wonder if perhaps you might not like to accompany me on a little adventure." Thomas felt he couldn't have been more tentative than that.

"Now?"

"I shouldn't have asked you; I can't even imagine the amount of energy you must have expended during the last few days."

"No, Sir. I'm just a little surprised that you're undertaking an 'adventure' at this time of day. I don't know what it is, but I'd love to come along."

"Really? Hold on. Let me see whether I can get it lined up."

With Edward driving, they motored along the road that led out of town, southward to the Hammonds' house.

Two thoughts from which to form a fugue. The excursion to the Old Light timed at haphazard (as he supposed). The telephone message, elating without even being taken. Edward had believed himself to be coming home. But "home," the greater area taken to constitute that place, was changed. Not gone; burnished. He could think of no other word for it. Had its splendors, there all along, been unwrapped for the new adult he had become?

Nine rings! It would have taken at least three more, probably, for Duzey to get to the telephone once he had made up his mind to answer. Twelve rings, then. And the message wasn't even important. Had she just wanted to hear the sound of my voice? No, that is taking the thing too far. It is only that I want to hear the sound of hers. The asking theme just kept running on, holding the answering theme pinned.

Edward kept trying to fit into the framework of his usual life a new happiness which seemed to be running swiftly to madness. It looked like being madness of a kind to amplify itself until finally it should consume its host. And he welcomed, looked impatiently forward to that overwhelming.

And the madness was light, entering by way of the eye, and the hindermost part of the brain, to which the eye reports. Light that was the reflection of a uniquely congenial beauty. Thus, the process began; it would end (It would; Edward wanted it to) by flooding all nerve-links; end by being never far from any other thought. Nothing else could have this power. Only beauty. *And not every kind of it. Just this; and only to my eyes.*

Edward himself, at least, was content with this explanation of things, set in terms of on-the-spot psychophysiology. Which, of course, was all bunk, like "The Twelve Dancing Princesses."

Now, by way of preparation for the adventure, for they were getting close to the Hammonds', Thomas Strikestraw said to his grandson: "John has had a little stroke—not like the 'little stroke' I had when you were in the third grade, but a real one. There is a slight disturbance of his speech, but very slight. His gait is just perceptibly abnormal. But there are things he has trouble doing with his right hand and arm. He thinks he'd rather not have any help. So if he gets into minor difficulty, then just look busy. If it gets to be more than that, give him a hand without saying anything, and leave off as soon as you can."

"I'll try to be tactful."

"And I'm sure you will succeed. I just wanted to let you know, beforehand. I get impatient myself, with my little debilities, and they are nothing much at all." At Trent, they might not have believed this.

Again they were rolling along the road, this time the three of them, with John Hammond's John boat in tow upon its trailer.

"Mr. Hammond," Edward said, "has my grandfather taken time to tell you what this is all about? Because he has said nothing to me, except that it's supposed to be an 'adventure.' "

"Son, I don't care what it is, not as long as it gets me out of the house for a bit. Helen and Blossom have been in the back of the house, all day today and half of yesterday. They're cooking. And Helen has ordered some little artificial woodbirds, but with real plumage. I can't identify all of the kinds of feathers. Anyway, they're making place-card holders out of them."

Thomas said: "I hope I haven't dragged you out, if you have house guests coming."

"We haven't. They're all coming tomorrow. And when I say 'all,' I mean it literally. Most are staying for one night; some for two."

"Good God!"

"Edward, remember yourself."

"Yes, Sir."

"And, Edward, please call me John, since we're all getting to be about the same age now."

Even my grandfather's friends are taking me on as an equal! And the telephone rang twelve times. I am coming into my own. And he had tried to address Lavinia as "Mrs. Ashfield," when saying Goodbye, and she had asked him to use her Christian name, and Laurence had said, offhandedly, "And you already know to call me Laurence." A thing he hadn't known, but suspected. Edward felt he was taking his place in the world, that it was a great place. But was it a great world? The coming years would tell most certainly.

Now the three men were over the divide of inlet between shore and island. Edward stepped out of the boat as soon as her bottom ground upon the sand, took the painter, and pulled as hard as he could with the two others aboard, one of great frame and the other, his grandfather, now entitled to the epithet of "portly." So he said: "Come ashore, Grandfather," and handed him out. "John"—for John Hammond had said he would just wait in the boat while they inspected the tower—"please get out," and he took him by the forearm, which that proud man would not have offered; "I need more buoyancy to get this thing onto the beach. I'm assuming we won't be away from her for long, but I don't know the phase of the tide. Does either of you?"

Nobody admitted to knowing the phase of the tide. They strode toward the Light.

"Are we going inside, Tommy?"

"If we can get inside."

"What has made you suddenly so interested in this, Grandfather? The last time I tried to go in, the door wouldn't open. The time before that, when I was very young, the door could be opened. But there was nothing inside except a gridwork of rusted iron. I would have tried to climb it, too, but it had fallen away from high up out of my reach, thank God."

"Put the electric light on the door, now, Edward, please, so we can see where we're going. And to answer your question, while I do know—but I don't want to say, yet—what occurrence has made me interested, I do not know at all what we shall find." The electric spotlight illuminated the base of the tower, shouldered and subsiding tabby, sturdier brickwork, clear against the darkness in the beams of the electric lantern, up to a height of fifteen feet.

Nothing to either side turned back the rays; they were lost in darkness. And the bricken face of the Old Light, with, at grade, a door made of timbers, which was evidently plumb, hung before them in the beam.

Thomas stepped up. He thought it his place to do so. John and Edward, as well, thought it his place to do so.

The door, which was a right-handed one, when easily unlatched, swung inward without resistance. Edward shone the light inside. The floor was clear of debris. All of them entered. As Edward swept the light about: New timbers everywhere; a Chinese box-puzzle of closely framed lumber wrapped inside the walls of the tower.

When he directed the light upward, they saw that this complex joinery lined the interior of the tower all around, all the way, so far as any of them could see, to the top. Then, it seemed, there fell, like a decorative mobile—for although fixed, there seemed movement within it—down the central shaft, a series of cross-members, each offset from the one above, and from the one below, by an acute angle, seeming to twist as it descended, liked the loosened wingèd seed from a gigantic pinecone grown dry and come apart. As though the mightiest of all Scotsmen had tossed the caber straight upward, to the tower's top, as though it had then arched over onto the horizontal, and was coming down in a flat spin, in light from a stroboscope, leaving interval images of itself, falling slowly, the two ends inscribing a double helix upon the interior of the hive-like cone of timberwork.

The actual complexity was great. The shadows cast by the electric lamp multiplied it.

The men were overawed, as standing in a hallowed place or before a Gargantuan undiscovered monument. For Edward, the second in a day. Then, as the work became comprehensible, they could see that a circular stairway began its ascent just to their left. So Thomas knew: It had been Benjamin Ormond's own true voice and mind, and not the subtlety of the drug, which had summoned forth his declaration.

That Crone—the one with the silver scissors?

Her? She sent them out to be sharpened. They're promised for Friday.

"Think of the cordage!"

"Brought over in small stacks, over so many years!"

"Edward, I've brought the mantle lantern, fueled and already pressurized. Here." Thomas bent to light the apparatus. It gave off a startling brightness, very white, until he reduced the flow of carbureted fuel. "Would you take this with you, and climb the stairs? If they begin to seem at all unsound, then...."

"They won't, I don't think, thank you, Grandfather. I have looked at this work, and I believe I understand the principles of its construction." So Edward took the lantern and started upward within the tower.

"If you reach the lantern—by this he meant the topmost chamber—try whether you can't hang the light onto something. If you should be able to, then turn it up full, and leave it. I don't care how long it lasts. I just want it to shine as brilliantly as it can, for as long as it can."

"Yes, Sir. If I leave the lantern, I may need you to put the beam from the electric light up there, to help me see what I'm doing on the way down."

"Of course."

"And what the Hell *is* he doing, after all?" John Hammond asked, as they watched the lamplight circle and circle, upward and upward.

"I'm not sure of any of this, John. But we are possibly offering some small thing—just a beginning, you know, of course—to the dying."

"That's all right, then. That's all of us, isn't it?"

"I have always thought so."

As they watched, John and Tommy, the bright flame vanished; then a faintly illuminated rectangle first appeared, then abruptly vanished.

"Thank you for asking us in, John. It's late. Things are going on here."

"Horrible things. But at least in the guise of giving thanks to the Maker. Blossom is long gone. Did you know it's past midnight? But I've gone up to check on Helen. She is sound asleep.

"Since it's so late, and the house so settled," Edward said, "couldn't I go ahead and tell you both what I found and what I did? The staircase was sturdy all the way up; I don't think I felt it tremble even once. I reached sound flooring at the top, with a port. Mr. Ormond, if he's the one who did all this, wisely stopped the updraft. Otherwise, the thing would have been like a chimney…without a damper. Any little fire—say, one started by a tramp—could have undone all his work.…"

Thomas answered the unrepeated question. "Yes, I think all of it is his work."

"Could you stay awake long enough to listen to a little account of that work, at least as I understand it? Having seen it? I'm amazed by it. I want to talk about it. Can you listen?" John gave everybody a whiskey.

"Son, of course we can…would like to hear what's been going on inside there. Not many people have seen anything like it, I think"

"So long as I can be at home by four o'clock."

"All right. This is as simply as I can put it: We think of shoring up walls usually from the outside. In the Tower, it has been done from the inside. The advantages to that are, first, that the walls are battered inward, so that strengthening from inside is more effective, simpler; and second, it has been done without anybody's knowing about it."

"Benny buys bits of lumber all the time."

"Used to."

"But nobody wondered much about it."

Well, but now no more is needed. The work is all done."

And are we the only ones, since we are the only ones to have seen it finished, to have wondered about the coming-about of the World? Or, have *we seen it finished?*

"In the stair, he used the newel. That's what we call the post at the bottom of the stair-rail. But in an architectural sense, stricter, it means a system in which successive levels of the stair are connected by vertical members. Mr. Bennie's construction has newels both to the center and to the outside of the stairs. That takes almost all stress off the old masonry itself.

"He seems to have started at the foot with nine pairs of four-by-fours. Pressure-treated. He attached stair-stringers to these—ones that were a little shallower to the outside, and a little steeper to the inside. He would have had to calculate the dimensions and build these himself."

John said: "There had to be a little tapering, in order to allow them to spiral.?"

"Yes, Sir."

"But not so much I expect. Because the circumference of the tower is great."

"At the base, anyhow. Inside, though the angle of the battering changes twice—three pitches in all. But where these uprights ran out, others were fixed to them in two ways: Mortising and through-bolting, and, on the other faces, hurricane-strapping. As you go up, the treads get narrower and less deep. A third of the way up, the nine pairs of uprights give way to only six."

"And, let me guess, Edward, at two-thirds of the way up, the six give way to three?"

"They do. That's when you're thankful it's dark."

"We saw the light flare then disappear in a rectangular silhouette. Was there a hatchway in the floor?"

"Yes."

"And you left the lantern?"

"Hanging from an iron rod and blazing like the sun."

"What about the spiral thing in the center?"

"Timbers to keep the uprights apart. They could tend inward, with battering at all, and the tendency is greater where the battering-angles change. I don't think much. However," and now Edward's eyes gleamed with the light of the visionary or with that of the lunatic, "with the cross-members spiraling about, they could not shift inward. It's in fact an illustration of how the whole thing works: Wooden beams, on grain, can bear great weight without compression or much deformity. But they don't lengthen with heating, either. Not excessively. Every board foot in that construction is held in position by at least two—and usually three or four—other members, from which it can't shift."

"Then, nothing left to Chance?

"Not that I could see."

John said: "How did you come to understand all this, Son?"

Thomas said: "How did Benny?"

"I can't tell you how Mr. Benny figured it out in the beginning; all I had to do was examine what he had done, assuming I do understand it correctly."

They all said goodnight, then, and exchanged futile wishes for an orderly observance next day. And then the Strikestraws left for home. Neither of them looked back for the light in the tower.

Upriver, in Ben Ormond's room where only a very dim nightlight shone at floor level, onto one of the old man's retinae there fell a little point of light (a weakened, diffuse smudge appeared at the same time upon the other, but Benny had shut off the pathway from this eye). He pressed the call-bell. He was surprised to find it answered by Sarah Whitman. "You were here all afternoon, Darling. Why are you here still?"

"So I can celebrate with my family longer over the Holiday."

"Your daughter?"

"Yes, Sir, and my husband's people—they have become my family, too."

"Ah. That's good. Now, I'm sorry to bother you at this time of night. I didn't know it would be somebody who had worked all day, too."

"All afternoon. Mr. Ormond! You have never been any trouble to me."

"When do you come to work next?"

"Not until Saturday afternoon. That's grand, isn't it?"

"Yes, it is. And I believe it means I won't bother you again. Now, I know I'm not supposed to see more than a little. But sometimes it's more than that. And I do now. A bright light, downriver. Will you help me mark it on the windowpane? Will you? So that when the sun comes up tomorrow, I can tell where it has been coming from? Because I think I know."

"Of course, Mr. Ormond."

"Will you call me 'Ben,' or 'Benny'? I don't mean any impertinence."

"Of course I will. It's not impertinence…not at all, Ben, but a privilege I shall treasure. But, now, you are saying that you want me to make a mark on the windowpane?"

"If you can; if they won't mind."

"The only one to 'mind' would be me. And of course I don't. Wait! I have the perfect thing!" And it seemed she went and came back in the same moment. "This is an oil pencil we use for marking syringes and test-tubes. Now, I'll put on a light so you can tell me where to make the mark."

"No, don't, or I'll lose the brightness."

So with Benny directing, and Sarah moving the pencil, they were finally able to find exactly where the beam passed through the windowpane on its way to Mr. Benny's eye, as he rested in his accustomed position. Before Sarah went out, she kissed Mr. Benny and said: "I hope you'll have a comfortable Thanksgiving Day, Ben. Good night."

"Thank you. Goodbye." It had been wonderfully palliative. Benny even thought it might be curative.

"You don't think you could have pieced out that…splendid, really…that splendid array of timbers, unless you had been able to see it completed?"

"No, Grandfather, I am afraid I could not have."

Thomas thought over this. "Do you think we have seen the world completed?"

"I have wondered about it, of course. And I believe we have. Or its maturity. Geologic changes still occur…."

"And new species continue to arise, old ones depart, but not many; they don't queue up to receive names anymore.

"It's at odds with Genesis. But we can't let a consideration like that stop us, or where should we be? Overall, though, I believe this world is more or less the world we get. Give or take."

"Then why don't we understand its coming-about?" They walked up the steps from the garden in pitch darkness, and into the kitchen. It was brightly lighted. As he glanced about, it seemed to Edward that Rhodë had prepared for siege. All *batterie* in place and in cooking-trim.

"A lot of people believe they do understand its coming-about." Thomas put on Rhodë's apron. "A lot of people believe a lot of things. I don't know whether it means those things are so, or whether people feel they must make up their minds about what they believe, and register it somewhere, in order to go on. Like a move on a board. When the player takes his hand from the piece.

"I think we must learn to delight, somehow, in uncertainty. As before unwrapping a gift."

Edward climbed the stairs as much in brightness as his grandmother had seen gather about him as a child. But now the light originated in his heart and flesh. He went to the front of the upstairs hallway and raised the window there. He stepped out onto the roof. Its light slope seemed to rise to meet him. Upon the plinths in the parapet, beings, or shades of beings, stood watching. He could hear the river murmur as it slid past. And he heard it brake.

He looked to his right, far to his right, the way he had in childhood done in order to see the lily pool from the dining room window. There was only darkness. He looked leftward. The Howells' house, three doors up the row, was set conspicuously forward, and angled slightly more to the south than those in rank with it. No sound, no movement.

There! In the lampless windows upstairs: As he stood among more Expectations than Dreads, all sculpted from shadows of the ghost of marble, Edward saw, in reflection—faintly fluid reflection—the Old Light, the First Light, burning. And he remembered:

"*...Once launched, we quest our way. Each next light is loftier; each blazes with a mightier fire. Somewhere, our right reckoning gradually turns to knowledge—partial at first—but finally our courses become wholly true, as What has been wholly Other becomes wholly Known.*"

The beacon burning again, sending forth its gleam, but high above an unpeopled island.